Fionn: Defence of Ráth Bládhma

Also by Brian O'Sullivan

The Beara Trilogy:
    Beara: Dark Legends
    Beara: The Cry of the Banshee (forthcoming)

The Fionn mac Cumhal Series:
    Defence of Ráth Bládhma

Short Story Collections
    The Irish Muse and Other Stories

Fionn: Defence of Ráth Bládhma

The Fionn mac Cumhal Series - Book One

BRIAN O'SULLIVAN

IrishImbas Books

ISBN: 978-0-9922545-7-5

ACKNOWLEDGEMENTS

Special thanks to Marie Elder and Susan Hutchinson-Daniel for all the support.

Many ancient Fenian Cycle texts were essential for the completion of this work. These included *Macgnímartha Finn* (The Boyhood Deeds of Fionn), *Acallam na Senórach* (The Colloquy of the Ancients), *Tóraigheacht Dhiarmada agus Ghráinne* (The Pursuit of Diarmuid and Gráinne) *Aided Finn meic Chumail* (The Death of Finn Mac Cumaill) and many more.

Thanks and credit to Marija Vilotijevic for cover development. Thanks and Credit also to Chiaki & Nasrin (Chronastock) for use of their image on the cover.

Foreword:

This book and its characters are based on ancient narratives from the Fenian Cycle and in particular from the *Macgnímartha Finn* (The Boyhood Deeds of Fionn). The *Macgnímartha Finn* was a twelfth century narrative that attempted to collate a number of much earlier oral tales about Fionn mac Cumhal and the Fianna. It was originally edited by Kuno Meyer in 1881 for the French journal Revue Celtique.

Many of the personal and place names used in this novel date from before the 12th century although many have common variants (Gaelic and English) that are in use today. For those readers who would like to know the correct pronunciation of these names, an audio glossary has been developed and is available at http://irishimbasbooks.com/ .

Prologue:

Ireland :192 A.D.

The animal appeared in the afternoon, when the best of the sunshine had faded. The first indication of its presence was a shudder of movement between the distant trees, then slowly but surely, the shadows congealed to form a grey timber wolf.

It took time before the beast emerged into the wide clearing that separated the two sections of darkwood. There it paused, cautiously assessing the surrounding terrain as it sniffed the chilly air.

Seated on a patch of rock at the opposite side of the clearing, Muirne Munchάem observed the predator's arrival with a tremor. She had traversed that same space not much earlier and her footprints – two staggered lines of blunt impressions – were still visible against the otherwise virgin surface.

Although a young woman of less than twenty summers, Muirne was close to the limit of her physical endurance. Two weeks of trekking through the Great Wild, trudging through the snow-stained forest and woodland, had sapped her of vitality. Despite her youth, the journey had been arduous, due in no small part to the weight of the child in her swollen belly.

She'd stumbled upon the clearing around noon, halting to recover her strength and enjoy the rare sensation of sunshine upon her face. Despite the internal drive to press onwards, she'd been unable to rouse herself and had tarried, reluctant to leave the sunlight for the relentless gloom of the forest that lay before her.

She bit her lip as she continued to watch the animal. *Na mactíre* – literally, "the sons of the land" – were not uncommon but few sightings had been reported for a very long time. Prior to her flight from Dún Baoiscne, Muirne had made a point of listening into any discussions concerning wolves, hoping to identify a time for travel that would increase her chances of avoiding such an encounter.

Muirne Munchάem feared wolves. As a child, she'd spent many evenings on the palisades of Almhu, her father's stronghold, listening as the creatures circled unseen in the darkness below. The blood curdling howls echoing out from the surrounding gloom had terrified her, despite the solid height of the tall stone walls, the fortifications patrolled by kinsmen with iron-tipped spears.

Predators by nature, the wolves generally avoided men. Over several generations they had learned the painful lesson of sharpened metal and tended to focus their energies on easier prey: the deer, hare and other wild animals that inhabited the surrounding countryside. On occasion, they were still known to attack humans, however such attacks were mostly restricted to the weak, the isolated, the foolish or the unlucky. Two seasons earlier, a warrior travelling on horseback to Cruach had dismounted to attend to nature's call, carelessly leaving his weapon in the scabbard attached to his saddle. His grisly remains had been discovered later and the tracks indicated that the horse had bolted, leaving the man defenceless against a passing wolf pack.

Dagán, the storyteller at Almhu, had a favourite tale of one particularly harsh winter when a starving pack of wolves had penetrated the *ráth* – the ringfort – where he'd lived in as a child. The animals' desperation had driven them through the narrow gateway to attack the tethered livestock and their handlers. Although the pack had eventually been driven off, the settlement had lost two cows and one of the men died of the injuries he'd sustained.

Muirne, too, had experienced the animals' deadly nature. As a young girl, she'd been present when a wolf pack had set upon a group of women and children collecting winter flowers in the nearby woods.

She remembered the attack predominantly for its ferocity. They had been chatting and laughing, passing through a pleasant glade on their way back to the fortress, when a horrific howl had halted them in their tracks. An instant later, the little glen was seething with a mass of grey-coated wolves.

The bulk of the pack had launched themselves upon her cousin, a happy, ten year old boy who'd been running several paces ahead of the group. Surging like a wave of shadows over the terrified child, they bore him to the ground. The vicious sound of snarling and ripping flesh had, mercifully, drowned out most of his screams.

The remainder of the wolves had launched themselves at the larger party. Panic-stricken, the women and children had dropped their baskets and scattered. As the group fled, two girls had been knocked to the ground by the pursuing animals. Several women, including her cousin's mother, managed to escape by climbing onto the branches of the nearest trees. Helpless, a babe clutched in one arm and another younger child hanging desperately from her dress, the woman could only cling to the higher branches and scream her despair as her son was dragged into the forest and, literally, eaten alive.

The attack would have ended even more tragically had it not been for the timely arrival of Fiacail and Torlach, two youths from another clan who'd been passing by on their way to visit Almhu. Hearing the screams, they'd rushed towards the commotion and, wielding their weapons, charged straight at the wolf-pack.

The sudden appearance of the boys took the wolves by surprise. Startled, the attack had wavered as the animals withdrew in momentary disarray. Fiacail howled at the top of his voice as he swung his axe in vicious, humming arcs. His companion, meanwhile, took the opportunity to grab the two fallen girls, who were screaming in pain and bleeding profusely from lacerations to their arms and legs.

The taller boy had hoisted the children up to the women in the safety of the trees then quickly clambered after them, calling to his friend to follow his example. By then, however, the pack had reassessed the situation. Realising that this new threat was not as intimidating as originally supposed, they began to advance once more.

The majority of the wolves returned to feast on the remains of Muirne's unfortunate cousin, now little more than an unrecognisable pile of gore and bone between the distant trees. Three of the larger animals, however, converged on Fiacail, hemming him into an open space beside a deep gully that cut him off from the safety of the trees.

Everyone watched helplessly as the boy was pressed backwards. Whirling the axe to keep the snarling animals at bay, he backtracked slowly, keeping his head as he tested the ground behind with his heel before placing his weight on it. Suddenly, the nearest wolf lunged for him but the boy managed to sidestep the attack, swirling the axe to strike the beast in the ribs with the blunt edge of the blade. It yelped as it landed heavily, stumbling and twisting around to snarl at its opponent.

The two other wolves growled menacingly, gnashing their teeth as they circled for the next attack. The remainder of the pack, having devoured what remained of their initial victim, also drew close, aligning with their fellows to circle around and test the boy's exposed side.

Fiacail was saved only by the arrival of a party of warriors from Almhu. One of the girls, miraculously, had made it to the edge of the forest and encountered a group of men returning from the hunt. The warriors arrived at a run, javelins and clubs in hand. Realizing that they were outnumbered, the wolves had simply disappeared, absorbed back into the shadows of the surrounding trees. Nothing remained of their presence apart from the bloody remains of Muirne's cousin and the wails of terrified women and children spilling from the trees like the juice of bitter fruit.

Since that event, Muirne had never lost her dread of the animals and it had only been her desperation that allowed her to overcome her fear and set out on this perilous journey through the Great Wild.

'Malach,' she muttered quietly to herself, then paused to wonder at why she'd drawn on the name of her deceased cousin.

An unconscious prayer perhaps.

Or a self-fulfilling prophecy.

She released a long breath and tightened her grip on the ash staff she'd used as support during her journey. Just beyond the distant tree line, the wolf paused, nuzzling the ground as it sniffed the earth.

It follows my spoor.

She stiffened, her hand automatically dropping to her stomach, as though to reassure the swollen belly. It was an unconscious reaction, an instinctive maternal response.

The wolf halted abruptly, somehow sensing it was under scrutiny. Raising its head, it stared directly across the flat in Muirne's direction and, even at that distance, she could sense its pitiless evaluation. An icy bead of fear trickled down her spine as her eyes scanned the distant trees for other signs of movement. If the animal was part of a pack, she would have little chance of surviving the encounter. The thought provoked a tremor of despair that she fought to overcome.

Fight. Fight for your child.

If the animal was a lone wolf, ejected from a pack, it would be more cautious without the support of the others and, therefore, less likely to attack. If she kept her head she and her baby could avoid a confrontation and come out alive.

Across the snow, the creature had not moved but continued its cold assessment. Muirne stood and raised her staff, brandishing its full length above her head. Apart from a small iron dagger, it was her only weapon and a poor one at that. From a distance, however, the slender pole would have the appearance of a spear. If she was able to maintain the illusion of an armed and capable opponent, the wolf would likely keep its distance. If it saw through the deception, identified her for what she truly was: a lone, terrified girl – it would not hesitate to come for her.

Turning her back on the animal, she gathered several handfuls of snow and coated the exposed patch of rock she'd been sitting on. When the rock was completely covered, she pulled on a fur hat and mittens and strapped a bulging leather satchel across her back. A moment later, she started on the rough trail up the incline leading to the trees high on the hill above her.

Moving slowly, she forced herself to maintain a steady pace, to disguise any indication of the fear bubbling up inside her. Burdened by the weight of her stomach, however, she was distressed to find how heavily she was breathing by the time she'd reached the tree line. Over the past weeks, she'd grown accustomed to the increasing weight of her belly but it was a dangerous restriction at a time when she could afford no such vulnerability.

Halting at the tree line, she turned to look back at the clearing and a queasy sensation curdled in her stomach. Much smaller from this height, the figure of the wolf was still clearly visible as it traversed the clearing. Slowly, cautiously, but advancing nevertheless.

Alarmed, she plunged forward into the forest, the high, closely packed trunks immediately filtering the sunlight and swathing her in shadow. After the brilliance of the sun on the expanse of white snow, the sombre environment of the forest was claustrophobic, the eerie silence sinister and unnerving. As she shuffled through the brittle scrub and briars, she imagined evil faces in the twisted bark and branches but comforted herself with the fact that, at least, the ground beneath the canopy was free of snow and relatively easy to traverse.

She maintained an uphill path through the trees, in the direction of a gap in the crest that she'd spotted from the clearing. As she climbed, an occasional easing or thinning of the trees permitted her to see the undulating forest spread out around her as far as the eye could see, the smooth green mantle broken in places by individual clearings and waterways. Off to the west, the mass of the Sliabh Bládhma mountains was tantalisingly closer than the last time she'd seen it. Working her way around them she would reach the serpentine weaving of a broad river. One of the tributaries feeding this waterway, she'd been informed, originated from the valley where Ráth Bládhma was located. Another day's walk at least.

Shivering, she bowed her head and trudged onwards, a solitary figure engulfed by the immensity of the forest.

***

After a time, fatigue crept up on her and she could hear the sound of her heart pounding from the effort of climbing. Her awareness of time and place began to fade, her step faltered and her fortitude was eroded by the ongoing exertion. The cold temperature under the trees did little to revive her. When she inhaled, the frigid air burned her throat. Each breath she released stuttered out like the vaporous gasps of a damaged bellows.

Exhausted, she came to a halt and braced herself against a tree, sucking in deep, greedy breaths, until her heartbeat slowed and her blurred vision began to clear. Peering uphill, she found that she was unable to perceive either the ridgeline or the cutting through the densely packed trees and scrub. For one horrible moment, she was convinced that she'd lost her way. Overwhelmed by despair and exhaustion, she was tempted to give up, to collapse onto the frozen ground and sleep until the frost, that lulling thief of life, came to pluck her final breath away. In the end, it was only the insistent presence of the child in her belly that kept her on her feet.

She'd regained her breath and was on the point of pushing onwards when a sudden instinct prompted her to twist her head, just in time to catch a flicker of movement from a distant thicket. She held her breath, stared, then released a muted whimper as the wolf slowly, brazenly, emerged from the trees.

From somewhere inside her, a great fury erupted. Wielding the staff with renewed vigour, she shouted at the creature and advanced, stamping her feet. The wolf, unmoved by this display of aggression, simply stood its ground and regarded her almost sullenly. Slowly, its lips curled back, exposing a set of vicious-looking fangs coated with strings of mucous-like saliva. A threatening growl echoed in the empty air.

Bending down, she grabbed a nearby stone and flung it but, unfortunately, the recent changes to her body weight affected her aim. The missile landed on a sliver of snow several paces in front of the animal. The beast glanced at it contemptuously before returning its attention to her, a wide snarl drawn along its muzzle.

Grasping another stone, she threw again and this time her aim was true. The missile struck the animal in the side of the head, drawing an immediate yelp. Startled, and momentarily unnerved, it turned tail and fled back into the cover of the vegetation.

Muirne exhaled in relief but knew it was a short reprieve.

It will attack soon.

She forced herself to start walking again, controlling her breathing and maintaining a slow, measured pace while scanning the forest for any further sign of her pursuer. There was now no doubt in her mind that the wolf was actively stalking her. Unless she was able to find a secure refuge, it was only a matter of time before it attacked. In desperation, she halted to look up at the surrounding trees and wondered if she could climb the higher branches. Immediately, she discounted the idea. Scaling those brittle, lower branches would have been a challenge at the height of her physical ability, impossible in her present condition. In truth, such a course of action would have done little more than stave off the inevitable. The wolf had her scent. He would merely wait her out until sleep or the cold took her and she fell from the tree.

She struggled onwards, so consumed by the sheer effort of walking that it took a moment to realise she was no longer moving uphill. Raising her eyes she stared around to discover that she'd actually entered the pass she'd been seeking, the cutting spotted earlier from her resting place in the sun. A wide, barren gorge bordered by low granite cliffs on either side, it carved its way through the upper section of the ridge for several hundred paces before dipping gradually, veering downhill in the westerly direction she needed to follow.

Elated, she advanced with renewed buoyancy, slowing her pace for the downhill section where the thawing ice made the surface dangerously slick.

It was in this gorge that she finally discovered a potential refuge, a cave at the base of a particularly steep crag to the northern section of the gorge. In fact, it was more of an alcove than an actual cave, a tight hollow beneath the overhanging cliff face, enclosed from behind by the curving rock and, at the front, by a contorted wall of tangled tree trunks. Sometime in the distant past, a cluster of ancient pine trees had tumbled from the summit of the cliff above. Now they lay twisted, interwoven branches wedged tightly together to present a substantial barrier that reduced access to the hollow to a narrow gap between the logs and a bulky rock that protruded from the cliff.

Approaching this restricted opening, Muirne Muncháem threw a quick glance inside, surprised to find that the interior was larger than she'd expected and the floor comprised not of rock but compacted earth. Further investigation revealed that much of that space was cluttered, strewn with broken slabs of rock, the ancient droppings of previous animal occupants, and a substantial mat of dried vegetative matter blown in over the years by the prevailing wind.

As she edged into the enclosure, Muirne threw a wary eye back at the wolf. The animal had grown bolder, reducing the distance between them and now stood back along the pass, watching warily from a fish-shaped rock less than forty paces away. As she moved out of sight, it released an anxious whine.

It's hungry.

It would not be long now, she knew. The beast's hunger was almost at a point where its craving would overwhelm its natural caution and it would attack. Ravenous and tenacious, it would not be stopped, forcing its way through the tight little aperture to get at her.

Unless she could prevent it.

She immediately set to building a fire at the entrance, placing it close enough inside the rocky overhang to remain sheltered from the wind or rain. Scooping up the cave's accumulated debris into a little mound, she overlaid this base with dried twigs and branches. She then proceeded to build a second, additional mound of fuel using larger branches and segments of wood broken from the ancient tree barrier.

From her satchel, she produced two sharp pieces of flint and holding them at the ready, assessed her situation. It would be a delicate business. The blaze would need to be sufficiently substantial to discourage her pursuer from entering, yet not so large or so high that the ancient trees might, themselves, catch alight.

A sudden rustling sounded outside. Startled, she panicked and struck the two flints together. Several bright sparks sprinkled over the pile of kindling and it ignited almost instantaneously. A moment later, the first yellow flames had taken hold and a small cloud of greasy smoke rose, tainting the air with a distinct odour of pine.

As the fire began to take hold, she added some of the smaller pieces of wood, gradually feeding larger portions until it was blazing strongly.

Outside the shelter, above the sound of the wind, she heard a frustrated whine and she shivered with relief.

The temptation to sit and rest for a moment was almost overwhelming but she forced herself to remain standing. Her ordeal was not over. The wolf was still outside, growing ever more desperate. She had merely bought herself a brief respite, a respite she would have to utilise if she was to survive.

With an exhausted sigh, she reached into her bag and withdrew the iron dagger.

It was time to get to work.

***

Eventually, there came a time when she was simply too tired to do any more. Her body was coated with sweat, her hands worn raw from her labours. Eyes clouded from exhaustion, she clumsily waddled two or three paces to the rear of the cave, panting deeply as she ungainly lowered herself onto one of the flatter slabs.

Outside, the sunlight had all but faded and the gorge was growing rapidly darker. A cold gust brushed through the gap, stirring the flames and throwing a dirty yellow glow onto the bare rock behind her. Despite the sudden flurry and the failing light it remained quite warm within the makeshift refuge. Muirne drew a forearm across her sweat-dampened cheeks and forehead and leaned back against the smooth base of the cliff, appreciating the cool touch of the stone against her neck.

When she'd recovered her breath, she forced herself off the rock, turned and kneeled to use it as a platform for her next piece of work. Grasping the nearby staff, she dragged it onto the flattened stone then, using the iron knife, began to sharpen one end, carving it slowly to a narrow point. Soon she had fashioned a crude but serviceable spear. Twisting the haft in both hands, she lay the point in the ashes of the fire to harden it, watching as the white wood curdled and carbonised.

Eventually, she pulled the staff from the ashes. Raising it to eye level, she held it out before her and examined its length with a critical expression. As a weapon, it had its limitations but, realistically, it was the best she could achieve in the circumstances. If the wolf got past the fire and penetrated her defences, its length might serve to keep its jaws from her. For a time, at least.

Task completed, she lay the new spear aside and slumped back onto the rock. Now there was nothing else she could do but await the dawn and, hopefully, outlast the beast that lurked outside. By morning, she hoped, the wolf would have moved on, compelled by its empty belly to seek food elsewhere in the forest.

A ripple stirred through her stomach as the child shifted inside her. The infant was restless, she supposed. Possibly in response to her own distress.

While she'd been working, she had continued to feed the fire and the stock of larger wood segments was substantially depleted. She could, she knew, break or cut some more from the tangled branches of the fallen pines but she was reluctant to undermine the structure of her principal defence or, possibly, create new openings that the wolf might attempt to penetrate. With a sigh, she continued to stare at the fire, watching how the flames curled greedily around each precious item of fuel from her meagre stockpile.

Muirne yawned.

She was exhausted and desperate to sleep but could not afford to do so. Outside, the predator maintained its vigilance. If she stopped feeding the blaze, it would take its chances as soon as the flames reduced.

Then it would be on her and one day, far in the future, some other passing stranger would discover this cave and find her gnawed bones.

With a scowl, she brushed such defeatist thoughts aside.

Fight, damn you. Stay awake. Save your child!

The exertions of the day were working against her. Her shoulders sagged beneath the weight of fatigue, her eyelids flickered and drooped. In desperation, she slapped herself across the side of her face then immediately repeated the action across the other cheek. The sting from the blow jolted her to alertness but, despite the tingling sensation, she was obliged to repeat the process several times as fatigue wore her down.

So tired. So tired.

Her eyes closed.

And snapped back open.

It was completely black outside the cave. There was no sound to be heard but the crackle of flames. She jerked upright, staring around in panic. Had she fallen asleep? How long?

She glanced towards the fire, horrified to discover that it had shrunk to half its original size.

Cursing under her breath, she hurriedly leaned forward to grasp some of the remaining lumps of wood and tossed them into the blaze. Staring down at the little pile she'd created earlier, she realised with a sick feeling that there were less than eight or nine logs remaining. Certainly not enough to last till morning.

Groaning, she raised herself awkwardly off the rock. Now she had no choice. She would have to cut more wood from her precious defensive wall.

One more effort. Just one more.

She was reaching for the knife when a ferocious snarl spilled into the cave. Suddenly, the wolf was there, filling the gap as it launched itself over the flickering barrier, black eyes locked directly on her.

With a cry, Muirne staggered backwards, dropping the spear in her panic. The beast cleared the fire, great jaws wide and slavering. Landing on the inside, its snarl transformed to a surprised yelp for it tumbled, not onto the floor of the cave but into the shallow pit she'd dug out of the earth after setting the fire.

Spurred on by her terror, Muirne reacted with frantic alacrity and sheer instinct. Grasping one of the broken stone slabs from the small heap she'd prepared, she hoisted it in both hands, advanced on the hole and flung it down with all her strength. There was an unpleasant, liquid crunch as it struck the wolf on the top of the skull. The animal crumpled.

She immediately hoisted a second boulder and flung it after the first. This time there was a softer crunching noise, no less repulsive, as the missile struck the creature's side, smashing the ribcage beneath.

Gasping for breath, Muirne grabbed a third rock but, on this occasion, she paused for the creature was sprawled unmoving in the hole below, a viscous yellow liquid pooling around its muzzle. She hesitated momentarily but then launched it, smashing the creature's head with the gratifying crackle of bone and gristle.

Several moments passed before she finally found the strength to draw back from the hole and stagger against the rock wall. Collapsing onto the rocky floor, she huddled, shivering, heart pounding, mouth sour with the taste of adrenalin.

The beast was dead.

She had survived.

Her child would live.

She released a low keen of relief. Hands tightening about her knees, she rocked silently backwards and forwards.

Some time passed before she finally ceased, roughly brushing away the tears that had formed beneath her eyelids. Hauling herself to her feet, she retrieved her woollen cloak and wrapped it around herself. Approaching the fire, she tossed the remaining wood onto the flames. With a sigh, she curled up as close to the snapping flames as she dared. A moment later, she had fallen fast asleep.

Chapter One

As ever, when winter showed signs of releasing its grip on the land, Bodhmhall was to be found to the north of Ráth Bládhma, overseeing the work being carried out on her *lubgort* [vegetable garden]. Over the three years since first occupying the *ráth*, she'd created an impressive series of raised stone-edged, earthen beds that stretched along the gently curving gradient of a nearby, north facing mound. The produce of her garden – an annual bounty of herbs, onions, carrots, parsnips and other vegetables – was of reliable consistency and quality. The nutritional variety it provided also proved popular amongst the inhabitants of the ring fort given a diet otherwise restricted to dairy and cereal products.

Perched on the crest of the mound, Bodhmhall brushed a fist-full of black hair back from either side of her forehead. With a deft twist of her fingers, she looped the strands into a more controllable shape and bound them in place with a bronze hair clasp. By anybody's reckoning, she was a striking woman. Tall and slender with a generous mouth and intelligent, brown eyes, her looks had been spared the ravages common to many of her contemporaries: the trials of childbirth and the arduous physical labour required to sustain the community. Daughter of Tréanmór, *rí* of *Uí Baoiscne*, Bodhmhall had enjoyed a privileged childhood in the fortress of Dún Baoiscne, something she increasingly appreciated as the years rolled by.

Standing with hands on her hips, she considered the garden as she planned out the next stages of work. It was too early for her efforts to produce any substantial results (the low temperatures ensured that any growth remained minimal to non-existent) but she was determined to do as much as practically possible to get an early start on the growing season. Experience had demonstrated that turning the cold earth of the raised beds helped to break down the cow manure mixed in over the autumn. When the warmer weather finally kicked in, the soil creatures would already be hard at work, merging precious nutrients to provide the initial spurt of growth for the herbs she needed to replace her dwindling supply of remedies.

She pointed to a patch of soil at the lowest ridge, positioned so that the gradient might drain the winter rains away.

'There, Cónán.'

Her hand moved, two slender fingers indicating another area.

21

'And there.'

With a sigh of resignation, a dark-haired boy of about eleven years moved forward, lifted a metal-headed hoe and began to turn the soil at the indicated areas.

Bodhmhall watched him work the earth, mixing in the remaining traces of manure with almost effortless ease. She felt no rancour at the boy's undisguised frustration. Working under her instruction could be taxing at the best of times and Cónán had demonstrated heroic tolerance to this point. Over the course of the morning, she had directed him from one section of the mound to another, a pattern of activity that, from his perspective, must have appeared meaningless. What the boy did not understand, however, was that his perspective differed substantially from her own. Where he saw indistinguishable lumps of frozen soil, Bodhmhall's *tíolacadh* – her 'Gift'– revealed patches that radiated with varying degrees of biological activity; the teeming life force of worms, ants, beetles, and other tiny creatures. Some of these – the areas that she directed him to avoid – glittered like a hundred, thousand stars in the sky at night; minute, exquisite sparks of brilliance. These, she knew, were the secret of her garden's success, the powerhouse that converted the base organic matter to a bountiful food source. She was adamant that such potential should be protected as far as practicable.

It was in her seventh year that Bodhmhall had come to understand how she differed from the other children at Dún Baoiscne. They did not perceive the flickering lights she associated with life in all its forms and therefore struggled to understand her reluctance to partake in the occasional activity that might extinguish such brilliance. Although she worked it out over time, Bodhmhall's innate stubbornness also meant that she did not attempt to alter her behaviour to align with that of her peers. This approach gained her a reputation for eccentricity but, more importantly, it brought her to the attention of Dub Tíre. And the cold scrutiny of the druidic order.

But that, of course, had been a lifetime ago.

Bodhmhall pushed such dark memories away, buried them deep within the soil of her garden. Over the years, experience had made her adept at dealing with such unpleasant reflections, developing numerous effective mechanisms and distractions to keep the dark thoughts at bay.

Like the simple action of gardening.

'To your left. Cónán. No, your left.'

Grumbling, the boy did as he was told.

'Don't be cranky, *a bhuachaill,*' she chided. 'You'll be glad of this effort when your stomach is riddled with gut cramp. That's where I intend to lay the *peirsil chatach* and there's no better remedy for the runs.'

She chuckled to herself for the boy was pretending to ignore her, sighing melodramatically as he helped her to turn the earth. Buoyed by the morning's accomplishments, Bodhmhall stopped teasing him and turned to gaze up the length of Glenn Ceoch – Valley of Haze – at a view that never failed to give her pleasure.

To her delight, the morning had dawned with clear skies, the habitual early chill diminished by the unexpected rays of watery sunshine. Bathed in this welcome glow, the valley had taken on a beauty that was even more dramatic than usual, patches of dew-lined pasture and the nearby stream glittering like silver in the soft, yellow hue.

Glenn Ceoch had been Bodhmhall's home since departing the fortress of Dún Baoiscne more than three years earlier. A wide V-shaped spread of flatland, it was enclosed on either side by two steep, tree-coated ridges that converged at the east of the *ráth* to form a steep and impassable barrier. The spring that fed the stream was located on the lower slopes of this formidable buttress, pooling in a small pond of clear water that emptied down onto the valley floor and flowed out to the west.

Set at the extremes of *Clann Baoiscne* territory, the isolated Glenn Ceoch was known predominantly for the bloody history associated with the previously deserted *ráth*. Two earlier attempts at settlement had taken place there many years before Bodhmhall was born. Both had ended disastrously with the colony destroyed, its inhabitants massacred by reavers. Despite the valley's excellent pasture and the potential of its loamy soil, there had been little appetite for a third attempt. Because of its history and isolation, the territory was still considered too dangerous, a section of the Great Wild best left to the wolves and bandits.

The decision to settle Glenn Ceoch, leaving Dún Baoiscne and the security of home and clan, was not one that Bodhmhall had taken lightly, even though she'd had limited alternatives at the time. In the opinion of her few supporters, the venture to re-establish a colony at that infamous location was doomed to failure. She had recognised the many valid reasons for such pessimism. The population of the proposed colony had been

23

ludicrously small: Bodhmhall; the woman warrior Liath Luachra; the old servant Cairbre – now her *rechtaire*; his woman and their three son: Cónán; Aodhán and Bearach. The supporting livestock had also been woefully restricted, consisting of little more than eight cows, four goats, four pigs and a selection of fowl. On the day of their departure, their entire possessions and all of their equipment – including the metal workings – had fit into three ox-drawn carts lent to them by Tréanmór. This unexpected act of generosity from her father had surprised her at the time until she realised that the gesture had not been a kindness so much as a desire to see the back of them as quickly as possible.

When the little caravan moved out of sight of the only home she'd ever known, Bodhmhall had felt great desolation and struggled to conceal her rising sense of panic from the companions who had so loyally aligned their fates to hers. Over the course of their journey through the Great Wild, a nerve-racking period of thirty-two days with the carts and cattle on the untamed topography,– that sensation had diminished only to return even more strongly when they reached Glenn Ceoch and observed the ruins of Ráth Bládhma for the very first time.

Their new home was a significant earthwork centred on the summit of a low drumlin. The original settlers had carried out extensive work to create a high, circular earthen bank that enclosed the central courtyard – the *lis* – surrounded, in turn, by a flat-bottomed ditch. After more than twenty-five years of neglect, much of the original structure had fallen into disrepair. Several sections of the embankment had caved away, sliding into the waterlogged ditch to bridge the *ráth's* principle defence and leave it exposed to attack from a number of different quarters.

Within the *lis*, there was little visible evidence of the previous colony apart from some rotted wattle, fragments of the ancient habitations buried beneath the fibrous roots of long-established grass. Work on clearing the area, however, had exposed several charred post stubs and a number of human bones, chilling reminders of the settlement's fate. Bodhmhall had immediately halted all other work and insisted on a cleansing ceremony, removing the remaining bones and burying them solemnly in the neighbouring woods.

Despite their miniscule workforce, the new settlers had launched themselves into the task of reconstruction with a vigour driven by their dread of the Great Wild as much as by their hopes for a new beginning.

Out in the isolated wild lands, livestock and goods were an irresistible draw for wolves and marauders. The shelter of the *ráth* offered their only realistic hope for long-term survival.

In many respects, the new colony was fortunate in that much of the original backbreaking labour had been carried out by the original inhabitants. In truth, all that remained – although it was a substantial piece of work – was to repair and to build on the original.

The initial efforts focussed on creating internal and external revetments to consolidate the earth embankment and prevent further collapse into the ditch. In those areas where slippage had occurred, the fallen detritus was removed and support posts inserted around the inward base. Once this was completed, gaps in the embankment were repaired using upcast from the trench.

Each member of the new colony had taken an active role in the reconstruction. Despite the gruelling physical labour, Bodhmhall had experienced a fierce sense of personal satisfaction as the results of her efforts came together. Ironically, the toil and sweat had also proven a welcome contrast to the years of stifling intellectual training imposed upon her by Dub Tíre during her druidic apprenticeship at Dún Baoiscne.

As Bodhmhall's *conradh* – military champion – Liath Luachra had assumed overall responsibility for the defence and security of the new settlement. Conscious of the fate of the previous colony and the ever constant threat of attack, she'd insisted on enhancing the earthworks with further fortifications, palisades constructed from split oak poles retrieved from the surrounding forest. She also oversaw the strengthening of the west-facing entrance, expanding the ditch further to create a causeway to the narrow gateway reinforced with sizeable blocks of stone.

The most substantial elements of the reconstruction took the little colony more than four backbreaking months of work but, on completion, they had a secure base from which to grow. Over the intervening years, their defences had been tested on two occasions when they'd been attacked by bands of passing reavers. In both cases, the attacks had been little more than opportunistic raids that they'd withstood by simply withdrawing within the walls. After one or two half-hearted assaults, both raiding parties had withdrawn, their urge for booty dampened by the effectiveness of the defences and the evident preparedness of its defenders.

Bodhmhall shivered as the sun disappeared behind a passing veil of cloud, uncertain as to whether the sense of unease she was experiencing was stirred by unpleasant memories of bitter times or simply the sudden physical drop in temperature. Reverting to one of her tried and trusted methods, she knelt and started to clear some weeds, intending to submerge her anxiety, once more, in the soothing routine of her garden.

It was not to be.

The 'Gift' manifested itself with its habitual subtlety, easing in so softly that it was on her before she'd even noticed. Her first inkling of its expression was an unpleasant tingling sensation tugging at her nerves like a loose thread snagged on a branch. Instincts stirred by some provocation she didn't quite fully understand, she straightened up and anxiously scanned the valley.

Something... there is something ...

She was only vaguely conscious of her heart rate increasing, the flush of blood pulsing through her veins. Then, all at once, it was as though every sense was intensified, each physical sensation magnified one hundred fold. The cheerful murmur of the nearby stream increased in volume until it had taken on the vociferous roar of a surging flood. The rustle of leaves on the surrounding trees crackled like static before an incoming storm. An overpowering smell of iron filled her nostrils and the very texture of the air seemed to scrape her skin.

For a moment her sight blurred then abruptly cleared to focus on the thick line of trees that bordered the far end of the valley. For some inexplicable reason, the sight of those trees suddenly terrified her and, somehow, even at that distance, she could feel them shiver as some invisible force brushed through them. Bundling up into a violent squall, the intrusion gathered impetus as it rolled down the length of the valley towards her. Unable to move, she helplessly watched it draw closer, stirring up dead leaves and moss, casting them skywards like a swarm of angry ravens.

She closed her eyes just before it struck, pummelling her with such ferocity that she was almost knocked from her feet. Somehow, she managed to maintain her balance, standing firm against the onslaught as it screamed and howled like a gale about her. Head bent and shoulders hunched, she channelled her energy into repelling an assault that was not physical so much as mental. Despite her skill at creating such intellectual barriers, she had the vaguest sensation of being probed by some intelligence, prodded like a farmer might prod an animal at a market to see how it would react. When she resisted, her response seemed to provoke an odd sense of outrage, as though the trespassing entity resented her ability to detect it. Enraged, it began to pummel her, to psychically strike again and again.

She had no idea how long the offensive lasted, how much time had passed before the air grew still, the roar dissipating to a jaded background wheeze. Numbed and emotionally drained from her efforts, she wearily opened her eyes. On the pasture south of the *ráth*, the small herd of cattle were lowing contentedly in the calm of the early afternoon. Beside them, the stream gurgled happily, like a gush of amused infants. Close by, bent over the vegetable garden, Cónán worked with quiet industry. Bodhmhall stared, struggling to understand what had happened. No one else had seen or heard anything.

Off to her right, on the western ridge, a murder of ravens suddenly took flight, crowing up from the trees in an angry flutter of wings. With a shudder, Bodhmhall forced herself to open her mouth and stuck out her tongue to taste the air. Almost immediately, she withdrew it with an expression of revulsion.

'Bodhmhall'.

Absorbed in her contemplation, she barely noticed this fresh disruption. Startled, she turned to find Cairbre the elderly *rechtaire*, standing beside her. The old man was studying her with quiet intensity, his left eyebrow curved upwards in a thoughtful arc. From his expression, it appeared that he had been standing there for some time.

'Are you not well, Bodhmhall? Was it the Gift?'

Somehow, she found the strength to nod.

'Does it bring good tidings?'

'When does the Gift ever bring good tidings?'

She immediately regretted her brusqueness. Cairbre was a quiet man, a gentle man and had been a loyal advisor to her family for as long she could remember. He did not deserve such discourtesy and yet she felt almost too overwhelmed and distraught to care. Taking a deep breath, she forced herself to calm her mind.

'Forgive me, Cairbre. The wind brought something new today. Something that leaves a taste of shit in the air. Even the ravens are disturbed.'

Cairbre, who was more familiar with her Gift than most, reacted to this news with concern.

'Should I alert the others, mistress?'

She shook her head in irritation, exhausted by the never ending burden of the Gift and its unsolicited, unwelcomed associations. Over the years, the *tíolacadh* had revealed many positive manifestations such as the 'light of life' but also negative manifestations such as the one she had just experienced. Either way, she had tired of them many years earlier. In the isolation of Glenn Ceoch, she had hoped to find respite, to avoid much that stimulated the Gift and identified her as a *bandraoi*, a female druid. She had achieved some success in this objective, experiencing no major expression of it for more than two and a half years.

Until now.

'I don't know, Cairbre.' She poked at a loose sod with the toe of her fur-lined boot as she attempted to work out what had just taken place. 'I think there is another *draoi* roaming the Great Wild,' she said at last. 'He or she has some deliberate intent but I was unable to tell what it was. It didn't bear me any specific malice or interest but it was not pleased to discover I could detect it.' She paused then, inspired by sudden flash of insight. 'It was seeking something. Or somebody. Whatever or whoever it was, it did not find it here so it moved on.'

She looked at the old man.

'Is Liath Luachra returned?'

'Not yet, mistress. No sign of her or Bearach.'

Bodhmhall frowned. Liath Luachra had left to hunt the local forests in the dark hours of the previous morning, accompanied by Bearach, Cairbre's second son. Vaguely conscious of the warrior woman rising from their bed, Bodhmhall had been too entangled in the viscous threads of sleep to waken properly and wish her safe travels. Now she regretted that lapse. The hunters had been due to return by nightfall that same evening but were a full day overdue. Although there were many reasonable explanations for such a delay, the thought of Liath Luachra out in the Big Wild at a time when a fellow *draoi* was stalking the land, filled her with unease.

Bodhmhall took a deep breath. Her mind was still reeling from her altercation with the intruding *draoi* and thinking of such complications was making her head spin. A sudden realisation helped to draw her back to more stable ground.

'You came to seek me out, Cairbre. What is it?'

'There's a wan, lady. Seeking refuge.'

'A wan?'

Even after all these years, Bodhmhall still found the old *rechtaire* difficult to understand at times. When he spoke, his barely articulate mumble was muffled not only by a dense mat of grey beard but by a thick, guttural accent as well. According to her father, he had been snatched as a child during a raid on the warm lands across the southern sea and this accent was the last vestige of his native tongue, unspoken since his abduction from his people.

Many years later Cairbre had ended up at Dún Baoiscne, traded on as spoils of war when his previous owner had perished on the battlefield. Purchased from a travelling merchant to provide crude brute labour for the maintenance of the fortress walls, his intelligence and natural aptitude for administration had gradually seen him transferred to lighter, more intellectual duties. Twenty-five years later, despite his tragic origins, Cairbre had adapted well to his environment at the *Clann Baoiscne* stronghold. Over that time he'd become a trusted assistant to Tréanmór's household, obtained his freedom and had even taken a woman of his own, another ex-slave who subsequently bore him three sons. All of Bodhmhall's earliest memories included the old man for he'd become her father's key administrative advisor. Consistently reliable in the running of the stronghold, he would probably still hold this position if she hadn't convinced him to accompany her and Liath Luachra to Ráth Bládhma.

'A wan, lady. A young wan.'

Ah! A young one.

Bodhmhall nodded, the mists of incomprehension finally cleared.

'Who is she?'

The *rechtaire* ran one wrinkled, leathered hand across his forehead then down the silver stubble of hair cut close to the scalp.

'I don't know her. She would not give her name.'

'She was accompanied?'

She held the old man's gaze and he shifted his weight awkwardly from one foot to the other. Every winter for the last few years, he'd suffered increasingly from the curse of stiffening joints. On their first winter at the *ráth* he had developed an awkward-looking walk that helped him avoid the stinging sensation in his knees. This year, he could barely move without the occasional hiss of pain.

'No company.'

Bodhmhall grunted in surprise. A single girl, a stranger, travelling alone in the Great Wild without escort or protection? She frowned, suspicion already forming in her mind. The arrival of a mysterious visitor in this isolated land so soon after the revelation of a hostile *draoi* could hardly be coincidence.

'The wan's with child.'

Bodhmhall's expression conveyed her otherwise silent astonishment.

'Near to dropping, I would say,' the old man continued. 'Yes. Definitely near to dropping.'

Unsure how to respond, Bodhmhall bit on her lower lip and gestured towards the settlement. 'Our guest is within?'

'Yes, lady. I left her in your house with Conchenn.'

'Very well. I suppose we should offer her the hospitality of the *ráth*.'

Wiping her hands on the rough material of her tunic, Bodhmhall left her instructions with Cairbre for the final section of the *lubgort*. Circling the embankment with a heavy heart, she curved around to the entrance of the ring fort and traversed the causeway leading up to the stone gateway. Aodhán, Cairbre's eldest son, was on sentry duty on the top of the stone structure. Taking a brief respite from his scrutiny of the surrounding countryside, he grinned and gave a brief wave as she passed into the passageway below.

A tall and pleasant youth, Aodhán had inherited his father's easy manner but was already an *óglach*, a competent young warrior. Like his brothers, he had undergone martial training with Liath Luachra since their occupation of Ráth Bládhma. Under the woman warrior's tutelage, both he and Bearach had become more than proficient with sword and shield while Cónán showed promise with the sling. All three boys were adept with the javelins and harpoons that lined the wooden rack on the gateway rampart, however Aodhán, in particular, had demonstrated an uncommon aptitude for casting weapons. After years of practice, the *óglach* was now lethal with javelins at distances of up to fifty paces, something the reavers had discovered, to their cost, during those early raids.

The *lis,* the central area of the *ráth,* comprised a wide circle that held two round houses, a small stockade for holding the cattle at night and a large fire pit over which a metal cauldron had been suspended. Two sturdy lean-tos had been constructed against the internal wall of the embankment to the left of the entrance. Predominantly used as a shelter for the *ráth*'s precious metal implements and tools, the structures also contained their supply of firewood, a resource well depleted over the cold winter months.

As she emerged from the gate passageway, Bodhmhall noted the ongoing consumption of firewood as Conchenn, Cairbre's grey-haired woman, fed the fire pit's insatiable flames. The bubbling of the cauldron's contents, a vegetable based broth flavoured with bones, was audible from the gateway. Clouds of steam coiled upwards into the frigid air like a veil of angry ghosts.

The smell of food made Bodhmhall's stomach growl and she realised she'd neglected to eat since rising that morning. Glancing at the sluggish, dark broth, she experienced a sudden, inexplicable craving for the fresh tastes and colours of summer: blooming red strawberries and raspberries, blackberries and blueberries, even the tangy sweetness of rowan.

Approaching the fire she ruefully discarded such notions. Summer was still some way off and harbouring such fancies was not only pointless but foolish to boot.

'Conchenn. Where is the visitor?'

Mute from birth, Conchenn said nothing but jerked her head in the direction of the nearest roundhouse. With this, she closed her eyes and raised her hands into the form of a pillow to mime a sleeping person. Bodhmhall smiled at the representation, nodded and turned towards the domed abode she shared with Liath Luachra. Pausing before the oak frame entrance, she stared at the leather flap, oddly reluctant to proceed any further. Privacy was a luxury that most communities could not afford but she'd grown fond of the personal retreat. Over the first year in Glenn Ceoch, she'd invested significant emotional and physical effort into creating that building, arranging the two concentric ring walls of hazel wattles and the insulating layers of straw. She'd also worked hard weaving the thatched reed roof. She had then spent a further two years making that space a home so the presence of an uninvited stranger unsettled her.

31

Setting her jaw, Bodhmhall lifted the flap and stepped inside.

The interior of the roundhouse was dark and it was difficult to see anything at first. Intimate familiarity, however, allowed Bodhmhall to automatically assign definition to the blurred shapes and contours; the curved brushwood sleeping platform, the narrow posts supporting the roof, even the wooden stand holding Liath Luachra's leather fighting harness.

A distinct scent of oil competed with the odour of wood smoke from the fire. Although not the most fastidious of housekeepers, Liath Luachra was meticulous when it came to the maintenance of her armour and weapons and spent hours cleaning and oiling them when the weather confined her indoors.

The central feature of the hut was the small, stone-kerbed fire pit where the fire she'd laid down that morning had settled to embers. It was still radiating sufficient heat to repel the chill from outside and its dull glow illuminated the fur-wrapped figure curled up on the floor beside it.

Bodhmhall stood and stared in silence as a gentle snore rustled through the confines of her living area. Their guest was facing the fire with her back to the entrance, however, the *bandraoi*'s unique Gift allowed her to see the blue-yellow hue of her visitor's life-force. Within that haze, but slightly lower, she could make out another separate glow; a strikingly vivid yellow.

Cairbre had it right, then. The visitor's with child.

She studied the fiery glimmer with curiosity, surprised by the intensity of colour in one that had not yet been born. In her experience most people, even those not yet fully formed, tended to exude a pale blue or green coloured aura. There were occasional exceptions like Liath Luachra where tinted flickers of orange or red could also be observed. She had never before, however, seen one burn as bright and intense as the flame from this unborn child.

Advancing towards the fire, Bodhmhall tossed in some scraps of dried turf from a wicker basket beside the hearth and stoked it up as quietly as she could. Puffs of blue smoke drifted slowly to the roof of the hut and there was a brief crackle as the turf caught alight. A sudden flicker of flame briefly illuminated the face of the sleeping figure. Bodhmhall's eyes widened.

She buried her shock in a surge of activity, busying herself until she had regained her composure. Crossing to a low, rough bench she grabbed a handful of dried herbs from one of the many that had been ground and stored in a series of little bowls, to be steeped as the need required. Sprinkling the herbs into a fresh clay beaker, she added some warm water from a pitcher sitting in the embers and started to stir. The sounds of swirling liquid and the sharp tap of a wooden spoon against the lip of the beaker did not rouse the sleeping woman.

Settling onto her haunches beside the fire, the *bandraoi* reached over and shook her roughly. It took several attempts before her visitor finally released a low moan. Rolling onto her back, the woman opened a pair of sleep-ridden blue eyes.

'Hallo, cousin,' said Bodhmhall.

The girl attempted to rise but was thwarted by the bulk of her stomach. Blinking and stupid with sleep, she succeeded in sitting upright on her second attempt and gazed about her in bleary-eyed confusion. She looked depleted. Pale and exhausted, despite her slumber.

Understandable, given the rigours of travelling in winter. And the weight of that child in her belly.

'Bodhmhall.'

The voice was husky, tight with tension.

Bodhmhall busied herself with her potion, silencing her guest with a raised forefinger as she poured the mixture from the beaker into a smaller bowl. The extended silence seemed to disconcert her visitor. She shrank back on herself, clutching her woollen cloak and drawing it more tightly about her.

She was scared, Bodhmhall realised with a start. Muirne Muncháem, Flower of Almhu, wife to her brother Cumhal, was scared.

Unsettled by this realisation, she stared at her visitor, once more recalling the spectral assault she'd repelled at the *lubgort*. The convergence of events did little to reassure her.

'I come seeking sanctuary.'

Bodhmhall's posture tensed as she glared at Muirne Muncháem. It was rare for her to experience true fury but she knew that the contorted emotions twisting up inside her could be nothing else.

'Sanctuary. You come to Ráth Bládhma, refuge of *An Cailleach Dubh* to seek sanctuary?'

Muirne blanched at the mention of *An Cailleach Dubh* – The Dark Hag – and Bodhmhall found herself unable to repress a bitter sense of satisfaction. It had been Muirne, after all, who'd originally contrived that cynical epithet and there was a righteous sense of balance in using it back against her.

Muirne let her head drop, unable to bear the wrathful expression of her host.

'Cumhal is dead.'

'What?'

Bodhmhall stared, her fury deflected but still too inflamed to completely absorb what the younger woman had just told her.

'Cumhal is dead.'

Bodhmhall studied the woman's face more carefully, scrutinising it for any sign of deceit, any trace of duplicity. The pain she saw in those features served only to confirm the tone of her words. Muirne was telling the truth. Which meant that ...

Cumhal!

Her brother, future leader of *Clann Baoiscne*, blond, vivacious and full of life was ...

Dead.

Bodhmhall stiffened, the news striking her like a blow to the stomach. Her guts lurched and shoulders sagged as though compressed by some sudden, unfathomable burden. Head whirling, she struggled to assemble some coherent thought through the maelstrom of questions and notions in her head.

Muirne tactfully looked to one side until her host gathered herself together.

'How?'

Under normal circumstances Bodhmhall would have been embarrassed by the catch in her voice, the exposure of such brittle weakness. Now, gutted by shock and grief, she simply didn't care.

'A battle with *Clann Morna*. There was a dispute about stolen cattle from an earlier raid. A confrontation was arranged by the *draoi* of both clans ...' Muirne's voice trailed off momentarily as an involuntary blaze of contempt flickered across Bodhmhall's features. 'It was to be a limited engagement, a clash of champions but *Clann Morna* treacherously broke the established tradition. The party from Dún Baoiscne was ambushed as it passed through Cnucha on its way to the agreed battle lands. Our men were taken completely by surprise. They fought well but they were overwhelmed. Cumhal fell. And seventeen other warriors.'

34

Seventeen!

Bodhmhall gasped. Seventeen warriors! Most of them individuals she would have known, played with as children and watched grow into young men. She shook her head in disbelief. Such a loss of manpower, of leadership, was catastrophic for *Clann Baoiscne*, a substantial threat to the ongoing survival of the clan.

'And Crimall. Is he —'

'Your other brother lives. They say he's fled to the West.'

'Lugaid the Lightning Stroke?'

'*Dead.*'

'Ernán mac Donn?'

'*Dead.*'

'Fergus?'

'Alive. But he will never use his right hand again.'

Bodhmhall paused. 'Fiacail mac Codhna?'

There was a silence as Muirne looked away. Her exhaustion was evident now, her posture slack, her natural beauty strained and haggard.

'He lives. He was at Seiscenn Uarbhaoil during the battle. A new love is said to detain him there.'

As always when distressed, Bodhmhall compressed her emotion beneath a mask of impassivity, submerging all trace of sentiment in the depths of a bottomless black loch, sunk and hidden deep within herself. The reaction was an instinctive response, a coping mechanism developed during her time with *draoi* Dub Tíre. She imagined her lips curve in a cynical smile, a grimace that was not reproduced on her face. The bitter lessons of that time, it seemed, served some practical purpose after all.

Fiacail? How typical! The man's cock has saved his life.

'My father?'

The Flower of Almhu shrugged. 'What do you expect? His favourite son is dead. His second son fled like a coward. All his plans died with Cumhal. Cumhal was the *tánaiste*, the heir destined to lead *Clann Baoiscne* to great deeds. There is no clear replacement.'

A burning sensation in the palms of her hands made Bodhmhall look down and she realised that she'd unconsciously gouged the soft skin with her fingernails. Blood was now trickling freely down the inside of her wrists. Folding them onto her lap, she exhaled slowly and drew upon all her reserves to focus solely on the issue confronting her. She nodded at the stomach of the younger woman.

'This is Cumhal's child?'

A protective hand dropped to cradle the bulge.

'Yes.'

'Huh.' A muted grunt of comprehension. Muirne's departure from Dún Baoiscne made some sense then. With their victory at Cnucha, *Clann Morna* would move quickly to establish dominance over their old rivals, *Clann Baoiscne*. A direct assault on Dún Baoiscne was unlikely given the cost in men needed to capture the fortress. They could, however, sue for peace under advantageous conditions. With the death of their future leader and the loss of so many warriors, *Clann Baoiscne's* power was seriously diminished. *Clann Morna* would be determined to eliminate any future challenge to their dominion by obliterating the hereditary lines of *Clann Baoiscne* leadership.

For Muirne, the ramifications were serious. If male, *Clann Morna* would demand the death of her child or, at the very least, insist on fosterage with one of their own. To cement their hold, it was also likely they would demand her union through marriage with a suitable member of their sept.

Bodhmhall sighed and got to her feet. She suddenly felt weary, much older than her twenty-three years. On leaving Dún Baoiscne, she had thought to leave this world of tribal politics and kingship squabbles behind.

Despite her personal anguish, she experienced an unexpected surge of sympathy for Muirne and the threat to which she was now exposed. Almost immediately, she smothered that reaction. Previous experience with Muirne Muncháem had too often demonstrated that such goodwill was unlikely to be reciprocated. In this particular case, there were also significant ramifications to becoming too involved.

'You are the raven, Muirne Muncháem. You bring pain and dismay wherever you descend to rest your feet.' She brushed her hands and sighed. 'Why have you come here?'

'I come seeking sanctuary.' The blond haired woman raised her hands, palm outwards. 'I have nowhere else to go. Would you deny me refuge?'

'Of course, I would. The wrath of *Clann Morna* is not a threat we would willingly bring down upon ourselves.'

The bluntness of the response took Muirne by surprise. She stared at the taller woman with wide eyes.

'Clann Morna does not know where I was headed.'

Bodhmhall ignored her. 'You turned your nose up at us for years with your airs and graces. Now, when misfortune pulls you from your heights of privilege you throw yourself at our door. You know full well you are neither welcome, nor have any rights to hospitality here.'

'Of course, I know! There are many places I could have sought help; family and bonds that owe me fealty and protection. Everyone is well aware that you and Liath Luachra bear me no love. Our antipathy is well known.'

'And yet here you are.'

'Because I carry Cumhal's child.'

Bodhmhall took a deep breath.

Clever. Oh, very clever.

The *bandraoi* scowled. Although not a stunt that she was in a position to appreciate, she had to admire the younger girl's political astuteness. As spouse to the *tánaiste* of *Clann Baoiscne,* Muirne automatically inherited the ancient rights of fealty due from the clan retainers, subject families and associated allies. Such networks of obligations and alliances had always cemented the authority of the ruling lineage. In times of adversity it was expected that these would be drawn on, that all favours would be called in.

Because of the circumstances behind Bodhmhall's expulsion from Dún Baoiscne, Ráth Bládhma and its inhabitants were outside of such conventions. Despite this, Muirne had come here in secret, gambling her safety on Bodhmhall's personal loyalty to her brother as opposed to the loyalty of clan obligation.

Yes. It was a very clever manoeuvre. *Clann Morna* would certainly not have expected it and by telling no-one of her destination, her location would be secure.

Provided Bodhmhall responded as anticipated.

She held the girl's eyes. Muirne returned the stare with an anxious expression then, unable to withstand its intensity, dropped her own eyes to the floor. 'Cumhal would always defend you,' she whispered. 'At Dún Baoiscne, when the people turned against you, he argued to let you stay. And yet ...' Her voice filled with bitterness. 'You would deny sanctuary to his son, your nephew. Your blood kin.'

'So it's a boy, then?'

'It kicks like a boy,' Muirne snarled and despite her fatigue, some of the woman's natural fieriness flared in her eyes. 'But you're *An Cailleach Dubh*. You tell me.'

With a sigh, Bodhmhall considered her guest and suddenly wished her gone. Departed with her tragic news, her lust for power, her games and abrasive personality. Right there and then, she wished nothing more than to lie down in the darkness, to grieve in silence for her brother, and to worry over Liath Luachra until she could find the strength to face the world again.

Of course, that was a luxury she did not have. Muirne Munchaém's gamble had been well played. Her loyalty to her brother, even deceased, was too strong. There were some responsibilities she could not shirk, irrespective of the circumstances.

She exhaled very slowly, as though she had been holding her breath for a very long time.

'You have the safety of Ráth Bládhma for tonight, Muirne Munchaém. But you have no friends here and the news you bring makes you all the more unwelcome. You also place *Muinntir Bládhma* in potential conflict with *Clann Morna*.'

'*Muinntir Bládhma?*' Her sister by marriage arched one eyebrow in surprise.

'We're our own clan now, Muirne. *Muinntir Bládhma.*'

Bodhmhall had plucked the words from the air. *Muinntir Bládhma;* the household of Bládhma. And yet as she'd said it the words had felt right to her. The settlement was not associated with any particular ancestor or family dynasty, nothing but the location in which they were settled. *Bládhma.* Its members were outcasts or misfits, every one of them. A disgraced *bandraoi*, a female warrior, an old slave, a mute woman, three landless sons. It was a new beginning for all of them.

Such aspirations were lost on the likes of Muirne Munchaém who continued with her habitual obtuseness. 'Well, *Muinntir Bládhma* has a limited future if it lacks the men to procreate. That is unless you intend to depend on the likes of your old slave and those boys I saw earlier.'

The *bandraoi*'s expression hardened but she could not deny the truth of her visitor's words. Over the past three years, the settlement had clawed its way to a state of relative security but it was still a precarious existence. Despite their achievements, it did not have a future while its population remained so restricted.

Not that she would ever admit as much to Muirne Muncháem.

With exaggerated assurance, Bodhmhall smiled and brushed a loose strand of hair back from her face. 'I understand you're tired after your hardships in reaching us.' She leaned forward so abruptly, her face so close to Muirne Muncháem's, that the other woman drew back in alarm. 'Nevertheless, you should not forget that you remain here by my leave.'

Bodhmhall got to her feet. 'I will leave you to rest now. You may use this roundhouse for tonight. I will consult my *rechtaire* and my *conradh* with respect to your request for sanctuary and inform you on my final decision after we have eaten this evening.'

Picking up the beaker that she'd let settle on the ashes, she gave it a final shake, added a dollop of honey from another pot and held it out to her visitor.

'Drink this. It will ease the pains and help you to sleep.'

Cowed, Muirne accepted the vessel but considered its contents with a dubious expression.

Bodhmhall stood up to leave. 'I may be *An Cailleach Dubh*, Muirne Muncháem, but I have yet to cause hurt to a child or a visitor in my home.'

Without waiting to for Muirne's reaction, she departed through the doorway. The thick leather covering dropped back in place with a heavy flap.

***

Bodhmhall's fury carried her several paces from the roundhouse before she was finally able to rein it in. Trembling, she halted beside the nearest lean-to, fists clenched so tight that the knuckles on her hands matched the colour of dirty snow. She leaned forwards, resting her forehead against one of the vertical support poles and felt the cool sensation of the wooden surface draw some of the anger from her.

She wasn't sure how long she remained standing there, staring at the ground, resisting the urge to fall to her knees and weep. It was all too much, and all at one time: Liath Luachra's disappearance, the assault from the *draoi*, the shocking news of her brother's death and now the arrival of her old rival.

Taking a deep breath, she released the air slowly in little gasps as she straightened herself up and pulled back from the support pole. Wiping the cold patch of skin on her forehead, she turned and strode across to the fire pit where Conchenn was seated on a reed mat peeling skin from a pile of wrinkled vegetables heaped in a wicker basket. Lowering herself onto the mat beside the old woman, Bodhmhall retrieved an iron knife and furiously started to hack the skinned tubers into smaller pieces.

Glancing at her in surprise, Conchenn considered her briefly then, sensing her turmoil, shuffled over on the mat to make room. Bodhmhall did not acknowledge it but she appreciated the old woman's gesture and felt a sudden gratitude for her silent presence, a perfect antidote to the vexing company of Muirne Muncháem.

Using an old druidic technique, Bodhmhall slowly submitted herself to the quiet rhythm of the physical action, the mindless repetition of cut, turn, cut and turn that allowed her to retreat deep inside herself. It was only there, in that monotonous routine, that she at last found the inner space to grieve, to mourn and empty her heart.

'Bodhmhall!'

Startled, she opened her eyes. The wicker basket was empty. A pile of perfectly chopped vegetables lay on the mat in front of her.

'Bodhmhall!'

She looked around in confusion, struggling to locate the source of the shout before spotting Aodhán on the gateway, beckoning for her to join him. For a moment, she stared dumbly at the slender guard then, abruptly, pushed the vegetables aside. Rising to her feet, she crossed the *lis*, brushing her hands against the rough material of her smock.

Several long strides brought her to the base of the ladder leading up to the rampart. Aodhán moved aside to give her room as she reached the top rung and stepped out onto the stone platform.

'What is it? What's wrong?'

The young warrior pointed wordlessly towards the northern end of the valley. Squinting, she stared in the indicated direction until she found what he wanted her to see; a faraway figure crossing the flatland at speed in the direction of the *ráth*. Despite the distance, she immediately recognised Bearach's distinctive stride.

Aodhán leaned forward, hands pressed against the edge of the wooden palisade. He said nothing as he peered at the runner but scratched at his beard with a wistful expression.

'Bearach's not carrying any game. And there's no sign of Liath Luachra.' He sounded equally perturbed by both observations.

40

'Why is he running at such speed?' The *bandraoi* unconsciously voiced her concern aloud but when she glanced at Aodhán and saw the expression on his face, a chill trickled down her spine. A sick feeling filled her stomach as she gazed around the valley, the familiar shelter of the surrounding hills suddenly appearing to close in around them like the jaws of a triggered bear trap.

'Aodhán, your brother and father are at the *lubgort*. Fetch them quickly, gather the livestock and drive them inside.'

The youth stared at her in alarm, a crease wrinkling across his forehead.

'What is it, Bodhmhall?'

'I think the *ráth* may be under attack.'

Chapter Two

They'd been stalking deer sign for the best part of the morning, following the meandering tracks through the frozen hill country east of Sliabh Bládhma. Liath Luachra estimated that there was one, possibly two, animals. Bearach was convinced there were at least four.

But then he'd always been an optimist.

Liath Luachra relaxed and slowly eased her grip on the javelin. She'd come to a stop in the murky shadow of one of the many trees coating the lower slopes and although she continued to scrutinise the terrain for movement, she was relatively sure the animals were not present.

As sure as she could be.

It was difficult to be certain from the most recent imprints they'd found. The snow cover was inconsistent among the hills and the substance of the previous fall had melted in the unexpected morning sunshine. Adding to the challenge was the fact the tracks alternated between dense wood land where the ground was still soft enough to leave a clear track, and rockier ground where the prints were easy to lose on the rough stone surface.

Liath Luachra exhaled a mouthful of ghost breath into the chilly air and watched the breeze snatch it away. Although she'd never admit to it, she didn't particularly enjoy hunting in winter. In her experience, the physical effort and the sheer discomfort greatly exceeded the rewards. Certainly there was no comparison to the hunt in warmer months. In summer, late spring and even early autumn you could simply choose a comfortable hiding site at one of the animals' favourite feeding grounds, easily identified with experience and patience, and wait for the animals to come to you.

In winter, of course, such an approach was impractical. The cold and the risk of hypothermia made it impossible to remain stationary or inactive for long periods of time. There was no real alternative, therefore, but to stalk the animals, to locate a trail in the snow and follow it, keeping downwind as much as possible in the undulating terrain.

In theory, this was relatively straightforward. Find trail. Follow tracks. Kill deer. In practice, of course, hunting deer required equal measures of skill and good fortune. At this time of the year, the deer had already shed their rich, red coloured coat for a greyish brown that blended perfectly into the background. This natural camouflage rendered the animals practically invisible when they were standing still and hunters were obliged to remain alert for minute traces of movement, the flicker of an ear or the glint of an antler.

Liath Luachra and Bearach had been moving ponderously all morning, passing through the woodland at a pace that allowed them to follow the sign while advancing silently. Avoiding the ridgelines and open spaces, they took only than three or four steps at a time. To counter the deer's sensitive hearing, they had tied sheepskin to the soles of their boots, muffling their footfall. They surveyed the ground ahead at regular intervals to avoid debris on the forest floor that might create noise and alert the animals to their presence.

Putting the javelin aside, Liath Luachra scratched at an itch inside her thigh but found relief impossible through the thick furs she was wearing. She slipped a hand inside the furs and then the wool leggings beneath, sliding her fingers down to the area of irritation. After a moment or two of scratching, she located a tick embedded in the skin. Teasing it out between her thumb and forefinger, she withdrew it for closer examination. Even in the dappled sunlight the insect looked bloated. It had feasted well on her blood.

Time to change the bedding again.

With an expression of distaste, she flicked it off into the trees then proceeded forward, using the limited vegetation and shadows to best advantage.

Even at a crouch, the warrior woman eased through the undergrowth with remarkable grace. Strong legs, toned from years of trudging the rugged landscape, bore her over obstacles with ease. An innate sense of balance allowed her to manoeuvre past barriers that would have tasked the most flexible of acrobats. She had wedged her thick, black, shoulder-length hair beneath a wool-lined leather hat to avoid the snagging branches but halted abruptly as something snagged her attention instead. Dropping to one knee, she brushed aside a tangled clump of fern to discover a small pile of deer dung half-hidden beneath the brittle, red fronds. Lowering herself onto her belly, she examined her find more closely, poking at the individual pellets with a broken twig. As she studied the droppings, she chewed thoughtfully on the inner side of her cheek.

With a sniff, she sat up, transferring her attention to her fellow hunter, Bearach, who had sidled up into the shadow of a neighbouring oak. A slim, dark haired youth of fourteen years, Bearach had always been her favourite of Cairbre's three sons for he laughed easily, a trait only one as solemn as Liath Luachra could truly appreciate. The boy also had a toughness to him that she respected. Although six years her junior, he'd forced himself to keep up with the gruelling pace she'd set on departing the *ráth* that morning and maintained until the first sight of deer sign.

'Bearach,' she whispered.

He glanced towards her and she pointed down at the deer spoor.

Slithering over to where she was crouched, he dropped to his knees and poked at the droppings, pressing one of the pellets with his index finger. It was moist and when he raised it to his nose, it remained fastened to the digit.

'It's fresh.'

'What else?' she pressed.

He looked at her blankly. Her face, pale from the winter season, was as inscrutable as ever and provided no clue to a possible response. She had noticed that when some people, particularly strangers, talked with her, their eyes often slid off to the right, distracted by the ladder of tattooed black lines that scaled the side of her face from below the ear to the forehead. Familiar with it to the point of indifference, the boy's eyes did not veer away.

'It's shit,' he hazarded.

'I know it's shit. What about the shape of it?'

'The pellets are small. Oval shaped.'

'Which suggests ...?'

'The deer have been eating leaves. Browse and twigs instead of grass.'

She nodded, satisfied with the response then waved him on to proceed ahead of her. The freshness of the droppings meant that the deer were not too far ahead. Up front, Bearach would be the first to sight the animal and have the best chance of making a cast. Patient and without complaint during the hunt, he deserved the opportunity and it would be good for his confidence to take the kill.

She continued to observe the boy with the critical eye of an instructor as he moved forward. Slowly detaching himself from the cover of the oak tree, he slipped smoothly from cover to cover down a steep, wooded incline that funnelled into a little valley between two broad hills. She nodded appreciatively as he changed direction at the appropriate times to remain concealed in shadow.

You've turned into a teacher, Grey One. A mentor of unblooded children.

The thought entered her head unbidden and she frowned, unsure whether the notion pleased her or annoyed her. Unable to decide, she ignored it and turned her attention to the surrounding landscape. Undulating hills and valleys shrouded by snow powdered forest as far as the eye could see. It was a beautiful sight and she took the time to appreciate what she was looking at.

It is good to be Out.

Her lips twitched in a rare expression of humour. Despite the cold and the discomfort it *was* good to be Out again. It had been a hard winter and three months of toil and domesticity at Glenn Ceoch had gnawed at her more than it had ever done before. The previous month had been particularly onerous. Preoccupied with treating a run of disease at *Coill Mór*, their nearest neighbors at more than a three day march, Bodhmhall had been away for much of that period, only returning to Ráth Bládhma two days earlier. During her absence, severe late winter storms had battered the land with depressing frequency to the point that Liath Luachra had barely ventured beyond the gate for weeks.

Constraints of any kind, physical or social, had always distressed Liath Luachra, legacy of an insane father who'd repeatedly chained her to a rock as a child. Consumed by fits of madness associated with his regular bouts of drinking, the deranged farmer had been convinced she was trying to poison him. The stomach upsets he suffered had, in fact, been associated with the rotgut liquor he consumed although that possibility had never seemed to occur to him. Instead, he'd interrogate her without respite, beating her when she tried to tell him the truth and then beating her when she made up lies in a desperate attempt to mollify him. In the end, she'd simply shut up and took the punishment, saying nothing as she nurtured a cold hatred in her hardening heart.

Now, many years later, her father was long dead but physical constraints still had the potential to send her into a sweat-stained panic. The living constraints at Ráth Bládhma, admittedly, were nowhere near as dramatic but they were still enough to spill her into that familiar pattern of behavior she'd come to recognize.

45

At first she would grow despondent, increasingly antisocial and withdrawing further and further inside herself. Attempts at interaction from the other members of the settlement would provoke a snarled response. Sensing her explosive hostility, they had wisely left her to her own company. Sitting alone in the empty roundhouse, she had fought the temptation of temporary oblivion from the settlement's supply of alcohol and, slowly but surely, felt herself fray at the edges.

It had been an immense relief when the storms had finally blown themselves inside out, dark clouds unfurling to reveal skies that were clear, if distinctly cold. Aodhán's complaints at the lack of venison had been a convenient excuse to pull on her furs, quit the *ráth* and leave all of its entanglements behind.

Most of the others were reluctant to stray too far from Glenn Ceoch or venture into the cloistered forests of the Great Wild beyond the valley entrance. She understood that. On a sunny day, the forest could be a pleasant place, a familiar friend with its abundant firewood, food supplies, and medicines. At other times, however, particularly when the weather changed, it could take on a dark and sullen personality, that familiar friend suddenly becoming menacingly unrecognisable.

Liath Luachra knew that she had something of a love-hate relationship with the Great Wild. Like most people, she was cautiously respectful of its sheer immensity, the potential for danger that lurked within the thick scrub or slunk through the shadows of the great trees. When humans walked within the forest, their voices echoed thinly amongst the towering trees and in places the green shadowed so much it was almost black. In the Great Wild, people could fan out, spread among its vastness only to be swallowed up by that immensity, never to be seen again.

She recognized that it was this exact same characteristic of the Great Wild that made it so compelling. There was something deeply attractive about a force so immense it could swallow up all trace of one's existence. Some nights, sitting alone on guard duty, she would stare out and shiver at the mysterious noises that echoed in from the encircling blackness. And yet, at the same time, part of her recognized the tug of that emptiness, the irresistible pull on her soul and it took a determined effort to resist the idea of dropping her weapons, clambering down the wall and giving herself up to that dark.

Liath Luachra breathed in, filling her lungs with bracing mountain air and slowly let it out again.

These things don't matter. Focus on the hunt.

She stared down to the heavily wooded valley at the bottom of the slope. From previous hunts, she knew this was a favoured haunt of many deer. The tree cover concealed a rocky fracture in the nearest hill and further in, this widened to a narrow canyon that cut through the hill and emerged out onto the twisted pass known as *An Bealach Cam*. The route, therefore, offered a secure and safe passage to the higher forest on the other side of the ridge.

Secure and safe, until today at least.

Taking a firm grip on the haft of the javelin, she pushed herself off the trunk of the tree with her free hand, using the gradient and the slippery grass to slide quietly down the slope.

Bearach was waiting for her at the entrance to the crevice. As she drew close, he put a finger to his lips and pointed at the ground where a hoof print was visible in a soft patch of exposed earth. Clucking her tongue quietly, Liath Luachra studied the track with interest. From the size of the imprint, the animal was likely to be a buck. And a big one at that. From the direction of the track, it looked as though it had passed directly into the canyon.

Bearach grinned with excitement, his teeth a broad slash of white in the shadows. Once again, she gestured for him take the lead. Javelin at the ready, he entered the rocky gap at a low crouch.

Several paces in, the tight walls of the fracture broadened out into a narrow canyon but the light remained murky, the high cliffs on either side filtering all power from the sickly, grey sunlight. Icicles dangled the length of the cliff tops on either side and the constant patter of dripping water echoed hollowly between the rocky walls. The vegetation here was sparse, consisting of little more than a few mildewed ferns, scraggly plants and a thick layer of moss that coated the various rocks and boulders. Three or four hundred paces down the passage, a dense clump of beech trees occupied the space where the canyon broadened out and marked its intersection with An Bealach Cam.

Bearach looked at her with an uncertain expression but she shrugged then nodded towards the trees. Possibly the buck was hidden there, possibly it had already sensed their presence and slipped forward into the pass.

Slowly, they advanced towards the little wood, weapons at the ready, Liath Luachra remaining a safe distance to the rear so that the boy could make a clear cast if the opportunity arose. Eventually, he entered the thicket but two or three steps inside the tree line she saw him lower his weapon, glance back over his shoulder and shake his head. The animals had moved on again.

Liath Luachra cursed. She could see that although the wood was less than twenty paces deep, it was clogged with interlinking branches, withered foliage and brambles. The resulting field of debris would be difficult to negotiate without making any noise. Unhindered by such requirements, the deer would be able to get ahead of them again, advance onwards from An Bealach Cam and disappear up into the higher ridges.

It took a time but they eventually managed to traverse the little wood without creating too much of a racket and it was Bearach who was first to step foot onto the floor of An Bealach Cam. A tight, but barren, valley weaving through a series of steep hills, it was still mostly covered in snow. Five hundred paces south of where he'd emerged, its steep sides flattened out to a gentle, downhill gradient.

From behind, Liath Luachra watched the boy step out of cover then halt stiffly as he stared down at the ground. Curious, she pushed her way through the last of the scrub and twisted tree trunks to join him. Emerging onto the pass, she realised what he was looking at: several lines of crushed footprints on the snow covered floor.

Bearach!

Liath Luachra grabbed the youth's cloak and yanked him backwards with her. The force of her action was such that momentum carried them both inside the tree line to land heavily on a layer of dead fern and brambles. Taken completely by surprise, Bearach was too startled to react at first, his exclamation of shock smothered by the hand clamped around his mouth. As he gathered his wits, however, and started to struggle, Liath Luachra brought her lips close to his ear.

'Quiet.'

Accustomed to obeying her commands, the boy ceased his attempts to break free. Slowly, she removed her hand and released him.

Bearach immediately shifted his weight off her and rolled to one side, completing the turn with a smooth upward movement onto the balls of his feet. He stared at her in an aggrieved manner which she ignored as she snapped a loop around the javelin haft and slung it across her back to join the other two. Gesturing for him to follow, she dropped to her belly and wriggled closer to the tree line, concealing herself behind the bulk of a bramble-choked elm. Following her example, the boy crawled closer and both stared out through the scrub at that section of the empty pass. There was no sound to be heard, no noise but the muted whisper of their own breathing and the lonely moan of wind gusting through the valley. Finally, satisfied that they were in no immediate danger, Liath Luachra turned her face close to Bearach. 'No-one,' she mouthed.

The boy opened his mouth to respond but before he had a chance she'd already risen to her feet, warily stepping forwards onto the open ground.

Shaking his head, Bearach stood up and followed.

Despite her conviction that they were alone, the woman warrior remained close to the edge of the tree line for a moment or two, eyes flickering from the western end of the pass to a distant curve at the eastern end where it veered a corner and disappeared from sight. Reassured, she approached the trampled snow and bent down to grasp a handful of the powdery material. Raising it to her nose, she sniffed, exhaled through her mouth and sniffed again.

'Not fresh.'

She stood, tossed the crumpled powder aside and headed for the mouth of the pass, studying the ground as she did so. From her interpretation of the scuffed surface, a large party passing through An Bealach Cam had entered from the east and temporarily halted at this point. A significant number of separate footprints had splintered off from the main trail to gather in smaller clusters, probably to converse with friends or comrades. Others had veered off to the side to piss against the cliff walls or amongst the trees where yellow traces of urine still stained the snow.

Liath Luachra collated different elements of the story written across the ground before her and finally came to her conclusions. Whoever they were, the party had not remained at the mouth of the pass for very long. Some discussion had taken place, there had been a brief respite for the men – they were all men's footprints – to catch their breath and wolf down some food. This much was clear from the scattered depressions where people had sat together and the scatter of crumbs and discarded scraps of food.

While they were waiting, the party had been joined by a single individual, possibly a scout, who'd entered the pass from the west. Perhaps this newcomer had told them something or perhaps they had simply rested enough. Whatever the reason, shortly after his arrival – his tracks were notably fresher – the group had assembled once more, formed a single column and headed out of the pass. They'd departed in a westerly direction, angling towards some hills that avoided the marshes and offered an easier track through the wilderness.

She raised her head to look Bearach in the eye.

'What do you see?'

The young man looked surprised to be tested at such a time but obediently bent down to examine the nearest tracks, using the tip of the javelin to sift through the layers of trodden snow.

'Twenty to thirty men.' He paused and bit his lip. 'Carrying a lot of weight. But moving fast. In a hurry. They didn't stay here long.'

His forehead creased in concentration and he glanced up at Liath Luachra.

'Bandits?'

She shook her head.

'Too many. And from the weight, too well equipped. It's a *fian*.'

Bearach stared at her in surprise. 'A war party? In winter? Travelling out here in the wild lands? That doesn't make sense.'

'No,' she admitted. 'It doesn't.'

'So where are they going? There aren't any settlements to the west except for An Coill Mór. Or maybe Ráth Dearg.' He scratched his chin then his hand rose to nervously pick at the pitiful moustache he'd been attempting to grow over the previous months. 'But An Coill Mór's at least three days march north-west. Ráth Dearg's more than four south west. With nothing but forest and marshland between.'

Liath Luachra gave a shrug.

'It doesn't matter. If they keep moving west, they can march to their heart's content. They're not our concern as long as they stay clear of Glenn Ceoch.'

'Shouldn't we warn An Coill Mór?'

'We don't have the supplies to make a three-day trip. Besides, Coill Mór is small. This war party will never find them.'

With this, she turned her back on the youth and examined the ground once more. Despite her apparent indifference, however, she was frowning. The tracks had roused her curiosity. Bearach had the right of it and his incredulity was well warranted. It was hard to believe a *fian* would be headed for either of the two other settlements out in the Great Wild. An Coill Mór was little more than a farm and had a total population of five people. Ráth Dearg, an admittedly larger holding, was the property of the old warrior Cathal ua Tuarsaig and his extended family. Back in the day, Cathal had the reputation of a ferocious fighter but he'd withdrawn to the isolation of the Great Wild many years ago. It was difficult to imagine anyone still cared enough or held resentment strong enough to lead a war party to attack him.

She exhaled slowly, feeling the weight of the boy's eyes on her shoulders as she walked parallel to the trodden snow trail, scanning the ground for anything else out of the ordinary. Suddenly, she gave an exclamation of triumph and gestured for Bearach to come closer.

'Here.'

He approached and she pointed out a faint deer print on an untouched stretch of snow. Several paces further on, there was another, similar print.

Having anticipated further discussion on the *fian*, Bearach looked at her with an expression of frustrated incomprehension.

'There's an animal that shows wisdom,' declared Liath Luachra. 'Veering east to avoid the *fian*. Let's follow that sensible example and do the same.'

With a wide grin, she turned and abruptly moved off in an easterly direction, quickly breaking into a powerful, ground-eating stride.

'Come on, Bearach. We may get venison for your brother's belly yet.'

***

By mid-afternoon, it was clear that they had lost the trail. Presumably alarmed by the presence of so much human activity, the deer had warily moved on, departing from its normal feeding territory and moving further into the Great Wild. It soon became evident that it was headed for the dense forest to the north-west where there would be little chance of finding them.

The hunters halted to discuss their options, disgusted by such a poor outcome after a long period stalking the animals. Disheartened, it took but a brief discussion for both to agree to return to Ráth Bládhma. Aodhán would, no doubt, grumble at their lack of venison but it was better that the settlement were informed about the *fian* even if they did return empty-handed.

No longer constrained by the need to stalk their quarry, the pair knew that they could now make good time and, if they pushed themselves, there was a good chance of reaching the *ráth* by nightfall. Despite their eagerness for the comfort of the hearth, however, the threat of the *fian's* potential return prompted Liath Luachra to ignore the direct route. Opting instead for a more circuitous path, the hunters followed the hills, staying inside the trees and avoiding any open flat land. Later that afternoon, her caution proved well founded when Bearach, who'd taken the lead, slipped on a loose section of snow while hurriedly traversing a stretch of open terrain. Tumbling face first into a nearby drift, he spluttered and brushed the snow from his face, then struggled to his feet.

'Liath Luachra!'

The hoarseness of the boy's voice would have alerted the woman warrior but, running close behind him, she'd already spotted what he'd seen; the worn trail of footprints. Twenty or thirty men. Moving in single file.

Frowning, she studied scuffed up tracks in the snow for the second time that day. Her lips pressed tight together as she went down on one knee, slipped a hand out of her mittens and scooped up a handful of snow. After sniffing she threw it aside and stood up again.

It was the same party. She was sure of it. Here and there, she recognised distinctive markings from the trail encountered earlier that morning: an uncommonly wide boot heel, the one-sided imprint of someone with a limp in their left leg, a sharp triangular impression of a damaged spear haft shaft used like a staff. On this occasion, however, the party was headed in an easterly direction, directly opposite to the one it had taken that morning when departing An Bealach Cam.

Which meant they'd curved in a wide semi-circle, looping back onto their original track.

Now why would they do that?

Her curiosity prickled, an incessant itch too deep beneath the skin to be effectively scratched.

They can't be lost. The sky is clear and they can work their direction from the sun.

Brushing the snow from her knees, she glanced south in the direction of Glenn Ceoch.

Bearach cleared his throat nervously.

'These tracks are fresher. Less than two hours old. We should get back to the *ráth* and alert them.'

Liath Luachra stared around at the empty landscape. Black, forest coated hills, broken here and there by white patches of snow. Apart from the long trail of broken snow there was no other evidence that the *fian* had passed this way.

'No.' She shook her head. 'We stay Out.'

Bearach stared, surprised by this sudden change in plan. Liath Luachra, however, continued to survey the surrounding landscape. Finally, her gaze ceased to drift, focussing in on one of the many forested ridges off to the south-west.'

'Up there.' She glanced at Bearach. 'I found a cave to the left of that cleft on the ridge last year. It won't be comfortable but it'll serve as shelter for the night.'

The youth continued to regard her in bafflement. Suddenly, his eyes flared with comprehension.

'The snow. They might see our tracks.'

'Leading them straight back to Ráth Bládhma.' Liath Luachra nodded. 'A *fian* that big, they'll have scouts out, covering the vanguard and flanks. We've been lucky so far. We've missed them on two separate occasions.'

She twisted her shoulder, adjusting the arrangement of the javelins strapped across her back.

'But this set of tracks is more recent. They'll be closer.' She nodded decisively to herself as though agreeing with the logic of her own conclusions. 'The best thing we can do now is to go to ground. Leave as little evidence of our existence as possible.'

***

By the time they'd climbed to the cleft on the hill crest, the sky was beginning to darken, the light turning brittle and grey. The wind had also increased, whipping icy gusts down from the summit to spatter their eyes and faces.

'There it is!'

Liath Luachra pointed towards a narrow slit in the side of a steep incline, just above the tree line. Pleased to find it exactly where she'd remembered, she approached the craggy cave mouth. It seemed a bit narrower than she recalled but it was definitely the place.

A rocky passage curled inwards from the entrance for a distance of about seven or eight paces before veering off sharply to the left. Here it widened to form a circular chamber with a high curved ceiling. In one wall, there was a wide ledge at the height of a tall man's head. Accessible using a rough series of hollows and notches that pockmarked the rocky surface, it provided a secure place to sleep.

Liath Luachra dumped an armful of kindling and branches onto the floor then left Bearach to coax a fire to life while she went outside and down to the trees to seek additional fuel. After returning several times with armfuls of the driest wood she could find, she hacked a number of branches from a nearby gorse bush and used them to plug the entrance to the cave. As a barrier, the spiny shrub did not present a serious obstacle, however its voluminous branches would serve as a credible windbreak to prevent the worst of the gale from entering the cave. More importantly, they would also help to shield any light from the fire that might seep out from the inner chamber.

When the gap was sealed to her satisfaction, Liath Luachra joined the youth, sitting by the small fire he'd managed to put together. Bearach had also laid their rations out on a flat rock beside the fire; two portions of salted fish, blood cake and some hard bread, all wrapped in broad, green dock leaves.

They ate the frugal meal in silence, the woman warrior chewing without relish on the tasteless hard tack. It was hardly a feast but it was certainly not the worst she'd eaten. With her habitual pragmatism, she accepted the food for what it was; simple replenishment to keep the hunger pangs at bay.

Beside her, somewhat more forthright, Bearach sighed and grimaced melodramatically with each mouthful.

'Some roasted meat would have been nice.'

Liath Luachra gave him a sideward glance, one eyebrow raised.

'You're as bad as your brother.'

'But Aodhán has a point. He likes his meat. This is like chewing dog turds. I wish we'd brought some decent food with us.'

Liath Luachra rewarded his opinion with a look of disdain. Tossing the empty dock leaves aside, she slowly got to her feet and then twisted her hips so that she could slip her right hand down the back of her woollen leggings. Bearach watched in growing bewilderment as she grunted loudly, forehead creased as though in immense concentration.

'What are you doing?'

'Be quiet. I'm trying to pull some nice fresh venison out of my ass for your dinner.'

He stared at her blankly then suddenly his head rolled back and a raucous guffaw echoed around the cave, resounding off the hard chamber walls to fill the enclosed space with laughter. Infected by his contagious good humour, Liath Luachra started to laugh as well and, for a moment, a great weight slipped from her shoulders.

When they'd finished eating the last scraps of food, Bearach climbed up to the rocky shelf to unroll their bedding; two double-layered wool blankets. He spread these out across a cushion of spruce cuttings that he'd trampled flat on the rock base and strewn with dead leaves bundled up from the cavern floor.

Liath Luachra regarded the sleeping arrangements with little enthusiasm. *Hard dreams tonight, then.*

'You go ahead and sleep,' she instructed the boy. 'I want to think and I need to be alone to work out the way of things. I'll come join you when I'm ready.'

Shrugging, Bearach retired to his bedroll and lay down, fully clothed, on the thin bedding. They would have no covering layer tonight, relying on their shared body heat, the fire and the shelter of the cave to keep them warm until morning.

Exhausted from the day's exertions, it did not take the boy long to fade and within a short period of time, a soft snore emanated from the huddle he made.

Liath Luachra remained seated before the small fire, adding some dry sticks then rubbing her palms together before the brief flare of heat they produced. Outside, the temperature would have plummeted but it was still pleasantly warm within the cave, the rocky walls reflecting the heat of the fire back on her. Later in the night, when the fire had died down, the accumulated heat would slowly seep out through the cave entrance, despite her best efforts to seal them in.

She glanced back over her shoulder and up to the ledge where Bearach was visible, sleeping quietly. She released a long sigh. Originally intending to travel alone, she'd allowed the boy to beat her resistance down with his good humour and boundless enthusiasm, somehow convincing her to let him come. She was still unsure how he'd actually managed to do that, to weasel his way past her habitual resolve.

The fire crackled and a low draught stirred the scent of burning pine up to her nostrils.

She had never been particularly good with children, unable to relate to their weakness, their innocence and complete dependency on adults. Her own childhood had taught her that there were only two types of people: those who were tough enough to survive and those who died. It was a simple as that.

And yet it wasn't, of course.

Three years at Ráth Bládhma had changed her beliefs on many things. Somehow, over that time, the routine domesticity and Bodhmhall's calming influence had mellowed her, worn down her more jagged edges. Until accompanying Bodhmhall to Ráth Bládhma she had never really known such an extended period of calm, of tranquillity. In the new settlement, for the first time in her life, she was surrounded by people she actually liked, people who respected her presence there as much for her company as for her martial skills.

You are getting soft, Liath Luachra. Life at Ráth Bládhma has made you soft and fat.

Sometimes she wished she could cut old memories from her mind, peel them away in the same way she'd peel the skin from a potato. If such things were possible she would have pared away all the pain, all the memories, long ago and tossed them into the air to let the wind take them away.

She chuckled at her own inanities. She was only fooling herself. The pain made her who she was. The pain made her hard and ruthless and, sometimes, ruthlessness was necessary to combat those who threatened you.

And there was always someone who would threaten you.

Someone like the fian.

The thought of the war party instantly dissolved any remaining trace of good humour, burning it off like frost on a sunny morning. She stared at the fire and cursed softly. For the sake of the boy she'd feigned indifference throughout the afternoon but the presence of the *fian* concerned her greatly, particularly as she could not work out the rationale behind it. It made no sense to rouse a war party at this time of the year, a time when most people were struggling to survive the hardships of winter. Its presence in these lands made even less sense. Settlements were few and scattered and none had sufficient booty to warrant a raid of such a large group of men, none that she was aware of at least.

And then there was the question of the *fian*'s erratic behaviour. Why would they make such fitful changes in direction? There had been no threat for them to respond to so they had to be searching for someone. Or something.

A chill trickled down her spine with that particular conclusion. Ráth Bládhma was isolated and had had no contact with other settlements since the beginning of winter. It was possible that some event had taken place, some political situation had changed that they were not yet aware of and which might have placed them at risk. With both Bearach and herself absent, the settlement had a single effective defender in Aodhán. The others, without doubt, would do their best to assist but, in reality, only Aodhán had the martial training needed.

Irritable and worried, she left the fire and climbed up to the ledge where Bearach was snoring. Lying down beside him on the uncompromising surface, she nestled in close to share his warmth but found that she was unable to relax. Sleep remained elusive, slithering away like a greasy eel between her hands each time she thought to clutch it.

She sighed. It was going to be a long night.

***

'Bearach. Wake up.'

The youth opened groggy eyes, struggling to come to full alertness. His hand moved, grasping for the dagger lying on the rocky floor beside the bedding. Liath Luachra, crouched alongside him, deftly moved it out of reach.

'You don't need to use that. Get up. We have to leave.'

She could barely see him as he sat up and peered blearily around. The fire had died out some time ago and now the little cavern was embedded in shadow as dark as a black pig's hole.

'It's snowing.'

For a moment he could only return her stare, struggle to work out what she was talking about. Finally, she saw comprehension seep into his exhausted brain. He understood. If it was snowing, they could travel without fear of tracks. They could return to their valley and Ráth Bládhma without fear of leaving a trail that might reveal its location.

Without further protest, he rolled off the bedding and started rolling up the blanket.

***

It was still dark when they emerged from the cave and into the icy air. Standing at the craggy entrance, Liath Luachra stared up at the perforated layer of white flakes cascading out of the darkness overhead. She shivered and pulled the hood of her cloak down lower over her forehead. The snow fall was not heavy but it was steady. The absence of wind meant that it would settle on the ground, leaving a fresh layer to obscure all trace of their passage. She exhaled slowly and a phantom mist momentarily frosted the air about her lips. Night still cloaked the land but her instincts told her that it would not be long before the first grey tinge appeared on the horizon, followed soon after by the streaky white blur of dawn.

'Stay close now, Bearach.'

The youth took a deep breath and nodded. Like Liath Luachra, he had packed lightly, bedroll and three javelins strapped tight across his back to allow maximum freedom of movement. Both wore their fur mittens, wool hats pulled tight over heads crowned with wide oilskin hoods.

They set off in a southerly direction, dropping from the hill to the flat ground that snaked between the ridges, trudging through snow that was ankle deep in places. South for Ráth Bládhma thought Liath Luachra. South for home.

Still struggling against the gluey clutch of sleep, the boy relinquished all responsibility for their path. Liath Luachra pushed them forward with her characteristic intensity but maintained a measured pace that kept them warm without causing the thick film of sweat that could pose a lethal risk if they were forced to stop and their body temperature dropped.

They'd been travelling for some time when the woman warrior stopped abruptly, so abruptly, in fact, that Bearach ran into her, buffeting his nose against the javelins strapped across her back. For a moment, the boy teetered and struggled to regain his balance. Ignoring his predicament, Liath Luachra peered forward into the gloom. Although Bearach knew better than to interrupt her when she was preoccupied, she sensed him easing up alongside, curious to see what she was looking at. Both of them stared at the dim smear of light in the distance, set at the base of a broad hill known as Drom Osna – the Ridge of Sighs.

'What is it?' Bearach asked at last, finally running out of patience.

'It's a fire. But it's distant. Or reflected off the trees. Hard to tell at this distance.'

Liath Luachra frowned up at the darkness stretched tight across the heavens and scratched her cheek with a mitten. The snow was easing but the sky was still black and viscous as a bog pool.

'Do you think it's that *fian*?'

She grimaced at the boy's enthusiasm, shaking her head in exasperation. 'They were headed east. They couldn't have come back this way so quickly. Besides, a single fire for so many? It ...'

Her voice trailed as off as her mind became absorbed with the possibilities. Eventually, she swore, unable to come up with a feasible explanation. Curious by nature, she hated not knowing the detail of things. 'Hell's testicles! This country is busier than a spring fair! People are traipsing all over the place.'

She bit her lip and squinted at the distant glow.

'Bearach,' she said at last. 'I'm going closer. I want to see who it is.'

'Wouldn't it be safer to go back to the *ráth*?' He stared at her with serious eyes from beneath the cowl of his hood.

'Safer perhaps. But we'd be no wiser on the nature of those parties tramping around our territory. Better to look them over before running back to cower behind the walls, no?'

Uncertain, the youth refrained from comment, stamping his feet to keep the circulation flowing.

Liath Luachra removed her javelins and blanket then divested herself of her heavy woollen cloak as well. She handed the awkward bundle across to Bearach. 'Keep these safe until I get back,'

'I'm not coming with you?'

The question took Liath Luachra by surprise and she looked at him blankly. After a moment, she pointed to a nearby clump of forest. 'You see those trees?'

He nodded.

'I want you to hide there. Stay out of sight when I leave. If you hear a noise, any commotion at all, you run directly for Ráth Bládhma and you don't stop until you get there. Understand?'

Bearach swallowed and nodded nervously, fingers struggling to get a decent grip on the meagre substance of his budding moustache.

'You don't stop,' Liath Luachra insisted. 'If there's trouble here you need to warn the *ráth* about the *fian*. Bodhmhall and Aodhán will know what to do but tell them if there's any trouble they should leave and make a run for Dún Baoiscne. They'll ... they'll protect our people.'

She grimaced involuntarily. Even naming the Baoiscne fortress out loud left a bitter taste in her mouth.

Without another word, she turned and started walking, intent on reaching the mysterious light. After only a few steps, however, something made her halt and look back over her shoulder. Bearach's face, staring miserably after her, was a pale moon amongst the shadow of the trees and she blinked, confused by the sensation it stirred up inside her chest. Unsettled, she shook it off, brushing all thought of the boy from her mind as she turned and focussed once more on achieving her objective.

The distant light proved an effective beacon, drawing her in towards it like a moth to a flame. Unhindered by javelins or blanket, she was able to move swiftly, slipping easily over the crusted snow until she reached the densely forested hill several hundred paces south of Drom Osna.

Pausing, she considered the light once more. It was a fire all right. Now that she was closer she could see that it was situated in some kind of hollow or depression at the base of the hill, just in front of what seemed to be a large cavern in the rock face. Although the source of the light was out of her direct line of sight, the glow from the flames reflected off the frozen surface of the leaves on the nearby trees and a light haze of ice crystals hanging in the air.

Foolish.

Liath Luachra sniffed in disapproval. The hollow was a poor choice to site the fire. Not only did it signpost their location but the occupants were more than likely night blind as a result of the fire's proximity.

All the better for me.

Moving at a low crouch, she followed the hill to a point less than a hundred paces from the cave. Here, she dropped to her belly and started to slide forwards across the snow. Fifty paces out, she stopped and lay motionless as she took the time to scan the trees for any flicker of movement, any unusually shaped shadows. She was relatively confident that she was safe where she lay. Around her the surface was rough and uneven, the snow folded up into low banks by the prevailing wind that would obscure her from most eyes.

She remained in the same position for a long time, before finally satisfied that there were no guards posted, none at the extremities of the hollow, none along the tree line of the lower hill. It was hard to believe but the occupants appeared to have taken no precautions of any kind.

What are these strangers thinking! They must have a death-wish.

She was about to move forward again when a sudden sound reached her ears and she froze in place. Startled, she drew her feet up, ready to take flight but as she listened to the low, humming drone, she began to relax. It was a chant. Someone below in the hollow was chanting.

Very thoughtful. That should cover any noise I make.

With one last sweep of the tree line, she began to move again, circling away from the hill to approach the hollow from a different angle. Further out from the hill the surface of the snow flattened out, becoming smoother and unblemished. Another slow, careful crawl brought her to within spitting distance of the lip of the depression but, spotting a fallen tree off to one side, she began to manoeuvre herself towards it, intending to use the trunk as cover when looking down into the hollow.

Easing in beside it, she lay with her face pressed against the trunk, her cheek stinging from the touch of the ice-coated bark. Shivering, she briefly regretted her decision to leave the wool cloak behind but almost immediately dismissed the notion. The extra fur-lined layer would have been welcome but the garment's bulk would have been too restrictive for what she needed.

Without warning, the chanting ceased. Once again, Liath Luachra froze in place. With shallow breaths, she sniffed the air but smelt nothing other than wood smoke and the sharp scent of snow.

Removing her right mitten, she gripped the wooden handle of her knife and drew it silently from the leather scabbard tucked into her belt. Placing the blade against her palm, she felt the coldness of the metal surface suck the warmth from her fingers. She hefted the weapon in the palm of her hand, comforted by its solid weight. If discovered, she had no intention of staying around to fight but the weapon would give her a slight edge – literally – if someone tried to stop her.

Drawing her knees up close to her chest, she carefully adopted a crouching position. Craning her neck forwards and around the side of the tree trunk, she cast a quick glance into the hollow, withdrawing back into cover in a smooth movement. Back in the lee of the log, she paused as she attempted to make sense of what she'd seen.

The hollow itself was wide, circular in shape and, unlike the land around it, empty of any snow layer whatsoever. In some ways that didn't surprise her. It was clearly a site of old knowledge, a place of the Old People who'd gone before and whose origins were now lost to memory. Two standing stones were situated at its centre, ancient monoliths for one of them had cracked in two a very long ago, the upper half tumbling to lie alongside the remaining stump.

The fire, an impressive blaze, was located next to the standing stones, surrounded by one or two sleeping forms lying huddled on the ground. As far as she could tell, there was only one person awake, a single figure seated on a rock before the flames, back turned towards her.

Liath Luachra bit her lip as she worked through the scene in her head again. It all felt wrong, smelled wrong. This group, whoever they were, were either insane or believed themselves under no threat of attack from man or wild animals. Curiosity burned her up inside.

She edged around the log again to get another look, shielding her eyes against the flare of the fire. The bedrolls she could see were occupied, the sleeping figures swathed in blankets and furs against the cold. Despite the size of the fire, it was impossible to distinguish their features because of the flickering shadows cast down by the flames.

In the cavern, beyond the blaze at the other side of the hollow, she caught a stir of movement. An equestrian snort confirmed the presence of at least one horse tethered within and she was suddenly very relieved that she'd decided to approach from downwind.

Fixing her eyes on the figure before the fire she studied it carefully. Wrapped in a shapeless black cloak and hooded cowl, any indication of sex or features were obscured. She continued to stare.

This isn't right.

Some intuition stirred a tremor of fear in Liath Luachra's belly and, unnerved, she decided to withdraw. Slowly backing away from the edge of the hollow, she saw the figure by the fire stiffen then stand straight up, turning slowly to stare directly at where she was hiding.

He can see me!

A spasm of panic spiralled through her and she almost screamed as she realised what she was staring at. There was something wrong with the face staring towards her, something terribly wrong. Even at that distance, she could tell that the figure had no eyes, nothing but an empty pair of ragged sockets. Beneath them, the nose had also been removed or cut back to the bone and the lips of its mouth had been crudely sewn together with rough black stitches.

For a moment, she was so terrified, so completely overwhelmed with fear that her bladder loosened. Ironically, the sensation of warm urine down the inside of her leggings distracted her, freed her enough to act.

Rolling desperately from the lip of the hollow, Liath Luachra got to her feet and took to her heels, no longer caring if she was seen, desperate only to flee the hideous sight behind her. The knife slipped from her fingers but she ran on, boots stirring up puffs of snow as she left it discarded in her wake.

The sound of cursing rose up from behind her, raised voices and muffled demands for clarification hurled into the night. Stirred by the uproar, the horses started neighing furiously. Even though she was running, she could hear hysterical high-pitched laughter so close that it terrified her until she realised it was her own.

Despite having succumbed to a fully-fledged panic, some part of Liath Luachra recognised that she was reacting completely out of character but, inside her head, her mind continued to scream, drowning out all rational thought. She felt her intellect diminish, reduced to an animal-like terror, a clutching desperation to put as much distance as possible between herself and the creature behind her.

After that, everything blurred. She was cognisant of nothing but the most basic of sensation: red fog, pain, the never-ending impulse to run, to keep on running.

At some point, she stumbled, hit the ground and cracked her head against something solid. Although stunned by the impact, the blow had the additional, secondary, effect of clearing her mind and for a moment, it was as though some tight mental leash had been loosened.

Where ... Where am I?

The sky was light, if slightly overcast. From the position of the sun, it looked to be well past dawn. Apart from a few shadowed patches, the snow had for the most part melted away. She gasped in pain as she tried to raise her head and discovered that she was lying on some frosted stones, the frozen detritus of a dried-out river bed. Her body was twisted on the uneven surface, blood pooling on the large boulder where she'd hit her head. Physical sensation overwhelmed her and she was suddenly wheezing, barely able to breathe in freezing air so cold it scalded the back of her throat. Her head pounded from the stress of extreme physical effort. She was, she realised, barely on the right side of consciousness.

Gods! How long have I been running?

She vomited then, the meagre but warm contents of her stomach creating minute swirls of vapour on contact with the freezing stones. Too exhausted to move, she lay where she had fallen, threads of saliva and phlegm dripping from her lips. She was close to passing out when she felt the terror building up inside her head again, a hollow wave of dread surging up to engulf her once more.

Then she was up and running again.

Out of the river bed stones, scrambling up the snow coated bank.

Deep into the forest.

***

For a time, nothing existed but the seething of dreams, a darkness thick and murky as swamp water. It was a slight rustling that finally roused her to consciousness, a rustling and a soft whistling that sounded like a tune she'd heard as a child a very long time before.

The memories flooded back as she drifted upwards, to awareness. Memories that stirred a hollow sense of panic.

That face!

She became aware of a soft weight pressing down on her chest. It took a moment to understand that she was conscious again, that the blue-whiteness filling her eyes was the play of clouds splayed across the heavens. Not the ethereal blank backdrop of nothingness.

The transition to sensory perception was not as gentle as her visual recovery, accompanied by a discomfort as deep as a battle wound.

It hurts.

Awake now, she could feel the ache across her entire body. Intense but profound, as though she had done herself some great internal injury. Although the pain felt acute it was also oddly generic and difficult to isolate. The muscles in her legs, however, burned with a distinctness of their own, as though the very tissue and sinew had been stretched beyond its limits. A ferocious thirst arose in a throat that was parched and dry and sore. Her stomach rumbled, ravenous for food.

Another rustle.

She struggled to rise but found she was lying on her back, spread-eagled on a bed of furs. Each hand and leg had been separately tethered to a small stake in the ground. A heavy fur cloak had been tossed across her chest.

'Are the rages still on you?'

The voice, masculine, came from behind. She struggled to raise her head and although she succeeded in tilting her neck at a slight angle, she was unable to make out the speaker. Fortunately, the source of the query moved into view a moment later, taking a seat on an overturned log lying on the ground by her right hand.

He was a young man. Broad shouldered and handsome with a full moustache and a thick mane of black hair that spilled down to his shoulders. The thick strands had been tied up in braids around his face, exposing the tattooed patterns on his left cheek and forehead. His noble heritage was evidenced by the embroidered, coloured tunic and pants of good quality. A green wool cloak hung draped over his shoulders, fastened beneath his chin with an elaborate bronze pin.

Liath Luachra struggled to focus and she blinked, pupils and eyelids burning. Her stomach hurt from heaving. Her joints were swollen, disjointed by strain. Her scalp and face felt scratched and torn and a headache pounded inside her temple. She stank of sweat and stale urine.

She ignored the pain. She knew how to deal with pain. It was the restraints that terrified her, the unfamiliar sense of powerlessness. She tried to speak but the word came out as a hoarse croak, her parched lips unable to articulate the sounds correctly.

'Gaaahh.'

The response, oddly enough, seemed to satisfy her captor for he gave an easy smile. 'Good. The rages have passed.'

With a nod, he rose from his seat and pulled a long knife from the scabbard on his belt. Unable to move, Liath Luachra watched him approach with mounting apprehension, glaring in defiance as he crouched down beside her. She forced herself not to flinch as he lifted the knife but he didn't seem to notice her relief as he used the weapon to cut the leather thongs around her right hand. Keen and freshly ground, the blade made short work of the bindings, the severed strips falling to the ground with a single slice.

Free at last, she made another desperate attempt to rise but it was a dismal failure. Her body, pushed beyond its limits, simply refused to respond to her mental commands. She was left lying as helpless as a fish left beached in the shallows by the departing tide.

Beside her, the squatting man continued to watch her as though anticipating some particular reaction that she was unable to provide. When it became apparent that no response was forthcoming, he sighed, slipped a hand underneath her back and hauled her into a sitting position. As she was pulled upright, the fur cloak shifted and slid off to one side. She was suddenly aware of the chill touch of air against the exposed skin of her arms.

Satisfied that she was not about to fall, the man grabbed a water skin lying on the ground beside them.

'Drink.'

He held out the leather container and she grasped it with weak hands, hauling it to her mouth to gulp the water down. Much of the liquid splashed down one side of her face but she succeeded in getting some through her parched lips.

After several long swallows, she continued to drink despite feeling sated. She could feel the water swell her internal tissue, filling her dehydrated body from the inside out.

Finally, she dropped the skin and considered the tall man who had returned to his seat on the rock. Stroking the tender, red welts on her wrists, a consequence of the bindings, she made a point of ignoring him while she looked around and assessed their surroundings although the effort set her head spinning. A muscle at the side of her face twitched, the nerve shot, but she ignored that too.

They were in a crude campsite. Located in a tight clearing, it was surrounded on all sides by forest, tall trees with wide, spanning limbs that blotted out patches of sky. She noted that her 'benefactor' had also constructed a rough lean-to, a shelter constructed with branches hacked from the surrounding trees. She placed a hand palm downwards on the ground beside her. It was cold but free of snow.

'Fiacail mac Codhna!'

The young man made a pretence at a bow.

'It always pleases a man to be recalled by the fairer sex, Liath Luachra.' He smiled, revealing the perfect set of teeth – *fiacla* – from which his nickname had been derived.

Her response was a growl.

'Even,' he continued, completely undaunted 'If it be for all the wrong reasons.'

'You had the good sense to cut me loose. Don't provoke me, big man.'

If he was in any way perturbed by the threat, the young man certainly showed no sign of it. He slapped his knee and roared with laughter, a deep, rollicking guffaw that only served to infuriate her further.

'You prancing cockerel. What are you doing here? For that matter what am I – '

She stopped in mid-sentence for she had suddenly noticed two other men sitting cross-legged on the other side of the little clearing, separated from her by a roaring campfire. Both were dressed in colourless, woollen jerkins and cloaks and bore the facial scarring and tattoos of seasoned warriors. Stocky and dark-haired, they shared similar pug noses and narrow foreheads, a strong resemblance that left little doubt of their close kinship. Although they were sitting half-shrouded in shadow, Liath Luachra was angry with herself for not spotting them straight off. Despite her open scrutiny, they stared back at her in silence.

'What are you doing here?' Fiacail completed the question for her. 'Well, there's an interesting tale.' He paused to reach back to the fire and pulled a wooden bowl from the embers. The strong smell of a warm meaty broth hit her nostrils and it took all of her self-control to prevent herself from licking her lips.

Fiacail handed her the bowl. Making no pretence of manners, she raised it straight to her lips and shovelled the steaming contents down her throat, ignoring the scalding it gave her tongue.

'You know,' continued Fiacail, politely ignoring her lack of finesse. 'It's always been a matter of some amazement to me, the efforts to which some young women will rise to seek out the pleasure of my company. Now, I'm hardly the one to brag but ...'

'Fiacail,' she snapped, tossing the empty bowl aside with a frown of regret. She could happily have gorged another bowl or two.

'But your approach was somewhat more original.' He grinned that infuriating grin, completely indifferent to her glowering expression. 'Never let it be said that Liath Luachra fails to make a dramatic entrance.' He coughed into his hand and took on the sombre tones of a professional storyteller.

'There I was, settled down with a fire, a warm meal and the congenial company of my kinsmen. He gestured towards the two men across the fire then widened his eyes for dramatic effect. 'Suddenly, who should come thundering out of the undergrowth but Liath Luachra, the Grey One of Luachair.'

He raised his eyebrows, shaking his head with an exaggerated expression of incomprehension.

'Not that we recognised you at first, of course. Your eyes bulging like a constipated toad, your mouth frothing, gibbering like a crazy woman. Without care or concern, you stampeded through our camp, trampled our little fire, and stomped on the girdle cake we'd been saving for ...'

Fiacail's melodrama tailed off quietly.

'Tóla and Ultán were particularly upset at the loss of that girdle cake. They'd been looking forward to the sweet taste for days. To be honest, I was none too pleased myself. That cake was a present from a close friend in Seiscenn Uarbhaoil.'

'Fiacail,' said Liath Luachra, her head drooping with fatigue. She closed her eyes as a pounding headache flowered up behind her temple. She had never felt so weak in her life. 'Please just tell me what happened.'

The young man considered her in silence. After a moment he nodded to himself as though he'd made some private, internal decision.

'Very well. Quite simply, you ran through our camp, tripped over the stones about out fire and hit the ground hard. The fall must have knocked the air out of your chest for you were wheezing and drooling, unable to even breathe. Despite this, you attempted to rise again, growling and snarling at us when we tried to restrain you. You truly had the strength of the mad, Liath Luachra. In the end, it took all three of us to restrain you, to tie you down so you could not harm yourself. Or us, for that matter. Despite your restraints, you kicked and you bucked for some time before you finally passed out.'

He looked her directly in the eyes but this time none of his earlier humour remained.

'You were possessed by a demon, Liath Luachra. If we had not stopped you, you would have run yourself to death.'

Chapter Three

Bearach was visibly flagging as he neared the *ráth*. By the time he'd reached the causeway and made it through the stone gateway he was, literally, staggering. Cairbre and Aodhán, waiting inside the safety of the *lis*, sealed the gap behind him with a heavy door. A thick slab of hard oak lined with rows of iron bolts, its outer panels had been reinforced with strips of metal, its inner panels inlaid with leather straps. The latter allowed it to be manhandled into position, flush against the protruding stone then securely fixed to four iron rungs set into the gateway. Once it was in place, a wooden brace was wedged firmly between the door and a large boulder. The final barrier presented a substantial obstacle to anyone intent on storming Ráth Bládhma.

With the entranceway secure, Cairbre returned to the gateway while Cónán was dispatched to the eastern side of the *ráth* to watch for any force attempting to outflank the settlement. Bodhmhall and Aodhán descended to the *lis* where Bearach was slumped against the wooden frame above the fire pit. Heaving great gasps of breath into the chilly air, he lifted a ladle full of water from a nearby bucket and poured the liquid over his head, sputtering and cursing at the cold of it.

'Where's the venison, brother?' Aodhán rested his weight on the shaft of his javelin, patiently regarding his brother. 'And what have you done to lose Liath Luachra?'

Scowling, Bearach ignored his sibling as he struggled to his feet to face Bodhmhall.

'A *fian*, Bodhmhall! At least twenty to thirty men.'

The *bandraoi* stared at him in shock.

'A *fian*! Out here in the Great Wild? Are you sure?' She cast a glance towards the older sibling, hoping for some form of reassurance. The worried expression on Aodhán's face did nothing to allay her fears.

'Yes, Bodhmhall,' the boy replied. 'There's no doubt of it.'

Bodhmhall paused to look around at the surrounding embankment and its upper wall of log pilings. The defences, which had always protected them so well in the past, suddenly looked disturbingly ineffectual. She bit her lip as she recalled a conversation with Liath Luachra shortly after their arrival at Glenn Ceoch, when work had just commenced on repairing the *ráth*. At the time, the warrior woman had been explaining how the ring fort's ditch and embankment were designed to protect its inhabitants from wildlife or opportunistic marauders. Even then, she'd made it clear that they would not be a meaningful deterrent against a determined attack from any kind of substantial force.

And twenty to thirty men is a substantial force.

'Liath Luachra?' she asked, trying to keep the concern from her voice but unable to tell if she had succeeded. 'Where is she?'

Bearach nervously cleared his throat. 'There was a fire -' The youth paused abruptly to catch his breath. Gasping a lungful of air, he tried once more.

'We saw a camp fire at Drom Osna on our way back to Glenn Ceoch. Liath Luachra went to go closer and get a better look. When she left, it was too far for me to see anything but I heard shouts and the sound of an alarm being raised. There was a lot of shouting so I ran.' He averted his eyes, face scarlet with the flush of guilt. 'I didn't want to run, Bodhmhall. But she told me I had to. That I had to come and warn you.'

The boy was clearly upset at having deserted his mentor. Bodhmhall attempted to console him, even as she did her best to ignore her own fears at her *conradh*'s disappearance.

'Do not feel guilt, Bearach. If Liath Luachra instructed you to run then you can be sure that it was the correct thing to do.'

She looked up at the slate-coloured sky. She sun had passed its peak and was starting its inevitable descent but there was little chance of darkness falling to shroud the settlement for some time yet.

'Douse the fire pit,' she instructed the *óglach*. 'I don't want the smoke to draw any strangers towards us. We'll use the hut hearths for the next few days. The smoke seeps through the thatch and won't be as visible.'

Aodhán nodded. 'Should we keep the livestock inside?'

Bodhmhall shook her head. 'No. But bring the cattle in to the near pasture. There's enough grass there to last for several days. Whatever you do, don't let them stray beyond the fences. The last thing we want is to have them wandering down by the entrance to the valley.'

The *bandraoi* looked about the settlement again, creating a mental list of the various tasks that needed to be completed. 'The pigs and goats can stay in pens for a few days. We won't have time to round them up if the *fian* find us. Tell the others to remain close to the *ráth*. If luck is with us, they will bypass the valley.'

71

Everyone remained resolutely silent on what would happen if the *fian* did not pass the valley.

'And Liath Luachra?' Bearach's voice had a distinct tremor. 'What should we do?'

Bodhmhall looked at the boy, the fear in his eyes reflecting everything that she herself felt in her own heart.

'We don't know where she is, Bearach. Even if we did we don't have the force to rescue her and could end up drawing the *fian* down on us.' She shook her head and sighed. 'No. We must place our trust in Liath Luachra's abilities. For the moment, at least, I'm afraid our friend is on her own.'

***

That afternoon, the *ráth* and its immediate environs formed the focus of an uncharacteristically frenzied activity as desperate preparations were made to prepare the defences. Conchenn and Cairbre worked on the food supplies, filling several troughs of water inside the compound and preserving what additional food stocks they could without the use of the main fire pit.

Cónán, meanwhile, drove the cattle outside to the fenced pastures alongside the northern edge of the settlement where they would graze before being driven back into the *ráth* again before nightfall. Once the larger animals were settled, he rushed off to locate the pigs and goats, some of whom had been wandering in the nearer sections of wood for days.

Bearach, recovered from his gruelling marathon, relieved Aodhán on the gateway, freeing his older brother to work on the preparation of two new javelins and a spear to be added to the selection already set into the gatehouse rack.

For her part, Bodhmhall spent most of the afternoon weaving a wicker panel that could be used to plug a gap in the eastern wall of the upper rampart. During the *ráth's* reconstruction, this final section had never been completed as they'd exhausted their supply of wooden pilings obtained at great effort from the nearby wood. Due to other, more demanding, priorities and the settlement's general lack of manpower, a gap of four or five oak pilings still existed. Located high on the inner embankment, this weakness had never previously been a significant issue but given the size of the *fian*, this breach was now the most substantial chink in the *ráth's* defences. The makeshift wicker barrier, although not a particularly effective measure, would have to do given the time constraints involved.

72

Immersed in her work, Bodhmhall lost all awareness of time and it was only a sudden drop in temperature that prompted her to look up and realise how late it was. Gazing down the valley, she was relieved to see Cónán herding the cattle closer to the *ráth* as the sun began to sink behind the trees at the distant valley entrance. She observed the darkening sky with some relief. Nightfall was not far off and soon the valley would be shrouded in a dark mantle more effective as a defence than the embankment and all of their javelins combined.

Determined to complete her task, Bodhmhall focused once more on the wicker panel. Finishing the final weave, she was manhandling the barrier into position when a stone flew past her head and glanced violently off one of the pilings. Startled, she looked towards the gateway where Aodhán and Bearach were gesturing furiously for her to join him.

Her heart sank.

Ignoring the sick feeling in her stomach, Bodhmhall left the panel leaning, unfixed, across the gap and hurried around the narrow earthen rampart to join the grimfaced youths.

'What? What is it?'

Wordlessly, Aodhán pointed towards the far end of the valley where three shadowy figures were barely discernible against the gloom of the forest.

Gods!

Bodhmhall swallowed a cold lump of mucus that had inexplicably formed at the back of her throat. She continued to watch in silence as the *óglach* alerted his father and his other brother. Cairbre and Cónán arrived on the gateway rampart as the strangers drew closer, each carrying a javelin and an iron sword.

'Cónán, take the eastern wall. There's three of them in sight but there could be more. I think – '

'Aodhán,' Bearach interrupted his brother. 'Something's not right. Look at the way they're running.'

Although clearly displeased by the interruption, the eldest brother grudgingly turned to reassess the approaching figures. The strangers had now progressed significantly further up the valley and were about half-way between the *ráth* and the valley entrance. Although almost completely engulfed by shadow of night at this point, it was still possible to see that the two individuals to the rear were carrying something between them. The creases in the *óglach*'s forehead tightened.

'Bodhmhall, can you ...?'

But Bodhmhall was already drawing on the full ability of her Gift, scrutinising the four bright flares that flickered in the distance.

'There are four individuals out there. One of them is being carried by two of the others. I can't see anyone else in the valley or up on the ridges.' She shook her head with certainty. 'No. Whoever they are, they've come alone.'

Aodhán released a sigh of relief as he stared out at the descending darkness. With a grunt, he reached down to pull a slender baton from a sheltered alcove built into the stone rampart. One end of the baton was heavily wrapped in gauze and smelled strongly of pitch. 'Stay back,' he told the others.

Striking two flints, he set the torch alight then grasping the haft, brought his arm back and launched it upwards and outwards into the night. For a moment, the fiery missile fluttered skywards then hung, momentarily frozen in the air, until it started its inevitable tumble. It struck the earth like a falling star, hitting the ground with a glimmering thump on the far side of the causeway.

The *óglach* was happy with his throw, marking his satisfaction with a tight nod. He advanced to the rampart's edge once more, the slim haft of a javelin gripped tight in his hand.

It didn't take long for the intruders to draw close. Although Bodhmhall could make out their glimmering life-lights, the others could not discern them in the gloom. As they halted before the causeway, however, the shuffling of feet was distinctly audible in the quiet evening air.

'That's close enough, strangers. Any closer and you'll have a javelin through your guts.'

Bodhmhall turned, taken aback by the aggressive quality in the young warrior's bellow, a striking contrast to the soft-spoken youth she'd come to know over the previous three years.

There was a muffled discussion from below then a strong male voice called up out of the darkness.

'I see *Muinntir Bládhma*. It is Fiacail Mac Codhna who stands here before you with no aggression in my heart. Can we approach?'

Bodhmhall felt a flurry of conflicting emotions.

Fiacail mac Codhna! Here!

From the corner of her eye she saw Aodhán glance towards her but she was too shaken to offer guidance.

'Step forward then, Fiacail mac Codhna,' the *óglach* shouted. 'Let's have a look at you.'

A tall figure limbered nonchalantly into the light of the burning torch. Halting beside its slight flame, he gazed patiently up at the ramparts. Bodhmhall released a hiss of pent up tension. It was Fiacail all right. Just as she remembered him. Handsome, poised, oozing confidence. His moustache was a little thicker perhaps, the hair slightly longer. There was also certain stiffness to his stance but, given the circumstances, that was reasonable. He had, after all, put his life on the line by stepping into the open, an easy target for any javelin that might come flying in out of the darkness.

Although it was unlikely the warrior could see anything but a dark blur beyond the small radius of illumination thrown out by the flames, Bodhmhall could not shake off the sudden conviction that he was staring directly at her. Folding his arms, he shouted up once more.

'I am accompanied by my men-at-arms, Tóla and Ultán, two loyal kinsmen who have been shadow to my heels since my very first steps. Also with us is your comrade Liath Luachra. She is ...' There was a flash of a grin in the flickering light of the torch. 'Having a little rest.'

Liath Luachra!

Bodhmhall immediately focused on the lowest of the four life-lights. Despite the distance, she now thought to make out the hue of the woman warrior's distinctive internal flame. A heavy weight fell away from the *bandraoí*'s shoulders. For what felt like the first time in an age, she found herself able to breathe freely again.

An angry muttering floated up from the darkness behind the warrior and Bodhmhall stifled a sudden, almost uncontrollable, urge to giggle. Although the individual words could not be made out, Liath Luachra's voice was instantly recognisable, the caustic tone unmistakable. The tension on the rampart dissipated in a nervous ripple of laughter. Relieved, the *bandraoi* reached over and touched Aodhán on the shoulder.

'I know these men. Fiacail is a friend.'

The young man held her gaze uncertainly and tossed an anxious look out at the figures in the darkness before nodding. Leaning forward over the rampart, he shouted down at their visitors.

'Very well, Fiacail mac Codhna. Approach and our gate will be opened to you.'

Cairbre and Bearach lit two additional torches from the supply in the gatehouse alcove then descended to remove the barrier. Ever vigilant, however, the elder *óglach* remained at his post, javelin in hand as he watched the newcomers traverse the causeway. Beside him, Bodhmhall drew a deep breath as she mentally prepared herself to greet their visitors. What else could this day possibly throw at her, she wondered. What else?

***

Fiacail was standing in the gateway passage when Cairbre and Bearach removed the barrier, almost completely filling the compact space with the breadth of his shoulders and the two, cloth-coated axes strapped to his back.

From the rampart, Bodhmhall watched how he acknowledged the Ráth Bládhma men with his usual confidence, nodding then haughtily striding past and into the shadowy *lis* as though the *ráth* was his own personal property. She swiftly turned her back to put her foot on the ladder as his eyes swung up to the ramparts. Although she couldn't see him, she could feel the weight of his gaze descend each individual rung with her. Stepping onto the ground, she took a deep breath before turning to advance into the circle of light thrown down by the flaming torches.

'I see you, Bodhmhall,' the warrior said.

'I see you, Fiacail.' She reached forward and embraced the big man, reaching up to put her arms around him. Abruptly, she pulled back, wrinkling her nose with an expression of surprise. 'You stink like a tanner's pit.'

'A healthy sweat,' he chuckled. 'Besides, is that any way to greet a dear friend?'

'Not so dear any more, Fiacail.'

Their visitor sighed, head dipped in mournful resignation. 'Ah, Bodhmhall. Will you never forgive a weak man's foolishness? You are still as beautiful to me as the flowers in Spring.'

'That was a well worn compliment the first time you offered it, Fiacail.'

76

A silence followed her retort, growing increasingly strained until it was mercifully disrupted by the bustle of Fiacail's men entering the compound. Struggling to negotiate a handmade litter through the gateway passage, they finally succeeded in entering the *lis,* laying it on the beaten earth with an expressive display of cursing and groaning. In the torchlight, Bodhmhall saw Liath Luachra's pale features stare up, cool and impassive, from the stretcher. Despite the show of indifference, she knew the warrior woman would be fuming inside, incensed at being returned to her people in such a helpless manner. The *bandraoi* felt a brief stab of sympathy for the two men who would have had to carry her and bear the brunt of her ill will.

Leaving the Seiscenn Uarbhaoil man, she moved forwards to crouch down beside her companion. Placing one hand on the other woman's shoulder, she squeezed and held her eyes for a very long time. Liath Luachra returned the stare in silence with her usual, aloof calm. Finally, Bodhmhall rose and turned back to the visitors.

'Fiacail, you and your men have our gratitude for returning Liath Luachra safely. The hospitality of Ráth Bládhma is yours for as long as you wish to accept it.'

The ritualistic declaration, uttered with the traditional sobriety, was somewhat undermined by a sudden snort from Liath Luachra. 'I didn't need their help. I would have made my own way back. Eventually.'

She struggled to rise from the stretcher and although she succeeded in sitting up, Cairbre and Cónán were obliged to assist her before she could get to her feet. Swaying precariously, she regarded her rescuer with undisguised hostility.

'You should rest,' suggested the big man.

'I am in my own home. I don't need your counsel here.'

Fiacail shrugged.

Further dissension was interrupted as Bearach, fresh from barricading the gate, hurried forward and excitedly threw himself on Liath Luachra. A titter of amusement fluttered through the little assembly as she staggered back under the impact, struggling to extricate herself from the enfolding embrace. Scowling, she pushed the boy away.

'I thought ...' said Bearach. 'I thought ...'

'You thought wrong,' she growled. 'I'm here, aren't I?

'Yes, but ...'

Stung by her unexpected hostility, Bearach gawped helplessly. Bodhmhall tactfully stepped forward, inserting herself between them as she directed the discussion to other topics.

'Bearach, Liath Luachra needs to rest and we need a keen pair of eyes on the rampart. Can we trust you to do this?'

The boy looked at her with a dismal expression but responded with a nod. As he trekked back to the gateway she made an apologetic gesture to the visitors.

'Forgive me, Fiacail. It truly brings me joy to see you again but I'm sure you understand our relief at Liath Luachra's safe return.'

The great shoulders shrugged. 'We were fortunate to be in the right time at the right place, Bodhmhall.'

'And the right place is Ráth Bládhma?'

The warrior's features tightened. He looked at her with an oddly cryptic expression that she was unable to decipher. 'A man cannot visit an old friend?'

'Of course. A friend such as you is more than a thousand times welcome.'

Fiacail smiled, somewhat pacified by the compliment.

'But when it requires a trek of several days,' continued Bodhmhall, 'such visits, by necessity, raise enquiry.' This time the *bandraoi* smiled coyly. 'Even for a wanderer the likes of Fiacail mac Codhna.'

The tall man's good humour faded and his face took on a pinched, drawn expression. He fiddled nervously with the ends of his moustache, a tic she would not normally associate with the brash and confident warrior.

'I come with poor tidings, Bodhmhall. I have travelled direct from Dún Baoiscne -'

Bodhmhall raised one hand to silence him. 'Then I already know of the tragic tidings you bring.'

Liath Luachra and Fiacail stared at her in surprise. She couldn't help but notice the sharp intake of breath from Fiacail's two kinsmen and the way they took a step back from her. The mysterious and terrifying powers of *An Cailleach Dubh* manifested for all to see! It took some effort not to snarl at them.

'You know?' asked Liath Luachra.

'I do. But perhaps we should first discuss a more critical matter. Bearach told us of a war party. We had feared you'd been taken by them.'

There was a brief silence as Liath Luachra's eyes took on a strangely haunted look. 'Yes,' she said slowly. 'We came across the tracks of a *fian*.'

'Are they coming in this direction?'

The shorter woman looked unhappy. 'They scatter tracks all over the land without any clear direction. It's as though they're searching for something. Or someone.'

'That's true,' Fiacail cut in, earning himself a pointed glare from the woman warrior. 'But the situation is worse than that. We also encountered the trail of a second *fian*.'

Bodhmhall felt a hollowness swell inside her stomach. 'A second *fian*?'

'Yes. We think there's about the same number of fighting men. Twenty to thirty warriors. They too seem to be wandering from direction to direction. I can't guess at what they might be searching for. I'm sure it's not for each other.'

Bodhmhall wet her lips with the tip of her tongue.

Gods! Two fian. Forty to sixty warriors.

It took all of her self-control to resist wringing her hands in despair. So many warriors was hardly a raid so much as a declaration of all out war. She hadn't seen such numbers mustered since her childhood when the fighting between Clann Baoiscne and Clann Morna had been at its height. 'Yes, well,' she began in as casual a manner as she could manage. 'It's possible that the object of their search is here at Ráth Bládhma.'

She proceeded to brush some imaginary dust from her skirts.

Once again Fiacail and Liath Luachra stared at her in consternation. The woman warrior's eyes flickered in comprehension.

'The *ráth* has received a visitor.' Her words were expressed as a statement, an expression of complete certainty. 'There is no other way you could have learned of Fiacail's news.'

Bodhmhall nodded slowly.

'Well, who is it?'

The *bandraoi* released a deep breath. 'It is Muirne Muncháem.'

This time Liath Luachra's reaction was not one of surprise but one of complete astonishment, a rarity for her. It slid from her features quickly enough. Her eyes hardened but despite her obvious shock, she refrained from comment, leaving it to Fiacail to express their shared bewilderment.

'Well, well. Muirne Muncháem. When I was in Dún Baoiscne, Tréanmór made no mention of her departure but -' The warrior paused and gauged her with a thoughtful stare. Before he could query Muirne's presence any further, she cut the subject short.

'Fiacail, I truly appreciate your efforts but Liath Luachra is in pain.' From the corner of her eye she observed the woman warrior raise one cynical eyebrow at this. 'I must beg your indulgence for such a poor welcome but I do need to treat her.'

She gestured to Cairbre, who had silently positioned himself behind her during the discussions.

'I'm sure you will remember Cairbre. He now acts as *rechtaire* for Ráth Bládhma and will occupy himself with your comfort and sleeping arrangements. For the moment, I would ask you to take your ease with our blessings. We will continue our discussions and celebrate your presence here later over food.'

Although the warrior would clearly have liked to discuss the subject further, he settled for a stiff smile. With a nod, he gestured for his men to accompany him and followed Cairbre towards the larger of the two lean-tos.

As their visitors departed, a light rain started to fall, tumbling down out of the heavens like a storm of aqueous needles. Ignoring it, Liath Luachra silently looked about the *lis*, nodding in approval at the doused fire and the livestock lowing softly in their pen. After a moment, she turned to consider the *bandraoi*. 'Why,' she hissed, 'is Muirne Muncháem in our home?'

'She came seeking sanctuary. What would you have me do? Cast a defenceless woman to the wilds?'

'Muirne Muncháem is hardly defenceless. That mouth of hers would knock an ox at sixty paces.' She briefly picked at a clotted scratch along her scalp. 'From the moment that woman arrived at Dún Baoiscne, she saw you as a threat, a potential competitor. She did everything in her power to undermine your standing there.' She growled a low, blood-curling snarl. 'She stood before our people and mocked you as *An Cailleach Dubh*. I should have slit her throat then. I certainly would do it now.'

'If you had slit her throat,' Bodhmhall pointed out. 'Then the people could, justifiably, have slit yours.'

'They would have had their work cut out.'

Bodhmhall made no attempt to conceal her scepticism at that particular argument.

'Muirne Muncháem is our guest.'

'Bodhmhall, she has proven herself no friend of ours. She poisoned your father's ears and used her influence to drive us from Dún Baoiscne. If she –'

Bodhmhall's eyes suddenly flared with all the authority derived of a privileged and regal upbringing. 'It was not Muirne Muncháem's influence with my father that drove us from Dún Baoiscne. You, of all people should know that.'

Taken aback by the *bandraoi*'s unaccustomed ferocity, the woman warrior uncharacteristically yielded the point. 'That's true enough,' she admitted, although it was a concession tainted with obvious bitterness. 'I stand corrected.'

'Besides, I have offered Muirne sanctuary for tonight. As *Taoiseach* of this settlement, that is my decision to make.'

Liath Luachra considered her with muted airiness. In all their years at Glenn Ceoch there had never been any doubt of Bodhmhall's leadership role. It had been Bodhmhall, after all, who'd successfully negotiated access to the land and the *ráth*, and who'd obtained the essential equipment and livestock. Everyone knew that without her influence and family connections there would be no settlement, although there'd never previously been any need to confirm this assumption so explicitly.

'Then you are truly your father's daughter, oh noble one.'

The *bandraoi* stiffened and for a moment it looked as though she might bite back at the sarcasm. Instead, her gaze softened.

'That was thoughtless. Forgive me, Liath Luachra. It's been a trying day and I'm close to the edge of my tolerance.'

Liath Luachra shrugged, her forehead creasing up in pain despite the slightness of the movement.

'Put your weight on me,' said Bodhmhall. 'I'll help you to Cairbre and Conchenn's roundhouse.'

'So Muirne Muncháem's sleeping in our bed as well then?'

Bodhmhall refused to respond to the provocation. 'Just lean on me.'

The woman warrior was no stripling but by wedging one arm under her shoulder, Bodhmhall was able to support her towards the roundhouse shared by Cairbre and his family. Stumbling through the wooden doorway, the *bandraoi* steered her to the nearest sleeping platform and eased her flat onto the fur-coated straw mattress. A small oil lamp placed on the stool to one side of the hut emitted a flickering, greasy light that competed with the glow from the small fire-pit.

'Wait here.'

The *bandraoi* left the dwelling, returning a short time later with a bowl of scented water in one hand, a bowl of oil in the other. Shuffling the heavy leather flap aside, she placed both carefully on the rush-strewn floor then sat on the platform where the other woman lay.

'Forgive me, Liath Luachra. I know Muirne's presence eats at you but you can't let that drive a wedge between us. She's here only because she has nowhere else to go. Her husband – my brother – is dead.'

Saying the words aloud served to release the truth of it. All at once, the strength that had sustained her throughout the afternoon finally gave way, crumpling like snow beneath a heavy foot. She began to weep. For her brother, for herself, for a childhood that was now truly gone and could no longer be retrieved.

Startled before the intensity of Bodhmhall's grief, Liath Luachra stared, unsure how to react. Awkwardly, she raised her right hand to stroke the *bandraoi*'s cheek.

'I've wronged you, Bodhmhall. In my own anger I ignored your family tragedy. I'm sorry. I grieve for your loss, *a rún*. As I grieve for Cumhal. I truly liked him.'

'My heart is low, Liath Luachra. I think it will break in two.'

'Then you must find the resolve to hold those halves together, dear one. Our lives may depend on it. These are dangerous times.'

'I fear I lack your resolve.'

'Bah! You have iron in you. You just can't see it as I do.' Liath Luachra levered herself up onto one elbow. 'I respect your decision Bodhmhall, but having Muirne here could come down heavily on us. On our people. Hiding out here in Glenn Ceoch we've avoided most of the bloodshed but now -'

She attempted to shift closer but flinched at the sudden movement. Bodhmhall wiped the tears from her face.

'That's enough talk of Muirne. You're wounded. Let me tend to your wound.'

'There is no wound. Just scratches.'

Bodhmhall stared, noting the stiffness in her voice.

'No wound?'

'No.'

'But you can barely stand.'

Liath Luachra rolled onto her stomach, face down into the furs and muttered.

The *bandraoi* considered her with open curiosity. It was unlike the *conradh* to be so circumspect. Although she had, admittedly, softened over the years, she was usually direct to the point of bluntness. Bodhmhall's lips twitched as she recalled Cairbre's initial assessment on meeting the woman warrior for the first time. He had summarised her as "a silversmith's hammer, the perfect instrument to deliver force directly and accurately to a specific point," an accurate, if somewhat ungenerous, description.

'Is this something you're reluctant to discuss?' Bodhmhall hesitated. 'Is this discomfort to do with Fiacail?'

A muffled voice emerged from the furs. 'Accepting help from your old husband causes me no end of discomfort. But no, that is not it.'

Sensing that this was a boil that would not be lanced with words, Bodhmhall retreated, dropping the subject as she helped the other woman out of her clothing: the grey wolf furs, the grey woollen tunic and leggings, the grey cloak, those dull and muted colours from which her name had been derived. Liath Luachra; the Grey One of Luachair. The warrior woman had always explained her colour preferences away on practical considerations. It made her, or so she claimed, more difficult to see during the hunt or when travelling in the Great Wild. Bodhmhall, however, had always suspected deeper motives.

By the time she got down to the inner garments, the rank smell of dried sweat was strong and pervaded the roundhouse. Removing the final items, Bodhmhall dropped them unceremoniously in a small pile at the side of the platform and considered the slim form stretched face down on the furs. With her hat removed, Liath Luachra's black hair now spilled freely down the left side of her back. Beneath the bulk of the furs, her frame was sleek and flat-chested but deceptively strong for all that.

Whatever her mood, however, she had spoken the truth with respect to her injuries. There were no visible wounds that Bodhmhall could see, provided one discounted the ragged set of old scars that ran from her shoulder blades down to the base of her spine.

Dipping a rag into the bowl of scented water, she started to wash the woman warrior, carefully wiping her skin clean and getting her to roll over or raise her limbs when she needed to get at the more awkward areas. The hand-bath did not take long and, on completion, she dried her off with a loose cloth. With a frown, Bodhmhall traced one line of welted tissue along Liath Luachra's back with the tip of her forefinger. She had become intimately familiar with the scars over the years but had never truly grown accustomed to the visual evidence of such severe punishment. Liath Luachra had never divulged how she'd come to receive them and, despite the *draoi's* best attempts to find out.

'Am I not beautiful?' The sardonic tone was not quite stifled by the furs.

'You are beautiful to me.'

'Sweet talker.'

Bodhmhall smiled to herself. Pouring oil into her hands, she rubbed the palms together and began to knead the woman's back and shoulders, fingers probing deep into the muscle beneath. Despite the absence of any fresh marks – apart from minor scratches and bruises – it was immediately apparent that Liath Luachra had suffered some immense physical trauma. Although the skin was relatively clear and responded well to the touch, the muscle and ligament beneath was tighter than Bodhmhall had ever felt it before and unusually striated in parts.

Transferring her attention to the lower limbs, Bodhmhall frowned at the swelling around the knee and ankle joints. From the extent of inflammation, it was now evident why Fiacail and his men had been obliged to carry her.

'You are dear to me, Liath Luachra. I feared the worst when you did not return.'

'I always return. You know that.'

'Mmm.'

Bodhmhall continued to massage, working the worst of the swollen tissue. It was warm inside the roundhouse and the crackling of the little fire was soothing. After a while, the *bandraoi* could feel the woman warrior relax beneath her fingers and she herself settled into a peaceful rhythm, lulled by the motion, the warmth, the silence.

'We saw a fire.'

The unexpected articulation took Bodhmhall by surprise. 'What?'

'Bearach and I. We were returning to the *ráth*. We saw a fire. At the foot of Drom Osna.'

'Uh-huh.'

84

The *bandraoi* nodded automatically, belatedly realising that Liath Luachra could not see the gesture. She continued to massage, the movement of her fingers focussed now on the inflammation about the back of the Grey One's knees, easing her touch in response to a wince from her patient.

Liath Luachra grew quiet and Bodhmhall could almost imagine her assembling her thoughts beneath that thick mane of black hair, rearranging the words to express herself more effectively. As though on cue, the woman cleared her throat.

'I was curious. I managed to crawl in closer to get a better look. Then -'

Bodhmhall listened wordlessly as the warrior recounted the events that followed, physically transferring her own mounting disquiet into her soft manipulation of muscle and tissue.

Later, when Liath Luachra had completed the telling, she grew quiet and remained lying face down in the furs, withdrawing into that impenetrable silence once again.

She's embarrassed!

Bodhmhall placed a hand on her shoulder.

'*A rún*, you are too hard on yourself.'

'I ran away. I ran like a coward from that ... creature. And I kept on running. I am less than I was, Bodhmhall.'

The *bandraoi* shook her head but, once again, the action went unobserved. 'No. That reaction was not truly yours but one provoked by another party. Believe me, you do not lack courage. You are fortunate to be alive.'

Liath Luachra twisted herself around and up off the furs so suddenly, so violently, that the *bandraoi* was taken by surprise and, instinctively, pulled back. The woman warrior's eyes drilled into her.

'You know what it is.'

Bodhmhall stared, too taken aback to answer.

'You do!' The exclamation was loaded with fresh conviction. 'What was that creature? Tell me.'

This time it was Bodhmhall's turn to work through the words. Several moments passed before she felt she had the right of it.

'This morning, out at the *lubgort*. I felt a great force, a great evil wash over the land.'

'What was it you felt?'

'It was One with the Gift.'

85

'One with the Gift?'

'Someone with the Gift. A *draoi* like me but with different ability. Where I can perceive life through life-light, this... thing is... a seeker of sorts.'

'A seeker?'

'Yes, something that has the power to draw in on people. It can perceive – feel – their thoughts. No-one can hide from it.'

Liath Luachra continued to observe her without expression, weighing up what she had been told.

'This morning,' continued Bodhmhall. 'When I felt its touch, I also had the sense that this individual was ... different. It felt tainted. Corrupted. At the time, I was too preoccupied trying to protect myself. Now that I've had a chance to think about it, I believe this *draoi* was not fully human.'

'Huh,' grunted Liath Luachra. She paused, awaiting further explanation but Bodhmhall had lapsed into silence, absorbed in contemplation of the morning events. 'Not fully human,' prompted the *conradh*.

'Hmm? Oh, yes. Back in Dún Baoiscne when I studied under Dub Tíre there were stories of such creatures. Tainted Ones, they called them. Men and women consumed and controlled to exist purely as the instrument of other, stronger *draoi*. Such *draoi* have the power to affect the minds of others, to provoke emotions and unnatural thoughts. I believe this is what you encountered at Drom Osna.'

'But what would a *draoi*'s minion be doing out here in the Great Wild? I don't -'

Liath Luachra halted abruptly as she saw the expression on Bodhmhall's face.

'Muirne Muncháem! I should have known.' Rolling onto her back, she snorted and slapped her forehead with the palm of her hand. 'Already, she brings troubles down on our heads. You should dispatch her. At once.'

'No.'

'But if this *thing* is as powerful as you say then it will find her. Is this not so?'

'I don't know.'

'Any yet -' The *conradh* paused as she worked through the ramifications. 'And yet, it appears to have missed her. How is that?'

'I don't know. I suspect I simply distracted it. It did not appreciate being perceived by another.'

86

Liath Luachra chewed slowly on the inside of her cheek. '*Clann Morna* seems extraordinarily intent on locating her. Two *fian* in winter? And now a *draoi* familiar? I know Muirne believes her arse shines like purest silver but it's hard to believe anyone else would value her enough to go to such efforts.'

Bodhmhall shrugged. 'The motives are hard to understand. I would need to acquire *imbas* to have the knowing of such things.'

'*Imbas?*' Liath Luachra stared at her in surprise. The secret rituals used by the *draoi* for the acquisition of *imbas* – forbidden knowledge – were not initiated lightly because they invariably took a heavy toll.

'It would not be my first choice,' Bodhmhall admitted.

'If you are seriously considering the *imbas* rituals,' said Liath Luachra carefully. 'You must be truly worried.'

'I am worried. This Tainted One ... its doggedness, its ruthlessness terrifies me.'

'Then get angry. Hate him.'

The *bandraoi* looked at her in confusion.

'That is how to deal with fear. If you hate your enemy, your hatred devours your fear. And your pain.'

'Hmm,' Bodhmhall responded, clearly dubious.

'Do not doubt yourself, Bodhmhall. Come, you're the talented one. You will work a scheme to save us from this creature.'

'It could be that this Tainted One is not the most significant threat. Rather we should be seeking to identify the individual who hides behind the Tainted One, who directed him out to the Great Wild to find Muirne Muncháem.'

With a sigh, Bodhmhall allowed her hands to drop to her sides. 'I have brought this threat down on us. You were right, *a rún*. I should have consulted with you before making my decision. I am a poor leader.'

'You're not a poor leader. You are an exhausted one, stretched in too many directions at once. Besides, I wasn't here and you had to make a decision.' She reached up to grasp Bodhmhall's wrist. 'Lie with me, Bodhmhall. Come close and hold me. We will lick our wounds and you can draw from my strength.'

'I'm afraid I can't, dear one. I must occupy myself with our guests.'

'Ah, our wondrous guests.' Liath Luachra growled in pain as she rolled over onto her side. 'First that prancing gadabout, now Muirne Muncháem. Truly, this is a day that improves with the passing.'

'You may not like Fiacail but he was correct in saying you need to rest. If you sleep your muscles will relax and heal more rapidly.'

'Perhaps.' The woman already sounded drowsy. 'But our visitors can wait. Spend a moment here with me and we can both rise together.'

'Very well,' the *bandraoi* relented. 'Just a moment, then.'

Bodhmhall lay down beside the other woman and drew a fur blanket up to cover them both. Nestling in closer, she closed her eyes and nudged her nose deep into Liath Luachra's hair, inhaling that reassuringly familiar scent deep into her nostrils.

Liath Luachra, Muirne Muncháem and Fiacail mac Codhna. Three of the most headstrong individuals she knew. All within one restricted space.

It was going to be a challenging night.

***

The wind had risen over the course of the evening. By the time the company were gathered at the larger roundhouse it had evolved to a screaming gale and even the blackness of night could not hide the tumultuous cloud movement above them. Traversing the muddy *lis* at a run, Bodhmhall felt a cruel sense of satisfaction. The inhabitants of Ráth Bládhma might well be cowering behind its walls but they were, at least, sheltered from the worst of the elements. For the two *fian* and the prowling Tainted One, this night would prove extremely uncomfortable, hopefully hazardous.

Such are the risks of mustering a fian so near to the close of winter.

Inside the roundhouse, the blazing fire-pit kept the interior at a pleasant temperature and several oil lamps threw a warm, yellow glow over the surroundings. With the exception of Cónán, Bearach and Liath Luachra, all of the company had settled onto the woven reed mats that surrounded the crackling fire and were sharing the last of the *uisce beatha* traded with Coill Mór earlier that year. The sharp, smoky alcohol, stored in two leather containers, had proven particularly popular with the guests from Seiscenn Uarbhaoil. Fiacail mac Codhna was effusive in his praise for the drink, holding up his wooden goblet to peer at it with heartfelt admiration. 'My bollocks have cramped, my guts are wrenching and my throat feels like its swallowed liquid fire. My head spins and it stings when I piss. Thundering arsefart, this is truly a man's drink!'

Bodhmhall smiled politely before casting a surreptitious glance at the doorway. Cónán and Bearach had drawn the short straw for guard duty above the gateway. Liath Luachra had agreed to join them once she'd completed an inspection of the *ráth*'s defences, something she'd insisted on doing personally, despite her injuries.

When all were settled, Bodhmhall nodded for Conchenn to commence serving. The old woman had done what she could to prepare a suitable feast at such short notice and in such restricted cooking conditions: fried pork chops from a freshly slaughtered pig, hot round loaves of bread, ash-roasted tubers and strips of a chewy meat that tasted like hare.

Muirne, despite several hours of slumber, looked drawn and haggard from her trek across the wild lands. Fiacail, as ever when presented with an audience, was the soul of good cheer: vivacious, hearty and effortlessly charming.

The food was passed about the circle, transferred from right to left. While the company ate, Muirne and Fiacail provided updates on extended family, friends and common acquaintances from Dún Baoiscne and Seiscenn Uarbhaoil. Any mention of conflict or politics, in particular the hostilities between *Clann Morna* and *Clann Baoiscne,* were studiously avoided.

As she nibbled on a leg of hare, Bodhmhall glanced again to the doorway, drawn by the flap of the leather covering behind Liath Luachra, the harsh, abrupt sound a clear measure of her mood. The Grey One circled the feasting group, halting to sit at Bodhmhall's right hand, deliberately inserting herself between the *bandraoi* and Fiacail mac Codhna. If their guest noticed or felt slighted in any way, he showed no obvious signs of it. If anything, he appeared happy to sidle over and provide Liath Luachra with more room while continuing a hearty conversation with Cairbre.

At first, the *conradh* contributed little to the conversation. It was only later in the evening that Bodhmhall noticed her lean slowly forward to listen in on a conversation which seemed to consist predominantly of Fiacail boasting of his achievements at Seiscenn Uarbhaoil.

'Is it true what they say, Fiacail?'

The big warrior turned to look at her, a hefty pig trotter in his left hand dripping grease onto the reed mats beside him. 'What is it that they say, Liath Luachra?'

'That you've coupled with over a hundred women.'

The warrior gave a pained expression as he munched on the pork, sucking marrow from the bone with a relish that seemed almost sexual.

'A man of breeding does not count the number of women he's bedded,' he answered shortly, smearing a patch of pig fat across his moustache with the tips of his fingers. 'After the first twenty, at least.'

There was a chorus of groans from the women, a quickly stifled cackle from Cairbre. Aodhán and Fiacail's warriors looked at the ground in an attempt to hide the smirk on their lips. Only Liath Luachra, who continued to observe Fiacail grinding the pork bone with his teeth, considered the response with any seriousness.

'Forgive me, Fiacail. I'm confused.' She slowly put her plate to one side. 'How does one distinguish between a man of breeding and a man who is inbred?'

The warrior chuckled, ignoring the veiled insult. 'That sounds like one of Bodhmhall's riddles.' He leaned forward even further so that he could directly address his host. 'What say you, Bodhmhall? You are daughter to a *rí* and I think the company would concede that you are the shrewdest of all those gathered here.'

Bodhmhall resisted the temptation to glance at Muirne's reaction to Fiacail's undisguised provocation.

'What do you think?' he insisted. 'What is the difference between a man of breeding and a man who is inbred?'

Bodhmhall stared into the flames and considered the question quietly. Silence descended on the feasting company as they awaited her response with undistilled anticipation. Slowly, she raised her head and smiled.

'Webbed feet,' she said.

***

Finally, the time for serious discussion was upon them. Bodhmhall pushed her wooden platter to one side, brushed greasy lips with the back of her hand and waited for the talk to subside about her. The individual conversations did not take long to peter out. All eyes had been on her throughout the meal, awaiting such a signal to indicate that the social part of the evening was over.

Fiaçail flicked a glance to his two kinsmen who, wordlessly, rose to their feet. Escorted by Aodhán and Conchenn, they quietly left the roundhouse.

When the others had departed, Bodhmhall raised her eyes and considered each of the four remaining individuals in turn. 'We should speak of Muirne,' she said.

No-one spoke but the tension was evident in the body language of those gathered around the fire. Muirne Muncháem's bearing, in particular, was tense and stiff as she awaited the decision of her hosts.

Bodhmhall turned to the Flower of Almhu.

'I will not insult you by softening the reality with honeyed words, Muirne. I have sought the counsel of my advisors. Both recommend that you be cast from Ráth Bládhma at first light.'

Muirne blanched but, to her credit, accepted the news with no other evidence of the despair she must surely have been feeling. Dropping her eyes to the ground, she nodded with stoic dignity. 'Of course. If that is the desire of *Muinntir Bládhma*, I will leave at first light.'

'You misunderstand me. That was the opinion of my advisors. It was not my final decision.'

Startled, Muirne raised her head to stare at her host with an expression that was equal parts hope and wariness. 'You do not share the opinion of your advisors?'

'In all honesty, I felt their advice sound. They recommend that which is clearly in the best interests of Ráth Bládhma. But -' She picked up a wooden spoon and absently tapped it against her knee while the others watched on. 'There are other factors to be considered. Duties of hospitality, family ties ...'

Her voice trailed off momentarily as she stared at Muirne's swollen belly.

'The future of *Clann Baoiscne* may lie within your womb and although I've given the matter consideration I'm unable to see a clear path through the thorns you plant before us.' She grew silent for a moment, as though planning her next words. 'I have decided that I will require further wisdom, I will seek *imbas* to identify the path that best suits our purpose. Until then, you may remain at Ráth Bládhma.'

Even as she spoke, Bodhmhall was surreptitiously assessing the faces about her. Muirne was pale but clearly relieved. Cairbre, calm and patient as always, simply awaited his mistress's lead. Fiacail mac Codhna, conversely, had a great grin plastered across his features. The warrior had remained uncharacteristically restrained throughout the evening's activities. Although he bore neither party any particular ill will, neither was he averse to stirring up a situation and then sitting back to enjoy the fruits of his devilment. For some reason, Fiacail often derived enjoyment or diversion from such situations. For the moment, fortunately, he seemed content to merely observe.

Liath Luachra as ever, appeared impassive. While Bodhmhall spoke, she remained resignedly silent, staring straight ahead into the fire as though preoccupied with some great internal deliberations of her own. Bodhmhall had informed her of her decision in advance, of course, but it couldn't have been pleasant hearing it when the source of such enmity was sitting directly across the fire from her.

Muirne's response, therefore, was particularly ill-judged.

'I thank the Gods that they have granted you the sense to meet your family duties.'

Bodhmhall saw the Grey One stiffen, the bread half-raised to her mouth, frozen in place. 'Family duties,' she spat. 'Do you not understand, foul-smelling flower! Your actions bring the wrath of *Clann Morna* upon us.'

'*Clann Morna* does not know I have come here.'

'*Clann Morna* may not know but they must strongly suspect it,' spat Liath Luachra. 'A *fian* beats the forests of the Great Wild searching for you.'

'A *fian*!' Muirne stared at her with wide eyes.'

'Two *fian*, in fact,' pressed Liath Luachra. 'And as if that weren't trouble enough, you and your unborn whelp have also attracted the interest of a Tainted One.'

'A Tainted One!'

'Yes. A seeker who now searches our land for you and your child.'

This further revelation prompted a shocked silence from their visitors. Fiacail looked as though he'd been struck across the face. Muirne looked back at them with a haunted expression. Her jaw began to quiver and for the first time since arriving at Ráth Bládhma, she revealed what she truly was; a terrified young mother.

This involuntary lapse did not last, however. Conscious of the fragility she'd inadvertently exposed, the Flower of Almhu clamped her jaw shut, grasped about clumsily on the floor behind her then pulled a bulky satchel forward. As the others watched on in curiosity, she plunged her hand inside and withdrew a wolf pelt which she defiantly flung on the ground beside the fire.

'This creature attempted to eat us: me and my baby. I swear to you all that anyone who seeks to harm my child will suffer a similar fate.'

There was a momentary silence as the others considered the pelt. The skin was rough and had been poorly skinned but from the size of it the animal had obviously been no cub.

'What did you do?' asked Liath Luachra at last. 'Lash it to death with your tongue?'

Muirne stiffened and her face grew red and ugly. For a moment it looked as though she might launch herself, belly and all, across the fire at the woman warrior.

Bodhmhall made a calming gesture. 'We do not need to -'

'That's what I like about you, Liath Luachra,' said Muirne, ignoring her. 'Many women lie awake at night dreaming of a cock between their legs but you, you lie awake dreaming that you're hung like a stud bull.'

There was a stunned silence in the wake of Muirne's outburst.

Oh Gods, no!

In despair, Bodhmhall watched the flash of lifelight between the two women, their internal flames blazing up as though someone had tossed oil on a bonfire. Muirne's was radiating a frightening yellow intensity that all but obscured the lower glow of her unborn child. Liath Luachra's, meanwhile was repeatedly expanding and contracting, red flecks growing brighter and brighter. Bodhmhall stared at them in alarm, feeling the situation spinning wildly out of her control.

'I'm hung like a bull,' said Fiacail.

The company was momentarily distracted as all eyes turned to stare at the broad-shouldered warrior. Fiacail, apparently oblivious to the consternation he'd provoked, was working to remove a sliver of meat from between his teeth with the point of a sharp knife. Putting the weapon to one side he looked around at his silent audience.

'What? Do you want me to whip it out and show you?'

'No!'

The startled chorus from the females was probably the first time all present had ever been in unanimous agreement. Fiacail, however, was unimpressed by their reaction. 'You don't need to act all high and mighty. At least two of you know this claim for fact.'

There was another startled silence as the three women looked at one another. Liath Luachra suddenly released a bark of amusement.

'Gods, Muirne! Oh, that is beautiful! You and Fiacail were slapping buttock skin!'

Bodhmhall stared in consternation from one visitor to the other.

'What? Is this true?'

Their visitor did her best to appear nonplussed but was visibly flustered by the unanticipated disclosure. 'Don't worry yourself, cousin. That was a long time ago. After your separation from Fiacail.'

Observing that her words had in no way placated the bristling *bandraoi*, the Flower of Almhu opted for an alternative approach.

'And I assure you, it took place before my marriage to Cumhal.'

'I wonder if my brother would have been so willing to wed had he known he was sipping such a well-tasted wine.'

Muirne's face clouded.

'Your brother was no stranger to midnight visits. In Dún Baoiscne he had his share of –'

'I'm aware of Cumhal's activities but he had, at least, the integrity to declare as much before the marriage. You, Muirne Muncháem, were presented to *Clann Baoiscne* as the unsullied blossom that would unite our two families.'

'I think –' said Fiacail. 'You mean the unplucked Flower'. With this he erupted into a howl of uproarious laughter.

Muirne, furious, staggered to her feet, her face flushed and angry. For a moment she looked as though she was about to bellow at Fiacail but then, to everyone surprise, she stopped and looked down at her feet. Bodhmhall followed her eyes downwards to where a small puddle was spreading across the floor.

'This council is concluded,' she said hurriedly. 'Please leave now.'

'Are you joking?' demanded Fiacail, completely unaware of what had just taken place. 'Things are just starting to get interesting and if you think –' His eyes fell on the puddle at Muirne's feet. 'Oh, look! Muirne's so angry she's pissed herself.'

'Get out!' roared Bodhmhall. 'Now, you fool! Muirne's waters have broken.'

The warrior stared at her in astonishment, transferred his gaze to the ashen-faced Muirne and then down to the growing puddle. His jaw dropped.

'Out,' snapped Bodhmhall. 'Now!'

Without further argument, Fiacail scrambled to his feet and scuttled from the roundhouse, Cairbre hot on his heels.

Bodhmhall turned to where Liath Luachra was standing, observing the flurry of activity about her with her habitual calm. The *bandraoi* regarded her uncertainly. 'You wish to stay and help?'

'I would sooner poke a stick up my ass and erect myself as totem,' said Liath Luachra, backing away, both palms held defensively outwards. With this she turned and left the roundhouse.

Taking a deep breath, the *bandraoi* turned her attention back to their visitor who was now backed up against the central pole, holding her stomach and staring down at it in dismay. When she finally noticed Bodhmhall standing before her, she gritted her teeth.

'Enjoy your moment, *Cailleach Dubh*. It must give you great pleasure to see me humiliated so.'

'Not really.' Bodhmhall pressed a hand against the other woman's belly then felt it from several different positions. 'This will be a hard birth,' she concluded.

Muirne grimaced against the pain and when it had passed she gave a dismissive shrug. 'Hard life, hard birth. There will be pain and then there will be none.'

And with that, the Gift suddenly manifested itself again.

It had been so long since she'd experienced a true vision that Bodhmhall wasn't quite sure what was happening at first. The walls of the roundhouse just seemed to recede then faded completely to black. The fire pit remained and Muirne Muncháem remained but Conchenn had disappeared. She tried to speak but no words came out. Slowly, remarkably slowly, the flames in the fire-pit appeared to subside but even as the light disappeared it was replaced by another light blazing out from Muirne's womb.

And then it was gone.

'... are you doing?'

'What?' Dazed, Bodhmhall stared at the red-faced Muirne.

'What are you doing? Why are you looking at me like that?'

Bodhmhall continued to stare blankly. Then the realisation hit her. 'It's the child, isn't it? Cumhal's child. They don't care about you. It's the infant they seek, the *fian* and that 'Tainted One'.

'What are you talking about?' Muirne glared in furious incomprehension. Bodhmhall shook her head with an embittered laugh. So stupid! The evidence had been there before her all this time but, preoccupied by other issues, her heart had not allowed her eyes to see it.

'Muirne Munchaem,' she said. 'You ask for your freedom and for your life.'

'You know that is why I'm here, Bodhmhall! Tréanmór and your family are in a position of weakness after the battle at Cnucha. It was only a matter of time before sufficient pressure was applied, before they were forced to offer me to *Clann Morna*.'

'And you also wish the life and freedom of your son.'

The Flower of Almhu groaned and gritted her teeth again. 'Of course I do.'

Bodhmhall frowned. 'There is something different about your son, Muirne. His inner flame flares like none I've ever seen before. All I can tell for sure is that there will be a high price associated with this birth, a price to give him life and a price to save him. I need to know if you are willing to accept this price.'

'There is always a price.'

'This is a price you may not wish to pay.'

The Flower of Almhu returned her stare. 'Will it save my son?'

Bodhmhall nodded.

'Then,' she said decisively. 'I will pay.'

***

As predicted, Muirne Munchaem's labour proved difficult. Although in a physical sense, the birth was not complicated – the infant was neither breeched nor twisted – the process was ironically hampered by the mother herself. Raised in isolation at Almhu under the unyielding tutelage of her politically-minded parents, Muirne has been taught everything there was to know about political machinations, tribal affiliations and leverage mechanisms. With respect to basic facts such as childbirth, however, she knew next to nothing. Ignorant and disconnected from the workings of her own body, she was close to panic when her waters broke and the contractions started.

For the first few hours, Bodhmhall worked to reassure the Flower of Almhu, to help her relax into the pattern of contractions, to focus on her breathing and control the pain while she applied steady pressure on the younger woman's lower back. As the dilation increased and the contractions closed in, Muirne's mind had fought the natural instincts of her body and she'd screamed in pain and terror.

For Bodhmhall, the ordeal was doubly distressing. Not only did the *bandraoi* have to deal with the immediate physical practicalities of the mother's panic, that panic was effectively reflected and magnified through the flames of Muirne's life-light and the life-light of her increasingly stressed unborn child.

To make matters worse, the increasing severity of the storm meant that the roundhouse shuddered violently, struck by a relentless series of ferocious squalls. In a surreal twist, the *bandraoi* also thought she could hear snatches of song amidst the howling gale and Muirne's terrified shrieks. It was only later she realised that Fiacail, evacuating the female-dominated roundhouse, had snatched a container of the *uisce beatha*. Retiring to the lean-to where his kinsmen were bedded down, the three men had started drinking, subsequently breaking out into a bawdy sing-song. The raucous singing continued endlessly from the little shelter, a masculine counterpoint to the high-pitched wails of childbirth.

It was well after midnight when the child finally emerged, entering the world in a slick coat of blood and fluid that did nothing to temper the brightness of its aura. Bodhmhall stared down at the newborn in her hands, radiating a glow that left her breathless and emotionally dazzled. To her surprise, the infant had the thumb of its right hand in its mouth. When she made to remove the thumb to clear the mucous, it released an immediate howl of disapproval.

'Is it is a boy?' gasped Muirne. Her face was pale and wet with sweat.

'It is a boy,' Bodhmhall confirmed. Muirne's instinct had proven correct, after all. 'He needs to suckle.'

Wrapping the infant in a fur blanket, she laid him down alongside his mother. Almost immediately, he settled in on the breast and started to suck. As she watched the mother with her tiny newborn nestled at her breast,

Bodhmhall felt something move inside her. She did not need the aid of her Gift to know that her world would never be the same.

Chapter Four

During the night, the storm had blown itself inside out. By morning, its fury had waned, the frantic winds calmed to an exhausted apathy. The air was still when Bodhmhall emerged from the roundhouse; still, not as cold but laden with a thick fog that dampened all colour and sound. Halting at the doorway, she considered the ghostly structures of the other roundhouse, the lean-tos and the almost invisible cattle pen where indistinct shapes moved and lowed softly. She was struck not only by the stark contrast in the weather but by how closely it mirrored the recent variations to her own emotional state. Retiring to her bed in the early hours, she had been exhausted, worn down by the escalating series of unforeseen events: the assault by the Tainted One, the disappearance of Liath Luachra, Muirne and Fiacail's unexpected appearance, the threat of a hostile *fian* and the subsequent news of her brother's death. The midnight delivery of her nephew, Muirne and Cumhal's child, had been the final straw, a physical exertion that had pushed her to her limits. Leaving the sleeping mother and child, she'd barely noticed the screaming wind as she'd traversed the *lis* to Cairbre's roundhouse, her head reeling into darkness as soon as she'd hit the mattress.

But my nephew is safe. And Liath Luachra is back.

She turned to look back inside at the sleeping platform where the woman warrior was a formless shape huddled beneath several layers of furs. Such things as this were the little anchors that held her in sheltered harbour, the emotional handholds that helped her maintain a grip on her sanity in such precarious times. Those and the opportunity for disconnection, the simple respite of a decent night's sleep.

Until the next challenge comes to confront us.

A harsh cough from the fog-coated rampart drew her back from such ethereal considerations. It was followed almost immediately by the rasp of a throat being cleared and a soggy, mucous-filled spit.

Staring up at the nearby southern embankment where the sound had seemed to originate, Bodhmhall stiffened in surprise when a naked man strolled out of the wispy brume.

Fiacail!

The warrior presented a somewhat surreal spectacle against the misty backdrop. Bareskinned, he nonchalantly wandered along that visible section of the rampart, absently scratching his left buttock, until he reached the eastern postern. Here, he finally drew to a halt, planted both feet apart and stretched two mighty arms towards the sky. Gazing up at the sun, glowing feebly through the mist like an ember in the ashes, he slowly began to chant.

'I greet you Warm One.
I see you up there through the mist.
Do not be shy.
Come share your glow.'

Bodhmhall stifled a giggle, recognising the early morning ritual the warrior had conscientiously practised during their time together at Dún Baoiscne.

'Does it ever answer you?'

Startled, the big man spun around on the soles of his feet, the smooth movement all the more impressive for a man of his size. Bodhmhall focused her attention on the warrior's face, doing her best to avert her eyes from the penis dangling low between his legs. When he saw her standing in the *lis* below, a broad smile spread across his features.

'No,' he answered. 'And this morning it teases me, hanging up there in the clouds like a veiled glimpse of a virgin's nipples!'

Bodhmhall shivered and pulled her cloak more tightly about her. 'It is cold, Fiacail. Does the chill air not chafe at your skin?'

'Pah!' He shook his head as though contemptuous of the possibility. 'The chill clears the head. It gets the blood flowing. After last night's drinking, this is a good thing.'

In truth, his voice sounded hoarse to Bodhmhall's ears, strained and rusty from the excesses of the previous night. The *bandraoi* was both surprised and impressed that he was not still abed and demonstrated such little sign of weariness.

Fiacail retraced his steps along the rampart to the point where he'd first emerged from the haze. Draped across one of the pine pilings were a pair of leather breeches and a cotton tunic that Bodhmhall hadn't noticed earlier. The warrior casually pulled them down and began to dress, clearly in no particular hurry. 'It is good to greet the day with a blessing,' he said. 'The Great Sky Father opens his sack to release light and colour onto the world. It is only proper to show gratitude for such a gift.'

Bodhmhall did not respond, casually averting her eyes as she waited for him to finish getting dressed.

When he was finally clothed, the man from Seiscenn Uarbhaoil looked down to consider her with an inquisitive eye. 'And you, Bodhmhall? As a *bandraoi* does the Great Goddess not answer your call?'

She shook her head as she walked towards the rampart ladder and started up the worn wooden rungs. 'You know she doesn't.'

'And yet she answers the entreaties of your fellow *draoi*.'

'So they tell us.'

'So they tell us,' he conceded. He gave a sad smile and she knew that he was thinking of an old story from old times, an intimate moment shared in the days when they'd also shared a roof and a bed beneath it.

Stepping onto the earthen rampart, she followed the sticky, mud-flattened surface around to the eastern section of the *ráth*. As he waited for her to join him, he peered towards the north, struggling to make out any detail through the hazy grey shroud. On a clear day, the position offered an excellent outlook over the valley's most impressive natural features: the silver flow from the eastern heights, the white, 'mare-tail' cataracts of the melted snow streaming down the steep rock slopes on either side. Today, although none of this spectacle was visible, its absence did little to detract from his good humour.

'I like it here, Bodhmhall ua Baoiscne. You have made a good home.' He drew nearer to her and the abrupt physical closeness prompted an unanticipated shiver and unbidden, long-forgotten memories of arousal. Disconcerted, she bit down on her tongue to keep the sensations in check. Fortunately, the big man seemed unaware of the effect his proximity had provoked.

'Many at Dún Baoiscne thought that you and your followers would be dead within a year. Some resent the fact that you are still alive.'

She swallowed and cleared her throat but there was still a bit of a croak in her voice when she spoke. 'They remember us then?'

'They remember you. They just don't speak of you.'

'So nothing is forgiven.'

He shrugged. 'You should not concern yourself with the thoughts of ... stiff minds.'

Bodhmhall felt a sudden surge of affection for the big warrior. Despite his faults – and they were many – Fiacail had been one of the few to offer

101

support prior to her expulsion from Dún Baoiscne. Given their fractious relationship and their tortured separation he had been the last person anyone expected to step forward in her defence. And yet, he had surprised them all.

'You are a good man, Fiacail mac Codhna.'

He eyed her in surprise. 'A good man? Easy, *Cailleach*. Did I not ruin your feast last night with talk of my monstrous member?'

Bodhmhall chuckled. 'Come now, man of Seiscenn Uarbhaoil. I know your intentions better than that. You deliberately introduced that topic to pop the boil of vitriol swelling up between Liath Luachra and Muirne Muncháem.'

Fiacail neither confirmed nor denied the tribute. Instead he closed his eyes and shook his head. 'Ah, Muirne of the Slender Neck. She truly is one like no other, is she not? It's hard to imagine her as mother to an actual human child.' He sighed. 'How does she fare?'

'She sleeps.'

'And the child?'

'A boy. He sleeps as well.'

'At least we are briefly spared that wailing. What a noise! I have not heard such screeching since the field of battle! Truly he is his mother's son.'

'Perhaps he was simply upset at being pulled from a warm womb before he was good and ready.'

'It's happened to me,' muttered Fiacail. 'Never screeched like that, though.'

Bodhmhall ignored him and turned away to look down over the valley. Faint rays of sunshine were finally starting to slice vague swathes through the wisps of mist and she could make out the blur of the individual cows that Cónán had just released from the *ráth*. Penned into the pastures beyond the ditch, they were chewing contentedly on the frost-coated grass. As instructed the previous evening, the boy had since left for the valley entrance, there to keep watch and provide warning for any sign of the *fian*. After the severe storm of the previous night and the murkiness to the morning, it was extremely unlikely that it would be abroad today but she was unwilling to take such assumptions for granted.

'Is it true that you slept with Muirne?'

The big man groaned aloud and held his palms outwards in a pleading gesture. 'It was the past, Bodhmhall. What can I say? I was grieving the death knell of all that we had. I consoled myself in the arms of another. This has always been the way of things.' Observing a distinct lack of sympathy in her reaction, he quickly added to his argument. 'It was a mistake. It served to ease my pain at the time. That was all.'

Bodhmhall closed her eyes and took a deep breath. She had forgotten how swiftly conversations with Fiacail could switch from fond to infuriating. 'You're right,' she conceded at last. 'Such arguments are in the past. Let us put them behind us, Fiacail. We are friends now. Let us turn our thoughts to the future.'

'I do turn my thoughts to the future. Why do you think I have come to Ráth Bládhma?'

Bodhmhall observed him with curiosity. 'I had understood you came to tell me of my brother.'

'That is true. I know how much you loved him. I preferred that you hear such terrible report from a familiar face rather than the unkind lips of some heartless stranger.'

'And I am grateful for that thoughtfulness. You travelled an immense distance, at great personal effort. You will always have my gratitude.'

'There is another reason for my presence at Ráth Bládhma. A second reason.'

Bodhmhall eyebrows tightened about her forehead as she assessed him with guarded equanimity. 'And that is?'

The big man shuffled awkwardly, shifted his weight from one foot to the other then back again. 'Will you walk with me, Bodhmhall? It would be good to inspect your exterior defences now that the day begins to clear.'

Puzzled, the *bandraoi* gave a silent nod of assent as she attempted to shrug off a foreboding sense of catastrophe. Procrastination from one such as Fiacail did not bode well for the nature of his news.

Descending to the *lis*, they proceeded towards the gateway where Bearach's form was silhouetted against the grey air on the upper rampart. They encountered Fiacail's kinsmen below the stone structure, lounging groggily against their spears. Although clearly nursing painful hangovers, both men stiffened and straightened up as they approached.

'Rest easy, brothers.' Fiacail gestured for the men to relax. 'Bodhmhall and I are going to examine the external defences. Take your ease. We will talk on my return.'

The men nodded at their leader but Bodhmhall noted how both refused to meet her eyes. Fiacail must have noticed it too for he raised it as they strolled through the gateway and out onto the narrow causeway.

'Take no notice of Tóla and Ultán. They're good men. It is not their intention to be rude.'

'No?' Bodhmhall struggled to keep the scepticism from her voice.

'They are cowed in the presence of the *Cailleach Dubh*. They do not know you as I do and have heard many wild stories of the infamous Ráth Bládhma where women direct and men obey.'

The bandraoi snorted. Fiacail chuckled and they traversed the little causeway in silence.

Circling around the ráth, they followed the ditch until they gained the *lubgort* to the east of the settlement. Bodhmhall halted to stare longingly at the vegetable beds then turned to find the Seiscenn Uarbhaoil man apparently absorbed in the assessment of the embankment parapet. 'You have a gap up there,' he informed her. 'Looks like some pilings are missing.'

'I know,' she said, unable to keep the frost from her voice. 'Now, do you intend to tell me of the second reason for your visit to Ráth Bládhma or are you intending to avoid the subject a little longer?'

Fiacail turned to her with an expression of exasperation. 'Gods, Bodhmhall. I'm not trying to avoid the subject. What I wish to discuss is not a topic that comes easily. I am attempting to assemble the right words.'

'Don't task yourself with garnishing the truth, Fiacail. Just tell me the nub of the matter.'

The big warrior stared at her for a moment then shook his head in aggrieved resignation. 'I should have known better than to try and embellish frank facts for you. The truth of the matter is ...'

'Yes?'

'The truth of the matter is that I have been thinking about the disasters that have befallen our people at Dún Baoiscne.'

Bodhmhall nodded slowly, wondering where this was leading.

'Disasters such as the recent raids, the poor harvests, the loss of our men at Gabhra -' His voice trailed off.

'Yes?'

'Well, I thought,' He hesitated once more. 'I thought that I might put myself forward.'

Bodhmhall stared at him and shook her head in incomprehension.

'Put myself forward as *tánaiste*,' he clarified. 'The next in line to lead *Clann Baoiscne*.'

'Oh,' Bodhmhall stared at him. After an awkward silence, she turned away and stared up at the trees on the eastern ridge in a belated attempt to conceal her consternation.

'You consider me unworthy of the title.' Fiacail's voice was tight and when she turned back to face him again she could see that he was genuinely offended by her reaction. 'And yet I am an eligible candidate. My line leads directly back to our ancestor, Baoiscne. I rule a wealthy holding at Seiscenn Uarbhaoil and can hold my own in combat against any three men.'

Listening to the aggravated tirade, Bodhmhall found little that she would dispute. The *tánaiste* was chosen from among the heads of the *righdamhna* – literally, those eligible males of 'kingly material' –elected at a full assembly of the sept. With Cumhal's death, that previously assigned position was now, once again, open for contention. Given that the single principle of eligibility was for the role to descend to the most worthy of the same male-line, Fiacail's bloodline and personal standing meant he met that basic requirement easily.

'You misunderstand me. I can think of few men more worthy.'

Startled by this unexpected acknowledgement, Fiacail considered her with suspicion. 'And yet I do not sense that I have your unequivocal support.'

'That is not true. You have my support. I just don't think the assembly, particularly the elders, will share my view. They will not support your candidacy.' She halted for he was regarding her with a look of complete bafflement.

'What are you saying, Bodhmhall? Have I not beaten off the cattle raids of *Ua Broinn?* Did I not overcome the champion of *Ua Gerrad* in single combat – their best man – in a matter of moments? I am the greatest warrior amongst the candidates and I tell you this: had I had been with your brother at Gabhra, we would not have been taken by surprise and we would not have lost seventeen men.'

Bodhmhall flinched. It hurt to hear it put so bluntly but she had to recognise the truth of his words.

'None of that is in doubt, Fiacail. But you forget an essential issue. Clann Baoiscne need neither a warrior nor a champion but a future leader to replace my father as leader when he dies. In the eyes of the elders you are a wanderer, a wastrel. Pleasant company, yes. Talented in war and strategy, there is no doubt. Nevertheless, you are also seen as a man outside the fold, a man with dubious associations to newer settlements such as Seiscenn Uarbhaoil. More importantly, everyone knows you as a man directed primarily by his cock. Do you think the people will allow themselves to be led by a tomcat who would sleep with their wives as soon as their backs are turned?'

The warrior stared at her over the length of a prolonged silence. Finally, he released a vexed sigh. 'You were ever unsubtle with your words, dear one.'

'As you were ever unsubtle with your actions. It is not my intent to offend you, Fiacail, but you know it is my way to expose the frank heart of a matter. I do not weave soft untruths and if ...'

'No, no.' Fiacail wearily waved her protests away. 'That is the reason for my direct query. Whatever may be said about your blunt response, I know at least that you will always tell me the straight of it.'

He stared gloomily down the valley where the mist was slowly dispersing. 'Perhaps it would strengthen my candidacy to have the daughter of Tréanmór, the current *rí*, standing by my side.'

The *bandraoi* grimaced, an expression not lost on her love from another lifetime.

'Oh, come, Bodhmhall. You know you are dear to me. Beneath that, admittedly stony, exterior, I suspect I am just as dear to you. We are a natural fit. You are the curving riverbank to my surging waters. You guide me, channel my force. You make me a better man.'

Bodhmhall shook her head for everything that Fiacail was now proposing reflected the other, unspoken, reason she knew that he would never receive the vote he desired. To put it simply, he lacked the necessary duplicity or guile for politics. He was at heart, despite his many other, less endearing qualities, the most truly honest man she had ever known.

'You forget recent history more easily than others, Fiacail. Events at Dún Baoiscne mean that any association with me would be to your, considerable, disadvantage. Besides -' She brushed several loose strands of hair back from her face. 'The truth of the matter is that I will not be by your side. The riverbed has long since shifted. If ever we were the natural fit then we are certainly so no longer. You made your choice many years ago. I have since made a choice of my own.'

He sighed, scratched one cheek in exasperation.

'Liath Luachra?'

'Liath Luachra,' she confirmed.

Fiacail muttered something under his breath.

'What was that?'

'I said that Liath Luachra is humourless. "The Grey One" suits her.' His bushy eyebrows closed in and his jaw tightened as he struggled with her response. 'She does not make you laugh as I did.'

'She does not make me cry as you did.'

Fiacail's expression darkened but when he spoke again his voice had a flatness that she had never heard before.

'She will never provide you with children. I know the prospect of children has been a yearning dear to your heart.'

'There are things that are more important than children.'

'Of course, but Liath Luachra lacks one of those as well.'

'I wasn't talking about that, Fiacail.' She threw her hands in the air. 'Great Mother, give me strength!'

The *bandraoi* turned and made to stamp away then caught herself.

If anyone must stalk off, let it be Fiacail. He is on my land.'

Infuriated, she rounded on the warrior. 'It is true Liath Luachra can never offer me children. But there is one thing that she can, and does, offer. Something you never could, Fiacail. Faithfulness.'

The big man rubbed a stubbled jaw with the palm of his hand.

'Ah.' He nodded slowly. 'Faithfulness. Right.'

As the *bandraoi*'s eyes flared, he raised one palm in a soothing gesture. 'You let your anger twist you up, Bodhmhall. I'm making a joke. I'm fully aware fidelity and I have not been ... intimate. That is a fault I have regretted a thousand times since you left. Do you truly think I have learned nothing from that?' He kicked at a low stone and sent it spinning off into the undergrowth. 'Besides, I fear for your safety.'

'My safety?' Bodhmhall looked at him with bemusement at such an unexpected digression.

'Something is not right with Liath Luachra. Her milk is ... unclean.'

'Oh, please -'

'Hear me out, Bodhmhall. I acknowledge Liath Luachra's ... accomplishments. But, believe me when I say, she cannot be completely trusted. You have not seen her as I have seen her.'

'What do you mean?' The chill in her voice warned him that he was treading on precarious territory.

Before responding, Fiacail crouched to pick up a fallen branch and used it to strike out wildly at a cluster of wintered thistle. As the withered heads went spinning onto the nearby pasture, he turned to her. 'I mean that when we found her out in the Great Wild she had the fury on her. She is a berserker, Bodhmhall.'

Bodhmhall quietly cleared her throat, taking the time to slow her pulse and symbolically swallow the rage that bubbled up inside. It took an effort to regain her earlier composure but when she spoke again, it was with a voice that was calm and surprisingly measured. 'You have seen her fight. Did she seem to you to fight like a berserker?'

Fiacail looked as though he was about to contend the point but as he made to speak he halted abruptly. Cursing, he snapped the branch in half and cast the two pieces aside. 'No,' he scowled. 'If anything, she was the opposite. She was cold. Dispassionate. Merciless.'

'Exactly. When you found her in Great Wild, she'd just endured the assault of a Tainted One.'

'Ah, yes. The infamous Tainted One.'

Bodhmhall nodded. 'The same Tainted One I made mention of last night, who seeks Muirne Muncháem and her child. Such creatures are deadly. Most people who have the misfortune to stumble across them do not see the dawn of the following day. Liath Luachra crossed this creature and she survived.'

'Only because I found her. She would not have survived had I not been there to assist her.'

Bodhmhall kneaded her hands together then placed them behind her back. 'An act for which I'm sure she'll remain eternally grateful.'

The warrior glanced sideways at her with such a sceptical expression that she could not help but laugh out loud.

'Or perhaps not,' she conceded.

A sudden wail erupted from within the *ráth*, the insistent sound of a hungry newborn bleating out over the embankment to pierce the earlier silence.

Fiacail grimaced. 'The Great-Lunged One recommences his song.'

Bodhmhall considered the embankment with a weary expression. 'I should return.'

Fiacail gave her a look expressing much that remained unsaid. 'Just promise me one thing.'

'Yes?'

'Promise me that you will consider my proposal.'

'I will consider it.'

'With earnest consideration.'

'With earnest consideration. But I can offer you no reassurances, Fiacail. You know my mind on that.'

'I can ask for nothing more.' The warrior took a deep breath then stared up at the northern ridge, his back turned towards her. 'Go. I will remain here a little longer. Your words have provided me with grist to gnaw on for a time.'

Bodhmhall nodded. 'Do not remain too long. The *fian* still roam the Great Wild and last night's discussion must be reconvened. I would welcome your counsel.'

He nodded but, already, he looked distracted, absorbed in his own internal deliberations.

'Yes, yes. We will talk soon.'

***

When Bodhmhall returned to the roundhouse the smell of birthing blood had dissipated, supplanted by the earthy scent of peat smoke and the odour of cooked meat. Conchenn was sitting on a reed mat beside the fire, stirring a metal pot, when the *bandraoi* brushed through the leather flap. The old woman had been working assiduously throughout the night, preserving the remnants of the butchered pig. Bodhmhall stared, impressed by the sheer volume of clay pots lined up alongside her, filled to the brim with seasoned pork congealed in layers of yellow lard. Slow-cooked and stored in its own fat, the meat could be conserved for a significant period of time, an important reserve for those times when they might not be able to leave the *ráth*.

The old woman glanced up and Bodhmhall felt a surge of guilt for those worn features appeared even more lined than usual. Following the arduous delivery of Muirne Muncháem's baby, Conchenn had urged the *bandraoi* to retire and, exhausted from the day's events, she'd allowed herself to be persuaded. Conchenn, however, had stayed up during the night, not only tending to Muirne and her child but preserving a significant quantity of food as well. Bodhmhall sighed. With her steadfast endurance and lack of

109

complaint, it was often easy to forget that Conchenn was actually a very elderly woman.

Up on the sleeping platform, oblivious to the industry being accomplished around her, Muirne continued to snore. Curled on one side, in a foetal position, with the infant – swaddled in a thick wool blanket – tucked beneath her breast and now mercifully silent as it sucked greedily on one heavy nipple.

'Hello, nephew. And what do you have to say for yourself?'

The only response was a greedy sucking sound. The baby's eyes remained tightly screwed shut.

Fair enough. You have other, more pressing, priorities.

Leaving her nephew, Bodhmhall turned back to the old woman. 'Conchenn, enough. It's well past time for you to reclaim your bed. I'll stay to watch over our guests and finish what's left of the meat.'

As usual, the old woman did not dispute her instructions. Rising to her feet, she nodded and departed the roundhouse.

'You need not fret, Bodhmhall.'

The unexpected voice took the *bandraoi* by surprise. Startled, she spun about to discover Cairbre sitting in a shadowed section of the dwelling where the flickering of the flames had served to make him practically invisible.

'We preserved the last of the meat this morning. Only the scraps remain and we will use those later today.'

The *rechtaire* was seated on a well-smoothened log with a *fidchell* board across his knees. The wooden square, decorated with spiral symbols, was laid out with a grid of seven-by-seven squares, each with an individual pin-hole at the centre. A game of strategy, the *fidchell* board also held a set of black and white pegs inserted in the squares at two opposing edges. The object of the game was to move these 'warriors' using a restricted number of specific moves, to attain and 'capture' the opponent's side of the board. Cairbre occasionally liked to claim that the ebb and flow of a game of *fidchell* reflected great events on the political or battle field but Bodhmhall personally felt the metaphor overlaboured.

'You have found an opponent?'

The old man smiled. An enthusiastic player, he regularly complained about the lack of suitable adversaries within the settlement.

'Fiacail mac Codhna. We engaged in three matches earlier this morning.' His lips abruptly turned down to form a dissatisfied frown. 'That young man has a unique mind and can somehow think several steps ahead. He was clearly drunk but he succeeded in winning each match. I can only imagine that fortune was on his side.'

Bodhmhall refrained from comment. The *rechtaire* prided himself on his skill with the *fidchell* board and was put out by his defeat. Clearly, he had misjudged his opponent, a common oversight when it came to dealings with Fiacail. Because of his coarse, uncouth manner, many tended to underestimate the Seiscenn Uarbhaoil warrior's intelligence. Usually to their detriment. Fiacail might enjoy acting the fool but such rough dissimulation disguised the sharp intellect lying in wait for the unwary like a predator in the bushes.

'I imagine it was good fortune,' she agreed.

'Perhaps the Mistress of Ráth Bládhma would enjoy a game,' the old man suggested.

'Perhaps.'

With surprising dexterity for a man of his age and physical condition, Cairbre shifted the board from his knees and shuffled off his seat. Placing his treasured possession tenderly on the ground, he sat himself on the mat closest to the fire. 'Forgive me,' he said. 'My bones ache. I need to stay close to the warmth.'

She dismissed the apology with a brief wave of her hand. Settling onto a mat on the opposite side of the board, she watched as he straightened the pegs of the two opposing 'armies'. 'Whose move is it?'

'That depends. Do you wish to instigate the attack – in which case you should take the white – or are you, by nature, more of a reactive person?'

Bodhmhall raised one sardonic eyebrow. 'Do you feel one is better than the other?'

'Like life, that depends on the circumstances. Sometimes, yes. Sometimes, no.'

The *bandraoi* groaned. 'This is why you find so few challengers within Ráth Bládhma, Cairbre. You transform an entertainment into a tedious lecture.'

Cairbre grinned in silent apology. 'I have limited time to pass on what little wisdom I have garnered, Bodhmhall. Hence, I do so whenever I have the opportunity. This is all the more important now that *Clann Morna* are on

111

the move.' He paused and looked down at the board. 'They must feel bold indeed, dispatching warriors so far from their tribal lands.'

'The *fian* are not from *Clann Morna*.'

Cairbre paused in the action of reaching for one of his pegs. Raising his eyes, he stared at her in astonishment. 'I don't understand. Last night you indicated that the *fian* were dispatched from *Clann Morna* in search of Muirne Muncháem.'

'Last night, that was what I believed. This morning I am of the opinion the *fian* are not in search of Muirne but of her son. My nephew.'

Both turned to look across the room at the sleeping platform where the baby lay, a slight bundle beside its mother. He was sleeping again, satisfied from the recent feed.

'That seems ... difficult to believe.' Cairbre sounded dubious. 'It is a lot of trouble to go to for a mere babe.'

'My brother's son is no "mere babe". The *Gift* confirms there is something unique about him. That also explains the presence of the Tainted One.'

The old man looked her in the eye before thoughtfully scratching his nose. She could tell that he was struggling to curb his curiosity and refrain from the obvious question. 'No,' she said. 'I don't know *why* he is special. All I can tell for certain is that his life-light shines brighter than any other I have ever seen. I think this portends a rare and very special future.'

Cairbre tugged softly at his beard as he considered the possibility further. 'Does the *Gift* also confirm that the *fian* are not from *Clann Morna*?'

'No. It is suspicion rather than certainty but I am convinced of the truth of it.'

Cairbre looked over at the baby once more as though he might somehow observe what only Bodhmhall's sight permitted her to see. Disappointed, he huffed glumly.

'So if it is not Clann Morna who send the *fian*, who is it?'

'Someone who knows of the child's potential. Someone with the power and the resource to dispatch a *fian* and a Tainted One. A hidden hand who places them like pegs on your *fidchell* board.'

'And that is?'

She shook her head. 'I don't know.'

Cairbre grunted then abruptly reached up to twist the board around so that the black pieces were facing her. 'Then you must take the black pieces for you are responding to attack.'

Without waiting for a response, the old man plucked a white peg from its hole and moved it forward. The placement was an odd one, within the rules but one that situated his 'warrior' directly in her 'territory'.

She looked at him in surprise, momentarily distracted from their conversation by the oddness of his placement. 'Why did you move your peg there?'

'Why do you think I placed it there?'

'I have no idea.'

'Do you feel my move was aggressive?'

'Of course.'

'Then my objective is something at your end of the board. Perhaps, like the mysterious hand behind the *fian* there is something within your territory that I want.'

Bodhmhall looked at him and released a weary sigh. 'Is this a clumsy attempt at imitating our situation on the *fidchell* board?'

'It is clumsy,' he admitted. 'And hardly a true imitation.' With this, he reached forward, removed four white pegs from Bodhmhall's side of the board and placed them on the floor. 'That would seem a more accurate representation.'

The *bandraoi* regarded him sardonically.

'If what you say is true, Bodhmhall, Ráth Bládhma has acquired powerful enemies. We are at a serious disadvantage.' Cairbre fixed her with a look of surprising intensity. 'You must respond to these threats with rare ingenuity and fortitude if we are to survive.'

'I am aware of that, Cairbre. Would it were as easy as moving pegs on a board.'

'Leadership is never easy. If it were, we would all be leaders. No -' The *rechtaire* continued to hold her eyes. 'The problem with leadership is that it requires compromise and sacrifice. A leader must balance the eternal conflict of values and options.'

'What do you mean?'

'I mean that real leaders make difficult decisions for others when few realistic options are available. Many of us do not have the heart to make such verdicts for they involve compromise and sacrifice. The matter is further complicated for those leaders with a moral conscience in that it restricts the range of options they have.'

He paused to massage his face with the palms of his hands.

'One thing has become clear to me over the years, Bodhmhall. Those leaders who prevail tend to be men or women who are ruthless and brutal, individuals who can make harsh decisions with ease.'

Bodhmhall found that she had been unconsciously leaning forward as though to compensate for the old man's accent and the muffling effect of his beard. Sitting back once more, she composed herself and smiled. 'So you see no value in values?'

'From a social perspective, of course. From a political or military perspective - He paused. 'Let us just say that the greatest and most successful generals or politicians tend to be those who lack any restrictions of morality.'

'And where would you rate my father in this scheme of thought?'

Cairbre gave a knowing smile. 'Tréanmór is a skilful and a ruthless leader but he would not eat babies.'

'Somebody would,' Bodhmhall answered quietly, shivering as she remembered the clammy touch of the Tainted One. She tapped the top of the peg at the centre of the black set. 'And me, Cairbre. How would you rate me?'

'Untested, Bodhmhall. Until now you have had the luxury of authority without true responsibility. Because of our isolation here in Glenn Ceoch, you have faced little more than minor crises with minor consequences. The penalties we face in opposing the Tainted One and the *fian* are significantly more than you've encountered thus far. To survive, I fear you will be obliged to respond with a brutality and ruthlessness that is not your nature.'

'Such as throwing Muirne and my nephew out to the wolves.'

The *rechatire* shifted uncomfortably on the reed mat. 'You know that is one possible option. And by far the easiest although I suspect you lack the callousness to do this.'

'Then you suspect correctly. I offered them sanctuary and I will keep my word.'

Cairbre shrugged. 'That does you credit as a human being but it also means that you have removed one option from the board that would divert the hostility of your opponents. Consequently, you must find another alternative to counter the threat of the *fian* and the Tainted One.'

114

Bodhmhall frowned. 'We could remain hidden. Stay within the valley.'

'Is that truly a valid option?'

The *bandraoi* thought about that for a moment then slowly shook her head. 'Probably not. The Tainted One will locate our guests eventually. The *fian* are likely to follow.'

'Therefore, the options are -'

'To eliminate the Tainted One. Or flee to a safer location.' She bit her lower lip. 'In truth, I cannot think of a safer location. Even less than I can see how we could eliminate the Tainted One.'

'There is another option you have not considered.'

'Yes?'

'You could seek the protection of a benefactor who provides credible opposition to the *fian*.'

'There is no-one. *Clann Baoiscne* would not take us back.'

'There is Seiscenn Uarbhaoil.'

'Fiacail? He has but two men.'

Cairbre returned that doubtful look with a direct stare. 'He has but two men here and their presence effectively doubles the ráth's defence capability. Like as not, he has many more blooded warriors back at Seiscenn Uarbhaoil. That settlement is certainly far enough away to offer refuge from the fian in this territory. For the ongoing survival of the colony, an alliance between Ráth Bládhma and such an increasingly powerful household would be ... fortuitous.' He let the words hang there, their meaning effectively escalating in the subsequent silence.

Bodhmhall considered him with a wary eye. 'You have been talking to Fiacail.'

'No. But his desires are evident to the observant eye.'

'Then the observant eye will also know that the price is too high. I have lived in rare freedom for the last three years, Cairbre. I answer to no man, nobody instructs me on what I have to do. This is not a situation I would easily sacrifice. If I leave Ráth Bládhma I cannot bring my cattle or my *lubgort*. I would be nothing more than a refugee, dependent once more on the will of others.'

She sighed.

'And then there is Liath Luachra. I would not lose her and, do not forget, we are both very much in her debt. She has kept us safe these past three years. She has also taught your sons the skills they will need to keep their land.'

She paused to appraise the *rechtaire* with a critical expression. 'You reveal a surprisingly ruthless streak today, Cairbre. It is not a side to you that I have seen before.'

'I am old, Bodhmhall. Despite my years, I am selfish enough to want to live a little longer. More than that, I want my sons to live. I would gladly give my own life to achieve that aim.' He grew silent for a moment. 'I like Liath Luachra. She is flighty but she has an admirable fortitude. I am grateful to her but even Liath Luachra cannot defend us from fifty warriors. And should you align with Seiscenn Uarbhaoil ...'

'Yes?'

'There is a stronger chance that both you and my sons would live.'

'To Liath Luachra's detriment.'

'It is an option. Not a desirable one, I admit. But remember what I said to you. To survive you must respond with brutality and ruthlessness.' He tapped the white peg that he'd moved into her portion of the *fidchell* board. 'You have to counter the threat that confronts you, Bodhmhall.'

Chapter Five

The newborn started to cry again later that morning. Muirne
Muncháem, still recovering from the exertion of childbirth, continued to
sleep on.

Liath Luachra also managed to sleep through the unhappy wailing. It
was well after mid-morning when the warrior woman finally stirred and sat
up, her back aching from lying flat for so long. Confused and disorientated,
she pushed the furs away, squinting about at the unfamiliar surroundings
until she remembered where she was.

She grunted as she swung her legs off the sleeping platform. Grimacing
in anticipation, she stood and placed her full weight on them but felt little
more than a twinge in her knees. Her thigh and lower leg muscles were stiff
but the swelling in the joints had subsided dramatically and she could move
freely.

Bodhmhall's magic hands.

Rolling her neck from side to side, Liath Luachra felt the tensed-up
muscle crunch and crackle like twisted gristle. She looked down at the
sleeping platform with its mound of twisted furs. The *bandraoi* was no
longer there, of course, but the memory of her company left a pleasing
emotional aftertaste.

Bodhmhall's earlier presence was also evident in the thoughtful
arrangements of the roundhouse's interior. It was pleasantly warm for the
fire had recently been banked up with a fresh supply of wood. A fresh
woollen tunic and breeches lay beside the sleeping platform and a bowl of
warm water sat in the ashes. Liath Luachra used this to wash her face then
wiped herself dry with an old piece of cloth. As she pulled on the fresh
clothing, she felt altogether more human.

It was only then that she heard the cry of the infant and stood, head
cocked at an angle as she tried to work out what it was. After a moment,
she snorted.

Muirne's brat.

Despite herself, Liath Luachra couldn't resist pausing to listen again. She
was probably feeling oversensitive, she realised, but she couldn't shake the
feeling that this sound, so alien to Glenn Ceoch, heralded some
monumental change for Ráth Bládhma.

With a sigh, she settled herself by the fire, sitting on the solid slab of polished wood that Cairbre often mockingly referred to as his 'throne'. She had a hazy memory of the old man and one or two of his sons coming into the roundhouse to settle themselves on the other sleeping platforms at some point during the night. Too tired to do more than simply register their presence, she'd drifted back to sleep immediately and hadn't heard them when they rose to leave again that morning.

Rubbing the last of the sleep from her eyes, she stared at the fire and nibbled on a hard oatmeal cake. When the entrance flap brushed aside, a draught of cold air flushed through the interior and even with her back to the opening, Liath Luachra recognised Bearach's distinctive step.

'What is it, Bearach?'

There was a startled silence and she smiled to herself, knowing that she had surprised the boy.

'It's Bodhmhall, Liath Luachra. She wants you to join her and Fiacail mac Codhna. To discuss the defence of the *ráth*.'

The warrior woman turned with heavy eyes to consider the boy.

'These are the words she used? She "wants me" to come.'

The boy shuffled uncomfortably beneath her gaze.

'She didn't say it like that, Grey One.'

'I know, Bearach. I'm teasing. Thank you. You can tell Bodhmhall I'll join her presently.'

'I will.'

As the youth made to leave, she returned to her contemplation of the flames but the absence of any sound from the entrance flap caused her to swivel about once more. Bearach was still standing there, staring at her closely.

'Have I disappointed you, Grey One?'

'What?'

'Have I failed you in some way? Should I have come to support you at Drom Osna? I -' He paused. 'You do not speak to me. I feel shame that I have let you down.'

Liath Luachra stared at him, a series of furrows slowly forming along her brow. For a moment, she considered brushing the question off with a generic response but a surge of insight prompted her to hold her tongue. The boy was genuinely distressed, fraught with feelings of shame and humiliation similar to those that she, herself, had so recently confessed to Bodhmhall.

'You did not let me down,' she said at last. 'You followed my orders. If you had not done so, I would have struggled to trust you again. Bearach ...' She trailed off, choosing her next words with care. 'You are someone I would trust to walk the Great Wild with. I can think of no other person I would prefer to have at my side.'

The boy's chin lifted perceptibly.

'It's just ... you seemed distant when we were Out. When you came back you were silent and didn't –'

'Bearach, when we were Out I was contending with memories from times past, old poisons in my head that still taint my thinking. Such blemishes on my mood have no connection with you.'

The boy looked ludicrously relieved by her words, almost grateful. He hesitantly tapped the reed-strewn floor with the tip of his toe.

'I wish to be like you, Liath Luachra. I wish to be a *gaiscíoch* - a true warrior.'

She stared at him in genuine astonishment. A moment later, she started to laugh. It was a rare sound for her and one that was surprisingly soft, if tinged with an underlying melancholy. 'Ah, Bearach. You are truly the only one to make me raise a smile.'

'I make no jest, Grey One. I wish to be a *gaiscíoch* like you. One day I hope to equal your skill as a fighter, your ability to work through the fight in your head. I want to learn courage such as yours. You know no fear when you are Out in the Great Wild.'

'Ah, yes. The Great Wild backs down when I tramp through its forests. Wolves shit themselves and slink into the undergrowth at my passing. Even the Faceless Ones, the ghosts of hazy glades, hide and tell each other fearful tales of the dreaded Liath Luachra who will come through the shadows to take their heads.'

The youth blushed at her gentle mockery. Picking at a loose thread on the hem of his tunic, he wound it about his index finger, tightening it until the tip of the digit grew white.

'You are the best of us here in Ráth Bládhma.'

'Which only goes to show how little of the Out you've actually seen, Bearach. There are many out there who would best me in a fight.'

119

'But Aodhán says you beat Dún Baoiscne's finest warriors. He says they fear you, that your reputation for war makes them quake in their boots.'

'Aodhán needs to harness his tongue. And his fancies.'

'He told me about the day you first came to Dún Baoiscne with *Na Cineáltai* – the Kindly Ones – your *fian of* a hundred men. He says that you crushed their best fighters in single combat. Humiliated them. That you were too agile, too strong to be defeated.'

Liath Luachra ground her teeth together.

'I did defeat them. And, yes, I did humiliate them. But that was a mistake for which they never forgave me.' She shrugged. 'I understand that now. I'd probably have reacted in a similar manner if I was defeated by someone I considered weaker or in some way inferior.'

'But you showed them!' There was a shrill enthusiasm to the boy's voice that made her cringe.

'You have a warped understanding of things, Bearach. I accept that the fault is not yours for you base it on the tall tales of those who should know better. I will have strong words with Aodhán about putting such stories in your head.'

The boy looked confused, almost disbelieving. 'Aodhán has not spoken true?'

Liath Luachra shifted awkwardly on her seat. She was uncomfortable having conversations of such depth with anyone other than Bodhmhall.

'Aodhán's claims hold a sliver of truth. I did lead *Na Cineáltai* but that band never had more than ten men at any one time. They were brutal men, little more than killers -' Her voice trailed off. 'You must understand, Bearach, my life back then ... that was a different life. I was a different person. I had a haunting on me, a haunting so venomous that I became little better than a wounded animal: vicious, savage and very cruel.'

Unable to bear his trusting gaze, she dropped her own eyes to the floor. 'You have seen the way a dog will snap at a wound in its paw.'

The boy nodded slowly.

'It is the reaction of a stupid beast who knows no better. It experiences pain and immediately thinks it has been attacked. In its attempt to retaliate, to strike back, it hurts itself even more.'

She reached down into the fire and pulled a burning brand from the embers. Part of the wood had burned away and much of it was scorched and black but the tip was still red hot.

'That was the way of me back in those days. Except that I didn't strike at my own limbs. No, I was far too smart for that. I struck out at others instead. Bandits, reavers, murderers, sometimes even innocent people who merely looked at me the wrong way, at the wrong time on the wrong day.'

She placed the tip of the burning brand against the back of her left hand. Bearach stared in horror as smoke from the skin rose up, the stink of burning flesh filing the air. Liath Luachra showed no sign of even noticing. Her eyes flared with a ragged intensity.

'I had a belly full of venom, a heart full of gangrene and battle rage. This world had cut me to the quick and I was determined to hurt it back, to carve its filthy influence out of my heart. I hacked and cleaved a route through blood and sinew and bone when all that time my real target, the one thing I was truly trying to strike, was myself.'

She paused and took a deep breath as she dropped the firebrand back into the fire. Her forehead was sweating profusely. Her heart thundered and there was a sickly taste in her mouth. She focused her attention on these other physical sensations, refusing to acknowledge the pain in her hand.

'So yes, in a martial sense, that made me strong. It made me impervious to fear and, for a time, to pain. It also made me impervious to those things that make us human: compassion, friendship, affection.'

Her eyes raised abruptly to lock directly on the boy's. 'And that,' she snarled, 'is what you must sacrifice to be a true *gaiscíoch*.'

Bearach blanched and unconsciously stepped back. For a moment, she thought that he would run, flee the roundhouse, but he surprised her by holding his ground. Drawing on some inner reserve of fortitude, he advanced towards her once more.

'I don't care. I like you Liath Luachra. I would have you as my comrade and friend and remain your comrade and friend when I am older.'

The woman warrior stared back at him, her features empty of all emotion. Inside, however, her belly had clenched, twisted into a hundred thousand knots. Her throat constricted and for a moment she was unable to speak, almost unable to breathe. With great effort, she took a deep breath then released it again.

'I like you too, Bearach,' she croaked. 'I like you too.'

***

121

Liath Luachra remained staring into the fire for a long time after the boy had departed, her thoughts immersed in its blazing red depth. The intensity of their conversation and the ancient memories it revived, had left her feeling empty, confused and, surprisingly, tainted with feelings of guilt. This latter reaction angered her. Although selective with the details, she had been as truthful with the boy as she could. Gritting her teeth, she wrapped a damp flannel about her stinging hand.

Fool! What were you trying to prove with that display?

She closed her eyes and shook her head. It hurt to think. Even now, after all these years, it still hurt to think. She didn't really understand why she'd felt the way she'd felt, why she'd done all the things she'd done during her days with *Na Cineáltaí*. Although it was true that the distance of time gave some level of detached reflection, all she could really recall from that period was a great geyser of rage and a head-full of black noise created from her own internal fury. That rage had directed every action that she'd taken, every sword stroke she'd delivered, every merciless thrust she'd made. The irony was that, in her madness, she'd truly believed she was in control.

Oblivious to such irony, she had led her *fian* from one battle to another, from one massacre to the next and somehow, miraculously, survived when stronger, better men had fallen at her side. Over time, her reputation had grown. Men had gathered about her – *Na Cineáltaí* – attracted by her luck and a ferocity that put their own blood lust in perspective. Storytellers, men who did not know her but were enamoured by the concept of her gender and accomplishments, spun romanticised tales about the campfires of a strapping female that no sword edge could touch who, in time, became the most notorious of killers.

Ironically, that reputation had probably saved her life. On at least two occasions, she'd seen it in the eyes of the men she was fighting, men who recognised her from the fanciful tales of her fearsome savagery. Convinced of the stories' accuracy, they had also allowed themselves to be convinced that death was upon them. Under such circumstances, it was. She had left both men leaking their life's blood into the thirsty earth.

She had been lucky. She had survived because of Bodhmhall. At Dún Baoiscne, the *bandraoi* had found her, calmed her, treated her with kindness, and doused her fury so she could return to humankind. She knew that Bodhmhall still worried about her, monitored her inner flame using that perceptive *Gift* of hers for fear that, one day, it might flare up and consume the world once more.

Such a possibility made her fearful. She did not wish to revert. At the same time her experiences with the Tainted One had shaken her. She truly feared that the creature had broken her mind, released elements of the brutal, mindless warrior she had been. And yet, conversely, she also knew that in the days to come, that very person might be the only one who could save them.

***

Bodhmhall was standing on the causeway beyond the gateway, in the company of Cairbre and Fiacail mac Codhna, when Liath Luachra came to join them. Engaged in heated discussion, none of them noticed her approach until she coughed softly to announce her presence. All discussion halted as they turned to face her and, with a start, the woman warrior realised Bodhmhall was holding a baby in her arms. Her nephew.

The presence of the infant took her by surprise. As she stared, she saw Bodhmhall snuggle it to her chest. Almost immediately, the baby nuzzled its head in closer towards the *bandraoi's* breast.

'You won't find any nourishment there,' Bodhmhall laughed. 'Forget your hunger for a moment, little one. Take your first true look at the world.' She raised the baby in her arms as though to offer it a view of their surroundings. The gesture was not appreciated, however, for the baby whimpered, until she pulled it close again, tucking the furs in around it.

She looks happy.

Liath Luachra considered the joy in the *bandraoi's* face, unsure what sensation the sight provoked within herself: happiness, jealousy or, perhaps, simply no sensation at all.

Fortunately, Fiacail proved an effective distraction from such complex considerations. The warrior had a sour puss on him and was clearly unhappy as a result of his discussions with Bodhmhall and Cairbre. 'Where have you been?' he demanded. 'We sent Bearach to fetch you an age ago.'

Liath Luachra stared back at him without expression, despite her irritation at the Seiscenn Uarbhaoil man's presumption of authority. Bodhmhall, too, had evidently noted this transgression for she glowered at the big man. 'We *asked* Bearach to fetch you,' she corrected as she regarded the woman warrior. 'Are you recovered, Liath Luachra?'

'I'm well. Forgive my tardiness. I have been reflecting.'

'On what?'

'On Life. On Death.'

Fiacail was unimpressed with her response 'Plenty of time to reflect on death when you're dead. We have other, more urgent matters to discuss.'

'More urgent matters?'

'Well, there is the *fian*. And then of course, there is that cursed Tainted One who continues to haunt your settlement.'

Liath Luachra glanced at Bodhmhall, one eyebrow arched in question. Despite the earlier laughter with her nephew, the *bandraoi* looked drawn and worried.

'He is still out there, Liath Luachra. I felt his touch again, just before we gathered here.' The *bandraoi* could not hide a shudder of revulsion. 'He seeks Muirne and her son. I am sure of it now.'

'And he did not detect her?'

'No.'

'I thought you said such creatures were effective at closing in on their prey.'

'That is what I was told. My understanding is that they can detect a person not only by sensing their thoughts but also through their dreams.'

'So why has it not done that?'

'I believe it has. Or at least it's attempted to. I suspect that exhaustion diminishes a person's mental activity and, thereby, the creature's ability to sense them. Muirne had barely arrived at Ráth Bládhma the first time I felt its touch and she was in a deep state of exhaustion. When its mind passed over our home she had passed out and it became distracted with me instead.'

The baby in her arms whimpered again. Liath Luachra watched in bemused confusion as Bodhmhall rocked it gently back to sleep.

'This morning,' the *bandraoi* continued. 'The circumstances were similar. When the Tainted One came searching, Muirne was deep asleep again, this time exhausted by the effort of childbirth.'

Liath Luachra nodded and thoughtfully chewed on the inside of her cheek. 'Yes, that makes sense. I can remember feeling the creature's grip loosen when I fell in an old riverbed and was knocked almost senseless.' A sudden thought struck her and her eyes dropped to the sleeping infant.

'It didn't sense the babe?'

'The babe is too young to form real thoughts. There is nothing substantial for the Tainted One's net of notions to seize.' The *bandraoi* released a sigh, suddenly looking very weary. 'Our visitors have been very fortunate but it is only a matter of time before it returns and finds them. I cannot prevent that.'

'Perhaps we could somehow conceal Muirne from the Tainted One?'

All eyes turned to Cairbre who was staring into space, tugging pensively on his beard. When he realised that they were looking at him, he started and cleared his throat with an embarrassed cough. 'I mean, if Muirne cannot be detected while she sleeps perhaps we should keep her in that state of slumber.'

This time, all eyes turned to Bodhmhall.

'I suppose I could give her a draught to keep her in deep sleep,' the *bandraoi* said with obvious reluctance. 'But I cannot keep her like that indefinitely. She needs to eat and the babe needs to be fed.'

There was a brief silence while the group considered the possibility. 'A pity,' said Fiacail, at last. 'The prospect of respite from Muirne's tongue had much to recommend such a plan.'

Liath Luachra pulled her knife from its sheath and started using the tip of the blade to clean her finger nails. 'We have to eliminate the Tainted One,' she said. Although she was looking directly at Bodhmhall, from the corner of her eye she was surprised to note Cairbre nodding in muted approval.

Fiacail's response was less encouraging. 'Brave words,' he taunted and mockingly rolled his eyes.

'We were discussing such possibilities before you joined us, Liath Luachra,' Bodhmhall explained. 'It seems an impossible feat. This Tainted One is exceptionally powerful. It can control the minds of others. If it feels threatened, it can simply turn the mind of its attacker against itself.'

The woman warrior was not to be dissuaded. 'I see no other option if you insist on protecting the Withered Weed of Almhu. If we remain hidden within Glenn Ceoch, the *fian* are unlikely to find us. They'll eventually lose heart and depart. The Tainted One is another matter. He is the black wolf in the undergrowth. It's simply a matter of time before he locates Muirne and sends his pack to attack us.'

Once again, Cairbre quietly nodded his approval.

'Besides,' continued Liath Luachra. 'There's the question of redress. This creature attacked without provocation. That balance must be addressed. Such is the nature of things.'

Bodhmhall frowned. 'This is not a time for vengeance, Liath Luachra. You were lucky to escape with your life.'

'Perhaps.'

'There is no 'perhaps'. That creature almost made you run yourself to death. How would you prevent such a recurrence?'

Liath Luachra had no answer. Annoyed, she turned the question around instead.

'Do your *draoi* teachings offer any potential means for dealing to the Tainted One?'

Bodhmhall shook her head. 'No. You know my apprenticeship was terminated ... prematurely. In any case, even if I had completed my training, it's unlikely I'd have learned anything that might help to eliminate such a creature. This is unique to anything I've encountered before.'

'To challenge a Tainted One,' said Fiacail. 'You would need a plan. A good plan.'

Liath Luachra considered the warrior's contribution with quiet disdain. 'I have the basis of a plan. I need to work out some of the details but it consists of two distinct parts.'

'Which are?'

She paused. 'First, locate the creature. Second, beat it to a messy pulp.'

Fiacail roared with laughter, greatly amused by her bravado. Bodhmhall's response was a tired sigh. 'Dear one, you could barely walk when came back to us yesterday.'

'That was yesterday. Today, thanks to your care, I am feeling much improved.'

'The Tainted One could be anywhere out there in the Great Wild.'

'True. But I have a sense it will remain with its bodyguards at Drom Osna. The site provided good shelter and had the air of being well settled. If I take one more day to recover, I should be able to travel and find it again.'

The *bandraoi* did not look happy. Instead of arguing the matter, however, she turned to her *rechtaire*. 'Cairbre?'

The old man took a moment to think before responding. 'I do not know how Liath Luachra proposes to confront the Tainted One but on one fact she cannot be disputed. If that *draoi* is associated with the *fian*, they will locate Glenn Ceoch and come for us.'

'And you, Fiacail?'

The man from Seiscenn Uarbhaoil scratched his moustached upper lip as he considered the question. 'I'm sorry, Bodhmhall. I know this is your home but I am not so optimistic that I would face the wrath of a Tainted One. Neither do I like the idea of traipsing the country with two *fian* at my heels, however. By your leave, we will remain and accept your hospitality until the circumstances change.

'And if the circumstances change? If the *fian* find us?'

'This *ráth* is well constructed but if the *fian* find Glenn Ceoch, we cannot hope to defend it against such numbers.' He shook his head. 'I cannot ask my men to throw their lives away needlessly so I will run away as though my arse is on fire and my sweet-heart's mother seeks to kiss me.'

There was a disappointed silence following the big man's decision. Only Liath Luachra seemed unperturbed by his lack of commitment. She nodded slowly. 'You have no obligation to us.'

There was an extended pause until Fiacail, looking increasingly uncomfortable, broke the silence. 'Is there no-one from whom you can solicit protection?'

Liath Luachra and Bodhmhall looked at one another. 'There is only Dún Baoiscne,' the *bandraoi* said at last. 'But they are unlikely to offer refuge to *Muinntir Bládhma*.'

'No,' Fiacail agreed. 'In any case, *Clann Baoiscne* is broken. They will need time to muster what remains of their forces and after Cnucha they are too stretched to offer protection so far from their home lands.' He turned to Cairbre. 'You mentioned some neighbouring settlements you were on good terms with. Ráth Dearg and Coill Mór.'

The *rechtaire* shook his head. 'They're little more than farms. Combined, they'd provide less than seven or eight fighting men.'

'All the same.' He glanced at the surrounding embankment. 'On a defensive position like this, such a number could make all the difference. And, with a hostile *fian* in the area, it'd be in their best interests to join forces behind the safety of a fortification such as this.'

'It would not hurt to ask,' Liath Luachra admitted. 'Ráth Dearg owes no allegiance but Coill Mór is beholden to us after Bodhmhall's help with their outbreak.'

Cairbre delicately cleared his throat. 'If we are to approach them, I would suggest that we express any offer in terms of a proposal for improved protection as opposed to a request for united forces.'

Bodhmhall looked at him in annoyance. 'We are offering to provide them protection.'

'Of course we are.'

'So you should send a runner,' said Fiacail.

Bodhmhall glanced at her *conradh*. Liath Luachra nodded. 'We send a runner.'

'Who will be the lucky athlete?'

Liath Luachra thought for a moment. 'Cónán,' she said at last. 'Aodhán and Bearach would be more useful on the walls if we come under attack.'

Cairbre was plainly displeased with this suggestion. 'Cónán is too young,' he protested.

'He is young but he is competent. I have taught him to survive in the Great Wild and if he moves quietly and carefully, he will be safe. He is best placed to fulfil the role of messenger. Just as Aodhán is best placed to accompany me when I leave to seek the Tainted One.'

The *rechtaire* stiffened. 'You are casual with the lives of my sons,' he said, unable to disguise the sharpness in his voice.

'I assign tasks as I think best for our survival,' Liath Luachra snapped back. Seeing the obvious distress on the old man's face, her expression softened. 'I do not value your sons' lives cheaply, Cairbre. But to survive, we must all contribute as best our skills allow us.'

'I understand. To protect us from danger you must first place us in danger.'

Liath Luachra stared at the old man, unable to tell if he was being sarcastic or not. She sighed and decided to accept the words at face value. 'Very well. Let us ask Cónán's opinion. His views may provide some insight to the situation.'

***

Cairbre and Liath Luachra located Cónán at the far side of the *lis* where he was busy feeding the pigs in a rough, wooden enclosure. Unlike his brothers, Cónán had tended more to Conchenn's features than those of his father. Hence the thick strands of curly, black hair, the slimmer frame and deep blue eyes.

128

Those blue eyes watched anxiously as they approached, somehow sensing the tension between them. He put the bucket of slops on the ground as they drew up before him. 'Cónán,' said his father. 'We have words to speak with you. Words of importance.'

The boy nodded stiffly, wondering if he was in trouble for doing something wrong. As the proposed undertaking was explained to him, however, his features relaxed. To Liath Luachra and Cairbre's mutual surprise he proved overwhelmingly enthusiastic at the prospect of delivering their message to the other settlements.

Cairbre regarded him with a grave expression. Fearful that the child might not have fully comprehended the task and the risks involved, he insisted on repeating it again. Cónán, however, remained firm in his commitment. Disappointed, the old man shook his head in dismay and walked stiff-necked back to his roundhouse in silence.

Liath Luachra considered the boy and frowned.

'You are certain you wish to undertake this task?'

The boy looked around at the pigs and grinned. 'Of course!'

It was only then that Liath Luachra fully comprehended the rationale behind the boy's enthusiasm. The mission offered Cónán the lure of adventure, the opportunity to travel by himself but, most importantly, it offered a reprieve from the drudgery of his daily chores at Ráth Bládhma. What boy, she belatedly realised, would not jump at the chance.

'Very well,' she said at last. 'Let us see if you are worthy of being our messenger. Tell me, what is the code of the Warrior's Path?'

'Run. Run, hide and run again.'

And if you can't run and you can't hide?'

'Make your opponent pay dear for the challenge.'

The warrior woman nodded in satisfaction. 'That's good. Some of the things I've taught you have managed to penetrate that thick head of hair.'

Reaching into the deerskin bag that hung from her shoulder, Liath Luachra withdrew a long, iron dagger wrapped in a sheet of leather. Unfolding it, she hefted the weapon in one hand and held it out before him. 'This is for you.'

The boy stared in shock, his big brown eyes widened and his jaw dropped. '*Bás gan Trua,*' he whispered.

'*Bás gan Trua*,' the Grey One confirmed. 'Death without Mercy.' She handed the weapon to him with solemn formality. From her experience, when it came to weapons, boys always responded best to solemn formality.

It was an impressive-looking weapon. The blade was sharp and clean, its pommel overlaid with strips of red leather, wrapped tightly about the hilt. The guard was engraved with a design composed of interlinking straight lines.

'This weapon has saved my life on several occasions. You know it is a named weapon. It has taken lives but I pass it to you because your mission is important. You may need it to defend yourself.'

'Thank you Liath Luachra. I will care for it.'

'See that you do or I will tan your hide like a six year old brat.'

They shared a smile at that. The young boy brushed the mop of black hair away from a freckled forehead. Despite his size, Liath Luachra did not doubt that he would make a skilled fighter one day. He wasn't particularly adept at the sling or javelin but his natural adroitness meant that he would be good with a blade.

A blade such as *Bás gan Trua*.

'Now,' said Liath Luachra. 'Repeat your instructions for me one more time. Just like you did when your father was present.'

The boy groaned but did as he was directed. 'I will travel in stealth to Ráth Dearg. There I will find Cathal ua Cuan and inform him of the hostile *fian* and the Tainted One. When I have finished, I will give them our offer of protection.'

'Very good. And then?'

'Then I will travel in stealth to Coill Mór. There I will find Ber Rua and inform him of the hostile *fian* and the Tainted One. When I have finished, I will give them our offer of protection.'

'And that offer of protection is?'

'Ráth Bládhma offers food and shelter to you and yours at Glenn Ceoch. Come at once. Bring weapons. Travel in secret. Leave no trail.'

'Good,' said Liath Luachra. 'Now, get back to your work and practice the recital of the instructions. I will test you again before you leave at dawn tomorrow.' And make sure to spend some time with your family this evening. They are worried and will want to spoil you before you go.'

Cónán nodded, striving to look serious and mature but unable to conceal a grin of excitement.

Shaking her head, Liath Luachra walked away.

Boys!

Heading back towards her roundhouse, she glanced over to the central fire pit where Fiacail's kinsmen were chatting quietly. Despite the coldness of the hearth and the absence of flames, the two men were huddled about it as though seeking warmth from the ghosts of fires past. On a sudden whim, she abruptly changed direction.

Noting her approach, the two warriors stood up and she noticed how their eyes flickered to examine her facial tattoo before coming back to rest on her directly.

The taller one was the younger of the two, although this wasn't saying much as he looked to be in his late thirties at least. He had long, brown hair tied up in a knot at the back of his head, a trimmed beard and several battle scars on his right cheek. Over the previous days, Liath Luachra had also observed how he favoured his left leg when walking, most likely the result of a wound that had never properly healed.

The older man was scrawny with a tangled beard and hair streaked with grey. He was chewing absently on a boiled tuber, watching her without expression as she drew closer. Despite the thin face and sunken cheeks, she was struck by the intensity of his stare. His eyes had an unusual dullness about them that, somehow, gave the pupils an unusual severity. Something, she suspected, was not entirely right in that wizened skull.

'I see you, men of Seiscenn Uarbhaoil.'

'We see you, *conradh* of Ráth Bládhma,' the taller one replied. He was using a knife to cut his own tuber, popping the resulting segments into his mouth. The other man said nothing, just continued to stare.

'I wished to offer my gratitude to you for carrying me across the countryside. I have been preoccupied and have not approached you until now. I did not wish to appear ... unfriendly.'

The two men looked at each other then back at her. After a moment or two, the taller one sniffed and wiped his nose with the sleeve of his tunic.

'You called us a mindless pair of pig-fuckers. After that, you didn't talk to us again for the entire time we carried you. Until we came here of course. Then you told Tóla that he had a face like a stamped turd.' He clicked his tongue. 'Some might construe that as unfriendly.'

'Some ... might,' she admitted.

The taller man and Liath Luachra eyed each other for a moment then he surprised her by holding out his hand. 'I am Ultán ua Feata of Seiscenn Uarbhaoil.'

She took his hand. His grip was firm but unlike many warriors he didn't bother trying to impress her with his strength by attempting to crush her fingers.

'And this stamped turd is my cousin, Tóla.'

She jerked her chin in acknowledgment at the older man. After staring at her for a moment, he leaned over and whispered in Ultán's ear. The taller warrior grunted.

'Tóla says he knows you.'

Liath Luachra turned her attention to the scruffy older man. He was still staring at her with that disturbing gaze of his.

'Is that so? Can't he speak for himself, then?'

'He's very shy. He says you led *Na Cineáltai* for a time, back along the eastern coastline.'

'Then he'd be correct,' was her guarded response. Two mentions of *Na Cineáltai* in a single day. That was two times more than she'd heard it over the entire three years she'd lived at Ráth Bládhma. Although not one to put too much faith in portents, she felt an odd sense of unease at the coincidence.

'So, you'd be the one who killed my brother, Dalgún.'

The woman warrior stiffened, her fingers sliding down the side of her knife sheath as though of their own accord.

'So many years, so many men. Is that going to be a problem, Ultán ua Feata?'

The warrior shifted his weight and calmly scratched his beard, by all accounts very much at ease with the world. 'Truth be told, Dalgún was a bit of a prick. Never happier than when he was out causing a bit of havoc. Rustling here, raping there. A bit of murder if he could fit it in. That was old Dalgún. He was my kin but I consider the world a better place without his taint in it.'

Liath Luachra nodded but she did not relax her guard. Ultán may not have liked his brother but kin ties were strong, loyalty to family and clan notoriously stronger than to the individual members that made them up. She repressed a sigh.

Might as well get this over with.

'Are we going to come to blows over your brother, Ultán?'

The warrior regarded her as he chewed on his tuber. Slowly, he shook his head. 'No. I saw you fight once at Ros Déige, during the Samhain festival. With Flannán Mór as I recall. That was several years ago, of course.'

He laughed and tossed the remains of his tuber aside.

'You were without reputation back in those days. Just some unknown bitch scrapper. As for old Flannán Mór, he was a brute of a man. He bragged that he was going to beat you and then that he was going to fuck you to celebrate his victory.' The warrior reached up and picked at one of his scars.

'But I'd seen you practising in the woods. I could tell you were a fighter, that you were fast and strong. And that you had the ruthless instinct of a water rat.' A grin cracked that scarred face wide. 'I bet a skin of wine and an iron sword that you'd beat him and you did.'

She remembered now. The Ros Déige man had been big all right. Big and broad and loud and heavy. But he'd also been slow. And drunk, not the particularly smartest state to be in before a fight. He'd had strong fists but it hadn't done him any good for he hadn't been able to hit her when he swung, those big hands connecting with nothing but empty air. She'd hit back with meticulous precision and barely-contained fury but without any mercy. In the end, he'd passed out in the dirt, bewildered and bleeding, minus two of his front teeth.

'That bet set me up for a nice plot of land in Seiscenn Uarbhaoil,' Ultán continued. 'With that land I was able to take a wife. Good woman too. We had several pleasant years together until she died from the flux last winter.' Turning his head, he spat a lump of congealed white matter onto the surface of the *lis*.

'The way I see it, I owe you for that little success. Your fight brought me good fortune after a lifetime of bad luck.' He gave her a careful glance. 'Mind you, seeing as how I helped carry you half-way across the Great Wild, I'm pretty sure that debt's repaid by now.'

Relieved, Liath Luachra nodded. Both were smiling when Tóla leaned forward to whisper urgently in his cousin's ear. Ultán glanced askew at him, clearly startled by what he'd heard.

'What?' demanded the woman warrior. 'What did he tell you?'

'Well -'

133

'Spit it out.'

'He says -' Ultán looked uncertainly at the older warrior who was nodding and grinning with the unreserved enthusiasm of a simpleton. 'He says you have no tits. He likes his women with something a bit more substantial. He likes to have something substantial between the palms of his hands.'

'My foot's substantial. How'd he like that between the cheeks of his arse?'

Both men looked at one another and roared with laughter. Liath Luachra relaxed then. She knew these men, or rather this type of men. Violent, rough, but completely without guile or airs of any kind. Ironically, in many ways, she felt more at ease with this calibre of men than she did with some of the inhabitants of Ráth Bládhma.

'Come back and join us when you want,' offered Ultán. 'We have *uisce beatha* to share. We can get drunk and tell outrageous stories.'

'Thank you. Your offer pleases me.'

'The pleasure will be mine. And Tóla's of course.'

The old man sniggered.

'Just as long as that pleasure's self-produced,' she said.

Their laughter followed her across the *lis*.

***

Bodhmhall was waiting for her when she returned to their roundhouse. Sitting on a mat by the fire pit, she was holding the baby close to her chest, rocking slowly back and forth as she crooned a gentle lullaby. Liath Luachra regarded her in surprise then transferred her attention to the sleeping platform where Muirne was still stretched out, snoring quietly. Her eyes darkened and she frowned.

'Does Muirne Muncháem intend to sleep forever?'

The *bandraoi* responded with a guilty smile. 'I must confess, I put Cairbre's suggestion to good use in the end. I gave her a sleeping draught with her food that will keep her in deep sleep for another two nights, the longest period that it can be used without harm. With luck it will conceal her from the Tainted One's sifting touch for a little longer at least.'

'She will not hear us when we talk?'

'She will not hear us.'

Laying the baby down on a bundle of furs, Bodhmhall beckoned the woman warrior forwards. 'Come. Let me examine you.'

Approaching the *bandraoi*, Liath Luachra stripped out of her clothes and lay down beside the fire. Bodhmhall poured some oil into her palms, rubbed them together and tentatively began to massage the flesh and muscle about the woman warrior's knees. Probing the tissue carefully, she continued her examination down to the ankles before she finally lifted her hands.

'Your injuries are much improved. But you may need more than a single day's rest if you wish to travel at your usual pace.'

Liath Luachra sat up in agitation, her body abruptly tensing up again. 'We cannot wait that long. Cónán leaves tomorrow morning and you tell me that Muirne will awaken the day after. I must leave here well before she opens her eyes.'

'Rest easy, Liath Luachra. You cannot force your body to heal faster than nature allows. Be content that the damage was not more serious.'

'Content! How can I feel content when our lives hang in the balance?' The woman warrior slapped the furs in frustration. Gods! A few days ago, I had the luxury to be content. I had my own bed, I had my hunting, I even had time to feel happy.'

'Were you, Liath Luachra? Were you truly happy?'

The warrior woman looked to the *bandraoi*, surprised by the tone of the question. 'Why would you ask me that? Do you think I harbour secrets?'

'I am *An Cailleach Dubh,*' Bodhmhall replied cynically. 'No secret is unknown to me.' She began to clean the oil from her hands with a rag. 'Tell me. Do you regret?'

'Do I regret what?'

'Do you regret this life with me? I have seen you fret, Liath Luachra. I have seen your restlessness up on the ramparts at nights, pacing up and down, gazing out at the Big Wild. There's a hunger in your stance. A hunger that I don't understand but, at such times, I sense that if you leave you will not come back.'

Liath Luachra stared at her in silence. The *bandraoi*'s perceptiveness had taken her by surprise, forcing her to confront an issue that she, herself, had never fully addressed or articulated. She took a moment to slip on her tunic and leggings, using the time to get her thoughts together. 'Don't talk foolishness, Bodhmhall,' she said at last. 'I regret nothing of my life with you. I would not return to that which I was.'

She glanced at the *bandraoi* who was still watching her closely.

'It is true ... what you say. What you have seen of me on the ramparts. A part of me, a part of what I was ... it sometimes calls out. I can't explain it. At Ráth Bládhma it feels as though I am changing, becoming a different person. I am glad to change but it makes me anxious when I see how soft I have grown. I feel like a farmer, a planter, a teacher shooing Cairbre's sons away from beneath my feet.'

Bodhmhall laughed. 'You make us sound like a family of defenceless field mice.'

'In some ways that is what we are. A nest of field mice hidden away in a field of barley, ignorant to the threshers that cut down the world outside our view.'

She sighed.

'War is coming, *a rún*. The very ground beneath our feet is moving. We must tread warily, choose our alliances carefully. I fear I'm losing the skills I need to keep us safe in times of such death and destruction.'

Seeing Bodhmhall's lip quiver, she stretched over to stroke her hair. For all her strength and skill as a leader, the *bandraoi* had clearly been pushed to her limits. '*M'fhíorghrá amháin, an Chailleach Dubh*. My one true love, the Black Hag. You still have me. My heart is light with you.'

Bodhmhall, once again, took her by surprise, reaching for her, kissing her full on the lips. As she returned the embrace, Liath Luachra felt a delicious sensation spiral up within her.

She drew the *bandraoi* closer.

***

Later, once their breathing had stilled and silence dripped within the roundhouse, Liath Luachra felt the *bandraoi* drum her fingers along the tightness of her stomach, tangle an ankle about her leg to draw her closer.

'Wake up.'

'Uh.'

'Wake up.'

'Why?' she growled, irritable at being disturbed so close to the point of drifting off.

'Because,' said the *bandraoi*. 'I think I have a scheme.'

Chapter Six

Liath Luachra had hoped to leave the *ráth* in silence, to slip away quietly in the shadows of the early hours. Bodhmhall, however, had other plans. Snapping awake, she glared as the woman warrior attempted to slide silently off the sleeping platform.

'You would leave in the night again? Without saying farewell?'

'Bodhmhall,' Liath Luachra groaned. 'You know farewells weigh my heart. It was my intention to wake you just before I left.'

The *bandraoi* sat up and tugged one of the fur coverings about her shoulders. Heavy rain thudded against the curved ceiling above them, the fire had all but died and a chill was infiltrating the roundhouse. She peered over to where Liath Luachra crouched, attempting to rekindle the dying embers of the fire. In the blurry light of the single oil taper, it was difficult to see her clearly although the two pale, white circles of her buttocks gleamed eerily through the gloom. Down on all fours, she poured a powdery mixture of dry twigs and desiccated leaves onto the fire's dying remnants then gently blew on it. Finally, her efforts were rewarded with a thin sliver of smoke that rose upwards from the resuscitated embers. Soon, the fire was crackling in earnest, hungry flames gnawing on the kindling and larger sections of peat.

Rising from the platform, Bodhmhall moved to join her at the fire pit. She started to heat some porridge while Liath Luachra retrieved her weapons from where they lay on the far side of the sleeping platform, swathed in cloth. Lifting the heavy bundle, the woman warrior unwrapped it and removed each one individually before laying it onto the furs.

The first – a short, iron sword – was her favourite. This was also the one she'd had in her possession the longest, having acquired it as booty from the body of a warrior in Cuarrach during her first years as a fighter. She'd been particularly lucky on that occasion in that the warrior had not only been unskilled, but wealthy to boot. The weapon had obviously been commissioned from a skilled metal-smith for it had perfect balance and the pommel fitted her hand as though it had been specifically moulded for it. Given the circumstances, she hadn't known if the sword was a named weapon but she'd dealt with that by applying one of her own. With her usual pragmatism she'd named it *Gléas gan Ainm* – Weapon Without a Name.

137

Beside the sword she laid a long knife, the last of the three she'd owned. Although the remaining weapon was by no means the best, regular sharpening meant that it was still deadly enough. An unnamed weapon, its blade had not tasted human blood but she had no doubt there'd be plenty of opportunity to rectify that in the days to come.

The last weapon, a sling, consisted of a diamond-shaped, woven flax cradle attached to two separate lengths of cord, also fabricated from braided flax. Light and easy to make from common materials, the weapon was also easy to maintain. Over the years, she'd replaced the cradle on three occasions, the more stable braid, once.

Although scorned by many warriors, Liath Luachra had always appreciated the effectiveness of the sling as a long-range weapon. Some fighters were obsessed with the concept of valour in up-front, hand-to-hand combat. In her mind, however, all that mattered was winning and walking away from the fight at the end of it all.

She dropped a small cloth bag beside the other weapons. This contained her shot for the sling; ten smooth stones, all slightly larger than a thrush's egg. She'd personally selected each one from the great range that littered the local river beds to ensure uniform size, shape and smoothness; three qualities essential for consistent accuracy of the sling cast.

Bodhmhall looked up from the fire and shivered as she watched the other woman. 'Sit,' she said, holding up a wooden bowl of steaming porridge that she'd sweetened with dried honey. 'Eat something.'

It was only as she accepted the bowl and caught the whiff of its contents that Liath Luachra realised how hungry she was. Using her fingers, she scooped the porridge out of the bowl, stuffing it into her mouth despite the stinging heat. She polished off a second bowl in a similar manner before she was sated.

Rising to her feet, she hauled the red, leather body harness from its stand, slipped it over her head and tightened the various cinches and straps. Finally, she swung her shoulders and stretched her upper arm muscles to ensure it wasn't restricting her movements. After the harness, she pulled on a matching set of greaves and a short pair of leggings held up with string that knotted at the waist. The leggings were cut off above the knees. Not particularly appropriate wear for the weather but the forthcoming day would be one of movement. She had a substantial distance to cover and she'd need to be able to move swiftly and unencumbered. The cold weather would eventually oblige them to halt, of course. Even running at their best pace would not keep them warm for long in such poor weather. When they stopped to rest, she would change into the spare set of clothing in the wicker satchel she'd be carrying across her back.

Turning to that very satchel, she began to rummage through the contents, checking to make sure it contained the items she needed. Looking up, she found Bodhmhall standing beside her, a leather pouch held out in her hand. 'This is it,' said the *bandraoi*. 'It's not much but it should be enough.'

Liath Luachra took the proffered pouch and nodded.

'You are sure you wish to attempt this?' asked Bodhmhall.

'I don't think we have any choice. Besides, you thought it would work when you suggested it last night.'

The *bandraoi* released a drowsy sigh, eyes still bleary from their late night discussions. 'I thought it *could* work,' she corrected. 'But you have the right of it. At this point, we truly are out of options.'

Liath Luachra stared, struck by the weary resignation in Bodhmhall's voice. The *bandraoi* looked completely exhausted. She reached out and caressed her cheek. 'Have faith, Bodhmhall. Your scheme will succeed. And this way, you don't need to seek *imbas*.'

'Just come back safe, dear one. If your instincts tell you it is too hazardous, take no risks and return to Glenn Ceoch. We will develop another plan.' She paused. 'I would endure the *imbas* rituals a thousand times before I'd risk losing you.'

The woman warrior smiled. 'There's a thought to guide me safely home.'

***

When she emerged from the roundhouse, dawn was still a dim prospect in a sky darkly stained with clouds and sloppy with drizzle. It looked as though the world had been seized up during the night, immersed in water, shaken out and then soggily replaced. Heavy rivulets streamed from the lip of the embankment and the roofs of the buildings. The *lis* was a muddy quagmire of puddles, straw and cow shit from the livestock kept inside overnight.

Pulling on her oiled grey cloak, Liath Luachra tugged the hood over her head and stepped into the world of plummeting rain. She scurried quickly across the exposed *lis* towards the gateway where Aodhán was waiting for her, standing in the shelter of the stone overhang. Bearach was also squeezed in beside him, looking particularly put out that she hadn't asked him to accompany her. She ignored his indignant stare as she glanced down at Aodhán's booted feet. 'Better put those in your bag. It's best to run barefoot in this weather.'

With this, she slung the wicker satchel onto her back, securing it with two shoulder straps that she tightened further with a cord about the chest. Aodhán had a similar satchel but it was a lot smaller to allow for the set of javelins which he also carried.

'Do we need to bring all of these?' he complained. 'They're heavy.'

'Yes.'

'They'll be short of missiles at the gatehouse if the *ráth*'s attacked.'

'That's a risk we'll have to take. This is more important.'

The young man sighed but did not argue the point further. As he shuffled his own pack onto his back, Cairbre appeared, braving the cold and the wet of the *lis* to farewell his son. Sloshing through the mud, hems of his breeches drawn up like an old woman's skirt, he entered the shelter and wordlessly started to disassemble the barrier. The old man struggled with the task, his stiff limbs preventing him from getting a decent purchase on the heavy wooden frame. Before he needed to ask for assistance, his sons had moved in to help him.

When the barrier was finally put to one side, Liath Luachra watched as he embraced his son, whispered in his ear and patted him affectionately on the side of the head. Embarrassed by this display of emotion in front of the others, the young man did his best to appear gruff and purposefully avoided eye contact. Suddenly, Conchenn and Bodhmhall were there as well, scurrying in out of the rain to join them. The woman warrior shook her head as she considered the little gathering crammed within the gateway.

Everyone in settlement is here now.

Well, almost everyone.

She threw a quick glance towards the lean-to where Fiacail and his men were quartered. The weather had clearly been something of a disincentive for there were no visible signs of activity, no stirring at all.

Cairbre approached and touched her on the shoulder.

'Come back safely, Grey One.'

She nodded.

'And bring my son with you,' he added.

'I cannot make such promises, old father. But I will do what I can.'

'Then I would beg you to do your best. This is the second child I've farewelled in the course of two days.' Despite the deceptive calm of his words, anxiety was evident in the *rechtaire*'s eyes.

The price of being a parent. Who would want that?

Liath Luachra turned to Aodhán who was standing beside her, loaded and waiting. 'Are you ready?'

The *óglach* nodded.

'Well, then.'

Without another word, she jogged out through the gateway.

Towards the water-clogged pastures of Glenn Ceoch.

***

Several hundred paces from the *ráth*, Liath Luachra threw a glance back over her shoulder. The gateway barrier had been reaffixed but it was the lonely figure up on the stone rampart that momentarily drew her gaze.

Gods, Bodhmhall. Don't make me weak.

Turning her head forwards, she focussed on the trees at the end of the valley and did not look back again.

Breaking into an easy lope, Liath Luachra shuffled off the remaining stiffness of her injuries, the regular movement warming her muscles and unclenching any lingering tension. Soon, she had a smooth rhythm established, long strides steadily eating up the distance before them while Ráth Bládhma receded further and further in her wake. Close on her heels, she could hear the smooth beat of Aodhán's footsteps, the even stride punctuated by pants that were deep but regular and without strain. Despite the gravity of her mission and the discomfort of the rain beating against her face, she experienced a brief, exhilarating headiness as the wilderness exerted its pull. Once more, headed Out! Once more, to the Great Wild!

By the time they'd reached the half-way point up the valley, the runners were drenched, their clothing saturated, hair slick across their skulls, legs slippery from the rain and water kicked up from the sodden pasture. Liath Luachra's bare feet were cold but she ignored the tingling sensation. A lifetime of walking barefoot had left her with leathery soles that were accustomed to rough terrain and all but the worst of weather conditions.

As they neared the heavy forest marking the entrance to Glenn Ceoch, they slowed their pace, then halted to stare at the broad tree line stretched out before them. The thick forest, unnerving at the best of times, looked even grimmer beneath the grey curtain of pelting rain.

Liath Luachra raised her hand to brush the rain from her face as she considered the best path out of the valley. There were two possible routes, one located on either side of the stream that ran down the valley and disappeared into the trees. The first, and most commonly used, was a narrow path wedged between the forest and the base of the southern ridge. This tight trail followed the ridge for several hundred paces before branching out and subsequently merging into the flatland forest beyond the Sliabh Bládhma hills.

The other option was the precarious path through An Talamh Báite – *The Drowned Land* – a large section of flatland that stretched from the right bank of the stream to the northern ridge. Initially forested, the ground quickly transformed into a dangerous marsh caused from poor drainage of the widening valley stream and flow-off from the nearby ridge.

Liath Luachra considered the pros and cons of both routes. Because of the dense forest it would be extremely challenging for the *fian* to locate Glenn Ceoch unless they were exceptionally lucky or had a clear idea of its location. Under the current weather conditions, it was also likely that the rain would wipe away any tracks the runners might make. Nevertheless, the risk always remained that imprints left in the mud would solidify, leaving a clear trail for any keen-eyed tracker. 'We'll take the low route,' she said at last. 'Through An Talamh Báite.'

Aodhán looked at her in surprise. 'That'll take much longer.'

'It doesn't matter. We can't afford to leave a clear trail. We can swing south afterwards. The Talamh Báite route comes out at the far end of the ridge. If we do leave any tracks when we get through the marshland, it'll be too far away to associate with this area.'

Aodhán grunted, acknowledging the logic of her argument.

Traversing the stream, they entered the trees, relieved to get out of the open and into the relative shelter of the wide canopy of oak and pine. Little of the actual downpour penetrated the upper branches, however the irregular showers of individual drops that did get through were cold and uncomfortable. The interior of the forest was quite oppressive, sombre and filled with twilight shadows, a place where every direction looked the same for anyone unfamiliar with the area.

After a time, the character of the land changed, the forest gradually giving way to lower ground where the trees grew further and further apart and the ground grew increasingly soggy. Soon, the trees had all but disappeared, replaced by a scrubby swamp and wide pools of black water spotted with mucky isles of reed and willow. Taking their time, they plodded slowly from hummock to hummock, using a trail assiduously worked out over three years of habitation in Glenn Ceoch and marked by well-disguised reed pointers. It was slow, monotonous work and difficult to keep their footing on the treacherously greasy surface. On two occasions, Aodhán slipped, the second time falling deep into the bog water. Only Liath Luachra's quick reactions prevented him from being sucked into the bottomless mire. Dropping to all fours, she reached out and grabbed his hair before he disappeared beneath the surface, hauling him painfully back to more solid ground. As he lay wheezing and coughing, the *óglach* stared fearfully at the still waters that could so easily have been his grave.

'I thought my father asked you to protect me.'

Liath Luachra was too breathless to respond. She looked down at one of the mouldy pools, watching the patterns of silt swirling in the dark waters. This was Black Lung territory. Lung-rot country that the inhabitants of the settlement generally avoided given its association with disease. She briefly recalled one of her younger brothers from her childhood in Luachair. The boy had been little more than a babe but she'd been close to him and had enjoyed his company. He'd caught a fever after spending time with her parents in similar territory and ended up dying, coughing up phlegm and then blood until there was no more to cough up.

She shivered.

Old days. Best forgotten.

Bowing her head, she silently continued walking. Behind her, Aodhán considered her departing back and shook his head. Picking himself up, he tramped after her, following footsteps that were already filling up with black bog water.

***

The runners halted at noon, taking the time to eat, rest and change out of their sodden clothing. Oppressed with thoughts of the challenge they

143

faced, they spoke very little. To her surprise, Liath Luachra found herself missing Bearach, wishing the irrepressible youth was present to improve her humour.

Refreshed, they started out again but moved more slowly, with much more caution. Although only a few days had passed since Liath Luachra had last travelled in this area, the land now looked very different to her eyes. The snow, of course, had gone, melted away except for a few tenacious clumps clinging to the higher, colder sections of the ridge. The forest and scrub land looked even more bleak and dangerous without the virginal white mantle.

It was late in the afternoon when the grainy outline of Drom Osna finally came into sight, its forested bulk heaving about a closer hill like the body of a lethargic giant. By then, the rain had eased, the sun clawing its way through the clouds to spill a greasy sunshine over the land. The woman warrior drew to a halt and leaned against a nearby oak tree as she considered the route ahead of them. They were quite close to where the Tainted One's camp had been located, a short march north-east of their current location, by her reckoning. The approach to Drom Osna they had chosen had also brought them up against a wide hill. It ran in an east-west direction and, by Liath Luachra's estimation, lay directly between them and their destination. Although it wasn't particularly high, the slopes of the hillside rose steeply, culminating at a broad plateau that lay well above the canopy of the surrounding forest. After working the logistics through in her head, she pointed to a section where the climb did not look so precarious. 'We'll go up there.'

Aodhán looked at her quizzically. Like the warrior woman, he was familiar with the hill from a previous hunt. He knew that steep cliffs on the other side of the hill would prevent a descent to the north.

'You don't want to go closer?'

Liath Luachra shook her head. 'No. The last time I moved in close the Tainted One became aware of my presence.' Her eyes narrowed and her gaze briefly flickered around the surrounding forest as though fearful of his sudden appearance. 'That hill will give us a good view of their camp. Once we've confirmed they're still there, we can decide what to do next.'

Approaching the base of the hill, they scrambled upwards, grasping low hanging tree branches for support on the steeper gradient where the mucky, slippery slope made progress more challenging. As they climbed,

144

Liath Luachra became aware of a growing unease, a chaffing disquiet beneath her skin that she was unable to shake off. It was only when they reached the crest and paused to catch their breath that she realised what was disturbing her. There was no sound. No breeze, but more alarmingly, no birdsong. In an area that usually teemed with birds.

The hairs rose on the back of her neck and a nervous tickle passed down her spine. She'd never encountered such silence in the Great Wild before. Belatedly, she realised that she hadn't seen any animal sign for some time either. The local wildlife had fled, instinctively deserting the area in response to some undefined danger.

Perhaps not that undefined.

Dropping to her knees, Liath Luachra loosened the cord around her chest and removed the wicker satchel. Rummaging through it, she located the leather pouch Bodhmhall had given her. She glanced inside, relieved to find that the flask it contained hadn't leaked any of the contents so crucial to the plan.

The plan.

The woman warrior stifled a quick flicker of doubt. Bodhmhall's scheme was, admittedly, simplistic to the point of artlessness. She shivered involuntarily, possessed by a sudden dread of her inevitable confrontation with the Tainted One. Her skin crawled as she recalled the rogue *draoi*'s touch and interference with her mind. The incident had seriously shaken her, much more than she'd admitted to Bodhmhall.

Focus on your revenge. Do not dwell on tainted concerns.

The plateau on which they found themselves contained wide slabs of exposed rock interspersed with thick patches of scrub; predominantly gorse and bramble. The height provided good views of Drom Osna to the north and the surrounding forest which seemed to lap at its sides like a hazy green sea.

The pair spent some time negotiating the scrub at the centre of the plateau before reaching a dangerously narrow precipice on the northern edge that pointed towards Drom Osna like some accusatory stone finger. Peering over its craggy lip, the Tainted One's camp was immediately discernable, pinpointed by a tall plume of smoke to their south-west. Even at that distance, Liath Luachra instantly recognised the unusual depression with its standing stone and the cave behind it.

Six tiny figures were visible, five of them clustered about the cave mouth. From their posture and body movements alone, it was easy to tell that they were warriors, probably the Tainted One's bodyguards. Sitting in isolation by the granite monolith – just like the last time she'd seen him – was the hunched and hooded form of the *draoi* himself. Even as Liath Luachra's eyes came to rest on that distant figure, she somehow sensed a shift in its demeanour. The hooded head abruptly turned and stared up at the plateau.

Gods!

An icy flood of panic surged through her and she dropped closer to the ground, scuttling backwards from the edge of the cliff. Aodhán was immediately behind her. 'He saw us.' The *óglach*'s face was pale as he struggled to appreciate the enormity of what had just happened. 'He knows we're here. How does he know?'

'It doesn't matter.' Liath Luachra attempted to sound confident but her voice sounded thick and phlegmy, even to her own ears. With a grunt, she rolled onto her stomach and wriggled forward to peer down at the campsite again. The Tainted One had resumed his previous position before the fire with his back towards them but three of the other figures were nowhere to be seen.

Cursing softly, she pulled back from the edge, greatly relieved that she'd taken the precaution of choosing a view point that was difficult to access from the Tainted One's camp. Nevertheless, they were, once again, on the back foot, responding to events rather than instigating them.

She turned and kicked Aodhán in the side of the leg. 'Get up. We need to get off this plateau. Three of his bodyguards are coming to kill us.'

***

It was on the descent of the southern side of hill that Liath Luachra noticed the faint line of shadow, a kind of waning in the otherwise thick vegetation that curved through the forest below in a rough north-easterly direction. Back down on the forest floor, she immediately led the nervous *óglach* towards the area in which she'd seen it.

It didn't take long to locate what she'd seen and have her suspicions confirmed. Nodding in satisfaction, she stepped onto a beaten scrub trail that was wide enough for a single man to travel at speed. Liath Luachra had seen these before. Deer trails beaten into the bush by the repetitive

146

movements of the animals then appropriated by humans and worn down even faster.

Crouching, she studied the trodden earth. Beckoning Aodhán forward, she pointed out a number of footsteps in the muddier patches. 'They use this path,' she whispered. 'Regularly.'

Plucking a stem of grass from the side of the path, she popped it in her mouth and chewed on it thoughtfully. Humans, by nature, were creatures of habit. If the Tainted One's bodyguards were coming towards them, they would likely use an established trail, one they were familiar with and that they knew to be easier to travel.

'We'll set up and wait for them here,' she decided. 'Let them do all the running around.'

***

'You should not tell your brother such stories,' Liath Luachra whispered. She was sitting motionless on the exposed root of an oak tree off to the left of the little trail.

Aodhán, stretched the length of an ancient bough above her, looked down in surprise. 'What stories?'

She shook her head. 'It doesn't matter.'

'But - '

'Quiet. Something comes.'

The *óglach* scowled but dutifully lapsed into silence, pushing himself even flatter against the girth of the bough. Pulling the hood of her cloak up over her head, Liath Luachra drew the remainder of the covering about her before easing back against the trunk of the tree.

For a long time nothing happened despite the woman warrior's warning. Seasoned hunters, both were accustomed to waiting and remained completely still. While she waited, Liath Luachra raised her eyes to where the *óglach* was barely visible. Although Aodhán had seen some action during the attacks on *Ráth Bládhma*, she was conscious of the fact that these had been little more than skirmishes with long-range weapons. She had faith in the youth's ability but she did not know for certain how well he'd react in a combat situation. The truth was, he remained untested in the most brutal hacking and cutting into which hand-to-hand combat usually degenerated.

At that point, an even more intense silence seemed to overlay the forest. Liath Luachra, once more, became aware of the distinct lack of bird song. The burned flesh on her hand began to sting.

Fool! Think of something else.

She returned her attention to the trail. A few moments passed then there was a gentle rustle in the bushes about thirty paces away where the track curved out of sight. A male figure suddenly appeared, moving cautiously along the trail.

Liath Luachra studied the newcomer with wary curiosity. He was tall, dressed in unusually dark furs and wearing a leather helmet of a kind she'd not seen before. In his right hand he carried a single javelin, in his left, a vicious-looking metal war-axe. A long knife was tucked into the leather belt around his waist.

The key trait that fascinated her, however, was the bloody scarring and the black tattoos that covered most of his face. The latter markings, in particular, gave him an eerie feral appearance, one that was not altogether human.

Some sixth sense seemed to alert the Tainted One's bodyguard for he froze suddenly, warily scanning the nearby plateau and then the length of the trail ahead of him. As his eyes swept over her location, Liath Luachra fought the urge to move further into concealment, impressed despite her situation by the man's instincts, the sixth sense that was alerting him to her presence.

Despite sitting in the relative open, she knew she was practically invisible, her shapeless grey cloak blending easily against the mottled shadows of the forest background. It was only fear that would give her away. Fear, because fear provoked movement and any movement, no matter how miniscule, would catch the watcher's eye.

Fortunately, she knew how to control her fear.

This one's a killer.

She couldn't say how she knew but there was something in the man's face, something beyond the grotesque tattoos that left her in little doubt that he'd killed before. He exuded a savagery, an incoherent sense of violence that she'd only ever seen in the most crazed and lethal of *Na Cineálta*. She shivered: part fear, part excitement. A bitter smile formed upon her lips as she recognised familiar feelings she hadn't experienced for a very long time. The old instincts were returning, past habits reasserting themselves in response to that odd, peer recognition.

Like knows like.

Slowly, very slowly, she raised her eyes to meet those of the *óglach* who was looking down at her, his features tight as a drawn bowstring. 'Stay still,' she mouthed. She raised the fingers of her left hand off the ground beside her, out of sight from further down the trail, and gently mimed a pressing down gesture.

Stay where you are.

The bodyguard's impatience seemed to have prevailed over his initial instincts for he slowly straightened up and gestured to someone behind him. Two other shadowy figures emerged from the undergrowth around the curve to join him, both bearing similar tattoos and scars on their faces. Spreading out in single file, they advanced along the trail.

As they drew towards her, Liath Luachra assessed her opponents with predatory dispassion. The threesome was demonstrating a curious overconfidence that surprised her. While it was true that the Tainted One had most likely alerted them to the number of intruders they might face and that they had both the advantage of a superior force and the support of the Tainted One to call on, it was a mistake to assume that their quarry would flee.

Intent on reaching the plateau, the little war party passed their hiding place, each of the three figures going by without a second glance. Liath Luachra waited until the third warrior had passed then moved like a ghost. Slipping about the tree trunk that separated then, she lunged onto the moving figure in one smooth, single movement. Her left hand clamped about his mouth, her right swinging the blade upwards in a tight, deadly arc. There was a brief sensation of wet lips against her fingers, the stink of sweat then the knife entered through the skin at the base of the warrior's neck, up into his brain. A fountain of hot scarlet spurted from the wound, spraying the side of her face, the strong iron taste and smell momentarily blotting out all other physical sensation.

The attack had been so swift, so brutal, that the warrior had no time to cry out, to resist. He simply died. Instantly.

He slumped, a dead weight in her arms but she'd already transferred her attention to his comrades. Despite the relative silence of her attack, some subliminal instinct had alerted them to the threat behind them. The nearer

149

warrior slid to halt and glanced back. Seeing his murdered friend, he released a violent snarl and turned to rush at her, a metal-headed club raised high to smash down on her skull.

The javelin seemed to swoop in out of nowhere, taking him in the lower chest and slamming through the ribcage with such force that Liath Luachra actually heard the shocked 'oof' of expelled air. Slammed backwards, the warrior stumbled, fell to his knees, hands grasping the haft of the weapon embedded in his torso. Slowly, he toppled to one side and did not move again.

Seeing the fate of his comrades, the third warrior did not hesitate. He took off like a startled deer, leaping from the path and plunging down a steep forested incline where the trees and vegetation offered better cover. His decision proved fortuitous for a second javelin slammed into the side of the tree behind him just as he disappeared from view, glancing off the trunk at an angle and a force that smashed the haft in half.

Liath Luachra reacted just as quickly, hurtling downhill into the scrub at an intersecting angle to her quarry's trajectory. Her face slick with blood and sweat, her arms pumping. The warrior must somehow have sensed or heard her for he almost immediately changed direction, heading deeper into the forest in the direction of the Tainted One's campsite.

Cursing, she pursued him, doing everything she could to keep the dark silhouette in sight. Behind her, the heavy crashing of bush confirmed Aodhán's close pursuit.

At this point of the chase, speed was more important than subtlety. Soon, if he was unable to elude them or reach a place of safety, the warrior would start to tire and consider other, more desperate options.

Tree trunks spun by on either side as she hurtled downwards. A collision at this speed was likely to result in serious injury but she was relying completely on animal instinct, body responding and dodging the obstacles faster than her mind could even register them.

Briars and thickets raked at her face as she barged through clumps of scrub, twisted branches snagged her clothing and ripped her cloak but she was gaining on him, slowly but inexorably drawing closer. She could see him more clearly now, no longer a shadow but a distinct form flitting intermittently between the bulk of the trees. A great, involuntarily howl erupted from her throat, a bloodthirsty ululation that she knew would alarm him even further.

150

Less than fifteen paces ahead, she saw the warrior disappear into a thick clump of scrub. Even as the brush closed behind him, the forest resounded with a piercing scream. Startled, she skidded to an unsteady halt, allowing her momentum to carry her into the shelter of a nearby pine. She stared at the clump of vegetation ahead of her. The scream had sounded genuine but could just as well have been a clever ruse for ambush.

A heavy swish of vegetation from behind heralded Aodhán's imminent arrival. A moment later, he slid down the slippery slope, coming to an awkward halt beside her. Several paces in front of them, there was no sign of movement and no sound from the thick bush where the warrior had disappeared. Tightening her grip on the hilt of her sword, she tentatively edged forward, nodding at the *óglach* to circle in from the left. Weapon at the ready, she pushed her way into the bushes.

They found the warrior lying on the ground a few paces inside the scrub. The lower part of his leg was twisted at an unnatural angle, the ankle trapped in a narrow sink hole that was still partially obscured by dead fern and leaves. Clearly he'd stepped into the hole in the uneven ground and snapped a bone. Despite the fact his face was pale and tight with pain, his eyes were wild with hatred. He glared at them, his jaws clamped shut to prevent himself from screaming.

She recognised him immediately as the first warrior to step out of the bushes back on the trail and knew that, despite his injuries, he was still potentially lethal. Even as she watched, he attempted to reach for the axe which lay on the ground off to his right. Twisting his body in a superhuman effort to move his fingers closer to the blade, he was actually close to touching it when Liath Luachra stepped forward and kicked it further beyond his grasp. He screamed again, this time in a combination of agony and frustration.

Satisfied that they were in no immediate danger, Liath Luachra took a moment to catch her breath, to allow the extended dose of adrenaline pumping through her body to subside. Crouching down to rest on her ankles, she leaned forward, making sure that she remained safely beyond his reach. 'Who are you?' she asked. 'Why are you here?'

The warrior stared at her ferociously but showed no comprehension of what she was asking him. She was about to try again when he raised his head and spat directly at her.

It was a lucky shot. The spittle hit her squarely on the left cheek.

With cold eyes, she raised her free hand and wiped the sticky mess from her face. Slowly, she resheathed the sword and pulled her knife out, the blade still wet and sticky from the first kill. A globule of blood dripped from the tip as she held it up before him.

'Are you going to hurt him?' asked Aodhán.

She glanced at the *óglach* in irritation. 'You could say that.'

'Why?'

'He has information we need.'

'And once you get it?'

'Then I will kill him.'

Aodhán looked taken aback but rallied quickly enough. The eyes of the stricken warrior flickered from one of them to the other, clearly not understanding what they were saying but comprehending enough to know that they were discussing his fate. Without warning he snarled and released a withering vocal outburst. Although neither of the Ráth Bládhma warriors understood what was said, the ferocity alone give it sufficient context. Unmoved, Liath Luachra gave a groan. 'He doesn't speak our tongue.'

'I don't want to kill him,' said Aodhán. 'He's hurt. It doesn't feel right.'

'Aodhán, this animal would have slit your throat and laughed while you bled to death in front of him.'

'Well, he won't be cutting anything now. Look at him. He's helpless.'
Aodhán frowned. 'Perhaps we should make him prisoner.'

'We can't keep a prisoner. We have a mission to complete.'

'We could bind him.'

'With what? I have no rope. Besides, he has a broken leg. If we leave him out here alone in the Great Wild he'll die slowly from hunger and thirst. Or the wolves will get him. Is that what you want?'

The youth struggled for a suitable answer. While he attempted to come up with an alternative suggestion, Liath Luachra raised her knife and abruptly slashed it across the wounded man's throat. The blade was razor sharp and the blood gushed from the jugular in one enormous spurt. The warrior's body flopped a little as the spasms rolled through him but after a moment, it settled down, lay silent and unmoving.

Aodhán stared at her, eyes wide.

'These men are killers, Aodhán. They will kill your brothers, your father, your mother. They know nothing of the mercy you're willing to offer them and would bear you in contempt for it.'

He glared back at her but despite this defiance she was satisfied with his mettle. He had fought well in the ambush and although he'd be angry with her for a time she knew he had the iron in him to carry out the tasks assigned him.

Reaching down, she dipped two fingers into the dead man's bleeding throat then daubed the sticky fluid across the boy's forehead. Although he looked sickened, he did not flinch and the warrior woman grunted in satisfaction.

'There Aodhán. You are a blooded warrior now.'

She flopped back against the trunk of a nearby oak, the effort of the run and the fight suddenly catching up with her. 'And that was the easy part.' She took several deep breaths to clear her head as she stared up at the sun through the thin winter canopy. They had been travelling fast in a north-westerly direction. They couldn't be far from the Tainted One's campsite.

Shuffling the wicker satchel from her back, she removed Bodhmhall's pouch and withdrew the stoppered flask. Placing it gently on the ground, she eased the stopper loose and raised the container to her nose. She sniffed at the contents, wrinkling her nose as the acrid fumes hit her nostrils. Her eyes watered.

Aodhán looked at her, unable to contain his curiosity. 'What's that?' he asked.

She raised her head and gave a smile that was bitter and sad in equal measure. 'Magic potion,' she said.

***

Darkness was not far off and the Tainted One's campfire was blazing even more fiercely when Liath Luachra staggered out of the trees and into the clearing. Two of the tattooed warriors were sitting together by the cave entrance, sharpening the blades of their weapons. The shrouded figure of the Tainted One was still hunched down in the rocky depression, face towards the fire.

'Thickheads! Come and face me!'

Startled, the two warriors jumped to their feet and stared in astonishment at the intruder in their camp. Their eyes darted towards the Tainted One as though seeking instruction but, preoccupied with some internal deliberations of his own, the *draoi* appeared oblivious to what was taking place behind him.

A great rage surged through the woman warrior. She furiously swirled her sword, cursing when it slipped from her hand and clattered noisily onto the hard rock surface of the clearing.

'Inbreds!'

Reaching down for the sword, she tripped and fell face first onto the ground. When she'd finally clambered to her feet again the two warriors had closed in, holding a few paces back with weapons at the ready, glancing uncertainly towards the Tainted One.

Gods, these creatures are ugly.

Two pairs of pitiless eyes regarded her, cold pale slits in the black facial tattoos that assured her a slow and merciless death. Shuddering, she raised her shaking sword point to greet them.

She heard the whoosh of the javelin as it flew past her ear, taking the first warrior in the throat. The metal head ploughed straight through the muscle and sinew, emerging a hand's width in length from the back of his neck. The warrior looked surprised as his eyes stared down at the shaft protruding from his throat. Gurgling and choking, he dropped to his knees, his life's blood spilling down his chest.

Beside him, his comrade, stared in equal astonishment. Stunned, he turned to the forest just as another javelin came whizzing in to slam him high in the chest. The force of the missile was strong enough to spin him around and he collapsed beside his comrade. He lay there, groaning incoherently and struggling to raise himself off the ground as Liath Luachra stumbled up behind him. Taking the haft of her sword in both hands, she plunged the blade at a downwards angle, through the back of his neck. It sank deep, down into the torso to pierce his heart. The lifeless body slumped forwards and rolled over on one side.

It was at this moment that the hooded figure finally deigned to stand and turn towards her. Beneath the heavy cowl, it wasn't possible to see the Tainted One's face but from the stiffness of his stance he was obviously appraising Liath Luachra with some alarm.

'What?' she bellowed. 'The Tainted One is surprised?'

She attempted to glare but the dark figure seemed to blur and waver before her eyes. She gasped suddenly as she felt him enter her, pushing her will aside, forcing himself inside her head. The sword fell from her hand and clanged on the rocky ground, her limbs no longer responding to her instruction.

Panicking, she started to scream, a howl of anger, outrage and fear as she felt her awareness shrinking away. A flood of power colours hit her then, exploded before her eyes and, somehow, the shadows seemed to slip, to loosen as though in revulsion of what they'd grasped. A great shudder passed through her, a sense of spiritual and emotional loathing, the mental equivalent of a retch.

And then her mind was back. He was out of her head.

She raised her eyes, looked over to where the Tainted One was now hunkered down, shivering and holding his head in his hands as though in immense pain.

'What's wrong?' she sneered. 'Can't hold your drink?'

She started to laugh then, feeling the *uisce beatha* sliding smoothly through her veins, uncoiling like a snake in her guts and spinning her mind in erratic patterns. 'And yet, it's *An Coill Mór's* best stock.'

Grasping the fallen sword, she staggered forwards to the shrouded figure. With a brutal yank, she reached down and wrenched the hood away to reveal a bald, wrinkled skull. Two empty black eye sockets stared up at her, the sewn-up lips quivered, mouthing their silent scream. Without even thinking, she plunged her sword deep into its gut, felt the blade slide effortlessly through the frail frame, encountering almost no resistance.

There was a strangled gasp. Nothing more.

Releasing the Tainted One, she let the body collapse and tottered away, her head reeling. Bodhmhall's scheme, despite its simplicity, had somehow succeeded. Distracted by Liath Luachra, the Tainted One's bodyguards had focussed their attack on her while Aodhán had snuck in close to take them out. The rogue *draoi* himself had been poisoned by the flavour of her *uisce beatha*-stained mind.'

We are alive! We are alive!

She fell to her knees and vomited.

Chapter Seven

The mood within the *ráth* remained subdued following Liath Luachra and Aodhán's departure. As she stood on the gateway, staring after the figures now faded into the falling rain, Bodhmhall could not shake the sense that the soul of the little community had departed with them.

Practical realities promptly dispelled such sombre musings. The intense rain wasn't long in driving the remaining inhabitants of the *ráth* indoors. The sole exception was Bearach who, as the last permanent member of the community with martial training, was obliged to remain on guard duty. He made a sad figure as he stood alone in the shelter of the stone passage overhang.

Bodhmhall joined Cairbre and Conchenn in their roundhouse but did not remain with them for long. Despite their attempts to maintain a brave face, it was obvious that the elders were preoccupied with concerns for their two sons out in the Great Wild. Excusing herself, the *bandraoi* returned to her own dwelling where Muirne and her son lay side-by-side on the sleeping platform.

The Flower of Almhu was still deep in slumber from the sleeping draught but, by Bodhmhall's estimation, would awaken sometime later that morning. The *bandraoi* still felt a trace of guilt for drugging her guest but knew that the need to remain undetected from the Tainted One outweighed such concerns.

Until Liath Luachra confronted him, at least.

Bodhmhall felt a caustic bitterness in the pit of her stomach as she recalled Cairbre's words:

You have had the luxury of authority without true responsibility

It was hardly a consolation to know those words were no longer valid, given that she'd just sent the one person most dear to her out to confront a lethal *draoi*. Especially with a scheme based on a notion she'd had no opportunity to validate.

Once again she immersed her anxieties in a series of simple physical tasks: stoking the fire, cleaning the pots, rearranging the ingredients for her herbal remedies. Although menial, each offered distraction and an element of control that she desperately needed. Within the dim interior of the roundhouse, however, her eyes were repeatedly drawn to the distinctive yellow glow of the sleeping baby.

Moving closer to the sleeping platform, Bodhmhall stared down at the two sleeping forms. She was struck by how serene Muirne Muncháem appeared in slumber, the tension lines from her scheming visage markedly absent in repose. Reaching down, she lifted the infant from the platform and cradled him gently in her arms. Swaddled in his warm wrapping, the babe looked strikingly small and vulnerable.

Who chases you, a bábóg? What do they want from you so badly that they would send a small army out into the Great Wild to chase you down?

She wondered vaguely whether it could have been some fault of the parents that had triggered such an apparently unwarranted pursuit. Some great offence, perhaps, some grievous harm caused to another party by accident or intent.

She quickly discounted the possibility. Muirne Muncháem's abrasive personality might have the potential to provoke such a reaction but she doubted that it would have happened in practice. The Flower of Almhu was simply too astute to risk offending someone with the power to raise a *fian* – not to mention a pet *draoi* – to their cause. A similar argument held for her brother. In many respects, it was even less likely given Cumhal's popularity and the general respect in which he had been held by friend and foe alike.

Until the battle of Cnucha.

She frowned and turned a suspicious gaze on Muirne.

I wonder if she has told me all that I should know.

The baby burped, distracting her from such misgivings. Bodhmhall gently stroked the soft skin of his cheeks with her fingertips. She felt an immense swell of tenderness at the realisation that this child would be her final connection, her last remaining tie to her sibling. With a sudden but completely precise sense of clarity, she knew that she would give her own life, do whatever it took, to protect this child.

A leanbh go deo. May you always remain so innocent.

Laying the infant back on the sleeping platform, she tucked the furs snugly in around him. Satisfied that he would not wriggle free, she returned to the fire and sat on the reed mat. The direct heat of the fire was comforting. Staring into the flames, she felt her eyelids grow heavy and realised just how tired she was from the previous night's planning and the early start. She closed her eyes for a moment.

Just a moment.

Just one, very, short moment.

'Bodhmhall.'

'Uh!' The *bandraoi* started, opened her eyes. Somebody shook her shoulder.

'Bodhmhall. You are needed.'

She looked up. Fiacail was standing over her, talking at her but she couldn't seem to catch what he was saying. 'What?' she asked, struggling to tear her mind free from the tangle of clinging cobwebs. 'What? I don't understand. What are you saying?'

'I said,' the big man looked at her impatiently. 'Strangers have come to your valley.'

***

'The boy fetched me when he saw the signal.'

'The signal?' In her fatigue, Bodhmhall stumbled on the lower step of the rampart ladder. Although the rain had mercifully ceased, the rung was still wet and coated with a thick layer of slimy mud transferred from the surface of the *lis*.

'The signal,' Fiacail repeated from the platform above her. 'I sent Tóla out to monitor the western path into the valley. It seemed a sensible precaution to have him replace your boy, Cónán, given your lack of warriors. If the *fian* do locate us, we'll need as much warning as possible to prepare. A short time ago he signalled that there was a group of people approaching. Bearach spotted the signal and came to fetch me but the intruders are already half-way up the valley.'

'Half-way up the valley!' She stared at him in alarm.

'Don't worry. I wouldn't think they're too much of a threat.'

'What do you mean?'

'See for yourself.'

Grasping Bodhmhall by the hand, Fiacail hauled her up onto the platform where she stumbled forwards to the rampart wall. Peering down the length of the valley, the *bandraoi's* eye immediately fell on the line of figures moving in the direction of the *ráth*. Her forehead wrinkled in

158

confusion. There were fewer than ten figures, some of them significantly smaller than the others.

Children!

'We need a better means of alerting the *ráth*. Fortunately, this lot don't look like the *fían*.' Fiacail stood close beside her, observing her reaction. 'Do you know them?'

'Yes,' she nodded. 'It is *Muinntir Ráth Dearg*, Cathal ua Cuan's people from the Ráth Dearg settlement.'

'Ráth Dearg?' he exclaimed harshly. 'I don't see any men. Apart from that shambling old relic at the back.'

'That's Cathal ua Cuan himself.'

The warrior looked at her, his forehead furrowed. 'This is ... not good, Bodhmhall.'

The Seiscenn Uarbhaoil man said no more but Bodhmhall knew what he was thinking. The plan to defend Ráth Bládhma had been dependent on convincing the men from Ráth Dearg and Coill Mór to join them. Given the bedraggled little group coming towards them, that was looking less and less like a feasible option.

Dismayed, the *bandraoi* climbed up onto the pilings of the rampart to get a better look at the approaching group. Even at this distance, she could tell that they were a dispirited, wretched band. Heads bowed, they trudged towards the *ráth*, beaten and exhausted. Bodhmhall's heart stirred in sympathy, knowing that they would have had a hard time of it out in the forest in the previous night's storm.

Only one member of the group, Cathal ua Cuan; the bald, grey-bearded, but still surprisingly muscular *Taoiseach* of Ráth Dearg, appeared to move with any clear sense of purpose. Keeping to the rear of the party, with one miserable looking infant perched on his shoulders, he was urging the shambling, mud-streaked refugees onwards, jadedly herding them towards the settlement. It was only when they halted, numb with exhaustion, before the causeway, that he pushed his way forward. Standing in front of his little group, he stared up at the *bandraoi*.

'I see you, Bodhmhall.'

'I see you, Cathal. Don't stand out there in the cold. Bring your people in.'

The old man took her at her word, making no attempt to explain his presence. Taking the child from his shoulder, he dropped him onto the ground, ushered the women and children ahead of him, and silently followed as they filed through the stone gateway and into the *lis*.

Cairbre and Bearach awaited them inside, guiding the exhausted company into their roundhouse where they immediately collapsed around the fire. By the time Bodhmhall and Fiacail came in to join them, Conchenn was serving up hot broth, passing it out in wooden bowls that were snatched from her hands by the ravenous children.

The *bandraoi* noticed that Cathal ua Cuan was the last person to receive food, accepting it only when every other member of his family had been taken care of. She watched as he held the proffered bowl in large, calloused hands. As he started to sup and allowed himself to relax, however, it was as though everything gave way. The old man stumbled unsteadily to one side and would most likely have fallen if Fiacail hadn't reacted with his usual swiftness, catching him by the arm and guiding him to the support of the centre roof post. Leaning against the wooden pole, Cathal slowly slid to the floor, his back against the pole, his two legs spread out before him. Bodhmhall noted how the skin on the soles of his feet was raw and torn, two of the toes on his left foot blackened as though from snow rot.

All that way from Ráth Dearg under such conditions. He is a tough man.

She was impressed. Crotchety and coated in filth the old warrior might be but he'd still managed to push himself beyond the abilities of many younger men in his struggle to protect his family. She was familiar with the man's reputation for toughness, of course. In his day, Cathal had been a warrior of some repute, Back in Dún Baoiscne, he'd served as a respected and intimidating bodyguard for Guaire – Bodhmhall's grandfather – for many years. However, with Guaire's death and Tréanmór's subsequent rise to the position of *rí*, the old warrior had become surplus to his new leader's requirements. Keen to establish his own distinct political and military reign, Tréanmór had wanted a fresh contingent of younger, fitter warriors. Cathal had been summarily discarded and put out to pasture with the older fighters.

A proud man, Cathal had not taken the insult well and had departed Dún Baoiscne for Ráth Dearg – The Red Ringfort – named for the red fern that grew in abundance in the area. The land had previously been linked to his mother's people but they'd long since died off or moved away. Cathal had re-established his own family holding there with his three boys, their wives and servants.

Bodhmhall raised a beaker to his lips and he gulped from it in great, greedy draughts.

'You look weary, Cathal.'

'I am weary, girl.' He paused to wipe his mouth with the back of his hand and his eyes took on a worn, despairing look. 'Bodhmhall of Ráth Bládhma, I come to beg your mercy. Without your help, my family will die.'

'You have it and welcome, Cathal.'

Relief tumbled from the exhausted old man. 'Thank you, Bodhmhall. Thank you.'

'What happened, Cathal? What are you doing here? Did Cónán bring you our message?'

The ancient fighter wheezed and for a moment she thought he was going to pass out but his characteristic toughness reasserted itself. With obvious effort, he forced himself to sit upright.

'Yes, Bodhmhall. Your boy came to us with your message. We encountered him on the trail less than two days ago. We were already on our way here.'

Off to the side, Bodhmhall heard Conchenn give a hiss of relief and saw how she reached out to grasp Cairbre's hand.

'Three days before that, our settlement was attacked by reavers. They came out of the morning fog, slaughtered our men, killed our animals. They took the *ráth*.' The old man sighed. 'Would that he'd come sooner,' he continued miserably. 'But that was not his fault. He gave us what food supplies he carried for the little ones would have died without it. Afterwards, he left to take his message to Coill Mór.'

Bodhmhall considered this news gravely. 'Your boys?' she asked.

'All dead.'

She shook her head in dismay. She hadn't seen Cathal's sons for many years but she remembered them as bold, handsome young men.

So much death. So much unnecessary death.

Fiacail was not so sympathetic. Reaching down, he took a firm grip of the old man's filthy tunic and shook him roughly. 'Your attackers, man. Who were they? Who drove the *fian*?'

The farmer shook his head and stared at them in incomprehension.

'T'weren't a *fian*. These men were foreign reavers.'

'Foreign reavers?'

'They weren't of The People. They spoke some bastard tongue I've not heard before and they had strange markings on their skin and faces. Some of them had black faces. Others wore necklaces or ornaments made out of human teeth. Or ears and fingers.'

He closed his eyes and shuddered, clearly thinking about the fate of his sons' bodies.

'How many of them?' demanded Fiacail.

Cathal shook his head. 'I don't know. Fifty, maybe.'

Bodhmhall and Fiacail looked at one another.

Fifty men. The two fian have joined together.

'You're sure?' asked the big man. 'They were not *Clann Morna* men?'

Cathal released a scathing, hysterical laugh. '*Clann Morna*? No. *Clann Morna* speak our tongue and, for all their faults, they don't kill unless they have a clear plan in mind. This band were savages. They attacked us for the sport. Our settlement posed no threat to them. We had little of value to a band like that. Nothing except for food.' He paused. 'Or the prospect of entertainment.'

Bodhmhall looked at him. 'What do you mean?'

'Those men hungered for murder, Bodhmhall. They may have been famished but, mostly, they were just hungry for blood. The better part of them just sat up on a hill overlooking the *ráth* to watch their comrades ransack our home, hack my sons to pieces and laugh at the sport of it. My eldest -'

He choked on a sudden sob and had to stop for a moment before continuing.

'My eldest son's wife – Elec – tried to save her man. She was a brave girl, that one. Ran out at them with a scythe, she did. Fearless. Courageous. But those animals didn't care. They just grabbed her, tore her clothes from her body and took it in turns, ripping her apart out there in the open.'

He closed his eyes and for a moment it looked as though he would be unable to continue. 'She did not die a pretty death.'

Although the old man was visibly distraught, Fiacail refused to ease up on his interrogation, intentionally pushing the desolate man with further questions.

'They killed your men and yet you, your women and children managed to escape. You were lucky then, weren't you? How did a fat old man like you get away?'

162

Cathal sniffed, blearily wiped a hunk of snot away with the sleeve of his jerkin. Suddenly he rallied, glaring up at the warrior with unexpected ferocity. 'Oh, yes Fiacail mac Codhna,' he responded, bitterness dripping from his words. 'I was lucky. So very lucky. I had all the luck of a fat old man who outlives his sons.'

The bitter retort had no impact on the big man's thick skin. 'You did not fight.'

'With what would I fight? I had no weapon to hand. Besides, someone had to protect the children and the women of my other sons.'

'Then they are truly fortunate,' said Fiacail blithely. 'That a warrior of such fearsome reputation would preoccupy himself with them.'

Cathal was too wearied to react to the insult. Fiacail shook him again.

'How did you get away? Were you hidden? Did they not see you?'

He released the old warrior who slumped, disconsolate, against the post.

'No. I'd taken my grandchildren down to the river to fish. The trout bite better on the cusp of dawn. We were on our way back with our catch when heard the screams. I hurried the children as fast as I could then, just in sight of the *ráth*, we ran into Cumann and Gnathad who were fleeing the carnage.' He pointed at the two women in the group. Both were now sitting by the fire pit. The older one, an attractive woman with fair hair tied up in a braid, was breast feeding a young infant of less than two years. The younger one, a dark-haired maiden of about sixteen or seventeen years, stared into the flames with a haunted expression.

'We stood at the edge of the forest and stared at the *ráth* but by then those savages had captured our home and massacred everyone. There was nothing I could do but run, try to save what remained of my family.'

'So, in your flight you simply outran them. You and your weak-kneed wretches.'

'Yes!' the old man snarled. 'No! I don't know!' He appeared flustered, confused. 'They must have lost interest in us. They were too busy enjoying their sport. I –'

But Bodhmhall could take no more of the interrogation.

'Fiacail, let the man be. Can't you see he's overcome with grief?' She lifted a damp cloth and wiped the elder's brow then leaned forward to whisper softly into his ear. 'Rest easy, Cathal. You are in a place of safety. You have delivered your kin and fulfilled all responsibility. Your duty is done. All that remains now is to rest.'

163

The old man looked up at her with despair-filled eyes. Without warning, those eyes rolled into the whites and his head rocked back against the pole. He began to snore.

Fiacail stared at the comatose old fighter then turned to the *bandraoi*, his eyes wide in amazement. 'You bewitched him?'

She wrinkled her lips in a cynical gesture and held up the beaker. 'This mixture has soporific qualities, as Muirne Muncháem has also discovered. It relaxed Cathal sufficiently to allow himself to rest, to forgive himself for something that was not his fault.' Her eyes narrowed. 'A well deserved rest. It was cruel to press him so mercilessly, Fiacail.'

'Yes,' the Seiscenn Uarbhaoil man admitted. 'It was cruel but we needed to know what happened. It's best to draw the facts from people before they get their wits about them, before their minds start to play tricks with the truth.' He paused. 'Let us go away from here, Bodhmhall.'

With this, Fiacail turned and departed the roundhouse. Surprised, she followed him outside, across the *lis* and up the ladder to the southern rampart. Here, he leaned silently against the wooden pilings and stared across at the woods, slowly rocking himself backwards and forwards on the heels of his feet. Bodhmhall studied him with curiosity.

'What is it, Fiacail?'

He pursed his lips for a moment before he answered. 'This attack on Ráth Dearg. It doesn't make sense.'

'What do you mean? The *fian* attacked them and killed their people. That is what *fian* do.'

'Cathal claims it was not a *fian.*'

'*Fian* or not, they were probably desperate for food and shelter. They've been out in rough country, exposed to brutal weather for several days at least. There's not enough game to be had to support a band that size. Ráth Dearg had shelter and plenty of cattle to give them fresh meat.'

'Mmm.' The big warrior did not appear convinced. 'That may be -' he said.

'But?'

'But I believe that there is more to it than that.'

'Why?'

'Because there were survivors. Survivors that should not have been able to outrun them. Including those two.' He nodded his head to indicate the two Ráth Dearg women Cathal had referred to earlier. Both women had come out to the *lis*, the fair one pulling the dark-haired girl by the hand. Bodhmhall watched as they sat on a log outside the roundhouse. When they were seated, the first woman attempted to feed her friend from a small bowl of broth. Judging from the dark girl's lack of response, she did not appear to be having much success.

'You cannot tell me,' whispered Fiacail, 'that hardened men who have not known the company of women for such a time would willingly let such a catch escape. Particularly that fair one. She'd rise a head on any a man.' His eyes lingered for a moment longer than necessary before he shook his head with quiet conviction. 'No, they would not have let them go. Not unless there was another purpose.'

Bodhmhall's face grew pale. 'The *fian* are following them here.'

'I think you have the nub of it. We've suspected the *fian* have been seeking Muirne Muncháem for many days now. We know their Tainted One has failed to locate us. If I was in their position, I'd be growing anxious too. They have no line of supply and they're in unfamiliar territory so they'd have had to resort to some other stratagem. They would have -'

'They would have attacked the settlement,' concluded Bodhmhall. 'And allowed some survivors to leave, knowing they would head straight for the nearest refuge: Ráth Bládhma.' She nodded her head in reluctant appreciation. 'That was quite clever.' The ramifications of what she was saying suddenly registered. She stared at the warrior in dismay. 'The *fian* may already be upon us!'

Fiacail scratched his chin. 'Not yet. Like you said, this *fian* will be exhausted, starving. They'll probably have sick men with them. I think they'll make use of Ráth Dearg to recover their strength and resupply. But they will have sent scouts to trail Cathal and his people.' He stared towards the west. 'They're probably out there now. In the trees at the end of the valley or the woods along the base of the ridges, watching us as we speak.'

Bodhmhall looked about in alarm. 'Will they attack?'

'I don't believe so. Now that they've found Glenn Ceoch, they'll have sent runners back to their comrades. The rest – probably two or three men – will remain here to keep an eye on us, to study our defences, the number of fighting men we have and so on.'

'But those runners will return with the *fian*?'

He nodded. 'Yes. Let us say two days to run back to Ráth Dearg, three days march to return.' He did the calculation in his head. 'I think that within five days Ráth Bládhma can expect a full scale assault.'

Bodhmhall shivered, her worst fears confirmed.

'Can we intercept the runners? Somehow prevent them from reaching the *fian*?'

'It's too late. They'll be moving fast, in a straight line to a predetermined destination. It'd be difficult to catch them up. Besides, even if we did give chase, there's always a risk of losing their trail then having to backtrack and find it again.' He paused to consider her keenly. 'We should use what time we have more wisely.'

'More wisely?'

'Making preparations to leave.'

Bodhmhall silently held his gaze.

He sighed. 'You have no intention of leaving, do you?'

'Are my intentions so easy to read?'

'Your features have a determined set to them that I recognise of old. It does not bode well.' He unstrapped one of his battle-axes from his back and tossed it by the haft with casual skill from one hand to the other. 'You cannot stay, Bodhmhall. Impressive though your defences are, they will not hold against fifty men. Besides, you have but a single, unblooded warrior to defend your walls.'

'Liath Luachra and Aodhán will return soon.'

'After defeating a Tainted One?' His look was sceptical. 'Bodhmhall, I would spare you the pain but you cannot count on their return.' Ignoring her obvious resentment, he pressed his argument. 'Even if they do come back, that would give you a total of three warriors against fifty. You have heard the fate of the Ráth Dearg woman.' He paused to regard her anxiously. 'It would be a painful and demeaning death for those women who remain here.'

The *bandraoi* fidgeted nervously with the polished black stone pendent that hung from a leather cord about her neck. A present from Liath Luachra on their departure from Dún Baoiscne, it was her single piece of jewellery and her most cherished possession. 'What, then, is your counsel?'

'I would have you flee. Cairbre tells me there is another secret route out of the valley to the east and that, although dangerous, it can be traversed with caution.'

'I do not wish to go to Seiscenn Uarbhaoil with you, Fiacail.'

The warrior stiffened. 'That thrust cuts deep, *Cailleach*.'

'It was not intended as a thrust, Fiacail. You know I am one to speak plainly.'

Fiacail remained uncharacteristically silent. Bodhmhall waited as the silence stretched on, wondering if she should say something. She was relieved when he suddenly responded again.

'If you do not want to come to Seiscenn Uarbhaoil with me, then at least travel to some other refuge where you can hide until it is safe to return. This is a good settlement but it is not worth your life.'

'And where would we go?'

Fiacail looked at her in surprise.

'There is no refuge to be found in the Great Wild,' she insisted. 'The nearest place of safety is back in *Clann Baoiscne* territory.'

'And what of it? You are the daughter of Tréanmór. There are plenty in *Clann Baoiscne* who would welcome you in. You have much to offer.'

'That's true. Some would probably take me in. And possibly Liath Luachra because of her reputation with the sword. But what about my nephew, Cairbre, Conchenn and their sons? And then, there is the responsibility of sanctuary we owe to Muirne and now to Cathal's family as well.'

'That responsibility does not extend to your own death, dear one.'

'Don't feign such ruthlessness, Fiacail. You have seen those Ráth Dearg children. They are on their last legs. It's a miracle Cathal got them here across that distance without losing any of them.'

'Yes. He is a tough old thorn, I'll give him that.'

'If we move those children now, before they've had a chance to rest, it's likely that many of them will die. Here, at least, we have food and shelter if we can defend the *ráth*.'

Fiacail reacted furiously, tightening his grip on the axe then swinging it in a tight arc. 'You cannot ask me and my men to stay and fight, Bodhmhall.'

'I have not asked you to stay.'

'Not with words but with silences.'

'What?'

167

'You do not ask me to stay yet you dangle the bloody consequences of my departure in the air between us.' He gave an irritated growl. 'And then, of course, there are the physical silences.'

'The physical silences?' Bodhmhall stared at him in confusion.

'When I am near you I sense veiled possibilities, airy prospects without the anchor of firm commitments. It is not your fault but it ... Gaaaah!'

He suddenly slammed the axe into the nearest piling, embedding the metal head deep into the wood. The blow was so violent that the long haft quivered for several moments. Fiacail cursed and grasped it with both hands but it took several strong pulls before he finally wrenched the weapon loose. Bodhmhall looked on, too shaken and too perplexed to speak. When she finally found her voice she was relieved to hear it had a steadiness she did not feel.

'I regret you feel such unintended enticements.' She moistened lips that suddenly felt dry and cracked. 'It's true I have placed silent burdens on you. It was my hope that, as my friend, you would offer help without condition.'

'Bodhmhall, I want to be your friend. I want to be loyal and honourable and to offer you help without condition. Alas, my *bod* wants something substantially more ... fundamental. When I am near, when I smell the scent of your skin, desire billows out the crotch of my leggings.' He stared at her in desperation. 'Woman, I have not had sex for weeks!'

She gaped at him for a moment then gave a nervous laugh. 'Well, milk the bull, Fiacail! We must all relieve ourselves when strained with desire that needs sating.'

A small smile cracked the corner of his lips. 'It is a lonely sport, *Cailleach*. Much improved with company.'

'Ask Muirne, then. By all accounts she is not unfamiliar with the dimensions of your needs.'

This time it was the warrior who laughed. 'Even I am not so desperate that I would poke an ill-tempered bear.' He shook his head then, conceding the ludicrousness of the situation. 'Very well, dear one. I will take the matter in hand, as it were. When my needs are slaked and my thoughts free from desire, I am sure that I can be your friend.' He breathed in and then exhaled long and hard. 'Gods, it is good to have such intentions out in the open.'

The *bandraoi* rested an arm upon his shoulder. 'You are a true friend, Fiacail and my gratitude to you is sincere but can I call on you then to remain for a further two days? To help defend the *ráth* until the children have rested, until -'. She hesitated. 'Until Cónán, Liath Luachra and Aodhán return. I ask this boon as friend and clan. I regret I can offer nothing more than gratitude and the friendship of my heart in return.'

'Not the friendship of your thighs?'

'Not the friendship of my thighs.'

The Seiscenn Uarbhaoil man chuckled. 'A shame. Very well, *Cailleach Dubh*. As your friend I will remain for another two days but you cut the timing fine. You will need a headstart on the *fian* if you wish to escape them. The children will slow you down.'

'I understand that. Nevertheless, I must give Liath Luachra the grace of two days to return if she is alive.'

'That is fair. I do, however, counter with another offer.'

'Yes?'

'If Liath Luachra does not return within two days, you will accompany me to Seiscenn Uarbhaoil. Your people are also welcome. I will protect all those to whom you currently offer sanctuary.'

Bodhmhall was silent for a very long time. Even as she worked through the offer and its ramifications in her head, she had the strangest sensation of the wooded ridges on either side of the *ráth* crowding in more tightly about them. Her head began to spin. 'I will make my decision at the end of the second day. When Liath Luachra returns.'

Fiacail laughed. 'You drive a hard bargain Bodhmhall ua Baoiscne. You may not have your father's looks but, by the Gods, you have his obstinacy. And his teeth.'

'Given the relations between my father and I, that may be a careless compliment. But I accept it in the manner it is offered.' She leaned back against the pilings, suddenly drained from the effort of the conversation. 'Are things between us settled to your satisfaction, Fiacail? I would have some time on my own.'

'As, apparently, must I. But no. There is still the matter of the scouts.'

The *bandraoi*'s shoulders sagged. She had completely forgotten about the scouts.

'I think that, at the very least, we should deprive the *fian* of whatever information they've gathered. Don't you?' He leaned his axe against the stone rampart. 'I am of course familiar with your dislike at being called on to use your abilities but given the ...' He trailed off for Bodhmhall was

169

already peering out over the pilings, drawing on her Gift. She looked about the valley for a long time and the concentration must have taken a heavy toll for when she allowed herself to relax again, her face was drawn and worn.

'It's still bright,' she said. 'And the valley teems with life-light but, possibly, there's someone in the woods below the northern ridge. Over th-'

She made to raise her hand and point but Fiacail promptly slapped it down. Outraged by his rudeness, she glared at him but he quickly moved to calm her. 'Let us not alert them,' he suggested in a quiet voice. 'To the fact that we know they are here.'

She nodded tersely, struggling to stifle her temper. 'I believe they are below the northern ridge. But I cannot be certain.'

Fiacail shrugged. 'It doesn't matter, I suppose. Tóla will follow them and identify where they set camp tonight, in any case.'

'How do you know that?'

'Because that is what I instructed him to do.'

She looked at him blankly.

'Forgive me for not conferring with you but you were asleep. I felt the precaution would be ... prudent.'

Bodhmhall watched him as he leaned out from the gateway into the *lis*, resentment from the imagined slight competing with a grudging admiration.

You were right, Cairbre. He does have a unique mind and thinks several steps ahead.

Unaware of her scrutiny, Fiacail bellowed; 'Ultán!'

A moment later, his kinsman appeared from inside the lean-to and stared up at his leader.

'Ultán, we go visiting tonight. Prepare your best blades.'

The dark-haired warrior nodded without expression and returned inside. Fiacail turned to fix the *bandraoi* with a look that retained no trace of his earlier arousal. 'You can rest easy, Bodhmhall. Tóla will continue to watch the entrance to the valley to make sure there are no further surprises. Bearach can keep adequate watch from inside the *ráth* but I suggest you keep your stock within and the door barricaded tonight.' He glanced up at the sky. 'Night will not be long in falling and Tóla will return with the dark. I will leave you now. There are many things to do. And one thing, at least, I am obliged to do on my own.'

***

170

It was mid-day when Muirne Muncháem finally regained consciousness. Preparing a remedy for one of the younger Ráth Dearg children, Bodhmhall saw her visitor stir, sit up, yawn and stare drowsily about the roundhouse. She watched with some amusement as Muirne's eyes fell on the Ráth Dearg refugees. Blinking in surprise, the Flower of Almhu stared uncomprehendingly at the unfamiliar children. Unconsciously, her left hand reached down to touch her baby as though reassuring herself that he was still there with her and hadn't suddenly grown up overnight.

Staggering off the sleeping platform, she stumbled forwards on unsteady feet. Bodhmhall sighed and rose to intercept her. Muirne was clearly aware that something very much out of the ordinary had occurred. She would be in a foul mood and it was beholden on a good host to protect her guests from the subsequent conflict.

Guiding the confused young woman to one side, she sat her down and offered her some fresh water as she explained what she had done. As anticipated, Muirne did not take the news well. Outraged that the *bandraoi* had dared to drug her, she was even more furious at the length of time she'd been kept unconscious. Fortunately, her grogginess undermined her anger and her outrage was further distracted by the urgent need to empty her bowels after two days of inactivity.

Bodhmhall watched her scurry through the doorway. The rush of air though the temporary gap behind her was cold but sweet. The cramped interior was already smelling strongly of body odor and damp, as though a pack of wet dogs had taken up residence. Having spent several days in the Great Wild, the children seemed loath to leave the security and warmth of the dwelling. Some of the older ones, seven or eight years of age, stayed close to Gnathad, the fair haired woman, and held her close. Two of the younger children were stretched on their stomachs by the fire pit when she entered, playing quietly with makeshift toy animals that Cairbre had created from pine cones and twigs. In some respects, thought Bodhmhall, they were the lucky ones. Too young to fully understand what had happened to their homestead or to recall much of the suffering endured during their travels to Ráth Bládhma, they would not be haunted by the experience.

Unlike Cumann.

Bodhmhall regarded the dark haired Ráth Dearg woman sadly. She was seated at the edge of the second sleeping platform, staring into space and rocking slowly back and forth as she keened quietly to herself. So far she

171

had not responded to any of their efforts at communication and seemed oblivious to their presence.

Later that afternoon, Bodhmhall helped Conchenn prepare a thin soup of pork bones and watercress. Although it lacked substance, the potage was tasty and immediately devoured by the children, prompting fresh concerns for the *bandraoi*. The population of the settlement had more than doubled and despite the *ráth's* access to dairy products and blood cake they wouldn't be long in eating through the remaining food reserves with such numbers.

When she'd finished feeding the children, the *bandraoi* examined her guests and treated their physical wounds. With the exception of Cathal's toes, these were relatively minor and she was confident that even the old warrior's feet could be healed with sufficient rest and care. Although not a healer by inclination, the Gift permitted her to assess the characteristic sickly hue that wounds took on when they became sore and tainted. From experience and experimentation, she had worked out that treating certain wounds with specific herbs and ointments had the ability to reduce and eventually extinguish these hues, thereby contributing to the patient's successful recovery.

As she ground up the ingredients needed to make a poultice for Cathal's feet, some instinct made her look over to where Muirne Muncháem was sitting, observing her with an indecipherable expression. On returning to the roundhouse, Muirne had quickly reestablished her dominance over the larger sleeping platform, defending any intrusion with an aggression that equaled the most territorial of beasts. At the time, Bodhmhall had been surprised that she'd not returned to their argument, something that the *bandraoi* was happy to forestall.

She sighed and put her pestle aside, preparing herself for another interminable conflict. 'What is it, Muirne? What poisons trouble your world now?'

'I misjudged you, Bodhmhall. I was wrong about you.'

She looked at the younger woman in surprise. Despite her earlier indignation, Muirne looked unusually calm, sitting quietly with the babe sucking greedily at her breast. It was a picture quite at odds with the combative personality Bodhmhall was accustomed to contending with.

'What do you mean?'

'As I said, I think I have misjudged you. Cumhal always insisted that you were uncommonly kind but I never truly believed him. And yet, when you did not need to, you took me in.'

'I took *him* in,' she nodded at the babe. 'My nephew. You were merely the vessel.'

The Flower of Almhu shrugged, the insult bouncing off her like a sword blade off a metal studded shield. 'Nevertheless, you offered sanctuary when many others would have turned their door to my face.'

Bodhmhall regarded her warily, unsure where the Almhu woman was trying to lead the conversation. A sudden peal of laughter from the fire-pit drew her gaze to where one of the little girls was lying on her back, convulsed with laughter. She smiled unconsciously at the welcome break to the otherwise dreary interior. Turning back to Muirne, she stiffened when she saw that she too was looking at the child, an open and benevolent smile on her lips.

Muirne, in her turn, was a little unsettled when she turned back to find the *bandraoi* observing her but she carelessly brushed her discomfort aside. 'And then there are these people from Ráth Dearg,' she continued, taking up from where she had stopped. 'I've watched you for some time and seen how you personally tend to strangers in your home. You display a generosity of spirit I'm unaccustomed to experiencing at first hand. At first, I assumed this was a pretense, an act on your part. Now, I'm convinced that it is genuine.'

Bodhmhall stared at her. 'Why would you possibly think I would play false in my efforts to help these people?'

'It's what I would do. I usually make a point of working to earn the goodwill of those in my company in case I should have need to call on their assistance sometime in the future.'

'If goodwill is not sincere, then it is surely impossible to sustain. Besides, I do not recall you working hard to earn my goodwill at Dún Baoiscne.'

'At Dún Baoiscne, I had no need of you. I had Cumhal. Besides, you were a potential rival.'

'And now?'

'And now? *Clann Baoiscne* is in the descent. We find ourselves in a similar situation. There is no time and no need for such rivalry between us.'

Bodhmhall exhaled long and slow. 'You truly are a twisted branch, Muirne.'

'I am the product of my upbringing. You cannot judge me for acting as I have been brought up to act. At Almhu there are no other offspring, no sons to bear arms or to defend the family name. I am sole heir to my parents' wealth,' Muirne continued. 'As a woman, I have no training in martial combat. Instead I am obliged to rely on those weapons that I can wield to best effect: my looks, my intelligence and my political skills.'

'Which you wielded well on my brother.'

'It's true. I did use them to charm him but it was a good match, linking our family to yours. From a political perspective at least.' She grew quiet. 'You may not believe me, Bodhmhall, but I truly liked your brother. He was a good man, a kind husband. His death leaves a scar on my heart.'

For just a moment the Flower of Almhu's eyes moistened, a reaction she countered in a bustle of activity. Raising the baby onto her shoulder, she patted him on the back in an attempt to burp him as Conchenn had shown her, despite the fact that he did not require it. The baby seemed to share in this belief for he immediately started to wail and she was obliged to set him back on the nipple.

'You and I, Bodhmhall. We are not that different. Were you not raised in similar circumstances, an instrument for your parents' great designs? You were, at least, fortunate enough to escape the fate planned for you.'

Bodhmhall considered her old adversary, wryly amused by the situation. It seemed unnatural but they appeared to be having a civil conversation, a genuine sharing of opinions and histories if not of confidences.

'I think you resided in Dún Baoiscne long enough to know that I was taken by the *draoi* as a child. I had eleven summers on me when I was removed from my family.'

'Yes, I had heard that. You were under the tutelage of Dub Tíre were you not?'

Bodhmhall stared directly at her but said nothing. Despite her misgivings, it was possible that Muirne was making a genuine attempt at conversation, albeit on a topic fraught with sensitivity. 'Yes,' she said.

'They say he was very uniquely talented.'

'He had some talent.'

'You sound as though you did not hold him in great esteem.'

The *bandraoi* felt something harden inside her and realised that her fists were clenched. 'That is because I knew Dub Tíre for what he truly was.'

Muirne nodded understandingly. 'So, is that why you killed him?'

She left Muirne in the roundhouse to share her scheming with the refugees from Ráth Dearg. Absorbed with their own problems, however, she couldn't imagine they would have much of an ear for her intrigues. It was no surprise therefore, when she saw Gnathad, the blond haired woman, emerge from the dwelling a short time later, trailed by three of the eldest children. An erratic breeze was brushing the sides of the *ráth* and the four stood by the empty fire-pit, staring miserably at the swirling ashes.

Bodhmhall approached the little group. 'I see you, Little Ones,' she said, addressing the children.

The young ones, two girls and a boy, looked up shyly. The oldest, a dark girl with long ringlets, nudged the younger, red haired girl in front of her. The younger girl stared in terror at the *bandraoi* then blurted, 'The wind makes my fingers sting, *Cailleach*.'

Bodhmhall considered the little girl. Her cheeks and the bridge of her nose were spattered with freckles and she had wide blue eyes that were gaping at her with dread.

I see my reputation has spread to Ráth Dearg, at least.

'Put your fingers into your armpits,' she suggested. 'Like this.'

After some initial reluctance, the girl also attempted it and seemed pleased with the result. 'It works!' she declared with enthusiasm, her earlier dread evaporated.

'Of course, it does.'

'I have to show my grandfather. He likes tricks like that. He says I'm his favourite.'

'Cathal? Is he your grandfather?'

'Yes,' she nodded sagely. 'He's *Taoiseach* of Ráth Dearg. Do you know him?'

'We have met.'

The girl nodded.

'I'm cold too,' the little boy announced suddenly. He couldn't have had more than five or six years on him and he was small with long, dark hair and a pale face. He wiped his cheeks with the back of his hands and sniffed.

'It is cold,' Bodhmhall agreed. 'But, here in Ráth Bládhma, if you're cold you can go back inside the roundhouse and be warm. Better than out there.' She gestured towards the gateway.

'You mean out with the bad men?' asked the redheaded girl.

'Yes,' said the *bandraoi*. There didn't seem to be any point in being untruthful, given what these children had already been through.

'Why do the bad men want to kill us?'

'I'm not certain. But your grandfather and I will stop them.'

'Good.' The little girl gave a surprisingly adult nod of approval, a gesture she must surely have picked up from one of the older members of her settlement. 'They killed Elec, Bran's mother. Didn't they, Bran?' She looked encouragingly at the little boy who stood there, tears welling up in his eyes.

'Bamba!' The fair-haired woman who'd remained to one side observing the conversation finally intervened. 'Don't bother our host. Take Bran with you and go off to play. Now!'

The redheaded girl gave her mother an impatient look but did as she was told. Taking the little boy's hand in her own, she led him away, following her elder sister who'd already wandered over to the pens to watch Bearach feeding the goats.

Bodhmhall considered the young woman. She was only slightly shorter than the *bandraoi* herself and had bright, intelligent eyes, red from shedding too many tears of late.

'You are called Gnathad, are you not?'

The woman nodded. 'Thank you for helping us, Bodhmhall ua Baoiscne. I will see that the children do not forget your kindness.'

Bodhmhall nodded. 'They are yours?'

'The two girls. As you heard, poor Bran's parents perished back in Ráth Dearg. We are his family now.' Gnathad's earlier composure suddenly looked close to cracking.

'I'm sorry, Gnathad. You have seen much suffering these past few days but yet I see you occupy yourself with all the Ráth Dearg children. And your friend. The other girl.'

'Cumann?' She released a soft sigh.

'Your friend is not well.'

'She was always a delicate girl. I think this has all been too much for her. She saw her husband die.'

'As did you.'

The Ráth Dearg woman's head drooped. When she raised it again, her jaw had a determined set to it. 'My husband used to tell me I had a heart as stout as a tree stump. He ...' Her voice trailed off and she swallowed. 'I find

- that is why I try to help. When I help others with their pain I cannot feel my own.'

Bodhmhall nodded in sympathy. 'I promise you, Gnathad. We will do everything within our power to protect you and your children.'

'Thank you, Bodhmhall. I know your offer is sincere but if the *fian* come there is little you can do. I have seen the enemy and Ráth Bládhma simply doesn't have enough warriors. They will flow over your walls like an incoming tide. Nothing you do can prevent that.'

She paused to pull a woollen cap from her pocket and clamped it down tight about her head. 'That is why I came out. To look for you.' Gnathad shuffled nervously, scraping a wound into the mud surface of the *lis*. 'I was talking with Muirne, the girl in the roundhouse who has a baby. She made me think of you.'

Bodhmhall nodded, wondering where the girl was leading to.

'She says that you are a healer, a potion maker. She says you gave her a draught, a sleeping draught that made her sleep.'

'Yes,' said Bodhmhall carefully.

'Can you make potions to sleep forever? With no pain?' She looked away in embarrassment. 'Forgive me, Bodhmhall. It shames me to ask but this … this is for Cumann and my children. I do not want them taken by the *fian*.'

Bodhmhall stared at her with a freezing heart.

But she had no words to say.

Chapter Eight

Liath Luachra floated up to consciousness on a bitter wave of nausea and a headache that felt as though she'd been hit with a club. The physical sensations were familiar, of course. She'd had bad hangovers in the past but this would surely qualify as one of the more painful.

Peeling her eyelids apart, she attempted to make sense of the blur that materialised before her. When her eyes finally cleared she could see that she was in the cavern, lying on a fur blanket that stank of wood smoke, stale sweat and other, more objectionable, body odours. A few paces away, seated on a curved rock between her feet and the cave entrance, Aodhán was wrapped in an unfamiliar fur cloak, presumably obtained from one of the dead warriors. Preoccupied with the task of reattaching a pointed metal head to the haft of a javelin, he hadn't noticed her come to her senses.

'Aodhán,' she croaked.

The *óglach* raised his head and glanced towards her.

'How long?'

'You've been in dark sleep all night and all morning. The sun has already passed its peak.'

Liath Luachra cursed.

It was sheer will power that got her up. Ignoring the pounding in her head and the brewing clouds of nausea, she pushed herself off the rough blanket and onto her feet. Despite the effort, it actually felt better once she was upright, although her entire body trembled. Stumbling on shaky legs towards the mouth of the cavern, she stood and gripped the rock wall for support as she inhaled the cool, fresh air and peered outside.

It was another grey day, cloudy but fresh. It wasn't too cold and, to her immense relief, it wasn't raining. A short distance in front of the cave entrance the rocky depression lay empty and forlorn in the muted sunlight. There was no sign of the warriors or the Tainted One and with the numbing effects of the hangover she could almost have convinced herself that the events of the previous day had never happened, that it had all been some twisted dream.

Stepping outside, she padded swiftly forwards and allowed the downward momentum to carry her into the rocky hollow where the standing stone was located. From this central point, it was possible to see that the depression was not a natural feature as she'd originally assumed but had been hand carved out of the rocky surface. She considered the standing stone with fresh reverence, wondering at the effort it must have taken the Old Ones to set it there in the first place. Despite the fractured upper section, the monolith was still more than a head taller than her. The granite surface was smooth to the touch, sanded down by wind and rain over the ages. Traces of the spiral patterns that would have once coated the entire rock remained, but they were faint and coated in parts by tufts of moss or lichen.

The scuffle of leather soles on rock made her turn. Aodhán had joined her and was standing behind her, filling the space with his mute presence. She stared numbly at the young warrior for there seemed to be something different about him, a new sense of self-assurance behind his habitual competence. All of a sudden it struck her. He had grown up. He had become a man.

'Where did you drag them?'

Silently, the *óglach* pointed to a nearby break in the tree line.

Liath Luachra grunted and started in that direction.

She found the bodies just a few paces inside the forest, strewn like tumbled lumber amongst the damp grass and scrub. In death, they looked smaller than she remembered, but then her memory was, understandably, hazy after the quantity of *uisce beatha* she'd consumed.

A full flask. I'm fortunate to be breathing the fresh air of a new day.

The two warriors sprawled beneath a thick holly tree, half obscured by the shadow thrown down by the branches. In the half-dark, the ugly faces appeared even more repellent, contorted with those facial tattoos and blackened lips that made them look like apparitions from an exceptionally evil nightmare. One of them had gone so far as to file his teeth down to jagged points to make his appearance all the more terrifying. Liath Luachra made to shake her head in disgust but the ripple of pain that shot through her head stopped her before she'd completed the action.

A small patch of dried blood had formed beneath one of the warriors. Despite the cold, it had already attracted the interest of ants although the insects had yet to start feasting on the open wounds. The nose and ears of the nearest warrior looked as though they'd been nibbled on during the night. A fox, she guessed. Possibly a rat.

Leaving the warriors, she moved to examine the third body which had been dumped a little further into the trees.

Because of the shadows, the Tainted One could have been mistaken for a pile of bones wrapped in a ragged blanket. It was only as you got closer that it became identifiable as a body. You could also have been forgiven for assuming it to be someone's ancient grandfather at first, some old man quietly passed away in the middle of the forest.

Until you looked at the face, of course.

Then, with its sewn-up mouth and empty eye sockets, it looked like nothing so much as a vile, unnaturally large, rag doll.

She stared down at the spindly legs poking out from beneath the dirt-stained robe and wondered how the creature had ever managed to stand upright. Studying the Tainted One's corpse through slitted eyes, teeth tight against the throb in her skull, she found that the sight prompted strong feelings of hatred and revulsion. Despite her triumph, she still felt beaten, sickened at what he had been able to do to her. Was that insult redressed, she asked herself. Was this really a victory?

But she already knew the answer to that.

'What should we do Grey One?'

Aodhán at her shoulder again. The *óglach*, understandably, was growing impatient, keen to return home to protect his family. She looked up at the sky, pale grey patches through the prickly green leaves of holly. Her stomach still churned, they'd lost most of the day and they'd have to camp overnight in the Great Wild on the way back but, like Aodhán, she felt an overpowering need to leave this haunted place.

'We return to Ráth Bládhma. We've achieved what we set out to do.'

'Will you be able to run?' Aodhán eyed her uncertainly.

Her response was a glare. Her chin set in a stubborn line.

The *óglach* shrugged.

'You did well, Aodhán.'

He looked at her in surprise, unaccustomed to such unguarded praise from the stern warrior woman.

'Listen, carefully,' she continued. 'What do you hear?'

Curious, the *óglach* cocked his head to one side and listened as he stared around the glade. After a moment, he shook his head. 'Nothing,' he said. 'Nothing but the wind in the trees. The call of the thrush.'

Liath Luachra nodded. 'Exactly The wildlife has returned, Aodhán. If nothing else, we have made this little corner of the world a safer place.'

***

180

They had to stop twice for Liath Luachra to throw up on the way back. The first time wasn't long after leaving the Tainted One's campsite. Stirred and jiggled by the physical action of running, the contents of her stomach refused to stay down and she abruptly spewed up off the side of the trail. Bent over, one hand grasping the bark of a large oak for support, she was grateful that she'd tied her hair up with a leather thong as the last involuntary spasms racked her body and vomit dripped from her mouth. Gasping for breath, she considered the expelled material, surprised to recognise hard tack from the previous day and even traces of the porridge that Bodhmhall had made prior to their departure from Ráth Bládhma.

The second time she threw up wasn't much further along the trail but at least, on this occasion, little else came up except bile. She was also able to keep down the water that she swallowed afterwards.

Travelling north-east, they made poor time because of Liath Luachra's condition. Locating a series of deer trails, however, they managed to avoid the worst of the rough terrain and by mid-day they reached the marshy land of Guada. Here, they stopped to rest and eat strips of smoked venison and blood cakes. Liath Luachra was relieved to find she was able to keep everything down.

On the far side of Guada, they regained the thick forest and although, at one point, they encountered a small pack of four wolves, the animals did not attempt to harass them. In the rough land of Catrach, the pair scrambled up a small, tree-coated hill, bashing their way through thick briars to reach the crest that offered them their first open view of the land ahead of them. Unfortunately, the low, forest-coated Bládhma hills far to the north were still not visible.

After taking a brief moment to rest, they continued their journey, pausing only to quench their thirst at a tree-shrouded glen with a wide stream that flowed in from the West. Throwing themselves down onto the bank, the two travellers drank deep, Aodhán plunging his sweaty head into the freezing water to refresh himself at the same time. The *óglach* still had his head immersed in the water when Liath Luachra tapped him urgently on the shoulder. Raising his head, he stared at her with a quizzical expression as rivulets of water trickled down his face.

Without speaking, she pointed towards the middle of the watercourse where a grey rag was bobbing gently downstream, a red patch of blood visible on its surface. The *óglach* looked at her then both simultaneously turned their eyes upstream to the moss-coated boulders marking the waterway's entry point to the glen.

'The *fian*?'

The woman warrior stared longingly towards the north then responded with a weary shrug. It was a detour she did not need but they could not return to Ráth Bládhma without identifying the source of the bloody rag.

'We will have to see.'

They traced the stream back to where it curved through the boulders then proceeded onwards, into the woods. Although not familiar with the local topography, Liath Luachra suspected the watercourse originated from a hillside spring some distance away. With the recent bad weather, this would have merged with several other tributaries draining rainwater from the higher ground. The cloth could have originated from any one of these but she didn't think it would have travelled far. The stream was littered with fallen trees and brambles and it would not have taken long for the cloth to snag in one of these.

Keeping the stream to their left, they advanced through the forest, taking time to survey the ground ahead of them for any sign of movement. Fortunately, the deluge of the previous day now worked in their favour for the ground underfoot was still saturated in places, the soggy dead leaves and debris dampening any sound from their footsteps.

The dark forest stretched away in a semi-circle of infinite tunnels formed by the shadowed oak trunks and the slender branches spreading overhead like the rafters of a great hall. The space between the trees was relatively uncluttered by scrub, nevertheless they moved slowly, keeping to the shadows.

This precaution proved fortuitous a little while later when they stopped and crouched to confer in an almost silent whisper. Liath Luachra was just about to rise to her feet again when a figure suddenly emerged from the trees, thirty paces to the southeast.

The travellers froze.

There was a distinct aura of lethality in the newcomer's demeanour. A tall man, he was clad in leather and furs that bore the trace of recent bloodstains. He carried no weapon in his hands but there was a nasty-looking hand-axe tucked into the waistband of his leggings. A forehead engraved with those disquieting tattoos marked him as an associate of the Tainted One's bodyguards.

The newcomer halted abruptly, staring straight ahead at the point where they were squatting. Unsure whether the warrior had spotted them or not, the woman warrior's hand tightened about the hilt of her sword. She tensed, poised to snatch it from its sheath and attack when he suddenly, and very unexpectedly, pulled his trousers down and yanked out his penis. Liath Luachra stared in shock as a watery arc sprang out before him, glinting dully in the fading light.

Hearts pounding, they watched in silence as the warrior urinated, oblivious to their presence. Finally, to their immense relief, he finished, grunted, and turned on his heel, disappearing back into the trees from where he'd first emerged.

The two Ráth Bládhma warriors looked at each other, too shaken to speak. Recovering from the shock, they quickly hurried after the warrior. With the fading daylight, the shadows continued to thicken but they were able to keep him in sight, a darker patch moving through the grey wisps ahead of them.

After a short distance, the warrior took a steep path that descended into a very narrow gorge heavily clogged with fern and holly and, further in, with a thick copse of oak. Here, Liath Luachra and Aodhán paused, unwilling to proceed further for fear of being trapped within the tight confines of the cliffs on either side. The *óglach* looked at Liath Luachra, his face pale and sweating.

'Stay here!' she mouthed.

Moving forwards, she skirted the entrance and proceeded along the cliffs to the left. Despite the deepening darkness, she kept several paces from the lip to avoid being seen from below. It wasn't long before the sounds of a large body of people reached her ears: heavy blundering noises, the clatter of metal and wood, the murmur of voices punctuated by an occasional guffaw or coarse laughter. A moment later, she caught the first trace of wood smoke and the smell of roasting meat.

She grudgingly conceded that the *fian* had chosen their campsite well. The narrow glen was not only close to a supply of fresh water, but its position and depth meant that it was well protected from the prevailing wind and impossible to detect unless – as was the case with Liath Luachra and Aodhán – it was stumbled upon.

Further along the cliff top, the vegetation cleared. Dropping to her stomach, she wriggled closer to the edge and looked down to catch her first glimpse of the gorge's occupants. Her heart sank as she counted five – no six – campfires. Large clusters of men had gathered about the fires, many of them packed tightly together within the confined space, lying with limbs overlapped like a tangle of murky tree roots. A wordless growl of frustration rose in the back of her throat as she looked over the shifting mass of bodies. She hadn't seen so many warriors together in one place since the old days, a period she'd thought behind her forever. As far as she could tell, the warriors were all part of the same group as the Tainted One's bodyguards for they looked similar: dark-haired, dark eyed, filthy faces layered with those terrifying tattoos and scars. Most looked to be heavily armed for there were numerous spears, javelins, short metal swords and axes gleaming in the light of the fires. She also saw a number of circular, black coloured shields interspersed amongst the bodies and vegetation.

The single most disturbing aspect about the gathered warriors was their personal ornamentation. Many of them wore necklaces which looked to have been made from human teeth or ears, although at this distance it was difficult to be sure.

One fierce looking warrior, situated by the trees almost directly below her, had somehow convinced or coerced his comrades to pull back from the fire to give him some space. This hardy individual was standing stark naked despite the cold, revealing a torso coated in black tattoos and hands dyed bright red to the elbow. He appeared to be performing some strange kind of ritual dance, breathing in noxious fumes from a bowl in his left hand as he swayed back and forth to some internal rhythm that only he could hear.

As Liath Luachra watched, she saw him cease his dance and reach down and tug some meat from one of the bubbling pots. It was only as he raised it to his mouth that she realised he was holding -

A human hand!

A stream of nausea ripped through her as she saw him tear off a chunk of flesh with his teeth. Unable to watch, she scuttled desperately backwards, despite the risk of being heard. Twisting around, she slithered back into the brambles and scrub deep within the trees and, shuddering, grasped the rough solidity of a nearby pine. Hugging onto the rough bark until it hurt, she struggled to control her panicked wheeze.

Corpse Gnawers. Flesh Eaters.

For the first time in her life, Liath Luachra felt the bitter stab of despair, of complete and utter hopelessness. Like the Tainted One, such men were lost, beyond salvation of any kind.

And they were coming to Ráth Bládhma.

***

The Ráth Bládhma warriors passed a restless night camped as far from the *fian* as they could safely travel in the dark. Uncomfortable and distressed by what they'd learned, sleep did not come easily and was intermittent at best throughout the dark hours.

They broke camp before dawn, eager to get as much distance as possible between themselves and the *fian* and to alert the settlement to the approaching threat. They travelled quickly, unhindered by a hangover on this occasion, and much more familiar with the territory they were traversing. Despite their progress, Liath Luachra could not shake off the sense that they were travelling too slowly. The burden of what she'd seen in the *fian*'s camp the night before weighed her down in a spiritual, if not a physical, sense.

It was late afternoon before the hills of Bládhma appeared in view. When they finally neared the *ráth*, they were strung out from their encounter with Tóla at the entrance to Glenn Ceoch. Desperate to reach the settlement, they'd been hurrying along the path below the southern ridge when the Seiscenn Uarbhaoil warrior had lurched out of the bush, alarming them with a high-pitched, blood-curdling scream. Their panicked reaction had greatly amused him. Delighted with his joke, he'd ignored their curses and laughed harshly as he disappeared back into the trees.

The two travellers found the *ráth* locked up tight as they drew close, the entrance barricaded, the livestock already interned and no sign of activity on the ramparts. At the outer edge of the causeway, they halted in shock, confronted by a pair of poles that had been set into the ground. Both bore a human head, impaled from the neck up and stained with drips of blood. Liath Luachra stared at them in alarm, recognising the distinctive patterns of the *fian* warrior tattoos. She looked to Aodhán who shrugged, evidently just as bewildered as her.

They were still examining the heads when Bearach and Cónán appeared on the gateway rampart and a series of delighted yells shattered the silence of the valley. The two brothers disappeared from sight but Liath Luachra could hear the distant scuffle as they descended to the *lis* to dismantle the gateway barrier. Moments later, they were outside, running across the causeway to launch themselves on their comrade and sibling.

Aodhán was understandably delighted to see his brothers, particularly the younger Cónán, and returned their embrace with enthusiasm. The warrior woman attempted a smile but despite the joyous welcome she was too dispirited to feel any real elation at their homecoming. Deflecting the boys' most effusive questions, she advanced onto the causeway only to be confronted by the sight of Fiacail mac Codhna arriving out through the gateway. The big warrior stopped in his tracks when he saw them, his demeanour stiff and strained as he regarded them both.

'I see you, Liath Luachra.'

'I see you, Fiacail mac Codhna. You do not seem overjoyed by our safe return.'

'I did not expect you back,' the Seiscenn Uarbhaoil man admitted.

There was an awkward silence as the two warriors eyed each other. Eventually, Liath Luachra relented and tossed her head towards the nearest post. 'These heads. This is your doing?'

'Yes,' confirmed Fiacail and from his tone she could tell that he was pleased with his handiwork. 'Two scouts from the *fian* come to spy on the defences and report back to their masters. Now, they report back a message that we see fit to convey.'

Liath Luachra considered the two heads once more. Under normal circumstances she would have been infuriated by such presumptive actions from a guest but she was too tired to feel any real emotion. Besides, she reasoned, it had to be acknowledged that these were not normal circumstances and Fiacail had protected the *ráth* during her absence. 'This may provoke their wrath?' she said at last.

He shrugged. 'I have found that in times of fear and doubt, it can be effective to act obnoxious or bold. It makes people think twice about confronting you.'

'Then you must be constantly terrified.'

His expression darkened. 'Maybe you should ask their opinion,' he suggested, tossing one thumb towards the two heads.

'We can ask their comrades,' she said quietly. 'The *fian* are close. They will be in Glenn Ceoch the day after tomorrow.'

That shut the Seiscenn Uarbhaoil man up. He looked at her and, for just a moment, she saw her own fear reflected back at her. Then, as suddenly as it had appeared, the expression was gone, smothered beneath a beatific smile. Fiacail was Fiacail once more; grinning, scoffing, irrepressible as ever.

'Yes, we know. They are following the trail left by some refugees from Ráth Dearg.'

'Cathal ua Cuan's people?' The news took Liath Luachra by surprise.

'The very same. They came in a few days ago. As did a group from Coill Mór with Cónán this morning. They'd found tracks of *fian* scouts sniffing around their settlement so they timed their departure well.' He grinned. 'The *ráth* now has a substantial defensive force to call upon. Twelve fighters, by my reckoning. That includes Cathal ua Cuan, the four Coill Mór men, my Seiscenn Uarbhaoil contingent and your own Ráth Bládhma defenders.'

'There are forty-three of them,' she said. 'I counted. Three times.'

Once again, her words acted like a blow to his good spirits. He laughed, but to her ears, the laughter sounded strained, the threat dragging his humour down.

'When they carry out a full scale attack on the *ráth,*' said Aodhán, keen to make his own contribution, 'we will not be able to fight them off. Even twelve fighters are not enough to repel that many warriors.'

The tall man rubbed his chin, dragging finger nails through the thickening stubble. Finally he looked from the *óglach* to the woman warrior. 'Well, aren't you the pair with dry balls,' he muttered. 'Sprinkling misery on everyone's spirits.'

Liath Luachra returned his glare without expression. She'd had her fill of talk. At that moment, all she wanted to do was enter the *ráth,* find Bodhmhall and rest.

'Liath Luachra!'

The call drew her attention to the gateway where the *bandraoi* had suddenly appeared, an expression of immense relief spread across her features. She rushed across the causeway to grasp the woman warrior by the shoulders.

'Liath Luachra! And Aodhán! I did not dare hope and now –' Overcome by emotion, she was unable to finish the sentence. She stared at her *conradh,* the smile fading in confusion at the flat and listless response. 'The Tainted One,' she asked. 'Is it not –'

'Dead. But we are not safe. The *fian* are coming. They will be here the morning after tomorrow. Their trail follows the longer path from Ráth Dearg. Aodhán and I took the steeper Searc Beag path to gain a day on them.'

The news struck Bodhmhall hard for her face paled, stark against the raven darkness of her hair. She clutched anxiously at the stone pendant about her neck but, despite her evident trepidation, she recovered quickly, her voice remarkably composed when she spoke again.

'We'd assumed they would follow the refugees from Ráth Dearg.' The *bandraoi* frowned and bit her lower lip. 'But to have our fears confirmed adds unwelcome substance to them. Is there any chance that ...?' Her voice trailed off as she saw the bleak expression on the Grey One's face.

Liath Luachra quietly shook her head. Bodhmhall was hoping against hope that the *fian* would not locate them but it was not something she could reassure her of, no matter how much she wanted to. The Grey One cleared her throat, wondering how to break the news of what she'd seen in the gorge the previous evening. Before she could speak, Fiacail stepped forward, pushing himself into the conversation.

'There are issues of consequence that we need to discuss. The people are gathering and will seek clear direction.'

Liath Luachra glanced at him in surprise.

'We have called an assembly,' Bodhmhall explained. 'The people are coming together within the *lis*, even as we speak. That is why the *ráth* has been secured so early.'

The warrior woman nodded and turned to Cairbre's three sons who were standing alongside, listening in with evident interest. 'Aodhán, go in with your brothers. Get them to give you some food. Bodhmhall and I need to confer with our guest.' She emphasised the last word for Fiacail's benefit, a gentle reminder of his status at the settlement.

The *óglach* glowered, clearly resenting the fact that he was being dismissed with his younger brothers. Nevertheless, he did as he was asked.

When the boys had disappeared inside, Fiacail quickly got to the point. 'Our predicament worsens.' He looked briefly at Liath Luachra as though she were somehow responsible then directed his full attention to Bodhmhall. 'There are over forty warriors arching on us. The fate of Ráth Bládhma lies in your hands, Bodhmhall. People want to know what fate awaits them.'

188

With that, he paused. A deep but intense silence stretched between the warrior and the *bandraoi*. Liath Luachra looked from one of them to the other, unsure of the meaning behind those words but sensing the stress they caused Bodhmhall. Reaching over, she placed a hand on the *bandraoi's* arm. 'We should leave. We should release the cattle, pack whatever we can tonight and head into the Great Wild at first light tomorrow.'

The *bandraoi* held her gaze. She seemed to have aged several years since the warrior woman had last seen her, a mere three days earlier. Some of that was fatigue and tension, of course. But there was more to it than that. Her eyes seemed to have had lost their lustre, their usual erudite confidence. Instead, she looked burdened. And sad, so very terribly sad as she slowly shook her head. 'I have had this conversation with Fiacail. There is nowhere else to go. Nowhere we can take the refugees.'

She looked at each in turn then turned to stare at the tattooed head on the pole beside her, the mouth hanging open, the eyes wide and vacant. 'Our options continue to dwindle,' she said in a low voice. 'Cairbre was right.'

'There is Seiscenn Uarbhaoil,' insisted Fiacail. Again he looked at her with an intensity that seemed at odds with the simplicity of his words.

'The children will never make it to Seiscenn Uarbhaoil. I will stay and fight.'

Liath Luachra looked at her in surprise. 'If it is your intention to stand and fight then we must develop a plan to undermine the *fian's* advantage in numbers.'

Fiacail gave a scathing laugh. 'And how would you propose achieving that?'

The woman warrior didn't appreciate his belligerent manner but she was too deflated to argue the point. Instead, she settled for a shrug. 'Skirmishers. Two or three warriors placed on the outside to split their forces.'

Fiacail considered the possibility. 'Yes,' he admitted grudgingly. He kicked idly at a clod of earth to send it tumbling into the ditch. 'It's possible they could be provoked, somehow. Perhaps a proportion of them could be drawn away from the *ráth*. And I like the idea of being proactive. Waiting inside the *ráth* for them to attack at their leisure does not sit well with me.'

'Sit well with you? Running for Seiscenn Uarbhaoil with your tail between your legs, the subject is hardly going to be a matter for your concern.'

Fiacail frowned and scratched his forehead. 'There has … There has been a rethinking. My men and I will remain.'

Gods!

Liath Luachra stared. Bodhmhall, however, beamed at the big man with heartfelt gratitude. 'Fiacail, I …'

'Did you really think,' he said awkwardly, 'that I could just walk away and leave you to your fate?' Fiacail shuffled self-consciously and looked away.

'Yes,' said Liath Luachra, before the *bandraoi* had a chance to respond.

Fiacail scowled. 'Were it just you, Liath Luachra, I would have run away, cheering. Waving a banner and telling all I met of my happy news.'

The woman warrior tensed but Bodhmhall stepped between the two, physically separating them. 'Enough,' she warned, some of the old fire glowing in her eyes. She reached forward and put a hand on Fiacail's shoulder.

'I cannot lie and say your support is not very welcome, Fiacail but -'

'Just accept the offer as it is gifted, Bodhmhall,' he interrupted, his stance surprisingly rigid. 'Freely given. Without condition. Let us discuss it no further.'

Liath Luachra continued to watch the Seiscenn Uarbhaoil man with suspicion, resenting his evident closeness with Bodhmhall. Despite her glare, Fiacail ignored her until he was ready to return to practical matters.

'I agree that the idea of skirmishers has merit. But their exposure would be a concern. The woods on either side of the valley are not deep and bank up onto steep cliffs. Places of concealment will be limited. Skirmishers would be hard pressed to escape any structured pursuit.'

With this, he turned to look back at the embankment and its upper layer of pilings, assessing the force of fighters needed to hold it. 'The *ráth* would need to maintain a sufficiently strong defending force but we could get Tóla or Ultán and one of your *óglachs* …'

'No,' said Liath Luachra.

Unaccustomed to interruption, Fiacail's eyes narrowed. 'What?'

'I would go out.'

'You are *conradh* of the *ráth*.'

'I am also the logical choice. I know this valley, every hiding place, every nook and cranny and the surrounding territory better than anyone else. The raiders would not be able to corner me.'

At first.

'Besides', she added. 'I am relatively certain your men would not follow my instructions without your leave.'

The warrior looked at her grimly then nodded, acknowledging the truth of what she was saying. 'If you are Out who will lead the defence of the *ráth*?'

'That will be Bodhmhall's decision. If it is truly your intention to remain then my counsel is that you fulfil that role.' She glanced at the *bandraoi.* 'What say you Bodhmhall?'

The bandraoi nodded slowly. 'Your battle expertise would be welcomed, Fiacail. We have none at Ráth Bládhma apart from Liath Luachra who could do this.'

'Very well. In that case, I accept.' He nodded grimly before glancing sideways at the silent warrior woman. 'To relinquish your command to a more seasoned fighter. That is wise, Liath Luachra.'

'Do not flatter yourself. These are perilous circumstances. And, as Bodhmhall says, our options are limited.'

The Seiscenn Uarbhaoil man's eyes glowered but he kept his temper reined in. 'Who would accompany you as skirmisher?' he asked, his voice low and tight.

'Bearach.'

Fiacail was surprised. 'Not Aodhán? I would have thought him more experienced.

'I've spent more time Out with Bearach. He moves with greater comfort in the forest than his brother. Besides, when the *fian* attack, blooded men will be needed on the walls to oppose them. Aodhán's eye and hand are lethal. It would be wise to place him on the gateway with the javelin rack. From there he can cover the causeway.'

Fiacail did not look convinced. 'He is a good caster.'

'He is the best I've ever seen. And I have seen many casters.'

'And how many javelins do you have in that rack?'

'Fifteen.'

'I see. So if he casts each javelin with complete precision that will still leave twenty-eight opponents.'

Liath Luachra gave an infuriated glare but he raised his hand to pre-empt the inevitable retort.

'I do not mock you, Grey One. I can understand how such a defence might work with small groups of raiders but this is a seasoned battle band. These men lust for the kill and intend to sate that lust with Ráth Bládhma blood. There are too many of them and javelin casts from a single man will not stop such a horde, no matter how good he is.'

She shrugged again, her fatigue smothering any urge to bite at Fiacail's response. She looked instead to Bodhmhall who had remained uncharacteristically withdrawn throughout most of the exchange. 'You have nothing to say, Bodhmhall? You are *Taoiseach* of this settlement, after all.'

The *bandraoi* brushed the question aside with a brief gesture of her hand. 'We will discuss such details later. At the moment, the people await us.'

Her eyes came to rest on Liath Luachra and she regarded the woman warrior with unsettling intensity. 'When the talk and the feasting is over, when you have eaten and rested, I would have words of consequence with you, *a rún.*'

Liath Luachra returned her stare and, despite the fatigue, the despair and the grief, she suddenly knew the worst was yet to come.

***

When they entered the *lis*, Liath Luachra stopped in surprise, shaken by the sheer number of people within the *ráth*. At first glance, including the children, she estimated there were at least twenty to twenty-five people gathered. Most of these were huddled about the central fire-pit which was now blazing with a freshly laid fire. Above it, hoisted on a metal crane was the iron cauldron from which a mouth-watering smell emerged.

Reluctant to talk any further, the woman warrior hurriedly veered to the right, leaving Bodhmhall and Fiacail to drift off to the left where a small number of fighting men had congregated. Moving close to the embankment wall, she circled the *lis,* intent on achieving the refuge of her roundhouse. Close to one of the lean-tos, however, she was intercepted by Bearach, eyes bright with excitement from the uncustomary activity and, of more immediate interest to Liath Luachra, holding a bowl of hot stew in his right hand.

Seeing the warrior woman's eyes fix on the steaming bowl, Bearach handed it to her with a grin. She began to eat right there, standing without ceremony beside the lean-to as she shovelled the warm meat broth into her mouth.

She finished the bowl and, with a sigh, closed her eyes to enjoy the physical sensation of warm food resting snugly in her stomach. After a moment she opened her eyes and released a satisfied belch.

The boy's grin widened. 'Aodhán told me of your adventures. I knew you'd be hungry but that you'd want to avoid the company so I convinced my mother to give me some food for you.'

'Thank you, Bearach. That was thoughtful.'

'I also know you enjoy your solitude at such times so I will not stay to disturb you.'

'Good.' She nodded and made to step around him but he hadn't finished.

'Except to say that should you need me I stand ready.'

She nodded again, this time decidedly more abruptly.

'All you need to do is call my name. I will come at a run.'

The woman warrior frowned and was about to berate him when the boy suddenly started to giggle and shake with laughter. Despite her poor humour, she could not prevent the grin that cracked the corners of her lips.

'Little bandit. I missed your stupid jokes out in the Great Wild.'

'Will you take me?' he asked eagerly. 'The next time you go.'

The humour slid from Liath Luachra's face.

'Yes,' she said hoarsely.

***

She had intended to head directly to her roundhouse to sleep but impressed by the rareness of such a large gathering, Liath Luachra decided instead to remain and listen to the talk for a little while. She remained to the rear of the crowd, inconspicuous beside the sloping lean-to. From there, she studied the little crowd with curiosity.

Muirne Muncháem was there of course, up towards the front with her infant in her arms, desperate in case she should miss anything. Standing beside her were two heavily armoured men; two Coill Mór warriors she recognised from one of her visits to the settlement. Ber Rua, the grizzled, lanky leader of Coill Mór had moved forwards and was scaling one of the ladders to the rampart beside the stone gateway A tiny subset of *Clann Faoill*, Ber Rua would probably have led his tribe in a number of cattle raids on *Clann Baoiscne* back in his youth, long before leaving to establish his own colony in the Great Wild. Back in the more populated tribal lands, the different clans would generally have avoided each other. Out in the isolation of the Great Wild however, the limited resources and the need for trade and cooperation meant political directives were often ignored and interaction a lot more common.

That evening the settlement was enjoying a rare treat, dining off the meat of a dairy cow slaughtered and roasted over a spit next to the cauldron at the central fire pit. The beef was an extravagance. Bodhmhall, knowing that there was little likelihood of surviving beyond another two nights, had obviously decided that they might as well have one good last meal, to build up their strength and, at the very least, deprive the *fian* of one valuable prize.

Liath Luachra worked the blade of her sword with a whet stone while she watched Fiacail move onto the gatehouse to address the assembled refugees. Despite her cynicism, she had to admit that he presented a good spectacle. Tall, ruggedly handsome and charismatic, he had truly been blessed by the gods for he also had a natural flair for presentation. All in all, thought Liath Luachra, he would have made a great leader of men had it not been for his weakness of wandering around, tripping over his own cock.

As she watched, the *Seiscenn Uarbhaoil* man place himself at the edge of the gatehouse so that he could overlook the little crowd. Bodhmhall and Ber Rua now stood on either side of him, emphasizing the impression of united force.

It was a cold evening but somehow the tangible atmosphere of fear hanging in the air served to make it feel colder. Everyone knew that an attack was inevitable; the horror stories had already been spread by the survivors of the Ráth Dearg attack and the people were justifiably scared. Wrapped in cloaks, heads draped with long hoods, the little crowd puffed clouds of vapour into the air and looked longingly at the roasting meat as Fiacail made to speak.

'You all know I am not a man to beat about the bush so I will keep this simple. Our enemies will be here the day after tomorrow.'

A low mutter rumbled through the crowd.

'You all knew this was coming,' Fiacail continued, his voice carrying well in the still evening air. 'You knew that your safety here was temporary, just

194

as you knew the only option to fighting was to flee into the Great Wild where your demise, although more prolonged, would be no less inevitable.

The force arraigned against us is not insubstantial. I will not lie to you. Having said that, we have a number of advantages that they do not. Firstly, it is Ráth Bládhma who holds possession of all the food and shelter. The *fian* will have been marching for three days to get here. They will be cold, they will be tired and whatever food supplies they managed to obtain at Ráth Dearg will be near exhaustion.'

An image of rotten teeth gnashing around finger flesh flared unbidden in Liath Luachra's head. The woman warrior felt the bile rising in her throat and almost gagged but by focussing intently on the edge of her blade she managed to repress it.

'They will be looking for a quick victory. An easy victory. They anticipate no opposition. They will expect us to lie down while they sweep over us, overwhelm us in a single attack.'

He paused for dramatic effect.

'If they do not achieve that, if we as a group can fend off that initial attack, then I tell you without a taste of a lie, they will lose heart.'

Liath Luachra looked around the *lis*, surprised to see people nodding and firming their jaws in anger.

'If they attack a second time,' Fiacail continued, 'and we can hold them a second time, they will be in a desperate situation. They will be discouraged and most likely flee.'

He grew silent as he looked gravely down upon them.

'We are fighting for our lives but we *can* survive this challenge. We can survive but to do so you have to want to with all your heart and soul. Bodhmhall has asked me to lead the defence of Ráth Bládhma. This defence will not be easy so we will require every single able-bodied hand, every man, woman or child that can hold a weapon or a shield. Later, I will come around to you all individually, and tell you what I need you to do. For tonight, however, I want you to feast, to take strength from your loved ones, from your neighbours, from those that live and those that have died as a result of this attack.'

With that he turned away. The address was finished.

There were excited mutterings and discussions amongst those gathered as the three leaders descended to join them in the *lis*.

'Well that was lovely. Very rousing, I must say.'

195

Liath Luachra turned to find Cathal Ua Cuan standing beside her. The ancient warrior was holding an armful of split logs for the fire pits which he proceeded to dump inside the lean-to.

'You're not impressed.'

His response was a shrug. 'I've heard worse. Some battle leaders can blather on all day. They end up taking longer than the actual battle.'

'Why weren't you up there with the other *ráth* leaders?'

'I was asked to stay out of sight. Nobody needs to be reminded about the fate of my *ráth*.'

There was a strained silence.

'Fiacail's right about one thing,' said Liath Luachra, doing her best to sound optimistic. 'If the *fian*'s initial attack can be held off it will demoralise them.'

Cathal gave her a sarcastic glance. 'Of course! You're right. I don't know why we don't just charge out there now and take them on.' He snorted. 'Don't play games, girl. I've seen these devils up close. From what I've heard tonight, you've been lucky to survive two encounters with them but you know as well as I do that there's only one way this can end.'

Liath Luachra gazed at him stonily. She knew she had been lucky, exceptionally lucky up to this point. But she didn't need to be reminded of it.

The old man sighed. 'Mind you, if I succeed in hacking some vengeance for what those animals did to Ráth Dearg before they take me down, I'll obtain some satisfaction.'

'Can you fight then, old man?' she said, lifting the sword and examining the blade edge against the light of the fire.

The grizzled warrior returned her look, the wrinkles on his forehead converging to form a deep crease above his nose. 'I was fighting before you were even a grubby little notion in your pox-ridden father's head.' He glanced at the weapon in her hand. 'Do you have another sword I can wield?'

'We have no metal-worker at Ráth Bládhma. All our metal weapons have been handed out.' She paused as a sudden thought crossed her mind. 'I have a sling.'

'A sling.' Cathal turned and spat. 'Well, that's no good.'

'You're too good for a sling?'

'Nah! I've seen a sling kill a man, fair enough. It's these eyes. I can't see a target that's any way distant. My aim's all off. I could probably hit a tree if I aim at the forest.' He frowned. 'I couldn't guarantee it, mind.'

'We have javelins.'

'Same problem. I'm probably worse with javelins than with the sling.'

With an exasperated grunt, she bent down to pull a long chunk of wood from the woodpile and tossed it to him. 'Here.'

The old man reacted faster than she thought he would, plucking the wood out of the air with surprising ease. He weighed it in one hand.

'What's this supposed to be?'

'It's a club. With a little bit of work and imagination.'

'That'd take a damn-side more work than imagination.'

She ignored him. 'Fortunately you have another full day. The good thing about a club is you don't need good eyes. All you need to do is to get up close to your opponent and beat the shit out of him with it. Think you can handle that?'

With this, she turned and stalked away, the heat of his glare burning a hole in the small of her back.

***

Walking back towards her roundhouse, Liath Luachra could not shake the feeling she was losing control, that her world was unravelling about her. The crowd had responded well to Fiacail's words and the gift of food, demonstrating a surprising sense of vigour and aggrieved determination to fight and make the invaders pay dearly. She, however, felt no such inducement. She could not rid herself of the sight she'd seen in the dark woods and the threatening sense of evil continued to weigh on her shoulders.

At the entrance to the roundhouse, she stopped to look back around the little settlement, busy and crowded now, more so than she'd ever seen it before. Her heart felt heavy. In two nights time all these people would be dead.

To her relief, Cairbre and Conchenn's roundhouse was empty, all the refugees from Coill Mór out feasting on Bodhmhall's bounty. Her body seemed to weigh more than usual as she dropped onto the nearest sleeping platform, lying on her side and folding into a foetal position she hadn't used since childhood. Despite her fatigue, her fears kept sleep infuriatingly at bay and she lay there thinking about the past.

197

In previous battles, when faced with ferocious adversaries, there had always been sufficient forces, clever ruses or strategic advantage that she could use to counter the strength of the opposition. Here, at Ráth Bládhma, there was nothing. She had nothing.

Back then, she realised, there had also been another important difference. She'd been a different person, a brutal and ferocious killer who hadn't cared whether she lived or died. Now, that insane fighter was long gone, grown soft and domesticated, attached to people and things she did not want to lose.

Her lips curled in an unconscious snarl as she vented her resentment at the person she'd become. She needed the killer back, she realised. Without the savagery and violence of the old Liath Luachra, she – and Ráth Bládhma – did not stand a chance.

**

Somehow she must have drifted off for she awoke to the sensation of fingertips against her cheek. Opening her eyes, she looked up to find Bodhmhall bent over her, stroking her face. With a groan, she reached up and grasped the *bandraoi*'s fingers, pulling them close to her lips to kiss them fiercely. An unfamiliar scent hit her nostrils.

'You've been making remedies.'

'Yes.'

'It is not a smell I recognise.'

'It is not a draught I usually care to make.' The *bandraoi* bundled up her hair. And the topic with it. 'Enough of me. How do you feel?'

'Refreshed. But still tired. I could sleep a little longer.'

'I'm not surprised. It is not yet midnight.'

The Grey One squinted at her with one uncomprehending eye.

'I regret waking you when you need the rest,' the *bandraoi* continued. 'But there are matters of importance we need to discuss.'

Liath Luachra sat up, wiped her eyes with the back of her hand and looked around, surprised to find the dwelling empty except for the two of them.

'I asked those who were tired to sleep in our roundhouse,' the *bandraoi* said, reading her expression. 'Or to remain outside until we had spoken.'

The woman warrior cast her a curious glance but said nothing. Swinging her feet off the sleeping platform, she crouched by the fire pit and splashed water from a bowl onto her face. She took her time washing. Something in the *bandraoi*'s demeanour alarmed her and every instinct was urging her to shirk further communication.

'*A rún*, there is a task I would place on you. A task that will strain you to your limits, in every possible sense.'

Liath Luachra apprehensively reached for the red battle harness and pulled it on. She was unsure how to respond and, in the absence of any certainties, fell back on the structure of routine. In any case, it did not seem likely that there would be any further sleep that night. 'Name this task,' she said at last.

'I would have you escort Muirne and my nephew back to Dún Baoiscne.'

The warrior woman stiffened then turned to stare long and hard at the *bandraoi*. Flustered by the directness of that mute scrutiny, Bodhmhall struggled to compose herself. Although she remained seated on the sleeping platform, Liath Luachra could see how she dug her nails into the palms of her hands, a sure sign of disquiet.

'It is a miserable task to set you,' the *bandraoi* admitted quietly. 'But I have pondered on this for days and can think of no other alternative. If they remain here they will die. With *Clann Baoiscne*, at least, they have some hope of survival.'

Liath Luachra continued to stare at her, displaying no emotion at the *bandraoi*'s words. Contrary to most people, when she was surprised or shocked the woman warrior tended to grow increasingly still. It was a disquieting characteristic that Bodhmhall was all too familiar with for she shifted uneasily.

'I would also have you take Bearach and Cónán with you. And the eldest Coill Mór girls. They are the only ones that will be able to make the journey without slowing you down.'

Liath Luachra took a breath, holding her emotion in check. 'If I take Bearach and Cónán,' she said carefully, 'the *ráth* loses three defenders, three defenders that cannot be spared.

'Do you honestly believe three fighters will make a difference?'

'It might.'

'You were ever a poor liar, Liath Luachra. Despite Fiacail's brave words tonight, we both know we can't hope to survive the *fian*'s onslaught.'

'You say this and yet, you also tell me you intend to remain.'

'I cannot leave those who depend on me. Fiacail offers sanctuary at Seiscenn Uarbhaoil but the truth is few would survive such a journey. Cairbre and Conchenn are too old for such distances at this time of the year. Cairbre can barely walk in this weather as it is. Aodhán will not leave his parents.' She sniffed and rubbed her nose. 'He is a good boy,' she added softly. She raised her hands and briefly rubbed her eyes.

'The refugees from Coill Mór and Ráth Dearg will also remain. They have nowhere else to go. If they flee out to the Great Wild they will not survive for long without food or shelter. Like me, they would not be welcomed by *Clann Baoiscne*.'

'Those who stay will die.'

'Probably.'

'You will die.'

The *bandraoi* was silent. 'Most likely,' she said at last.

'And you are happy to send me away when you need me most?' She snorted. 'Your argument is flawed. The positions should be reversed.'

'That decision withers any joy I had, Liath Luachra. But it is my decision. You are the only one I can trust to guarantee my nephew's safety. His survival is essential. He is the future of *Clann Baoiscne*. He is more important than you or I or any other soul at Ráth Bládhma.'

'Not to me,' Liath Luachra countered bitterly. '*Clann Baoiscne* holds no importance for me. You are the only thing I care about.'

'But I am *Clann Baoiscne*. And *Clann Baoiscne* is me. Liath Luachra, if you truly care for me, for all that I hold dear, for all that I am, then you will do this for me.'

The warrior woman glared at her. 'This is shit!' she protested.

'No, this is fate.'

'Fate can stick its head up the arse of a poxy cow. I will not leave.'

'*A rún*, if you refuse then you condemn us all. On the night of my nephew's birth the Gift showed me there was a price to be paid, a blood sacrifice for his survival. Until now I'd always assumed that sacrifice was Muirne's alone but the price is much greater than that.'

'Such a price is no bargain. Walk away, Bodhmhall. Come climb the wall with me. Let the others face their fate and we will slip away in the darkness. I will protect you and keep you safe until we can find somewhere else to live in peace.'

The *bandraoi* shook her head solemnly. 'Do you truly believe I could live with myself after such an act?'

'This is …' The woman warrior struggled to speak, revealing the first true signs of anger. 'This is witless! Bodhmhall, you cannot ask me to do this. I'll have nothing in my life if you're not there.'

'Yes, you will. You'll have Bearach and Cónán to care for. And the *Coill Mór* girls. They will be your family now. They will need your support. As will my nephew. And Muirne, of course.'

'Muirne!' The woman warrior spat the name like a curse. 'Muirne! Muirne Muncháem has truly set the countryside aflame.'

'Even Muirne,' the *bandraoi* insisted. She has acted to save her child's life. Besides, she is just a pawn in the great scheme of things. As are we all. In a year's time, the sun will still rise in this valley every morning. Every night it will still sink again. This will never change and no-one will ever remember us. No-one will care.'

'I will care.'

The *bandraoi's* expression softened. '*A rún*, I would do anything in my power to spare you this but it must be done. You know that we've had more than our share of good fortune. Three years. Three glorious years that we have lived in peace, free of others who would constrain us or use us as chattels. If I died right now I would die grateful with the knowledge that I had, at least, these last three years with you.'

Liath Luachra's face contorted in silent rage as she attempted to assemble any argument, any emotional appeal that might make the *bandraoi* see sense. Deep in her heart, however, she knew the cause was already lost. Barely articulate at times, she could not hope to rival Bodhmhall's innate ability with words and reason. Looking at the *bandraoi's* determined gaze, it was also clear that Bodhmhall's mind was intractably set. Nothing Liath Luachra said, nothing Liath Luachra did, would divert her from the path she had fixed herself.

What hope is there now?

A wave of bleakness washed over the woman warrior. She felt a sudden, sinister coldness fill her heart, a growing nausea, a choking sensation that tightened about her throat.

And then it was there, that manic rage from the old days: viscous, cruel, and overpoweringly destructive. Fury washed over her like a powerful fever, blurring her vision with a bloody red haze, filling her head with white noise that sounded like distant screaming.

The *bandraoi* must have seen something for Liath Luachra saw her flinch. Bodhmhall stood and made to advance towards her but whatever flickered across the woman warrior's face made her stop and back away uncertainly.

Strained with a fury she could not vent, a desire for violence she feared to unleash, Liath Luachra lunged for the doorway. Pausing to snatch her weapons and her cloak from the floor, some instinct prompted her to glance over her shoulder to where the *bandraoi* stood terrified and wilted, staring at her with wide eyes.

'Liath Luachra,' she began. 'I –'

Without a word, the woman warrior plunged through the doorway.

***

The *lis* was still relatively busy. Cairbre, Ultán and a few of the Coill Mór warriors, wrapped in cloaks, chatted softly around the fire pit. The moon had disappeared behind the clouds however, so none of them saw the flicker of movement as she crossed to the gateway.

The barrier at the stone passage had been removed, the combined livestock driven outside, presumably for one last opportunity to feed before the *fian's* arrival prevented it. Atop the stone barrier, Tóla was on guard duty. Focussed on trying to spot anyone approaching the *ráth*, he did not notice her pass silently below and slip outside into the night.

A hundred paces from the *ráth*, Liath Luachra stopped and stood panting in the dark pasture, heart pounding, body sweating as though she'd run for days. With the sky obscured by heavy cloud she was completely blind, engulfed by a dense blackness that filled all space about her. She'd never known a night so dark and yet there was something comforting about that darkness, something … restful.

Gradually, she felt her heartbeat slow, her breathing ease. In the blinding black, there was no tinge of red and the sound of screaming ebbed away. It was, she felt, as though the darkness had suffocated the fury, snuffing its fire to a charred numbness.

Am I dead? I feel nothing.

Nothing.

She tried to make sense of it but no matter how she tried she couldn't get a grip on any particular emotion. Everything she smelled, everything she heard, everything she remembered, felt as though they were the sensations and memories of someone else. Someone she used to know.

She remained standing there for a long time for she did not know what to do. In her mind, she had no destination, no goal but to flee Ráth Bládhma. Even this was fruitless and pointless. In the darkened forest she would have no means of finding the path through the trees. If she did by some miracle locate it, she had no means of preventing herself from wandering off it again.

The simple truth was that she would, in all likelihood, become lost and spend the night curled up beside some shrub, shivering with the cold until dawn came and she could find her bearings again.

She didn't know when she'd started it but she suddenly realised she was walking again. In the darkness it was impossible to tell but she hoped that her natural sense of direction was guiding her west to the entrance of Glenn Ceoch.

After several hundred paces she stopped, startled to hear the distant sound of voices. Dropping to the ground, she paused and listened, her old martial instincts kicking in even if her mind was too numb to act.

Crawling on all fours, she moved through the damp, frosty grass in the direction from which the voices seemed to come. All of a sudden, the clouds cleared again and there, illuminated by the moonlight, less then fifteen paces away, she spotted Fiacail in the company of Ber Rua and Aodhán. All three were standing with their backs towards her, observing – and presumably guarding – the nearby herd of cattle. Frozen, she crouched lower in the grass, waiting for them to move so that she could continue on her way.

'Should we not bring them in soon?' she heard Aodhán ask the two older men.

The lanky Coill Mór man shook his head. 'Your *lis* won't be long stinking of cow shit with our combined herds. Besides, they won't have access to food once they're back inside the *ráth*. Best to let them eat their fill. They might be a long time inside.'

'I wouldn't think so,' murmured Fiacail, so softly Liath Luachra could barely hear him. 'The fate of the *ráth* will be decided within a single day. Probably in a single battle.'

Belatedly realising that the others were staring at him, he turned to face them, smoothening out this unintended gravity with an expansive grin. 'But there's little enough danger for another day at least. No point in us all losing a decent night's sleep.'

He jerked his head towards the *ráth*, which Liath Luachra could now make out as a dim outline against the meagre light of the internal *lis* fire. 'I'll remain on watch. I suggest you two take another beast back for the slaughter tomorrow morning. It'll strengthen the people's resolve and the smell of fresh meat alone will drive those *fian* warriors mad with hunger.'

'A man needs a belly of meat to fight,' agreed Aodhán, nodding gravely.

In the darkness, Liath Luachra rolled her eyes. One day a blooded warrior and already the *óglach* was spouting shite like every other thick brained fighter she'd ever known.

The clouds continued to clear so she crouched even lower in the grass as she watched Aodhán and Ber Run pass by, driving one of the cows ahead of them as they proceeded back to the settlement. When they were gone, her eyes returned to the Seiscenn Uarbhaoil man who continued to obstruct her route out of the valley. For a moment, she considered circling around him then realised that she'd have to make a significant detour to avoid disturbing the cattle. If the clouds closed in again, she would probably lose her way again and could end up blundering back into him.

To the dim, grey Gods with this!

Rising to her feet, she started walking directly towards the big warrior.

It took Fiacail a moment to hear the sound of her footsteps but, when he did, he swung about quickly, bringing a sharp-tipped spear to bear, level with her stomach. Recognising her, despite the gloom, he allowed the spear point to drop but he continued to stare at her. 'It must truly be the end of the world,' he said. 'If the Grey One weeps.'

Startled, Liath Luachra raised one hand to her face and found her eyes were damp, her cheeks streaked with tears. She stared in bewilderment at the wetness on her fingertips.

'I take it Bodhmhall's determined to stay, then,' continued Fiacail.

She stared voicelessly back at him.

He nodded to himself. 'Ah, yes. I thought as much.'

Somehow, the Seiscenn Uarbhaoil man's presence managed to rouse her when nothing else could. She could feel his voice poke the angers in her gut, stirring them to life again. 'Shit on your head, Fiacail,' she said in a dead voice. 'I will raise a drink in toast to your death.'

'Then drink deep, Grey One,' the big man said, unmoved by the insult. 'It should not be too long in coming.'

She brushed past him then. Intent on the distant shadow of the treeline she made three or four paces before a sudden thought caused her to spin about, the movement whipping the hem of her cloak with a muffled snap. 'Why do you stay?'

'What?' The big man blinked, blindsided by the question.

'Why do you stay to die at Ráth Bládhma? You have the option of sanctuary, of returning to Seiscenn Uarbhaoil.'

He peered at her for a moment, as though trying to work out where she was coming from with such a line of questioning. 'Because there is nothing else.'

Liath Luachra stared at him blankly. He returned her gaze with a soft chuckle.

'I do not expect you to understand, Grey One but the truth is I have no wish to return to Seiscenn Uarbhaoil. As an outsider, I was obliged to join in union with the daughter of the previous chieftain to cement my authority. That old fool was happy enough with the bargain. He had no sons to retain the land.'

He laughed sourly.

'But she, of course, is a pig. She has voice like a hoarse magpie and she wails at me incessantly. It is my intent to dissolve that union by not returning.'

'And yet you offered to bring Bodhmhall to Seiscenn Uarbhaoil.'

'I did. It was my intention to try and save her life. If Bodhmhall had agreed to come I would somehow have made the situation work.' He shrugged. 'But she knows her own mind, that woman. From your tears, I see her stubbornness has confounded you as well.'

Liath Luachra's face remained expressionless. By rights, she should have felt slighted by the comparison but now she found that she lacked any ability to care. 'That's no reason to stay. You could go to Dún Baoiscne. *Clann Baoiscne* would have you.'

'Of course they would. But they would only ever want me for my fighting arm. All I will ever be to *Clann Baoiscne* is Fiacail the Cock who is good in a fight. My ambitions grow beyond such limitations.' He laughed sourly. 'Do you know, I came here to Ráth Bládhma with aspirations of convincing Bodhmhall to return to Dún Baoiscne with me. With her help, I intended to make the role of *tánaiste* of *Clann Baoiscne* my own. And eventually lead *Clann Baoiscne* as *rí*.'

He grunted.

'Of course our *Cailleach Dubh* opened my eyes to that particular delusion. Bodhmhall knows me as I truly am. I probably could have been *rí* but I'd never have been a good one. I am too easily swayed by every ripe pair of buttocks that walk before me.' He laughed but it was a self-mocking laugh, cold and loaded with bitterness. 'I was only good when I was with Bodhmhall. There is not a day goes by that I regret not remaining with her.'

Liath Luachra stared, too dulled to respond with any true feeling. 'So you would prefer to throw your life away,' she said at last. 'Here at Glenn Ceoch.'

'If you give your life for a purpose you are not throwing it away.

'And remaining here has a purpose? What could it possibly offer you?'

'A battle. It may be a battle against ridiculous odds, it may be a battle to the death but oh, Liath Luachra. What a battle it will be!'

She regarded him with utter weariness. 'You will die.'

'Of course I will. But we all die at one point or another. In the end it is only the manner in which your name is remembered that counts. In the years to come, when people speak my name around the campfires they will remember me as Fiacail, Battler of Ráth Bládhma. Not Fiacail the Cock.' He paused for a moment and scratched his chin in thought. 'Maybe I will have a saga of my own.'

'And what of Ultán? And Tóla?'

Fiacail gave a tired shake of his head. 'Hah! This is their decision as much as it is mine. Ultán has never been the same since the passing of his wife. Now he himself is sickening from a growth in the stomach. He always knew this would be his last trip. He wishes to die with a sword in his hand.'

'And Tóla?'

'Tóla has no family, no loved one to return to.' Fiacail shrugged. 'The truth is no one likes Tóla. Seiscenn Uarbhaoil would express little regret if he did not return.'

Liath Luachra wrapped her cloak around herself and prepared to move on. 'You are a fool, Fiacail.'

'Perhaps. Perhaps not.' He appeared completely unperturbed by her disdain. 'In any case, you should clean that face of yours, Grey One. It will dishearten people to see the great Liath Luachra with tear streaks.' He grinned. 'No doubt it will also detract from that reputation of ruthlessness.'

'They won't see me.' She shrugged. 'Besides, who's going to know? They'll all be dead soon.'

She started to walk away.

'Liath Luachra.'

She turned to look back, surprised to find the Seiscenn Uarbhaoil man observing her with an uncharacteristically soft expression. 'If it is any consolation, you will find other ... other women that you can love. Other women you can feel attracted to. Those who - '

'You misunderstand, Fiacail,' she said, brusquely interrupting him.

'What do I misunderstand?'

'I feel no attraction to other women,' she said sadly. 'I have only ever loved Bodhmhall. But now, like you, she is already dead.'

Chapter Nine

It was fear as much as the cold that caused Bodhmhall to tremble. Although she knew this to be true, it did not prevent her from pulling the fur cloak tight about her shoulders, drawing the heavy folds closer.

It did not stop the shivering.

The *bandraoi* was crouched on the embankment just to the left of the gateway rampart. Here a crack in the pilings offered a safe vantage point from which to observe the terrain extending from the causeway to the woods at the base of the southern ridge without being observed in turn. This morning, unfortunately, that view was particularly restricted. A heavy mist had, once again, settled in over the valley, wisps and tendrils clinging to the surface and coiling about the *ráth* like an endless shoal of ghostlike eels.

As if we didn't have enough to contend with. The fates are truly against us.

In all, four of them were huddled below the ramparts about the gateway. As the central point of the *ráth's* resistance, Fiacail had insisted on maintaining a strong defensive capability there. Hence, his presence and that of the blooded warrior, Tóla. He had also taken Liath Luachra's advice and placed Aodhán beside the javelin rack above the entrance.

Bodhmhall, with her limited combat experience, was present not for fighting ability but because of her ability to detect the presence of life through the brume. In such a mist, that talent could prove critical when the *fian* finally made their presence known. With the Gift, Bodhmhall could alert them as to where the enemy was massing and from which direction they intended to launch their assault.

In addition to this role, Fiacail had also assigned the *bandraoi* the more physical responsibility of screening the gateway defenders from missile attacks. It was for this reason that she was hugging a wide, rectangular shield, her nerves causing her clasp it tighter than necessary. Constructed from a light wicker frame, it was stuffed with straw and overlaid with three layers of leather. Two straps had been worked into the side so that she could grip it at an angle when raised. Although not solid enough to impede a direct assault or a spear cast with force from a short distance, it would help to deflect any missiles coming in at an angle. It would also reduce the visibility of the Ráth Bládhma defenders, making it more difficult for the casters to target them effectively.

A similar defensive cluster had been placed at the eastern end of the *ráth* at the gap in the pilings. This consisted of Ber Mór and his wife Lí Bán, Ultán, a Coill Mór warrior, and Gnathad as their shield bearer. The two remaining Coill Mór warriors were situated at the apex of the curving northern and southern ramparts. If they came under pressure, they would be supported to the south by Fiacail's group and to the north by Ber Mór's.

All in all, it was a fragile line to hold back the great wave of anticipated warriors.

Because of their vulnerability on the ramparts, a reserve force had also been stationed at the centre of the *lis* to the side of the pens where the livestock were hemmed in tightly together. Under the command of Cathal ua Cuan, this particular group had responsibility for supporting the rampart defences, responding to any intrusion where a section of the rampart was in danger of being overwhelmed.

Although no expert in warfare, even Bodhmhall could tell that this reserve force was woefully inadequate for it consisted uniquely of Cairbre, Conchenn, and Cathal himself. With the exception of her *rechtaire*'s single short iron sword, none of the others were armed with metal weapons, obliged to make do with a club and a long spear. Bodhmhall clutched her stomach, feeling a sudden nausea at the thought of these frail elders attempting to oppose a swarm of violent and hardened warriors.

Bodhmhall winced, recalling the previous evening's Council of War. At some point over the course of the discussions, she'd argued strongly for making someone available to assist with the inevitable wounded that would result from the conflict. The stifled – almost embarrassed – silence of the warriors that followed her words had abruptly stilled that proposal. Only now could she see how naive she had been. They had no-one available to help the wounded. Indeed, during the forthcoming battle, there would be no opportunity to care for injuries. The fate of Ráth Bládhma and all who lived within it – wounded or not – would be decided in that very first assault.

She picked nervously at the hem of her skirt. One edge was already torn and threadbare from the repeated attention and she could feel the fear swell inside her, gnawing away at her courage. Her stomach felt bitter, her bladder heavy with a desperate urge to urinate despite having just relieved herself a short time earlier.

Utilising a technique learned during her training with the druidic order, Bodhmhall attempted to calm her mind, to free it of the mental images that threatened to overwhelm her. Bowing her head, she closed her eyes. Breathing in through her nose, she focussed on the physical sensation of air brushing against the inside of her nostrils as she drew up a memory: a pool of still, black water. The restful image was of a pond on the outskirts of Dún Baoiscne where she'd played as a child.

After a time, her mind slowed, the intrusion of physical distraction lessening although her senses remained alert. She felt herself grow calm and as she sank deeper into a more relaxed state she could feel the fear fall away from her.

Later, when she opened her eyes, she found she was thinking rationally again, despite a lingering sliver of anxiety that refused to go away. Holding her hands out in front of her, she was pleased to find that the shaking had ceased.

She shifted her position on the compressed earth of the embankment as she regarded her comrades. Beside her, Aodhán was repeatedly shifting a javelin from one hand to another. Every time the weapon changed hands, he wiped the palm of his free hand on the knees of his leggings.

Fiacail, conversely, looked as nervous as a block of granite. Sitting quietly with his back against the rampart, his eyes were closed as he sharpened the blade of one of his axes with a whetstone, using the sensation of touch alone to guide his actions. Despite his outward composure, Bodhmhall knew him well enough to know that his mind would be swirling with strategies and counter strategies, as he attempted to work through a counteraction for every assault the *fian* might launch at them.

Fiacail, she realised, had owned those axes for as long as she had known him. Both weapons were identical, long wooden handles with ornate carvings that extended up to a wide metal head. Bodhmhall had never seen him use them in combat but had frequently observed him during his regular practice sessions, noting the skill in which he swivelled one weapon in each hand in complicated but well-controlled arcs. Attached to his wrist by leather loops inset into the haft, he actually guided the blows by extending his thumb along the handle. Given what she had seen him do in practice, she had little doubt that in a true battle situation those axes would be lethal.

Of the four, Tóla was the most animated. Since his return from the valley entrance with news of the *fian*'s imminent arrival, he'd been grimacing and gesticulating to himself up on the gateway, wordlessly mouthing inaudible insults as though in silent argument with some individual that was invisible to the others. The *bandraoi* found this behaviour baffling but was grateful for the distraction from the reality of their imminent annihilation. On a bizarre and completely incongruous whim, she briefly considered calling the warrior Ultán over to interpret his friend's behaviour.

Foolish. Your mind is slipping.

Resting her shield against the embankment, she raised herself off the cold surface to peer through the crack in the pilings, staring out at the fog-smeared view. Beyond the ditch, nothing but wisps of fog were visible. Hidden in the murk, the distant woods were utterly quiet, bereft of any birdsong. Similarly, despite the settlement's expanded population, the only sound from within the *ráth* was the grainy rasp of Fiacail's whetstone and the intermittent low of a disgruntled heifer, eager to reach the pasture.

Where are they? Tóla said he heard the fian approaching the valley. They must be close.

And then they were.

She tensed as the first vague blur of life-light flickered into being. First one, then another and a moment later, another again.

'They're coming.'

Her words created a flurry of muted activity. Aodhán stiffened and gripped his javelin tight with both hands. Tóla put his finger to his lips to silence his invisible companion. Fiacail sat up, blew some dust off the blade of his axe and lay the whetstone aside. 'How many can you see?' the big man asked.

Bodhmhall peered out at the gloom. 'Three.' She looked again, staring patiently until she was certain. 'Only three.'

'Aah.' Fiacail relaxed. He slumped back against the wall and yawned. 'An advance party, then. Rest easy. They'll look around and wander away once they've satisfied their curiosity.'

He closed his eyes and seemed to drift off to sleep. Bodhmhall stared at him in disbelief. Despite his calm assurances, she turned back to look through the crack, her apprehension mounting as the three dancing flames advanced, flickering like flames in a draught as they eased through the mist-shrouded trees.

The route they had chosen was a good one. The woods at the base of the southern ridge offered the most effective concealment when approaching the *ráth* although the foggy conditions now made such precautions superfluous. It also brought them to within three hundred paces of the settlement, separated by nothing more than a wide strip of pasture.

With that habitual competence of hers, Liath Luachra had pre-empted the arrival of the *fian* at this particular point. It was at that exact spot, in fact, that she'd originally proposed to place the skirmishing party.

The *bandraoi* bit her lip.

The thought of the warrior woman still hurt like a bruise on her heart. She wondered briefly where Liath Luachra might be. On the night of their clash, the flare of violence and the colour of her internal flame had been truly terrifying. When she'd fled the roundhouse and the settlement, Bodhmhall had truly believed she would not return.

The following morning, when she had reappeared, haggard and forlorn, Bodhmhall had struggled to contain her relief. Their reunion, however, was neither celebration nor reconciliation for when the *bandraoi* had approached and reached out to touch her, Liath Luachra had brutally shrugged her hand away. The hostility of the glare thrown at her had left the *bandraoi* reeling.

You cannot complain. It is your own fault.

She unconsciously raised a hand to massage the space beneath her left breast, a physical symptom of her emotional distress. The good intentions behind her actions offered little consolation. By putting loyalty to her nephew and clan before that of Liath Luachra, the *bandraoi* had betrayed the woman warrior's trust in her. Despite a lifetime of treachery and violence, Liath Luachra had a unique sense of integrity and brutal noblesse. She did not offer her trust lightly.

That afternoon as the warrior woman had prepared the little party of refugees for leaving the *ráth*, the *bandraoi* had watched from a distance. It had been impossible to work out what was going through the Grey One's head, why she'd returned or why she'd agreed to guide Muirne and the children to Dún Baoiscne given her earlier opposition. Whatever her reasons, Bodhmhall sensed that the closeness, the mutual affection and

212

respect, everything that had kept them together in fact, had been irretrievably lost.

It was early afternoon before the little group was finally ready to leave the settlement, loaded down with clothing and as much provisions as they could carry. Before they left the *ráth*, the *bandraoi* had, once again, approached the warrior woman to attempt some form of appeasement but the stony expression on her face had driven her away. Bodhmhall watched each one of them step through the gateway with a sinking heart: Bearach; Cónán; Muirne with her nephew strapped tight to her chest in a wraparound shawl; the Coill Mór children; and, of course Liath Luachra.

When the last of the group had passed through the gateway, the passage was sealed. No one climbed up to the ramparts to call out. No one attempted to wave them off. Everyone knew that this was a final farewell, a reversed parting where those who stayed were the ones who were leaving for good.

The *bandraoi* pushed such thoughts aside. Present circumstances allowed no respite for the luxury of relief, of grief or self-pity. She continued to stare out through the gap, noting how the scouts, shielded by the thick fog, had confidently advanced beyond the tree line. She watched the firefly lights approach the *ráth* south of the causeway, stopping abruptly just a short distance from the ditch. They had, she realised, spotted a post bearing the head of one of their comrades.

An angry voice floated up to where she was hidden, its harsh, guttural accent emphasised by the anger and menace in its tone. She shivered, understanding nothing apart from the implicit threat of things to come. Slowly, the flickers moved, continuing their circuit of the *ráth* before heading back in the direction they'd come from.

'They're leaving. They're going away.'

Aodhán looked uncertainly from Bodhmhall to Fiacail and back again. For her part, Bodhmhall hung her head, suddenly feeling weary beyond despair. She just wanted this to end. One way or the other.

'Don't worry,' said Fiacail. 'They'll be back soon enough.'

***

The morning dragged on interminably as the inhabitants of the *ráth* waited for the full force of the *fian* to appear. Nerves stretched, they watched the morning mist dissipate, dispersed slowly by the delicate motion of a gentle breeze. When the watery veils finally cleared, they stared around at the empty valley. There was no sign of the *fian*.

'I don't understand,' Aodhán said to the Seiscenn Uarbhaoil man. 'Haven't they conceded the advantage? Surely it would have made more sense to launch an attack in the mist.'

The big man shrugged but said nothing.

'Maybe they're gone.' The *óglach* suggested hopefully.

A cold glare quickly shut him up.

To relieve the stress on the defenders, Fiacail sent them down to the *lis*, one-by-one. There, they took a few moments to feed themselves on beef stew from the cauldron above the fire pit and to stretch their limbs before returning to the ramparts to be replaced by one of their comrades.

Despite the breeze and the low temperature, the off-putting smell of shit and urine from the confined cattle was growing increasingly rank. The goats and pigs, meanwhile, milled around the interior grunting, making noise and generally getting in the way.

By mid-day, Bodhmhall was standing upright, leaning against the pilings as she stared around the valley. There was still no sign of the attacking force.

Where are they?

Although the mist's dispersal meant that her Gift was no longer required, the *bandraoi* remained in place. She still had her duty as shield bearer to fulfil of course but she was also prompted by a desire to maintain her presence as leader of Ráth Bládhma. After three years of guiding the settlement, it had been no small thing to relinquish martial command to Fiacail despite knowing that this was the right decision. Without Liath Luachra, there had really been no other alternative. Ráth Bládhma needed a *conradh* to lead the defence and, of them all, Fiacail was the only person who offered any prospect of ensuring the settlement's survival.

It was early afternoon when the *bandraoi*'s keen sight picked up the first indication of movement among the trees to the west. Raising a hand to shield her eyes against the watery glare of the winter sunlight, she stared for a very long time.

'Fiacail.'

Hearing the tension in her voice, the warrior got up and approached. He stood beside her, peering up the valley then abruptly leaned his head forward and spat into the ditch. 'Ah well,' he said. 'We knew it was coming.'

With this, Aodhán and Tolá hurried over to join them. All four stood in a line against the pilings, staring. The movement at the far end of the valley was much more evident now, easily discernible as a mass of men approaching in their direction. A blast from a powerful horn was suddenly unleashed, the terrifying blare resounding off the ridges on either side. The hollow echo it produced was frighteningly loud and washed over the settlement like an incoming thunder storm. Within the *ráth*, the defenders stirred, nervously tightening their grip on their weapons and shuffling uneasily at their posts. Bodhmhall peered out at the nearing *fian* where individual figures could now be made out. The horn blasted again, rolling down the valley like another great thunder clap.

So many! Gods, so many!

Bodhmhall gasped and realised, with a start, that in her fear she'd forgotten to breathe. They'd always known a substantial force was being assembled against them. To see that horde of snarling, blood-crazed warriors advancing towards them, however, put a clearer reality on that fear. She looked towards the woods on either side of the *ráth*, seeing distinct flickers of life where additional men had been placed to prevent any attempt at escape.

The body of the *fian* was spread out in what at first looked to be a straight line but, as they drew closer, became a loose semicircle formed to curve around the settlement. Two hundred paces from the *ráth* the huge force halted abruptly and started to roar and bellow, battering the sides of their shields with their swords or clashing metal weapons together. Within the valley's narrow confines, that thunderous clamour froze the blood. Bodhmhall could feel her fortitude leeching away and it took all of her self-will not to falter.

It's happening. It's truly happening.

'Ignore it,' roared Fiacail, glaring around at each individual within eyesight as though to underline his words. 'They're full of huff and puff. They're only doing this to intimidate you.'

'They're succeeding,' muttered Aodhán. Fiacail glowered at him and the young man flushed.

Finally, the terrifying din subsided and petered out. The horde stood there waiting, staring at the *ráth* with features that were hungry for blood and full of hatred. Bodhmhall glanced around at the strained faces of the defenders. The men on the southern and northern walls had moved up to see what they were facing and their white faces said it all. Cathal ua Cuan had also arrived up on the gateway and stood there staring at the sight of the *fian*. Although Bodhmhall longed to hear him make one of his disparaging remarks, he simply blanched and said nothing.

Three figures broke away from the body of the *fian* and marched forward until they were within a hundred paces of the *ráth*. Here, they stopped to confer while they looked towards the settlement. The tallest of them was a thin, mangy looking individual wrapped in a grey wolfskin cloak. Bodhmhall studied him for he had an unusual, hatchet-like face: narrow and flat with a hostile edge. It was the cruelest looking face she'd ever seen, empty of any pity or compassion but, unlike his comrades, it was devoid of any tattoos.

Beside him stood a shorter individual with a beard that went down to his waist and hair that had been cropped close to highlight the tattoos on his skull. Both he and the taller man looked to be in charge for they did most of the talking and directed the third one forwards towards the *ráth*.

'A *techtaire*,' grunted Cathal. 'They're sending a messenger.'

Fiacail turned, startled by the presence of the older man and the two Coill Mór warriors who'd followed him up onto the gateway. 'Get back to your position, you old fool.' He turned to the Coill Mór men. 'And you. Go on! Get back.'

Surly but scared, the Coill Mór warriors did as they were told. The old man frowned and glowered at Fiacail but then, he too, began to descend the ladder to the *lis*. Fiacail looked around at the others. 'Everyone else, stay low. We don't need to let them know how many we are.'

The approaching *teachtaire* was a bald, stocky man with an oddly lumpy face distorted even further by the irregular patchwork of tattoos. He came to a halt before the causeway, his hostile squint looking up at the pilings for any sign of life. Bodhmhall crouched even lower although she was sure he couldn't possibly see her through the little crack.

'I think he wants to parlay,' she whispered.

Fiacail sniffed and scratched his nose. 'Given events as Ráth Dearg, I'd have thought these devils more interested in slaughter than talk.'

'They've lost their *draoi*, Fiacail. They may be treating us with caution.'

He pursed his lips and tapped them with the tips of his fingers. 'When you have a force that size you don't need to be cautious. It must be something else.'

He glanced at her and although he said nothing she knew what he was thinking. There would be no capitulation. No negotiation. The *fian* needed their food but they were not going to let the inhabitants live, no matter what greasy promises they offered.

She nodded. 'We fight. No surrender.'

'Good.' He nodded in approval. 'Still, I'm happy to waste a bit of time with the parlay talk. Enjoy these moments, Bodhmhall. Savour them for they are the sauce of life. You will live more with every breath you take now than you have ever lived in your life before.' He offered her a mirthless grin. 'Now, let's hear what this dog has to say.'

With that, he crawled towards the inner edge of the embankment. There, making sure he couldn't be observed from outside, he stood up as though he'd just mounted the ladder and wandered nonchalantly towards the rampart like a man out for a morning stroll. With a great yawn, he stretched his shoulders, making sure to face the opposite side of the *ráth* from where the *fian* were assembled. He made a point of taking his time before he happened to 'notice' the warrior below. Leaning forward he beamed down at the *techtaire* with his widest smile, as though recognising a welcome neighbour.

'Well, hallo there, friend.'

The Seiscenn Uarbhaoil man's voice projected well, sounding surprisingly clear in the gentle breeze. The *techtaire*, who'd been assessing the depth of the ditch while he waited, glanced up with a neutral expression although a quick flicker across his face revealed his surprise at being addressed by a male. The two axes strapped across Fiacail's back were not lost on him either.

Ignoring the greeting, the man called up with a hoarse voice rendered all the harsher from the strange, guttural accent. 'This is settlement ... The Ráth Bládhma?'

He watched stonily as Fiacail turned away, that cruel expression rapidly transforming to one of alarm as the big man grasped a javelin from the rack and flung it at him. The *techtaire* squawked, a mixture of shock and outrage, as the weapon thudded into the earth, quivering from the force of the impact as it protruded from the ground between his legs. An angry murmur

217

passed through the *fian,* sounding like the drone from an enraged swarm of bees. Fiacail paid it no heed.

'I don't recognise the accent of your mangled tongue, stranger, but when I greet someone I am accustomed to a response in kind.'

For a moment it looked as though the *fian's* emissary was about to snarl and it took a visible effort on his part to hold his rage in check. He glanced angrily back towards the two men behind him. The bearded man returned his stare mutely but the taller one slowly shook his head. Twisting about to face the *ráth* once more, the warrior's mouth turned upwards in a misshapen, gap-toothed smile that looked all the more feral for the lack of humour in his eyes. 'Greeting.'

'And greetings, once more, to you. What is your business in our valley?'

'We seek the habitat, the Ráth Bládhma.'

'Well then you are truly fortunate for you're standing before Ráth Bládhma.'

The messenger nodded, the false smile faltering from the effort of maintaining it. 'We understands …' He paused, his tongue struggling over a language that was a twisted stick in his mouth. 'We understands,' he tried again. 'A woman reigns Ráth Bládhma.'

'That's true. Alas, she is ... preoccupied. She is taking her bath.' He leaned forward and offered the messenger a conspiratorial wink. 'Women!'

Terror afforded Bodhmhall little space for offence. Clutching the handle of her shield with the grip of a drowning man, she stared, captivated by the interplay between the two men. The messenger gazed up at Fiacail, taken aback by the Seiscenn Uarbhaoil man's assured bonhomie, his hale and hearty demeanour.

'You have the woman? The Muirne Muncháem?'

The man's accent mangled the Flower of Almhu's name and although it was close enough to work it out, Fiacail pretended he hadn't recognised it. He shook his head in careful deliberation. 'I don't understand. Which one is she, then? So many women, it's hard to remember them all.'

'She is...' The *fian* warrior hesitated, struggling to remember the correct expression. 'With child.'

Fiacail nodded. A substantial pork chop suddenly appeared in his right hand and he chewed on it with exaggerated relish while pretending to give the matter great attention. Through the gap in the pilings, Bodhmhall noted how the *techtaire*'s eyes focussed on the meat and his tongue involuntarily licked his lips.

Fiacail was right. They are starving.

Fiacail wiped his mouth with the back of his hand. 'Ah, yes! The fat one. Yes, she's in here. Not my particular favourite but ...' He shrugged.

'Send her out. Give her to we.'

The big man shook his head. 'Now, now, little tattooed man. I thought I'd made my expectations of etiquette clear?'

The *techtaire* glared furiously at him and again glanced back towards his leaders. The two men looked on in flinty silence before the tall one gestured for him to proceed. With obvious ill grace, the warrior attempted a smile once more.

'With grace, we seek you to deliver us the woman named Muirne.'

Bodhmhall stiffened, suddenly divining why the *fian* were not attacking. *They want the baby alive! That is why they don't attack. They fear hurting the child.* That wouldn't stop them of course.

'Very well. Wait there. I'll see if she's available.'

Before the messenger could respond, Fiacail pulled back from the rampart and dropped back out of sight. With a sigh, he sat on the inner edge of the embankment, legs dangling down above the *lis*. Noting the spread of defenders regarding him in alarm, he gave a wide grin then made a jerking masturbation gesture with his right hand. Despite their fear, the Ráth Bládhma fighters grinned and stifled a laugh.

Heart pounding, Bodhmhall stared out at the *fian* emissary who stood abandoned at the front of the *ráth*. The infuriated warrior was at a loss. Face contorted into a snarl, he glowered at the top of the gateway, unable to leave without looking foolish in front of his watching comrades.

The *bandraoi* turned her gaze to Fiacail. Her old husband had surprised her. She'd known of his potential as a battle leader of course but few could have matched his nonchalant command and deliberate calm, his ability to maintain the morale of the settlement under such hopeless circumstances.

Sensing her attention, he glanced towards her and grinned. 'Maybe if we stay down they'll just go away.'

Bodhmhall suppressed a hysterical giggle.

'That was a waste of a javelin,' hissed Aodhán.

Fiacail shook his head. 'It served a purpose. They know we're ready to fight. They also think we can afford to waste a javelin.'

'But we can't.'

'True, but they don't know that. Now they're under the impression we have so many javelins we're happy to use one playing games with their messenger. With any luck, when they come in for the kill, they'll come in more cautiously to avoid a potential volley of missiles. We have a better chance of repelling a slow attack than a full-on wave of warriors.'

'You think we can beat them off?'

The big man shrugged. 'Anything's possible.'

'I would have kept the javelin. Better sticking out of a *fian* man's guts than out of the mud.'

The Seiscenn Uarbhaoil man stared coldly at the *óglach*. 'Boy, you can question me when your balls drop. Until that day, you just keep your words in a place where they won't end up putting you in harm's way.' With that, he tossed the pork chop aside and wiped his hands on his leggings. 'Now let me be. I need to focus. These mind games take their toll.'

Taking several deep breaths, he got to his feet and strolled back towards the rampart. There, arms folded, he leaned forward against the stone structure and looked down at the fuming warrior.

'Hallo again, foreign man. I see you.'

The messenger glared, unable to risk speaking for fear he would lose what little self-control remained.

'Alas, the woman you seek is engaged in a sleep of beauty. Given that she has a face like a pig's arse this is likely to take some time but you have our permission to wait outside.'

The warrior stood there, practically quivering with fury. 'Deliver the woman,' he snarled. 'Now!'

Fiacail grinned broadly. 'You know, for such a little arse-crack of a man, you make an irritatingly loud farting sound.'

The warrior would have responded had he not been grabbed roughly by the arm. Taken by surprise, he turned to find the bearded man had silently moved up behind him. The *techtaire* listened as his leader spoke harshly to him. When he'd finished, he turned moodily to face Fiacail once more, urged by the silent vehemence of his leader behind him.

'The Man of Blood say all those within will die but you ...' He regarded Fiacail with evident relish. 'With you, he promises that he will use his sword. He cutting your balls and wears them as necklace.'

Fiacail stared at him in silence before transferring his gaze to his malevolent companion. 'Then, by the Gods, your Man of Blood will blunt his blade. My balls are firmly attached and it'll take more than his little mouse paws to achieve such a deed.' Fiacail tossed him a contemptuous look. 'This conversation bores me.' He turned his gaze to look Aodhán in the eye. 'Now.'

The young warrior responded with a blur of movement. All of a sudden he was upright at the rampart, his arm pulling back then abruptly snapping forwards. The javelin left his hand before anyone truly had time to register what he was doing yet everyone heard it smash the *techtaire's* forehead, snapping his head back with an audible crack that knocked him clear off his feet. The Man of Blood staggered backwards with impressive alacrity then stared at the still-quivering body lying before him.

Bodhmhall looked on in shock. It had been an astounding cast. An exceptional cast. One that she would not have believed possible at such a distance. Its suddenness had also taken everyone by surprise, shocked them and sent a clear and simple message. Approach and you face death.

The hatchet-faced man near the massed *fian* looked on impassively. The Man of Blood, however, stepped forward and glared up at Fiacail with utter loathing. Placing a foot on the corpse, he caught hold of the javelin haft and yanked with both hands. The barb of the head had caught on the inside of the skull however and several strong upward tugs were required before the brain-smothered tip finally jerked free with a gory, squishing noise. Holding the javelin aloft, the Man of Blood took it in both hands then contemptuously snapped it across his knee. Tossing the broken pieces aside, he turned his back on the *ráth* and slowly sauntered back to his men.

'It starts,' said Fiacail quietly. 'Prepare yourselves. He will unleash them now.' For a moment, he seemed to falter, grabbing hold of the rampart with both hands as though for support. Composing himself, he reached over to cover the *bandraoi's* hand with his own great paw. 'I am sorry, Bodhmhall. So sorry for having hurt you.'

She grasped his fingers tightly in response, unable to speak for the fear that was choking her.

The Man of Blood, meanwhile had got as far as the taller, hatchet-faced man. He walked past him brusquely, ignoring the other's attempt to engage him.

Reaching his men, the bearded man drew forth a heavy sword and wielded it high as though to demonstrate to the defenders what fate awaited them. Opening his mouth he released a roar of pure fury.

'GAAAHHHH! You will die! A hundred times over. We will enter your flea-pit of a settlement, we will rape your women and burn their bodies on the bonfire. We will open the throats of your children, feed the earth with their blood as we feed ourselves upon your meat.'

Bodhmhall looked on in horror, momentarily oblivious to the fact that the horrific warrior was screaming in her language. Even at this distance, she could visualise the spittle flying from his mouth as he worked himself up to a frenzy, evidently working up his men as well given the increasing volume of snarls and bellows that rumbled through the ranks. Her Gift showed her a growing red aura slowly radiating out from the assembled warriors.

She shivered.

'I will rip the unborn child from the womb of Muirne Muncháem. I will eat it raw. And you, queen bitch of thorns ...' Bodhmhall shuddered for he seemed to be addressing her directly. 'I will slice your sex open with my blade and -'

Whatever the Man of Blood's intentions, they were abruptly cut short as his jaw exploded. Fragments of bone, flesh and even an eyeball erupted from his face, arching high into the air then landing with a plop on the ground before the startled warriors.

A stunned silence filled the valley as everyone, defenders and attackers alike, stared in complete and utter shock. Sagging briefly, the bearded man toppled sideways and collapsed onto the grass.

As the initial sense of disbelief wore off, all eyes turned to the woods south-west of the *ráth*, drawn by the movement of a figure emerging onto a slight rise in front of the trees.

Liath Luachra!

Bodhmhall's heart lurched with both shock and emotion as she stared at the familiar figure, the sling dangling from her right hand, her sword *Gleas Gan Ainm* in her left. The woman warrior stood staring at the assembled warriors, tall and straight ... and completely naked.

Without warning, she released a loud, blood-curdling whoop as she slid down the little slope, into a flanking group of three warriors who were staring gobsmacked at her breasts. Her sword flashed in the sunlight and the nearest of them stumbled backwards, both hands attempting to stem the blood spurting from his face. Then she was past at a run, legs pounding westwards across the pasture.

It took the invaders one heavy, shock-laden moment to drag their eyes from their fallen comrade. There was another stunned silence as they stared at the fleeing female figure then, with a furious roar, a whole section of the horde suddenly surged after her, howling with rage and desire.

Bodhmhall turned to stare at Fiacail, her mouth hanging open. 'What -' she started to ask but stopped for Fiacail was clearly as dumbfounded as her. Slowly a look of comprehension crossed his features.

'She's drawing them away. By the Gods! She's drawing them away.'

A similar conclusion appeared to have been reached by the tall hatchet-faced man for he was suddenly amongst his men, whipping them with a leather bullwhip, screaming abuse and driving them back towards their original goal. His efforts proved successful for although almost a quarter of his men continued their pursuit of Liath Luachra, the main body of the *fian* surged forward in response, howling with unbridled excitement. The now ragged force split into three sections, belatedly responding to some prearranged plan. One section headed straight for the causeway, two others veered off the sides, the first curving up to the north of the *ráth*, the second to the south. Several of the warriors ran in small groups, hauling long section of thin tree trunks strapped together with flax.

'To arms,' roared Fiacail.

Twenty paces from the causeway, the main section suddenly slowed, allowing a smaller group of four to five warriors to draw ahead, each carrying a cluster of javelins in their hands. Bodhmhall stared numbly as they drew to a halt and launched their missiles, watching entranced as they arched upwards then slowly started to descend towards her.

'Get down, woman!'

She felt a rough hand grab her by the belt of her tunic and hurl her down, then she was smothered by Fiacail's weight and the darkness of the shield frame pulled over them both. There was a loud crack on the gateway floor in front of her as a metal javelin head struck, spattering her face with chips of stone. Then the weight was off her again and she could hear Fiacail bellowing.

'Aodhán! Kill their casters! Kill them!'

She pushed herself up of the ground, her gaze moving up to where Aodhán was crouched. At first, the *óglach* stared in shock then something seemed to shift behind those eyes as all the years of training with Liath Luachra kicked in. A cold look of concentration came over him and, grasping a fresh javelin from the rack, he advanced at a crouch to the edge of the rampart.

Bodhmhall winced as another shower of missiles struck the gatehouse, one of them glancing off the pilings above her head.

They're keeping us pinned down! We can't stop them coming across the causeway.

'Come on, woman!' Fiacail again. 'Protect the boy!' A slew of javelins flew overhead, some slamming into the pilings, others sailing past to land in the *lis* where the elderly reserve force pulled back in alarm. One of the missiles embedded itself in the buttocks of a dairy cow, sending the wounding animal bellowing and bucking in paroxysms of pain inside the crowded pen.

Aodhán was flinging javelins back in return. Bodhmhall lifted her shield and was moving towards him when a heavy wooden pole crashed against the gatehouse's outer stone rampart. A metal hook at the tip slipped down the inside wall, latching onto the internal stone and securing the makeshift ladder in place. Even before it was fully secured, a foul head had appeared over the top of the rampart, an invader's filthy hand reaching over the rim to haul itself up. The *fian* warrior was still pulling himself up over the rampart when Tóla suddenly appeared beside her, driving a spear deep into his chest with such force that he tumbled back off the wall and disappeared from sight.

Another javelin glanced off the wall. The air was full of screaming. Bodhmhall pushed forward towards Aodhán, past Fiacail who was hammering an axe at the hook of another assault ladder, doing his best to dislodge it while he bellowed at the top of his voice. 'Shitheads! Pox breathers! Pig fuckers!'

The *bandraoi* heard rather than saw a missile whirring in from the left and instantly raised her shield to defend the *óglach*. A sudden blow almost knocked it out of her hands and a spear tip and two fingers of shaft erupted through the inner leather lining.

'Aodhán defend the gateway. Bodhmhall help him.'

Fiacail rushed past, headed for the southern rampart. The *bandraoi* glanced towards the south of the *ráth* and saw why the big man had left them. The Coill Mór man placed there was down, stretched limp along the embankment with most of his scalp missing. Three more of the improvised assault ladders had appeared, poking ominously above the pilings on that side. As she watched three, then four of the *fian* warriors climbed over the spiked wooden barriers. Struggling to free himself from the piling where his belt had become entangled, the nearest warrior didn't notice Fiacail approach or hear the whirr of his swinging axes. One came down in a vertical arc, burying itself into the back of the raider's skull. He hadn't even dropped in the time it took Fiacail's second axe to swing upwards, catching another warrior under the jaw with full force. The impact of the strike was such that the warrior was lifted off his feet and thrown violently back against the pilings.

On the northern edge of the *ráth*, things were going little better. The red-haired Coill Mór man stationed there was successfully holding back an attempted intrusion from one assault ladder but a second ladder had already latched on a few paces to the left of where he was fighting for his life. One *fian* warrior had already clambered over the barrier by the time Ber Rua got there to confront him. Young and impossibly agile, he responded to the Coill Mór leader's attack with almost contemptuous ease, ducking under the slashing sword then swinging up with an attack of his own. There was a clash of steel as his sword caught on the hilt of Ber Rua's knife, then both men were struggling hand to hand.

Protected by their comrade's efforts, two more *fian* warriors had succeeded in breeching the *ráth* and gained a foothold on the northern embankment. They were advancing on the red-haired Coill Mór man when a spear throw from Ultán took the foremost one in the back, knocking him off the rampart and into the *lis* below.

The Coill Mór man must have finally noticed the presence of enemies to his side for he glanced to his left, his face sweating and pale. Unable to protect himself from an attack on two fronts, he had no choice but to back away, retreating to his right and conceding the assault ladder.

Leaping over his writhing comrade, the second *fian* warrior immediately rushed forwards. To his misfortune, in his hurry to defend the ladder, he tripped over his fallen comrade's battle axe and momentarily lost his balance. Grasping the opportunity, the Coill Mór man immediately moved in, sliding his sword up to stab him in the stomach. There was a loud scream as the warrior fell, clutching the innards that were spilling from his eviscerated stomach. Ignoring him, the Coill Mór man immediately moved back to confront another warrior slipping in over the pilings at his previous position.

'Bodhmhall!'

She snapped about to see Aodhán stumbling backwards, his sword on the ground and a terrible gash down his left side. A *fian* warrior with long, black hair was pulling himself up onto the rampart, a bloody sword grasped in his right hand. She charged him without thinking, bringing her shield up to use as a weapon. He lifted his head just as she reached him, ramming the hard rim of the shield into the skin beneath his nose with all of the strength she could muster. The blow bowled him backwards off the wall, into the ditch.

She stared at the empty space and was about to release an ululation of victory when a javelin spinning in from the side glanced off her shield and struck her in the shoulder. The impact was enough to spin her around and this time it was Bodhmhall who went tumbling off the top of the gateway, landing with a heavy thump in the *lis*. For several moments, she stared at the muddy surface, disorientated and unable to work out what had happened. She tried to get up but the movement caused the haft of javelin in her shoulder to twist sharply.

She screamed.

Her vision momentarily turned red from the pain. Forcing herself to grasp the haft of the weapon, she attempted to pull it but wasn't able to get a firm grip. A bellow of rage from overhead caused her to look up to at the gateway where Aodhán's arm dangled lifelessly over the *lis*. To the left, she could also see Tóla repeatedly battering a *fian* warrior who'd managed to get over the rampart wall but was struggling to fight while supporting a bloody wound in the leg. Behind the Seiscenn Uarbhaoil man, another warrior was scrambling over the wall from the second assault ladder.

'Fiacail!'

Within the din and clamour of battle, the Seiscenn Uarbhaoil man should not have been able to hear her yet, somehow, by some miracle he did. Over on the southern wall, she could see him knock another warrior from the pilings. The big man had been joined by Ultán, who was busy wrestling on the rampart with another invader, stabbing him repeatedly in the side with a blood-smeared knife and hand. The Seiscenn Uarbhaoil warrior's face bore a terrifying animal-like rictus and he roared each time he plunged the knife into his enemy.

Glancing around, Fiacail understood the risk to the gateway immediately. Aodhán and Bodhmhall were down. Tóla was on his own, attempting to defend himself against one opponent and unable to prevent incursion from two different assault ladders. Despite this, the big man was in no position to help. With three separate assault ladders, the southern side of the *ráth* was taking the brunt of the attack and, between them, Fiacail, Ultán and the red-haired Coill Mór man were struggling to hold them back.

At the eastern edge, the wicker barrier blocking the gap in the pilings had been smashed aside and the Coill Mór warrior, Lí Bán and Gnathad were fighting valiantly to hold the *fian* assault back. Even as she watched, she saw the Coill Mór man stagger back, a spear haft embedded in his right eye. He quivered violently as he flopped to one side and slid off the rampart but the Ráth Dearg woman quickly grabbed his sword and started hacking at the incoming warriors. Lí Bán wailed in dismay, leaving her to fight alone as she ran to the aid of her husband on the northern wall.

Ber Rua was down and unmoving, although he'd evidently managed to stab his opponent several times before he died. The young *fian* warrior had dragged himself further along the rampart but, bleeding copiously, it was clear that he wouldn't be doing any more damage. The red-haired Coill Mór man was also down but had somehow managed to dislodge one of the assault ladders.

A single assault ladder now remained on the northern rim and it was this alone that allowed the reserve force to get there in time. Cathal ua Cuan mounted the internal ladder and ran along the rampart, swinging his club with impressive vigour for a man of his age. At the scaling ladder, a *fian* warrior with one leg over the pilings just had time to look up before the old man's club smashed his head in.

The old fighter did not stop there. Like Fiacail, he too had seen the danger at the gateway and hurried towards it, reaching it just in time to prevent the most recent invader from stabbing Tóla in the back. His first strike took the *fian* man behind the knee, swiping his leg up and knocking him flat on the ground. His second blow took the startled warrior across the side of the face, smashing his left cheek and eye socket.

The old man didn't stay to enjoy the screaming fruits of his labour but moved immediately to counter the next warrior on the scaling ladder.

Despite the limitations of his club, with the advantage of a secure footing and higher ground, he was able to successfully hold them at bay.

Bodhmhall breathed a sigh of relief and tried to ignore the torturous discomfort in her shoulder as she struggled to her feet. She staggered forwards but each step she took made the haft of the javelin quiver and the resulting agony in her shoulder was almost impossible to bear. Weeping with the pain, she stumbled on, intent on reaching the ladder to the northern curve where the reserves were now attempting to prevent the enemy from entering.

It was not a viable contest. Cairbre was no fighter and was barely able to move with his brittle bones. Despite this, she saw him chopping downwards, repeatedly striking a *fian* warrior's shield while Conchenn and Lí Bán, enraged with grief, poked ineffectually at the raiders through gaps in the pilings with the spears.

Bodhmhall slumped against the nearest roundhouse. 'Morag! Morag!'

The curly-haired woman that she'd so recently treated in Coill Mór tentatively stuck her head through the leather covering, a spear grasped tightly, if inexpertly, in her hands. The only adult not defending the wall – with the exception of the traumatised Cumann – she was the last line of defence to protect the children should the *fian* break through to the *lis*.

'Pull it -' Bodhmhall wheezed. 'Pull it out!'

Morag looked at her in alarm then stared with wide eyes at the javelin protruding from her shoulder.

'Do it!' shouted Bodhmhall.

The Coill Mór woman responded faster than Bodhmhall expected, grabbing the javelin haft with both hands and wrenching it free with a single tug. The sheer agony of the extraction caused Bodhmhall to stagger and for a moment she almost fainted. Hanging onto the doorway for support, she fought off clouds of unconsciousness as blood from the wound trickled down her arm. 'Tie it up,' she whispered and although she must have been barely audible, the younger woman quickly did as she was asked, ripping a piece of cloth from her tunic to wrap around the wound.

Lucky. You were lucky.

The javelin head had been unbarbed, it hadn't hit her directly but had glanced off the shield. Admittedly, the force had been enough to knock her from the gateway but the weapon had not penetrated so deeply that it couldn't be removed. The wound still burned like scalded flesh of course, and she was sweating and feeling nauseous, but she could move, albeit in a restricted manner. She had been remarkably lucky, even if the knowledge prompted little elation.

Leaving the startled Morag to return inside the roundhouse, Bodhmhall grabbed the blood-coated javelin and used it as support as she tottered towards the northern ladder. Up on the pilings, the invaders had managed to climb higher on the assault ladder despite Cairbre's efforts and the assistance of the women.

Bodhmhall pulled herself, one-handed, up the wobbling ladder. As she dragged herself onto the rampart, she heard Cairbre shriek in agony and looked up just in time to see an upward spear thrust take the old man in the armpit, the tip ploughing through skin and bone and erupting out through the tunic on the back shoulder. The *bandraoi* screamed in dismay as she saw her *rechtaire* driven back from the pilings and an enormous, tattooed warrior leaping over the barrier to take his place. Grabbing the spear haft, the *fian* man rammed the helpless elder back off the rampart to fall with a cry into the *lis* below.

Desperate to protect her man, Conchenn attacked with Lí Bán but the warrior simply swatted their spear thrusts aside with his shield. Spinning rapidly on one heel, he launched himself forwards and smashed the edge of the shield against the older woman's head. Bodhmhall could hear the sickening sound of Conchenn's skull splinter beneath the force of the blow. Intoxicated by the heady mix of physical violence and victorious achievement, the *fian* warrior roared with laughter as she too slid lifeless off the rampart.

She didn't know how she managed it but, somehow, Bodhmhall managed to reach the warrior just as he turned on the terrified Lí Bán. Unable to hold the javelin properly, she grasped it by the haft with her good hand, close to the metal tip, and jabbed it into the side of his neck. The *fian* warrior roared and swung about, instinctively swiping out with his shield. The flat surface smashed her violently across the chest, knocking her off her feet and onto the rampart surface. Glaring down at her with smouldering eyes, the *fian* man ignored the other cowering woman as he advanced on his newest target. Looming over her, he was raising his spear to a stabbing position when he suddenly shuddered and stiffened. Staring up at him, the *bandraoi* saw his face take on a bewildered grimace as he slowly dropped to his knees and then fell forwards, flat on his face beside her.

Terrified, mind still reeling from the effect of the shield strike, she stared at the axe head lodged deep in the base of the warrior's neck, the long wooden haft sticking up at an angle, still quivering from the impact. Shaking, she looked down to the *lis* where Fiacail was standing, his post deserted in order to save her. Chest heaving with exertion, he looked to make sure that she was alive than turned and ran back to the southern ladder.

Behind her, Bodhmhall could hear the sound of fighting as Lí Bán fought off another attempt at entry but found herself unable to rise to her feet. Dazed, she watched Fiacail cross the *lis*, struggling to get back onto the rampart where Ultán was in serious trouble.

Fighting off two fresh *fian* warriors, a third was clambering up over the pilings behind the Seiscenn Uarbhaoil warrior. Sensing the threat to his rear, he quickly slid backwards, smashing the newcomer in the face with the pommel of his sword.

Turning to face his two other adversaries, Ultán stepped forward only to get slammed backwards by a sudden spear to the stomach. Staggering sideways against the pilings, he stared down in disbelief at the shaft protruding from his belly, his hands burying inside his furs as he struggled to staunch the flow of blood. The nearest *fian* warrior didn't hesitate. Taking advantage of the distraction, he leapt forward at speed to grasp the haft and hammer it deeper into the Seiscenn Uarbhaoil man's solar plexus. Ultán screamed and attempted to wriggle free but he was caught, impaled like a fish on a spit. Ultán's opponent echoed the scream with his own screech of victory, leaving the older warrior to buckle and collapse as he raced on towards the approaching Fiacail.

Down to one axe, the big man swung the weapon in even more tightly controlled and menacing arcs. As the *fian* warrior sprang forward, he brought the blade swirling down in a deadly movement that the warrior successfully dodged by shifting to the rear. At the last moment, however, Fiacail changed the direction of the swing, drawing the weapon back up at an angle that allowed it to carve through the man's Achilles from behind.

There was a scream as the *fian* man's leg collapsed but Fiacail had already bypassed him, pausing only to kick him in the head and reach down to grab his fallen sword. Rising to confront his next opponent, he smiled grimly as the twisting blade threw spatters of blood over the nervously waiting warrior. Having observed the outcome of the previous skirmish, it was clear he was not going to be as rash as his comrade.

Slowly, the warrior advanced with his shield up and feinted a thrust at Fiacail's head. The big man stepped back then surged forward again, slashing the axe down and quickly following it up with a thrust from the sword. The *fian* warrior parried both assaults then shuffled forwards, punching out abruptly with the shield in an effort to force Fiacail back. The effort was his undoing for Fiacail had already swung his axe again.

Although the warrior attempted to block it, the curved metal head caught on the edge of his shield, snagging the lip. Muscles bulging from the effort, Fiacail slowly dragged the resisting shield lower and lower until the man's increasingly panicked features were visible. With lethal abruptness, he struck from the side with his sword, struck and struck again. The *fian* warrior gurgled as his throat blossomed red then a font of blood erupted from this jugular. His body fell to the rampart, shuddering in death spasms. Blood continued to gush from his throat until there was nothing left.

Over on the northern rampart, Lí Bán was huddled against the pilings, crying. Bodhmhall stared across to where Fiacail was spinning about, struggling to locate his next opponent. Bodies were stretched out on the ramparts all around him, blood was pooling at his feet. He whirled again, in confusion for no-one – no-one – was attacking him.

It took Bodhmhall several moments to work it out as well and it was only when she saw several of the *fian* retreating in scattered groups up the valley that she truly understood. The battle was over. The great wave had shattered upon the headland. Pummelled and maimed, the headland had survived. Ráth Bládhma had survived.

Bodhmhall looked over the edge of the rampart, down to where the crumpled bodies of Cairbre and Conchenn lay twisted and broken. She began to weep, for the elderly couple, for Liath Luachra, for all the others who had died when she had not.

They had survived.

Chapter Ten

Liath Luachra ran.

And did not look back.

The heavy pound of feet, punctuated by bellows and threats, told her everything she needed to know.

After thirty paces or so, the shouting eased off. Clearly her pursuers were saving their breath, intent on catching her. If they caught her, she knew there would be no mercy. They would pin her to the ground, most likely taking their own type of vengeance before finishing off what was left with a knife across the throat.

And they would catch her.

The woman warrior was tall for her sex and extremely fit but the undeniable reality was that no woman could indefinitely outrun a full grown man over a level stretch of ground. After a time, her head start on the *fian* would diminish, the distance between them closing inexorably as they wore her down. The single advantage she had was that she was encumbered by nothing more than her sword. The men behind her, dressed for battle, carried heavy leather or furs and weapons. That alone would slow them for a time. Until their greater stamina won out. And they closed the gap sufficiently to reach out and ...

And then, that was that.

After five hundred paces, her lungs were already burning from the effort, the initial burst of adrenaline slowly draining away. Despite her predicament, for one brief, insane moment she felt an urge to laugh. The tightness of her over-stretched lungs, however, meant little more than a merry wheeze escaped her lips.

Half-way down the valley she risked a quick glance back over her shoulder, the movement momentarily unsettling her stride and causing her to lose speed. Almost immediately, she'd straightened up again and was back in the rhythm, recovering that lost ground with a little extra effort. Those few lost paces had been worth it. She now knew there were at least ten to twelve of the tattooed warriors spread in a tight wedge about forty paces behind her. They were no fools though. They'd sent one of their younger men ahead running a good ten paces in front of them.

It was an old pursuit ruse, one she herself had used in the past. If there was nowhere for the person you were chasing to run to, you sent your fastest man to run him down while the rest of the party followed at a more measured pace. If the front runner tired, he dropped back and was replaced by a second, fresher runner. This meant the person being chased was forced to constantly run at maximum speed, quickly wearing himself out. If he tried to turn and fight, the front runner held them at bay until the others caught up. Either way the outcome was inevitable.

Liath Luachra knew, therefore, that engaging with the front runner was not an option. She had to outrun him. Granted, that wasn't going to happen on the flat, hence her desperate efforts to reach the twisted confines of the forest at the end of the valley. If she reached those trees, her natural agility and familiarity with the territory would give her the advantage.

But it still looked a long way off.

Even now, with death at her heels, Liath Luachra had no regrets at her decision to return to Glenn Ceoch. Although, the truth was she'd never actually left.

Following their departure from Ráth Bládhma, she'd escorted the little party to the most easterly point of the valley. Although in terms of distance it wasn't particularly far, the dense and twisted woods between took quite a long time to cross.

At the eastern apex of Glenn Ceoch, the sides of the valley closed in, terminating at a wide granite wall that rose to a summit of more than a hundred paces. It was a formidable barrier and, from all impressions, impassable.

Except through Gág na Muice.

Gág na Muice – the Pig's Crack – was a crevice situated at a height of about six men had they been standing on each other's shoulders. It was approximately three paces wide and noteworthy because of the thick flax rope that hung from its shadowed interior, dangling down to the base of the cliff. If it hadn't been for that rope, it was unlikely that anyone would have remarked on it given that there was little to differentiate it from the many other cracks pocking the granite surface. What could not be seen from the valley floor, however, was that the crack widened as it penetrated deeper into the rock. Even further in, it expanded into a relatively broad passage in parts, traversing the entire ridge to emerge in thick forest on the steep northern face.

On the far side as well, Gág na Muice was virtually impossible to detect. Liath Luachra had discovered it by chance, the lucky result of chasing a wild pig into it – hence the name – during a hunt less than a year after their arrival in the area. Recognising its value as an escape route, the woman warrior had brought the flax rope to the Glenn Ceoch side, secured it to a substantial boulder and dropped it into the valley. Keen to avoid the passage being discovered on the opposite side of the ridge, she'd forbidden hunting or travel through that section of wood for fear of leaving tracks. The risk of discovery remained but it was limited and, given the precautions taken, it was one she'd been willing to live with.

They'd scaled the cliff using the flax rope, Bearach hauling himself up first, followed closely by Liath Luachra. Cónán had then attached the end of the rope to each of the Coill Mór children in turn, so they could be swiftly lifted to safety. A similar process was used for the baby, although in his case, the rope was attached to a wicker food basket brought along specifically for that purpose. Lying snuggly inside, nestled in his blanket, he didn't seem to mind too much about being carted upwards, swinging loosely from side to side.

The Flower of Almhu had also needed to be pulled up by hand although, in her case, she'd helped by taking her weight on the footholds and handholds available, reducing some of her burden on Liath Luachra and Bearach. Cónán, as rear guard, had been the last to climb up. Nimble and light, he'd scaled the cliff face with such speed and alacrity, he made it look as though he hadn't even needed the rope.

When the little party was safe inside the crevice, Liath Luachra had pulled the rope up behind them with a dismal sense of finality. They were secure from any threat from the Glenn Ceoch side but the only escape route out of the valley had now been cut off. Ráth Bládhma was on its own.

The warrior woman had urged them to travel quietly through Gág na Muice but the uneven, rocky ground took its toll on the children and they were obliged to stop sooner than expected. They set up camp at an odd overhang where the walls on the opposing sides of the crevice bulged outwards at head height and met to create a long, tunnel-like cave.

'We'll spend the night here,' Liath Luachra informed them. 'The *fian* may have men out scouting the territory. I don't want to risk travelling until I know the route ahead is clear.'

She'd glanced down at Muirne who was preoccupied with her baby, cradling him and making soft cooing noises. Liath Luachra repressed a sigh. The presence of the infant was another complication. If he started crying the sound had the potential to alert any enemies in the area. She dismissed the issue for consideration at another time. There, deep in the ridge's stony heart, it would be impossible to hear them, no matter what kind of racket they created.

She'd looked at Muirne again, surprised by the lack of opposition. Her body language certainly suggested displeasure at the prospect of remaining in such a claustrophobic location.

She's scared of me.

The realisation had momentarily surprised her. Thinking about it, in retrospect, she realised how carefully the Flower of Almhu had been avoiding her since her return from Drom Osna. On the few occasions when they had crossed paths, Muirne had quickly scuttled off. Whenever this hadn't been possible, she'd turned her eyes to the ground and remained as silent and as unobtrusive as possible.

Liath Luachra shrugged. The Flower of Almhu's behaviour held little interest for her and she had enough to concern herself with at present.

When the little party was settled, Liath Luachra sent Cónán to scout the terrain at the northern end of the ridge but gave strict orders not to proceed beyond the bush-coated end of the passage. That night, they had no fire.

***

It was before dawn the following morning that Liath Luachra nudged Bearach awake.

'I'm returning to the entrance to the Glenn Ceoch outlook. Do you wish to accompany me?'

The boy was weary but nodded readily, just as she'd known he would. Like her he'd slept poorly and she'd heard him toss and turn while standing her turn on guard duty. What worried her most was that, since leaving the settlement, he'd barely spoken a word. The fate of his parents and his older brother weighed heavily on him.

Leaving Cónán to watch over the other members of their party, they hurried back along Gág na Muice, reaching the high ledge overlooking Glenn Ceoch just after dawn. The sight awaiting them filled Liath Luachra with dismay. The height of the ledge usually offered an excellent view of the *ráth*, visible over the eastern woods. That morning, however, the valley was choked with dense fog that blanketed everything in a thick veil of ghost breath.

Anxious and frustrated, she quickly backtracked along the passage, Bearach following dutifully behind her. At a narrow fissure to the left of the passage, she climbed up to a wide ledge on the side of the cliff. This slanted upwards at a steep gradient, eventually leading away from the cliff to a higher, flatter section of the ridge. Here, it connected with an ancient deer path that followed the upper ridge, parallel to the valley. Inaccessible from the valley floor as a result of some earlier rock fall that wiped out the only other adjoining path, the trail had not been used for several years. Although much of the original vegetation had grown back, the exposure of the ridge face to the worst of the elements had prevented it from being completely overgrown.

Pushing through the scrub, they successfully navigated the remaining trail without too much difficulty, finally reaching another set of steep cliffs at the ridge's most westerly point. A flat rock, bordered by furze provided a good point to overlook the forested entrance to Glenn Ceoch and they remained here for some time, hoping to catch a glimpse of the settlement through the slowly dispersing mist.

Time passed frustratingly slowly, measureable only through the gradual thinning of the heavy fog. Sitting there, Liath Luachra was struck by the uncharacteristic silence that filled the valley. It did not have that otherworldly character of the silence she'd experienced at Drom Osna but it was no less disturbing for that. Eventually, the reason for the unusual stillness became apparent. It started with a distant noise, a sound like the shuffling of many bodies through heavy bush. All too soon it became clear that this was exactly what it was.

They're here.

Soon, they could hear the tread of many feet through the undergrowth, the clink of metal, the coughs and voices of a large body of men. The *fian* emerged through the trees between the stream and the ridge where the two Ráth Bládhma fighters were hiding, barely visible at first although the fog had mostly dispersed. Grim and silent, Liath Luachra and Bearach watched the three, long lines of black-faced warriors moving quietly, spirits flagging at the sight of the full force assembled against the *ráth*. Bearach started shaking, a mixture of fear and repressed fury. He tugged repeatedly at the pitiful moustache he'd been attempting to grow over the previous few months. Inordinately proud of it, he'd used every spare moment to twist it or play with it, as though coaxing might make it grow faster. This time, however, there was a nervous desperation to the action.

The *fian* established a temporary camp in the thick wood close to the northern ridge, allowing Liath Luachra and Bearach to observe them in relative safety. The Grey One watched the strangers all morning, noting how they busied themselves in preparation for the forthcoming attack: sharpening blades, slapping each other on the back, generally talking each other up. There was no sense of fear in their preparations, none that she could detect in any case. If anything, she sensed an air of gleeful anticipation. Although she could not understand what the men were saying, it was evident that they knew what they were facing and it didn't perturb them. They were confident and brash, expecting little serious resistance.

One of their preparations confused the woman warrior at first. For a time, she'd been watching the warriors fell a number of young pine trees, all of roughly equal size and proportion. It was only when she saw them hack the branches down to stubby protrusions and strap the trunks together that their intended use became clear. A cold sensation trickled down her spine.

Ladders. They intend to cross the ditch and scale the ramparts.

Bearach, too, had experienced a similar revelation for he released an involuntary, high-pitched gasp.

'They will kill my family. My father, my mother.'

She turned to find the boy looking at her with desperate eyes, wordlessly imploring her to do something, anything, to save his family. The woman swallowed the cold, hard lump of phlegm that had suddenly formed in her throat but she said nothing.

'Liath Luachra,' he pleaded. 'We can't desert them. They need us.'

'You have a duty to protect your brother. And Muirne and the children. They need us too.' She frowned at that. The taste of the words was off. She was repeating Bodhmhall's words and they felt wrong coming out of her own mouth. She tried again. 'They made their choice. I cannot save them Bearach. This way, at least, you and the others will get to live.'

'What is the point in living?' Bearach answered miserably. 'If everyone you care about is dead then you are dead too.'

237

Liath Luachra turned away, unable to bear his gaze. She looked down on the invaders with silent, intense hatred.

A short time later Cónán startled them by sneaking up from behind to catch them unawares. Concerned by their extended absence, he'd followed their tracks back to the Glenn Ceoch overlook then up to the ledge and along the deer trail until he'd located them. At first, Liath Luachra was angry to see him, annoyed that he'd left the children unprotected. She quickly relented, however, recognising that the reaction was unfair. Ensconced in the Gág na Muice cave, the others were in one of the safest spots in the region so there was little reason to be too concerned about their safety. Her own delay in returning had been valid grounds for concern and Cónán had acted correctly.

She chewed on the inside of her cheek as she watched the dark-haired youngster. Like his brother, Cónán was greatly distressed at the thought of deserting his family. Moving nearer to Bearach, he sat down beside him and leaned in close. Liath Luachra saw the older brother reach over and put a comforting arm around his younger sibling. For some reason, she suddenly found herself struggling to breathe.

She looked down at the *fian* once more, the black-faced men preoccupied in the arrangements for the attack on the settlement. Her hand gripped the hilt of *Gleas Gan Ainm* so tightly her knuckles shone white.

'Very well.'

The two boys raised their heads to look at her.

'Very well,' she repeated. She cleared her throat. 'We will do what we can to help our people.'

***

While Cónán was dispatched to retrieve the flax rope from the Glenn Ceoch overlook, Liath Luachra outlined her plan to his brother. By the time she'd finished, Bearach was pale and looked decidedly nervous. He considered what she'd told him in silence for several moments. 'What about Muirne Muncháem and her baby?' he said at last.

'At the moment, that cave is the safest place they can be. Besides, it was Muirne Muncháem that tossed these thorns into our path. Now she must pick her way between them.' Seeing the look on Bearach's face, Liath Luachra gave a conciliatory growl. 'She will have Cónán with them. He'll take good care of them.'

238

Bearach nodded. They had agreed that the youngster would not be accompanying them.

Later, when Cónán arrived from affixing the rope on a cliff further down the valley, they told him what was intended and he wept for he knew it was unlikely he'd see either of them again. Unlike Bearach or Liath Luachra, however, he was still young enough to do as he was told. Returning to where the rope was secured, he watched in silence, therefore, as they slid down to the base of the ridge.

Having safely reached the bottom, Liath Luachra looked back up to make sure the boy had hauled the rope back up. Cónán's thin little figure made a forlorn silhouette against the sky. She turned to face his brother. Bearach looked scared, struggling to control his fear.

'You know what to do?'

He confirmed with a tilt of his head. 'I won't let you down, Liath Luachra.'

She looked at her young comrade, frightened but determined not to fail her, and felt a fierce surge of affection towards him.

'You are the only one who has never let me down, little bandit.'

She started to strip.

***

When Bearach had left her, Liath Luachra worked her way through the woods, headed east towards the *ráth*. Dropping to her stomach, she crawled as close to the settlement as she dared. Concealing herself in a leaf-filled depression at the edge of the trees, she quickly buried herself in the withered leaves in an effort to stave off the cold.

She was present, therefore, when the *fian* made their dramatic and clamorous approach, trembling at the thought of Bodhmhall and the others trapped inside the *ráth*. Silently, she watched as the force drew to a halt before the settlement and she regarded the three men who broke away from the larger mass of men with curiosity. These, she guessed, were the *fian*'s leaders and, therefore, potential targets for her sling. Given the likelihood that she'd only have time for a single cast before she was spotted, she knew she'd have to choose that target wisely.

To her surprise, the voices carried well in the still air and despite the distance, she was able to make out every second or third word being spoken. Listening in on the conversation between Fiacail and the *techtaire,*

239

she quickly dismissed him as a target. The *techtaire* was a translator, a foot soldier, and his death would have no real impact on the *fian*'s attack. Transferring her attention to the bearded one and the tall, hatchet-faced one, she attempted to assess their status. The presence of the latter intrigued her for he seemed to be an ill fit with the rest of the warriors, not least because of his lack of facial tattoos. At the same time, there was nothing distinctive that marked him as a leader. The bearded man, however, strutted about with an obvious sense of his own importance.

Hauling herself out of the leaves, Liath Luachra got to her feet in the shadow of a nearby oak, unravelled her sling and laid a bullet into the flax cradle. The eyes of all the *fian* warriors were focussed on the increasingly strained interaction between Fiacail and the messenger. Like them, she followed the exchange intently and was equally as stunned when the javelin sailed over the rampart to strike him down.

Gobsmacked, the woman warrior released a silent whistle of appreciation at the cast even as her eyes turned to the bearded man stalking back towards his hatchet-faced comrade.

Take them Aodhán! They're the leaders. Make a cast!

Despite her silent urgings, no other javelin came from the *ráth*. Unimpeded, the bearded man brushed past the taller man, and returned to the body of his men. Liath Luachra looked from one to the other and back again, desperately trying to judge the right moment, the right target to create the most debilitating disorder.

Then, supported by his snarling horde, the bearded man had started his furious tirade.

And, instinctively, Liath Luachra had loosed her bullet.

And then …

Well, then, she was running for her life.

***

She crashed into the shelter of the forest with the *fian* warrior just a few paces behind her. Achieving the shadowed embrace of the trees felt like being enveloped in a welcoming hug, a sensation she had little time to appreciate. The young warrior, fearful of losing her in the shadowed greenery, made one last, all-out effort to seize her.

Sensing his approach, Liath Luachra abruptly changed direction just as he tackled her. His extended lunge took him completely in the wrong direction and he hit the ground hard. Grasping the opportunity, she headed deeper into the forest.

The winter weather had thinned much of the woodland vegetation, reducing the lush undergrowth to withered stalks. Although what remained provided limited opportunities for concealment, it did form a tangled net of obstacles that she could use to her advantage. Confronted by a wide clump of desiccated fern, the warrior woman knew to make a desperate dive over it, just managing to clear it and roll back onto her feet, running. Sapped of energy, she'd paid for the effort but she'd extended the distance between herself and her pursuer. Behind her, there was a pleasing sound of thrashing and cursing as the young warrior attempted to barge through the ferns and became ensnared in the briars concealed at their heart.

Over the next few moments, she used every trick she could think of, every ruse, and every manoeuver to further increase the distance between them. Although at the limit of her physical capacity, the *fian* warrior was in a similar situation and she slowly succeeded in pulling away from him.

The distant sound of shouting alerted her that the remainder of the *fian* warriors had entered the forest and were calling on their comrade to reveal his location. Liath Luachra ignored it. Concealed by the tightening tree trunks, she'd managed to shake off the warrior and now she dropped on all fours, crawling off at an angle to the direction in which she'd been running.

Behind her, the *fian* had spread out and were beating the bushes in an attempt to drive her into the open. Contained between the steep ridge and the stream, the forest was relatively narrow at this point with only one direction really open to her; west towards An Talamh Báite. Despite this, the *fian* did not know for certain where she was and were obliged to search to make sure they didn't miss her. Slowly but surely, she pulled ahead.

When she felt she was at a safe distance, Liath Luachra rose to her feet and started to run again, stumbling now because of her fatigue. Soon the trees began to thin, the ground underfoot growing increasingly soggy as she got closer to the marshland. She followed a route different to the one she'd taken with Aodhán only a few days earlier, veering more in a westerly direction, away from the ridge. Sticking close to the remaining trees where the ground was firmer and offered concealment, she progressed deeper into the wetland.

After an exhausting flight, harried by the calls of the warriors behind her, Liath Luachra emerged from the last stretch of trees which descended a gentle slope to a rocky protrusion that poked deep into the grey marshland. Stretching out for several hundred paces on either side was a terrain of limp, black water interspersed with low hummocks of slimy grass and clusters of yellow reed. A soft mist lay low over the water, stretched like a sea of smoke between her and her intended destination,

Oileán Dubh – Dark Island – was the closest piece of solid ground from where she was standing. A wide, circular island, it consisted of a low, double-shouldered peak of black rock, encircled by thick evergreen woods.

Wheezing, Liath Luachra stumbled forwards onto the first mouldy hummock, dropping to her hands and knees as she hauled herself across the precarious terrain. She followed a safe route mapped out by little reed posts placed there over the previous summer when the path had been drier and more easily traversed. Each time she passed one of the markers, she plucked it out and flung it into the surrounding water. For every few paces she slithered forward, she anticipated a cry from behind but, miraculously, she reached the rocky surface of Oileán Dubh without any alarm being raised.

Getting to her feet, she staggered onto the island's broken surface, her muck-covered arms and legs trembling, her chest heaving from the effort. Despite the cold, she was sweating fiercely. Heart pounding, she slumped against some nearby boulders, grasping them with both hands to support herself as she caught her breath and looked around.

Holly and pine grew surprisingly thick and close almost down to the edge of the marsh although the undergrowth beneath them looked sickly and grey. Shadows seemed to flicker between the trunks but she knew it was only a trick of the light.

'Bearach!'

There was no response. Anxious, she nervously massaged the back of her neck. Lathered in sweat and swamp water, it was taut from stress. 'Bearach!' she hissed again.

Once again, there was no reply. Liath Luachra glanced around, unsure what to do, fearful that the boy had been captured or had somehow missed the assigned meeting place. She continued to lean against the boulder. There was no point in rushing off trying to look for him until she had recovered. She had a brief breathing space before the *fian* caught up with her and she would most likely need it.

Suddenly, Bearach appeared, scurrying out from the nearby trees. He hurried over to her, a great grin smeared across his face, her battle harness and leggings in his hands. Liath Luachra almost cried aloud in relief.

Tossing her the clothes, he moved to crouch by the boulders beside her. As she attempted to dress with shaking hands he grinned again but then as he looked back across the swamp, that grin suddenly faded.

'Liath Luachra.'

She turned and felt her stomach clench. On the far side of the little swamp, standing on the rocky promontory, one of the black-faced warriors was staring coldly at her across the water. She watched as he turned his head and released a shrill yell to alert his comrades. Moments later, they had all emerged from the trees and gathered to regard her closely as they worked out the best route across.

Eleven. There are eleven of them.

She was still tugging her leggings on when the *fian* men began to advance: sloshing, wading, pulling themselves over the slippery hummocks. Without the assistance of the reed markers to guide them, they were obliged to move slowly, avoiding the sucking pools as they crossed the treacherous terrain.

She waited until they were half-way across before she stood up, unravelling the sling that was still wrapped about her wrist. A humourless grin formed on her lips. They didn't like that. She could see the nearer faces snarling as they splashed and stumbled, heaving themselves over the slimy hummocks, but there was an increased urgency to their movements. Exposed in the open mire, they had no cover, nowhere to run to. And they knew it.

As she anticipated, they did the next best thing they could. They pushed themselves to move faster, stumbling, tripping, sinking knee-deep at times into the slippery mire before desperately hauling themselves out again. Some of them held small shields up to better protect themselves, others dropped down on all fours – as she had done – to improve their balance and purchase on the slippery ground.

Her first shot took a warrior directly in the forehead, snapping his head back and sending him spinning backwards into the water. Although nowhere near as dramatic as her earlier shot on the *fian*'s leader, from the crack of the stone hitting his skull she knew that particular individual wouldn't be getting up again. Incensed by the death of their comrade, the

243

warriors further increased their efforts. One of them, carrying a number of javelins across his back, unslung one of the missiles and cast it at her. Disadvantaged by the unsteady ground, his aim was off and it landed well to her left, sinking deep into the wet earth with a slapping noise.

You're next.

Her second shot missed but gave her the range for the third. By then the warrior had prepared a second javelin and was lining it up for a cast. Her shot hit him on the knee before he could release it, smashing his knee-cap.

The warrior screamed as he fell, slipping sideways off the greasy hummock and scrambling ineffectually to stop his slide down into the waiting marsh water. She saw him grab a handful of grass but in the wet, silt-like soil, the vegetation pulled loose and barely slowed him. He hit the water with a wet splash. There was an initial, panic-stricken thrashing but then the grey liquid engulfed him and he disappeared from sight.

'They're getting close.'

She cursed. Bearach was still there, crouched low beside her, peeping out from between the rocks, shifting the grip on his sword. No doubt he was cursing the decision to leave all the javelins behind at the *ráth* for use in the defence of the settlement.

'Go, Bearach. Leave now.' Her voice was terse. The remaining warriors were much closer and she hadn't thinned their ranks as much as she'd hoped. There was a positive side to their proximity, though, in that their closeness made them better targets. Her fourth shot hit a man in the throat, crushing his windpipe. He fell to the ground, hands clutching the flesh under his jaw and gurgling in agony while his friends slithered past him in the muck. Her fifth grazed another man in the shoulder but didn't take him down. Her sixth sent a small fountain of water splashing up beside him but she'd missed him again.

'Liath Luachra.'

Gods!

The boy was still there. His voice was tight. And rightfully so. The slime-coated forms were growing very close, the blood lust in their eyes clearer now as they slithered closer through the muck.

'Go, Bearach. Stay low so they don't see you.'

'But —'

'Go!'

244

Focussed on her next shot, she barely heard him run off. Her cast sent the seventh bullet smashing into another warrior's face, cleaving up through his chin and into his brain. He collapsed onto a mound and lay there, unmoving.

One more.

Her last shot took the young warrior who'd been chasing her, low in the chest. The impact of the bullet knocked him back and he fell to his knees, clutching his chest. She felt no emotion at the agony in his face, no sympathy or satisfaction, nothing but an abstract calculation of the remaining threat he might pose. It wasn't much. At the very least, she knew the bullet must have smashed his ribs, probably causing some serious internal injury. He would probably die from his wounds but, at the very least, he'd not be pursuing her again.

That's it!

There was no more time. The remaining mud-spattered warriors, admittedly depleted to six, were almost on solid ground. Although winded from the effort of traversing the marsh, they'd be even more determined to get their hands on her. Now that they had her cornered on the island, they wouldn't stop. She had to move.

She spun and started along the steeply rising trial where Bearach had disappeared a few moments earlier. The heavy gorse hid her from the *fian* warriors but as she was cresting the first ridge a gleeful roar informed her that the first of them had reached solid ground.

She felt the first sense of despair settle on her shoulders at that point. Earlier, on the ridge overlooking Glenn Ceoch, she'd come up with the scheme to draw some of the attacking force away from Ráth Bládhma. In that respect, she'd been inconceivably successful for the odds against the settlement had been substantially reduced. As part of that original scheme, she'd also planned to lure the warriors here to the swamplands to take out as many as she could with the sling.

Unfortunately, that was as far as she'd thought it through. She hadn't truly expected to make it this far. Now, physically and mentally exhausted, she had no idea what to do next.

I'm ready to die.

The unprompted reflection took her by surprise. She'd never previously experienced such a profound sense of resignation prior to battle. She'd certainly never approached it with such a sense of defeatist inevitability? Was she, she wondered, simply preparing herself for things to come?

'Liath Luachra!'

The call from the gorse and holly bushes beside the trail was so unexpected, so sudden, that she almost yelped as she skidded to a halt. Instinctively adopting a fighting stance, she brought her sword to bear but it was a familiar figure that stood up amongst the prickly shrubs.

'Bearach! By the Gods! Why are you still here? I told you to leave.'

The boy's jaw firmed and Liath Luachra cursed under her breath.

'I have to stay with you. Those warriors, they'll … hurt you.'

'They have more than that that in mind Bearach but they will pay dearly for it.'

'We can fight them.'

A shout from down the trail prompted her glance back over her shoulder. Her pursuers were coming.

Furious, she plunged into the thick bush, ignoring the prickle and scrape of holly spines against her skin as she grabbed the boy's shoulders and pulled him down to the ground. Whatever Bearach's misguided reasons for staying, it was now too late for him to escape. The only way off the island was across the marsh and attempting that would place them in a situation similar to that endured by the *fian* warriors. They would not have time to cross the marshland without being spotted and, out in the open, hindered by the boggy terrain they would make easy targets for their enemies' javelins. The irony was not lost on her.

Putting her finger to her lips, she glared at Bearach as they lay side by side. A moment later they heard the heavy tread of running feet and the sound of heavy panting. The warriors rushed past the holly bushes, following the deer path around to the east. When they'd drifted out of earshot Liath Luachra rounded furiously on the boy.

'Foolish child!' she whispered fiercely. 'You throw your life away for nothing. We cannot best six warriors.'

He bristled at that, resenting being called him a child. His jaw firmed and his eyes darkened with uncharacteristic defiance. 'You defeated six warriors with my brother,' he countered.

'Five warriors. Besides we had the element of surprise. And Aodhán's skill with a javelin.'

'We can still surprise them. You have me. They don't know I'm here.'

246

She wasn't really listening for she was already trying to devise a plan for getting the boy safely off the island. Possibly, she thought to herself, she could create a diversion on one side of the island, giving him time to get away on the other side. Alternatively, she could draw the warriors with a fire, and, when they came for her, he could slip across. If he was lucky, he –

'Grey One, they don't know I'm here.'

She looked at him, both surprised and irritated by the interruption. She was about to retort with a scornful dismissal but excited baying from the distant warriors momentarily silenced her. She listened carefully but they did not seem to be coming back. Clearly, they had found some old tracks and had mistaken them for hers.

Brushing the encroaching holly away, she sat up, pausing briefly to consider what he'd said and the various possibilities that offered her. Finally, she released a tired sigh. The boy had really left her with no option. They could not escape the island without being seen but neither was it large enough for them to hide indefinitely. Once the *fian* realised they'd lost her trail, they'd backtrack and beat through the scrub and forest until they flushed her out. It was only a matter of time before they were found.

'Little bandit!' she hissed.

Bearach dropped his head, knowing he had pushed her too far.

Liath Luachra fingered the crinkled burn on the skin of her hand, gaining an odd calmness from the pain it produced. She breathed deeply several times before she could speak again. 'If they split up we might stand a chance. But we'd have to be fast.'

'I'm fast,' said the boy, lifting his head, eyes bright with enthusiasm. 'I'm fast enough to be a *gaiscíoch*.'

Liath Luachra felt her heart sink.

***

A cold breeze brushed the surrounding oaks, the creaking of the branches making it difficult to work out the location of the warriors from the occasional yells echoing through the island forest. Liath Luachra cautiously raised her head from behind her refuge, a fallen oak tree stretched across a small clearing in the northern section of the island. Coated in a brown layer of dead leaves and other vegetative detritus, the clearing was encircled by thick woods that stretched off for more than a hundred paces on either side.

Slithering over to the tree line, she peered into the shadowy interior from where the last call had seemed to come. For a long moment she saw nothing, then a brief movement less than sixty paces away caught her eye. Three warriors. Moving cautiously through the trees in her direction. She chewed on her lower lip.

They've split up then, divided into two groups of three.

She slithered back into hiding behind the tumbled length of oak, lying behind its bulk in silence as she listened to the deep voices grow closer. The distinct swishing sound of heavy feet on old leaves alerted her that they'd entered the clearing. Despite the cold breeze, she was sweating and leaves were smeared to the skin of her arms and shoulders.

She waited until they were almost on her before she stood up to face them. Startled, they froze at her sudden appearance. Despite their numerical superiority, they cautiously surveyed the clearing for any sign of ambush. Liath Luachra slid over the rotting tree trunk and twirled her sword to draw their attention. The middle warrior smiled, revealing a mouthful of brown and rotten teeth. Adjusting his grip on the sword in his right hand, he drew a round shield a little closer to his left flank. Slowly, all three began to advance.

Suddenly Bearach erupted from the dead leaves behind them. Lunging forwards, he plunged his sword blade deep into the back of the hindmost warrior.

Good boy!

The stricken warrior screamed and swatted feebly behind him with his sword. Bearach pulled his own weapon free as his victim fell to the ground, blood from the deep wound already staining the leaves beneath him. His two comrades had whirled about at his yell, poised to confront this new threat and that's when Liath Luachra launched herself. The nearest one – armed with a hand-axe – sensed her attack and attempted to swing back to face her but he was too slow. Her sword strike took him across the front of his throat, the force of it tearing his epiglottis right out and spinning it off into the trees.

She barely had time to register the horrible gurgling sound he made as she slid past towards the remaining warrior. This heavy-built man had already closed in on Bearach and knocked him, dazed, to the ground but, hearing her approach, swung round to meet her. Her sword slashed down with all the weight of her body behind it but he deflected it easily, rolling it off the blade of his own weapon as he shifted to one side.

Halfway through the movement, the woman warrior abruptly changed direction, adjusting her momentum to lunge sideways at an angle to her original attack. Sparks flew as the two blades scraped apart.

Pulling away, Liath Luachra cursed. The warrior was an excellent fighter, constantly circling or adjusting his movement. Worse, he had a longer sword that gave him the advantage in reach while his hand strength meant there was no corresponding loss in dexterity. Despite the death of his two comrades, he didn't look worried. He knew that all he had to do was hold them off for a short time. Alerted by the yelling and the clash of combat, the other three warriors would not be long coming to support him.

He lunged forwards with surprising speed for a man of his size but she'd readied herself, anticipating the attack. She blocked the blow but the warrior's sword struck hers with such a violent clang that the vibration rattled through the blade and pommel, numbing her hand.

This time it was Liath Luachra who retreated. This man was too strong, too fast to defeat with agility or brute force alone. He yelled in excitement as he drove her backwards, the strength of his sword attack too strong to block effectively, his shield held well so that his flank was protected. She backed further into the trees, hoping that the *fian* warrior's mighty sword swing would be constricted by the closeness of the trunks. Realising what she was up to, he continued to press her but changed his onslaught from tight angled strikes to a series of well-targeted lunges that she struggled to avoid.

Suddenly, he moved so fast that he caught her and she bit back a yelp of surprise as his sword thrust cut through the edge of her battle harness, the flat side of the blade sliding cold and dangerous against her skin. Wrenching back, she managed to tear herself free before he could follow up but as she attempted to slide around the nearest tree trunk, she slipped on a wet patch of earth. Her feline agility permitted her to twist so that she landed on all fours but there was one horrible moment of realisation that she was completely powerless to defend herself. Looking up, she saw the gleam of victory in her opponent's eyes, his broadsword already swinging up in a vertical arc. In that instant, she tried to raise her own sword but knew that the downward swing of that heavy weapon would have the combined power of the warrior's two arms behind it. She didn't have a hope of blocking it.

I'm dead!

Suddenly, there was a dull thwack of metal striking wood and the warrior unexpectedly staggered. Shocked, both adversaries glanced up to where the weapon had snagged, the blade lodged deep into the bark of an overhead branch.

Even as the curse erupted from the warrior's mouth and he started to yank his weapon free, the women warrior was up. Rolling sideways, she twisted half-way through the roll to bring *Gleas gan Ainm* up in a tight arc, plunging it directly into his stomach with all the force she could muster.

She heard the big man gasp, more out of shock than pain, then blood and entrails were pouring over her hands and the hilt of the sword. Despite his injuries, the warrior would probably have remained upright if she hadn't kicked the legs out from under him. He crashed heavily to the soggy ground and she wrenched the weapon from his guts. He stared at her, eyes flared with hatred, agony and, she imagined, infuriated disbelief.

Bearach.

She wasted no time basking in her victory. The second group of warriors would be on them in moments and, this time, there would be no opportunity for ambush. Rushing back to the centre of the clearing she found, to her relief, that the *óglach* was up on his feet and although he was groggily wiping his face with one hand, he had his sword clutched firmly in the other.

'Bearach!'

He looked up at her yell, staring fuzzily at her as she grabbed him by the shoulders and started pulling him away.

It was something in his expression that warned her; an involuntary grimace, a kind of numbed appreciation of danger. It was only her instincts and keen reactions that saved her. She ducked and the sword blade from the assailant behind her went swishing overhead. Even as he struggled to regain his balance, she was up and running, pushing Bearach ahead of her.

The other warriors.

'Run!'

They made it to the edge of the clearing at a point where two faint animal trails veered off in different directions. She pushed Bearach to the right and took the left, yipping and screaming to draw the men after her.

Making no attempt at stealth, she ran as fast as she could, following the trail as it wound uphill then, abruptly, came out of the trees, onto the exposed hill top that formed the island's centre. Up on the hill, there was nowhere to hide, nothing to see. Nothing but bleak, black rock and a withered tree standing eerily at the very crest. Without slowing, she'd started round the curve of the slope when something in the rhythm of the pursuing footsteps alerted her. Something about it was wrong. Very, very wrong.

She glanced back over her shoulder and saw, to her horror, that only one of the warriors had followed her.

Bearach!

Her heart was in her mouth as she skidded to a halt. If her sudden about face disturbed her pursuer, however, he showed no sign of it for he came on to attack her without pause. He was a thickset man, squat and burly with no sign of a neck between his head and shoulders. What he lacked in neck, however, he more than made up for in muscle.

He came at her with a wild sword swing that she managed to dodge, then followed up with a stab from the knife in his left hand. The tip of this came closer than she'd wanted, nicking the skin in her shoulder.

Circling away, she held her own sword at the ready, looking for an opening. He gave her one, raising his knife hand too high on his left flank but her instincts immediately told her it was a ruse. Sure enough, when she feinted he reacted far more quickly than he should have, pulling back with his knife arm to reduce the point of contact and swinging down hard with the sword in his right hand. He'd obviously been prepared, waiting for her move. It was a simple trick. Probably an old trick he'd learned, one that he continued to use simply because it'd worked once before.

She backed away, blood trickling from the wound in her shoulder, and he leered at her with a face that only a blind mother could love; skin as tanned as leather, a livid scar across his forehead, artless black tattoos, a broken nose and a gash across his lips and cheek. He was also a formidable fighter, aggressive and vicious, but she was desperate. She had to end this quickly to get back to Bearach.

And there's only one way to do that. Get in close.

She slid forwards then, feinted an attack on his 'exposed' side as she'd just done a moment earlier. Once again, the warrior reacted in a similar manner, drawing back on the left and striking with the right. This time, she took a risk, switching her weight from her right leg to her left so that she could surge forward, low under his sword arm to slam his chest with her shoulder.

The swiftness of the movement caught him completely by surprise, bowling him over backwards. Somehow, he managed to grab her harness and drag her down with him and, just before they hit the ground, got in with the knife. She felt the blade enter her outer thigh, just below her hip. Unable to control the movement because of the fall, his strike slashed rather than stabbed, the blade cutting through the flesh of her leg at an angle instead of penetrating deep into the tissue. It still hurt though, burning with an intensity that threatened to overwhelm her. Aware that her sword was useless at such close quarters, she dropped it and slammed him in the face instead, using both fists. He roared with anger and tried to stab with the knife again but she had her knee down on his inner forearm, preventing him from raising it.

Can't hold him!

He was strong, much stronger than she'd expected. The pressure from her knee was also weakening as a result of the wound. The more she pressed, the more agonizing it became, to the point where she was close to blacking out. Desperate, she pummelled him again in the face with her free hand, momentarily stunning him while she wrestled the knife from his left hand. Before she had a chance to use it, his right hand broke free and slammed the haft of his sword against the side of her head. The blow stunned her and he used the opportunity to buck her off to one side but, instinctively, she continued to grapple, refusing to let him get to his feet.

He lunged on top of her then, fighting to get possession of the knife. Drops of spittle sprayed her face as they struggled. Wrestling on the ground, working to kill him, her mind was unconsciously registering the strangest details: the stink of his breath, the weight of his belly grinding against her as they fought.

Somehow, probably because of his sweat-lined palms, she managed to wrench her right wrist free, just enough to jab the knife in his stomach, to feel the metal sink deep into soft tissue. She was rewarded with a yelp of pain and although it wasn't a lethal blow it was enough to make him panic. Now, ironically, he couldn't get away from her fast enough. He couldn't get away from her at all, in fact. Liath Luachra had wrapped her left arm about his head and throat and although he could drag her backwards on the ground, he couldn't pull himself off her. She held him there in that twisted embrace and kept on jabbing, jabbing and jabbing with the knife until he'd stopped moving and nothing lay on top of her but dead weight.

She was weeping from pain and exhaustion by the time she finally managed to roll him off. Crawling five or six paces, she retrieved her sword and, with an effort, struggled to her feet.

The warrior's body was lying on its side. His mouth was open, as were his eyes but they were seeing nothing. His stomach, even concealed by the heavy leather jerkin, was a tattered mess of gore and blood, much of which was now spread over her as well.

She staggered back down the hill towards the trail, unable to run, stumbling on her bleeding, near-useless leg. Sword hanging limp from her gore-encrusted right hand, she wiped blood and snot from her nose with the other, never having felt so exhausted in her life.

She forced herself to lurch forward, growing increasingly desperate the further down the trail the got.

Moving too slowly. I'll never catch them up at this rate.

By the time she'd reached the clearing her despair was rising. The bodies of the three warriors they had ambushed were still sprawled there but there was no sign of anyone else.

Despite the pain, she pushed herself on, headed down to the marshland at the edge of the island. She was stumbling through the lower woods near the eastern shore when she heard a shout, then another and another. There was excitement in those cries. Amusement. And cruelty.

Through the trees, she suddenly saw Bearach running on the grey 'shoreline' with the two warriors in close pursuit and immediately realised what had happened. Realising that he couldn't fight them and live, the *óglach* had run. While Liath Luachra had been fighting for her life, he'd been running for his, leading his pursuers in a complete circuit of the island only to arrive back at the spot where everything had started, where they'd first set foot after crossing the marsh.

Red-faced and gasping, the boy was at the end of his ability. Unable to run any further, he backed up against the very same boulders she'd been leaning against earlier on and raised his sword to face his pursuers. Liath Luachra desperately tried to hobble faster but struggled to get through the crowded tree trunks. She yelled desperately as she staggered forwards but her voice was suppressed by the screen of the woods around her.

By then the two *fian* warriors had clearly had enough of their sport. Advancing on the terrified boy, they lifted their swords, ready for a quick kill.

'Bearach!'

Somehow he had heard her. He glanced towards the woods, squinted. Then the two warriors attacked.

She was so proud of him, so proud. For he fought like a *gaiscíoch*, using every trick and technique she'd taught him. His attackers were startled, taken aback by his ferocity, the deadliness of his strikes. Unsettled, they momentarily backed away, moving slightly further apart.

So that they could attack again.

This time they came from both sides and Bearach struggled to block or parry the flurry of blows. Despite that, the boy did not jerk away or flinch.

For Liath Luachra, it was as though everything was moving too fast. Although she had just reached the edge of the trees, it felt that no matter how rapidly she moved, she could never get there in time. Her anguish swelled, tinged with pride, as she saw how bravely he fought, courageously blocking one assault then whipping back to avoid a feint from the second warrior. Until fatigue overtook him. Fatigue and sheer bad fortune.

Moving backwards, he stumbled on a small rock, fumbling a feint from the first warrior to leave his right flank completely exposed to the second. The killing strike came from there, a low, upward sword thrust. Liath Luachra saw the blade go in, piercing the boy's side. She saw the eruption of blood gush out through his furs, heard his anguished scream of pain and fear, felt the pain as though she'd been stabbed herself.

And then there was nothing but hatred, nothing but wrath. Three years of repressed loathing, of frustration, of every poisonous unexpressed thought, all unleashed in one terrifying instant. She felt the black strength flow into her, savoured the bitter taste of utter ruthlessness. She moved forwards and, where before it felt as though everything was moving too fast, now it seemed to be moving impossibly slowly. Bearach was falling, taking an age to hit the ground. The two warriors, having heard her scream, were turning to face her. But incredibly sluggishly. Like two men moving in deep water.

Gleas gan Ainm slashed with almost contemptuous ease and she felt the impact of the strike right through the hilt. The blow sliced through flesh and bone, taking the first warrior's hand off at the wrist. It tumbled through the air, sword hilt still clenched firmly in the fist as a gush of blood sprayed over her hair and face.

The second warrior materialised beside her, but fuelled as she was by such unnatural hatred, he stood no chance. She hacked and hacked and when the screaming in her head finally faded, she was standing in a bloody mess, intestines and gore wrapped about her ankles. It took a moment to regain control of her breathing, the blood pulse pounding in her ears, the taste of iron on her lips. Her hands shook, burning from the fear-fury gush of adrenaline.

Bearach was on the ground, stretched on his back several paces away. She teetered unsteadily towards him, almost falling twice before she actually reached him and collapsed by his side. His eyes looked up at her but he couldn't move.

'I'm sorry, Liath Lu -. I ... I tried to be ...' He wasn't able to finish the sentence. She could feel the fear swell in her stomach once more.

He looked like a girl's discarded doll: limp, face a deathly pale, eyes large and full of fear. He tried to speak but no words came out. She grasped his hand and he gripped her with a desperation that made her want to cry.

'Bearach.'

His fingers loosened, releasing her own. His head slumped forwards onto his chest.

'Don't die, little bandit. Bodhmhall will heal you.' She resisted the urge to shake him, to force him to respond. 'Curse you, Bearach. You are my only friend. Who will I walk the Great Wild with if you're gone?'

She howled at him but he wouldn't listen, wouldn't respond. The only answer was the wind, soft and ghostly over the grey mud flats, and the melancholy cry of the marsh birds.

Chapter Eleven

Long after the fighting, the cries continued. Cries of pain, of loss, of grief. Looking about the battered, blood-stained settlement however, Bodhmhall found herself unable to express any such sentiment. Emotionally, she was spent and felt nothing but a deep-rooted, withering numbness.

We have survived.

She kept telling herself that, repeating the words over and over in her head. But she didn't really believe it. Ráth Bládhma may have survived but *Muinntir Bládhma* – the people that formed its heart – had not. Cairbre, Conchenn, Ultán were dead. Liath Luachra, Bearach and Cónán were missing. Aodhán had somehow survived the sword thrust to his side and still breathed but Bodhmhall did not know for how long. The *óglach* was now lying in his parents' bed, unconscious from blood loss. If he survived the night and any associated fevers he had a chance. She tried not to think about it.

Tóla too was badly wounded. The cut to his lower leg meant he could not set his weight upon it without great pain, a situation that was likely to last for several weeks at the very least. He would walk again but there was a strong possibility he would limp for the rest of his life. If the man could talk he'd probably disagree but, in truth, he'd been extremely lucky. The spearhead that pierced him had penetrated so deeply he'd nearly bled to death.

The cost had also been high for the neighbouring communities. At the very moment of victory Cathal ua Cuan had, tragically, been killed by a javelin cast from the departing *fian*. With the old warrior's loss, Ráth Dearg had no surviving menfolk and, of the original population, only Gnathad, Cumann and the children remained. As a settlement, it was no more.

Coill Mór had fared almost as badly. Ber Rua and two of his men were dead. Lí Bán and Ferchar – the red-haired warrior who'd fought so bravely on the northern rampart – were also hurt although the *bandraoi* was confident both would survive their wounds.

The injured were Bodhmhall's immediate priority following the attack. Once she'd got over the blunted realization that the fighting was done, that she had come through it alive, she'd somehow managed to move the wounded into Cairbre and Conchenn's roundhouse. There she'd examined everyone, dressed their wounds and treated them as best she could within the limitations of her own injury.

The intensity of the battle and these subsequent efforts took its toll, however. The aftershock had caused her to break down without warning on two occasions. The first time, in the privacy of the lean-to where she'd been gathering supplies, no one had seen her. The second time she'd been treating Lí Bán, a big-boned woman in her thirties. Despite a serous stab wound to her left breast, the older woman had found the strength to comfort the weeping *bandraoi*, to hold her and share in her shock and grief.

Later, after cleaning Aodhán's wound for a second time, Bodhmhall had sat, rested her head against the wall of the round house and promptly passed out.

It was almost dark when the *bandraoi* was woken by Tóla tapping her on her unwounded shoulder. Looking up, she saw the ugly man standing before her on one leg, a spear haft under his shoulder a crude crutch to support his weight. He grinned, made an odd chirping noise and gestured for her to go outside. Blearily, she struggled to her feet and left him to watch over the others while she struggled to the doorway.

The world was grey and fading to black as she emerged onto the *lis*. Heavy cloud obscured any sign of the sun sinking behind the forest to the west. Up on the gateway rampart, she caught a glimpse of Gnathad's slim figure. The woman was armed with a *fian* shield and spear, and stood beside a grim faced Morag, both staring towards the fading skyline.

Fiacail mac Codhna was waiting for her by the *lis* hearth, sitting on one of the logs, gazing long and hard into the flames. Despite being immersed in the thickest of the fighting, despite one deep cut across his forehead, the big man had somehow escaped with only cuts and bruises. Dried blood stained the front of his tunic but she knew that this was not his own. Unlike Bodhmhall, who'd spent the afternoon saving lives, the big man had spent his ending them, passing through the *ráth* and its immediate surroundings like a spectre of death, snuffing the life-light of any wounded *fian* warriors who still breathed. The bodies of those warriors who'd managed to breach the *lis* had been piled outside with their comrades in a grisly heap beyond the causeway, awaiting disposal.

There was no sign of the children but that did not surprise the *bandraoi*. She was aware that they'd been hidden inside her roundhouse during the course of the attack and doubted that they'd have been permitted outside

257

while the signs of slaughter remained so obvious. Earlier, Morag had also come to the roundhouse to tell her that she'd ordered them all to bed. Despite the fact that they'd been restrained inside for a full day, none of the children had resisted or complained. They'd understood that events of great significance and danger were taking place. They were scared and worried and did as they were told.

Bodhmhall yawned and took a seat on the log beside the Seiscenn Uarbhaoil man. She was still struggling to get her thoughts together and, with Fiacail, she would need to have her wits about her.

'The *ráth* is secure,' he informed her. 'I've got rid of the ladders. Some were too difficult to lift so I cut the grapple hooks and let them fall into the ditch. I've moved those I could carry inside. They can feed your fires next winter.'

She looked at him bleakly. There was no guarantee they would survive to the following winter.

Absorbed by the colours of the flames, the warrior missed the expression on her face. 'But enough of ladders. We should discuss what needs to be done next.'

'We need to find Liath Luachra. And the others.'

This time Fiacail raised his head and stared at her directly. 'The black mantle falls, Bodhmhall. It will be too dark to make out the form of things until morning.'

Although Fiacail's words were full of sense, for some reason the response infuriated her. 'Fiacail, you have fulfilled your role as *conradh* beyond anyone's expectations but I am *Taoiseach* of Ráth Bládhma. This decision will fall to me.'

'Fatigue unwinds your intellect, Bodhmhall. The decision may fall to you but so too does the night fall. Besides, Tóla says wolves are prowling the edge of the northern woods. They are been drawn by the scent of death.'

The *bandraoi* shuffled along the log, away from the fire. Even with the cold air, the heat from the blazing flames was intense. 'If Liath Luachra and the others lie wounded out in the Great Wild that is all the more reason to search for them.'

'And who do you propose that we send to carry out such a task? Apart from the other women, I am the only one who is not seriously injured. I am needed here to defend the settlement against attack. The *fian* may have run from battle but they may return to storm the *ráth* again.'

258

She looked at him dubiously. 'They will not be back, Fiacail. Before I fell asleep I used my Gift to search the valley. It was empty of human life-light. The *fian* has lost its leader and its spirit for battle.'

'I found no sign of that tall, hatchet-faced man. He's still alive out there and the fact that you did not see them there does not mean they will not return.'

'If you will refuse to help, I will go alone.'

'You cannot go. It is dark and if you are *Taoiseach* of Ráth Bládhma as you claim to be, you need to lead your people. They depend on you.'

'My people lie dead or scattered in the Great Wild.'

'You have other people now.'

She looked at him blankly.

'Those of Coill Mór and Ráth Dearg, Bodhmhall. They fought for Ráth Bládhma. Some of them died for Ráth Bládhma. Those that still live have nowhere to go back to so you must accept them into *Muinntir Bládhma*.'

Bodhmhall fixed him a furious stare but could not deny the truth of what he was saying. Beside her, the fire crackled mockingly. A log collapsed to one side wafting a fresh blast of hot air over her. She attempted to pull the cloak from herself but, for some reason, the clasp holding it in place proved difficult to unfasten. After several attempts, exasperated, she yanked the garment off over her head and furiously tossed it onto the ground. She glared at the warrior, daring him to make a deprecating comment but he remained steadfastly silent, focussed once more on the dance of the flames.

Gods! Fatigue makes me absurd. Fiacail speaks the truth.

The realisation provoked a fresh wave of despair but she managed to regain control of her emotions. Sliding back along the log, she put a hand on the big man's shoulder and was about to apologise when a sudden noise from outside the *ráth* stilled her. Heart pounding, she turned to stare in the direction of the gateway, beyond which the strange, high-pitched yipping seemed to be coming.

'It is not Liath Luachra,' said Fiacail.

'What?'

'It is not Liath Luachra. It's the wolves. They feed on the fallen.'

Bodhmhall returned his gaze, ashen-faced.

'Do not fret,' he said. 'All of our people are within the walls.'

'Not all of them.'

Fiacail sighed and looked away.

***

The following morning, they prepared their dead for burial, the women working with Fiacail to lay the bodies of the defenders in a line between the western rampart and the lean-to. Hampered by the wound to her shoulder, Bodhmhall was unable to provide much assistance. Over the course of the night, the pain had worsened. Fortunately, it hadn't disturbed her sleep. Physically and emotionally exhausted, she had not stirred until the first light of dawn.

In a way, she was grateful for the burning ache. The pain meant that she could feel something and anything was better than the numbing stupefaction that continued to cling to her like a damp cloak she could not discard.

Returning briefly to the roundhouse, she checked on her charges. Lí Bán had deserted her sickbed, struggling to cope with the pain of her wound but insisting on being present for the burial of her man. Ferchar was still unconscious. During the battle, he'd received a blow to the head and although he occasionally came to his senses, even at such times he was groggy, confused and suffering greatly from head pain.

Aodhán remained pale and feverish but he had not passed away in the night. There was still hope.

She left the sleeping men and slipped quietly outside, crossing the *lis* to the gateway ladder. Yet another grey day; dark, lumpish layers of cloud hovered above the ridges on either side. Using her Gift, she scanned the valley but could see little to indicate any sign of human life. There was certainly no sign of Liath Luachra's distinctive fire.

Glancing down to where Fiacail had dumped the bodies of the *fian* warriors, she noticed that there seemed to be less of them than she remembered. Several of the remaining bodies bore signs of mauling and she shuddered as she recalled the horrendous sound of ripping flesh from the previous night. Yet another task, she realized with dismay. Once they'd buried their own dead they would have to dispose of their enemies. If not, the rotting flesh would draw even more wolves into the valley.

Although she could not dig, her one good hand meant the *bandraoi* could help carry their friends to the edge of the southern woods for burial while Tóla kept watch from the gateway. It was here, looking down at Cairbre and Conchenn's remains, that Bodhmhall finally let go of the dormant heartache lying inside her like a bitter seed. The two elders had been a constant for the entirety of her existence, from her early days at Dún Baoiscne to more recent times at Ráth Bládhma. Their absence was incomprehensible, like new knowledge that did not quite fit inside her head.

She sat for a moment with Cairbre's head in her lap, keening quietly as she caressed the old man's wrinkled face. His eyes were closed and his features relaxed but such repose could not be confused with sleep. His skin was white and cold to the touch. The *bandraoi* struggled to conceive how Ráth Bládhma could prevail without Cairbre and the tireless Conchenn. The old man had been the perfect *rechtaire*; calm, measured and so very, very wise.

Not so wise if he followed you to Ráth Bládhma.

She could still recall the moment she'd asked him to accompany her to start a colony in the distant Sliabh Bládhma hills. At the time she hadn't really expected him to accept her offer. He had, after all, a relatively comfortable existence in Dún Baoiscne. His prompt acceptance, therefore, had taken her completely by surprise. It was only much later that she understood that decision had been driven by love for his sons. At Dún Baoiscne, despite his achievements, Cairbre would always be remembered as a freed slave and he held greater aspirations for his sons. By accompanying Bodhmhall and assisting in the creation of a new settlement at Ráth Bládhma, his boys would not grow up as 'sons of the slave' but as landed freemen in that community.

She bent down and kissed the cold forehead.

'*Coladh sámh, a* Cairbre. Sleep well. Rest gentle on soft beds where your bones no longer give you pain.'

It was hard, emotionally draining work to bury their dead deep enough so the wolves could not touch them. The task took Fiacail and the women the better part of the morning. Shortly before noon, as they were laying the final body to rest, a yell from the settlement made them look up in alarm. Bodhmhall looked towards the gateway where Tóla was gesturing urgently to the east. Turning towards the thick forest that bordered the converging of the valley walls, she caught sight of several figures making their way towards them.

Cónán! Muirne Muncháem and the children.

She glanced down at the freshly turned earth where Cónán's parents were buried and winced in sympathy for the boy. He would come looking for his parents and, as *Taoiseach*, it would fall to her to impart the terrible news to him.

She closed her eyes and wished a close to this endless day, this endless grief.

***

That afternoon, they released the cattle onto the nearest pasture. The winter grass wasn't substantial there as it had been intensely grazed over the days leading up to attack but it was better than nothing and would pacify the hungry animals until other arrangements could be made. Fiacail and Morag accompanied the cattle outside, keeping them close to the settlement and watching for wolves, the grey shapes still skulking around the trees in the northern woods.

By mid-afternoon, to everyone's surprise, Bodhmhall insisted on driving the livestock back inside the settlement. At first, the reluctant animals resisted, unwilling to leave the pasture, but stinging blows from some slender ash branches quickly convinced them otherwise.

As the cattle passed through the passage below her, Bodhmhall stood at the rampart and stared across at the northern woods then down at the pile of remaining *fian* bodies. Earlier, during the process of moving the cattle outside, they'd found one of the *fian* warriors half-submerged in the watery soil inside the livestock pen. During the battle, the invader had apparently fallen from the rampart and landed in amongst the cattle. Unable to rise because of his wounds or the closeness of the animals, he'd been trampled to death or had simply drowned in the piss and shit-stained sodden earth. Fiacail had regarded the compressed corpse with complete dispassion before dragging it from the sucking mud and tossing it outside with the others.

The bodies will draw the beasts, not to mention the risk of sickness. But it must wait. There are more urgent tasks I must take in hand.

Bodhmhall returned to check on her patients. Ferchar had regained consciousness but remained dizzy and confused. The *óglach* was still unconscious and hot with fever but his breathing was regular. She changed his bandages once again before making sure that the glow about his wound had not intensified. Satisfied that there was little else she could do for them, the *bandraoi* pulled on a heavy cloak, armed herself with a spear and headed outside.

A soft drizzle had started to fall over the valley, saturating the trampled *lis* and making it even muddier then it already was. Tramping across the sludge, she arrived at the gateway to find Fiacail waiting inside the passage overhang, running a whetstone along the length of an axe blade. He held the weapon up against the weak light of the leaden sky as she drew to a stop before him. Despite his efforts, a deep nick remained in the lower section of the blade.

'You leave us then? You intend to go in search of the Grey One?'

His eyes moved from the spear in her hand to the bandaged shoulder barely visible beneath the folds of her cloak.

'I have done what I can for the settlement. Liath Luachra and Bearach need me now.'

Bodhmhall took a deep breath as she prepared herself for another vexed confrontation with the Seiscenn Uarbhaoil man. To her surprise, Fiacail simply nodded and got to his feet, slotting the axe handle into a leather sheath slung across his back. 'Very well. I will accompany you.'

Bodhmhall stared, startled by the offer but also extremely grateful. Fighting for her life, she'd had no opportunity to observe in which direction the Grey One had fled after that initial bolt to the west. To find Liath Luachra, she would need to locate the woman's trail and she was no tracker. Having someone like Fiacail to help her – a competent woodsman from an early age – significantly improved her chances of finding that trail.

'I did not think you liked Liath Luachra.'

'I don't. But I like you.'

They left the *ráth* with the gateway passage sealed behind them. Tóla and Cónán stood careful guard on the ramparts although in Tóla's case it was more a case of 'sitting' guard. Bodhmhall threw a worried glance at the young boy. Cairbre's son was still red-eyed and shaken. She felt guilt at leaving him with such responsibility given that he'd had so little time to grieve the loss of his parents. But grieving was a luxury none of them could afford.

Following the stream that meandered slowly to the west, they travelled quickly until they reached a point approximately half way down the valley. Here they slowed and moved in more of a zig-zag pattern, back and forth across the pasture, with the big man pausing occasionally to study any tracks they intersected. The earth was still relatively soft due to the recent rains and the imprints they found were well defined but she could tell that

Fiacail was not happy. With all the movement from the *fian* warriors, much of the valley floor had been trampled, making it difficult to distinguish the warrior woman's trail from all the others. Two hundred paces from the edge of the forest, however, they had a stroke of good fortune. Fiacail stopped abruptly and bent down to examine a small imprint on the ground. After a moment of quiet deliberation he glanced up at the *bandraoi*. 'It's the Grey One.'

Bodhmhall regarded the imprint. All she could see was a muddy footprint, not much different from the many others around it. 'How can you tell?'

'The imprint of the toes point away from the *ráth*.' The big man shuffled forward on his knees to rest his fingers on another imprint. 'The distance between the steps is also wider than normal.'

'So the person who left these tracks was running.'

He nodded.

'But that could have been anyone.'

'True. But the imprints are less distinct than the others. That means the runner was lighter. We know Liath Luachra is lighter than most of the *fian* warriors. She was certainly carrying less weight.'

To demonstrate what he meant, Fiacail indicated another set of tracks where the full outline of the foot was more deeply indented in the earth.

Fiacail tugged on the end of his moustache. 'The first runner was being followed by about ten others. That could only be Liath Luachra.' He raised his head and stared towards the trees. 'At least she made it to the forest.'

That statement alone gave Bodhmhall cause for hope. Liath Luachra knew this territory better than anyone and thrived in the shadowy hug of the Great Wild forests. If she'd made it to the trees then her chances of survival had substantially increased.

They advanced towards the forest, noting how the closer they got to the trees, the more the tracks of the pursuers appeared to converge. Soon, all trace of the woman warrior's tracks was obliterated, trampled by the heavy tread of the mob behind her. Bodhmhall looked at the ground in concern.

'Fiacail, do you think …'

The big man looked at her. 'It's impossible to say. All we can tell for certain is that more than ten men followed Liath Luachra into these woods. And none of them came back. We will only know by proceeding further.'

The flurry of tracks entered the forest between a pair of towering oak trees that gave the vague impression of a gateway. Inside the forest, the shadows and tightness of the trees became immediately oppressive. Despite the shadows, the trail was easy to follow at first as much of the undergrowth had been disturbed, branches and shrubs broken or crushed from the passage of so many feet. Further into the shadows, however, the tracks spread out as the pursuers diverged in different directions but always continuing roughly westward.

Fiacail stopped and squatted to consider the tracks. He snapped a twig from a nearby branch and chewed on it thoughtfully as he considered the ground. 'Clever girl,' he said at last. Noting the *bandraoi*'s worried expression, he quickly clarified the comment. 'She gave them the slip. They spread out to search for her although ...' He paused. 'The tracks all seem to be moving north-west. What lies in that direction?'

Bodhmhall's face was troubled. 'Marshland. A small island then nothing. From there, it's impassable. There's no way out.'

They exchanged worried glances.

'Let us continue,' the warrior suggested. 'The trail is over a day old but we must travel carefully. Our enemy may be about and there are always the wolves to consider.'

The *bandraoi* reached over suddenly and caught the Seiscenn Uarbhaoil man's arm. 'Thank you, Fiacail. Thank you for helping me.'

'You are my friend,' the big man answered. 'Besides, my dislike of the Grey One does not blind me to the reality of things. She drew off more than a quarter of the *fian*'s force, thwarting their plan of attack at the very last moment. We barely held the walls as it was and that was only because they were confused and fewer in number.' He tossed the twig aside and got to his feet. 'No, I am not blind.'

Bodhmhall gave a tired laugh then quickly caught herself. For one blissful moment she had forgotten but now, after the tragedy of the last few days, the laughter felt wrong, disrespectful. 'You are a fool, Fiacail. A beautiful, wonderful fool.'

They continued onward, moving slowly, keeping as low as possible in the darkly dappled undergrowth. Bodhmhall began to sweat, the pain in her shoulder intensifying from the continuous movement. Ignoring it, she focused instead on her Gift, using it to look ahead for any telltale light of

265

human activity, desperate for a glimpse of Liath Luachra's flame to brighten up the gloom.

Suddenly Fiacail hissed and dropped to his knees. The *bandraoi* froze. The warrior was staring directly ahead towards a particularly thick section of trees. He turned his head slowly towards her, pointed at his eyes and then towards the trees.

Bodhmhall shook her head and dropped her palm in a slanting movement to indicate the sharp drop of the terrain beyond the trees. She could not see through the earth to what lay beyond.

As they waited, Bodhmhall heard what had alerted the warrior: a noise, a kind of drawn out scrape that lasted for several heartbeats than stopped before repeating again. It stopped, a moment passed and she heard it again. Bodhmhall grasped her spear but it was more out of fear than any deep-rooted intent to fight. She was no warrior and even if she wasn't injured she would have struggled to use the weapon effectively.

The sound came again. Louder this time. Fiacail gestured urgently towards a withered oak tree behind her that they'd passed a moment earlier. The tree looked to have been struck by lightning in the past. Its upper branches were black and bare, and its bark was peeling. The resulting gap in the canopy layer above them allowed grey light to filter down onto the floor of the forest. 'Get back,' he whispered. 'Behind the Great Oak.'

Bodhmhall scuttled back towards the shelter of the giant trunk and watched as Fiacail pulled both axes free from the sheaths on his back. He flexed his shoulders in preparation, eyes fixed on a natural parting in the bushes directly ahead of him where a number of the *fian* tracks appeared to congregate.

Suddenly, a mud-coated figure appeared through the leafy gap, stumbling forward with an awkward movement that matched the scraping sound then abruptly straightened as it stopped. If it hadn't been for that characteristic glow Bodhmhall wouldn't have recognised her. Coated in several layers of mud, face covered in blood, leaning heavily on a roughly cut staff, bloody bandage about her thigh, it was the Grey One.

'Liath Luachra!'

The woman warrior started, fumbled clumsily for her sword but struggled to pull it free of its sheath. Bodhmhall stepped out into the open and the figure froze when she saw the *bandraoi*.

'Liath Luachra, it is us!' Bodhmhall stared in surprise for the Grey One was dragging a makeshift litter behind her, the source of the scraping noise. As her eyes moved down the wooden frame she saw the pale, lifeless, figure of ... Bearach.

Bodhmhall gasped, raised her eyes from the body to the warrior woman and opened her mouth but didn't know what to say.

Liath Luachra filled the silent space. Her teeth were chattering, whether from the cold or exhaustion, it was impossible to tell but she forced herself to speak. 'Bearach is my friend. I couldn't ... I couldn't leave him to the wolves.' With that, she slumped on her staff, looking lost and for the first time that Bodhmhall could ever recall, vulnerable.

Bodhmhall moved forward, catching her by the arm before she collapsed.

'Enough, *a rún*. Enough. Let us go home.'

***

The woman warrior was in a bad way but Bodhmhall was confident she would survive. The knowledge kindled an internal warmth, giving a renewed sense of hope, of pale blue skies finally breaking through the winter gloom.

Liath Luachra was in the roundhouse with the other injured, stretched on the sleeping platform previously occupied by Lí Bán. In the warmth of the dwelling, her shivering had finally ceased. Bodhmhall examined the woman warrior's body in the flickering light of an oil lamp, wiping her with a fresh cloth as she cleaned the worst of the blood and muck from her wounds. The Grey One's face and, in particular, the left side of her head was swollen and badly bruised. Blood matted her hair and left ear. The latter concerned her at first but when she examined it more closely she found that it was due to a cut in the inner earlobe.

The Gift allowed her to see to the initial glimmer around the bloody cut in her thigh. She knew that if she did not deal to it, by tomorrow the surrounding flesh would become hot and stretched, the tissue within, pink and raw. The wound was deep and must have been extremely painful to walk on. She couldn't begin to imagine how the woman had managed to drag a heavy litter all that distance from An Oileán Dubh.

Bodhmhall sighed as she recalled the sight of the slender body strapped into the litter.

One more body. One more member of Muinntir Bládhma gone.

It had been almost dark when they'd finally returned to the *ráth*, too late to place Bearach in the earth beside his parents. Overnight, the body was resting in one of the lean-tos, watched over by Cónán until it could be buried in the morning. Her heart was heavy for Cairbre's youngest boy. In the course of a single day he had lost his parents and now, one of his older brothers as well. The only consolation she could offer was that Aodhán's condition appeared to be improving. Some colour had returned to his cheeks and he'd woken briefly shortly after their return. He'd even managed to swallow some stew and water before dropping off again.

The *bandraoi* raised a beaker to the Grey One's swollen lips. 'Drink,' she said.

The woman warrior swallowed greedily, spilling half of the liquid down her neck. Bodhmhall wiped the moisture away. Despite the familiar surroundings, Liath Luachra remained visibly tense, unable to drop her guard and relax. Unconsciously, she was fighting her physical exhaustion, the effort putting a quaver in her voice and making her hands tremble.

Bodhmhall put the beaker to one side. 'Regret weighs heavy on these shoulders, *a rún*. I was wrong, I was so wrong and ... you came back. Despite everything, you came back and saved us.'

Liath Luachra looked at her, trying to give her full attention but clearly struggling with the pain. 'Your plan,' she croaked. 'It was shit.'

'It was shit,' Bodhmhall agreed. 'It was shit. I had thought our fate settled, that by sending you away with my nephew you would both survive. People say I am a wise woman and yet I displayed all the wisdom of a simpleton child.'

For a moment she thought that the woman warrior was coughing then realised what she was hearing was a hoarse chuckle.

'Then we share that idiot wisdom. For my part, I thought to walk away, to leave you and my friends to the fate you consigned yourselves to.' She gripped the *bandraoi*'s hand with surprising firmness. 'I could not do so. I have changed living here, living with you. I have scoffed at your words these past years, Bodhmhall and yet all the time you spoke true. Belonging here, being part of *Muinntir Bládhma*, it has given me ...' She gave a crooked smile. 'You are dear to me, *An Cailleach Dubh*.'

Bodhmhall rested her free hand on the woman warrior's cheek. 'And you are dear to me, Grey One.'

Liath Luachra finally lay her head back and closed her eyes. 'Sometimes, Bodhmhall … sometimes, I think … I think …'

Whatever she intended to say remained unsaid. Bodhmhall waited, listened carefully but no further words came from the injured woman. There was no sound but the soft rhythm of breathing.

Bodhmhall glanced down at the beaker. She'd been using the sleeping draught with restraint but it had done its work. Fortunately, as it was the last of her existing supply.

She sat there quietly, staring at the unconscious woman warrior for a time, a bitter ball of anger swelling in her throat from the thought of what she had lost.

Muirne.

Bodhmhall took a deep breath then, assuring herself that the Grey One was unconscious, bent to examine the wounded thigh more closely. Biting her lower lip in concentration, she used a sharp knife to open the scab and gently pressed the skin on either side to squeeze out accumulated blood and fluid. The little quantity that did ooze from the wound already gleamed bright, heavy with life-light.

The *bandraoi* washed the gash out with an astringent solution made from flowerless plants found in the woods at the far end of the valley. It was the same herbal remedy she'd used on Aodhán and Ferchar, a liquid that reduced the life-light of injuries and which she'd successfully used in the past. Repeating the cleaning process several times, she finally plugged the hole with a salve before stitching the edges of the torn skin close together again with a needle and thread.

She was shaking with fatigue when she finally emerged from the roundhouse but she knew she had to ignore it. There were still a number of critical tasks to be completed before she could rest.

She advanced towards the *lis* hearth where Morag was sitting with the children, feeding them a meal of bread and broth. The children looked up in alarm at her arrival and she belatedly realised that her hands were still covered in blood. Hiding them awkwardly behind her back, she turned to address the dark-haired Coill Mór woman. 'Morag, get the children to bed when they've finished eating and gather the others. I am calling an Assembly.'

***

While Tóla watched from the gateway rampart, the remaining adult occupants of Ráth Bládhma assembled around the hearth. For Bodhmhall, although she did not reveal her feelings, the gathering was marred by those haunting absences from the last Assembly and the subsequent War Council. Of the original Council, only herself, Fiacail, and Muirne Muncháem were present. Prompted by Fiacail's suggestion, the *bandraoi* had also invited Gnathad, Morag, and Lí Bán to attend. As the big man had correctly pointed out, they had all made sacrifices for Ráth Bládhma and deserved an opportunity to have a say in the decisions that needed to be made.

Cónán had also been invited to attend. Like the others, he had proven himself over the previous days and Bodhmhall felt it important to have a symbolic recognition of the input his family had in the settlement to date. It was a little gesture but it was an important one.

Once again, the *bandraoi* waited while the others ate. The meal was simple fare, a stew of beef and tubers, washed down with water and a shared ladle of flat beer. Although most people ate sparingly, Fiacail mac Codhna devoured everything that was set before him, working his way around a bowl twice the size of the others to shovel the contents into his mouth. Beside him, Muirne Muncháem, more demure and nervous about the discussions to come, poked half-heartedly at the contents of her own bowl while her baby cooed quietly in a fur blanket at her feet.

Bodhmhall coughed and pointedly cleared her throat. 'We should begin,' she said as the muted discussions about her wilted. She turned her gaze to Morag. Since the battle, the Coill Mór woman had taken on all responsibility for feeding and looking after the children. Earlier, Bodhmhall had asked her to extend that responsibility to include the settlement's remaining adult population as well. The dark-haired girl who'd lost her man during the battle had been eager to occupy herself, to fill up any opportunity for reflection with work. Bodhmhall could sympathise.

'Morag? The food supplies. Will we last the end of winter?'

The Coill Mór woman brushed a curtain of black curls away from her eyes. 'We have many fewer mouths to feed and spring is already on us. We will not go hungry.'

Bodhmhall nodded her thanks and gestured towards Fiacail. 'All are aware that Liath Luachra's wounds keep her from her role as *conradh* at this time. I am grateful to Fiacail mac Codhna who has agreed to act in her stead until she has recovered.'

Fiacail quickly wiped some sauce from his chin and stood up to address his little audience. 'The defences of the *ráth* are solid. The gateway barrier was untested during the attack, the pilings are sound. I have used the *fian*'s ladders to close the gap in the eastern rampart.' He grinned at Bodhmhall. 'You will not be using them for firewood after all.

With respect to weapons, we now have a surplus from the dead *fian* warriors but we lack the hands to wield them. We are fortunate that Cónán has returned. With the exception of myself he is our only other able-bodied fighter. Morag and Gnathad have demonstrated that they can be called upon if the need arises but they lack battle experience. Lí Bán has also indicated her enthusiasm to defend the *ráth* if we are attacked but she is not yet sufficiently recovered.'

'*If* we are attacked,' repeated Bodhmhall as the big man sat down. 'Therein lies the issue. We have no means of knowing if there will be another attack. We are ignorant both as to the identity of our aggressors and to their true intentions.'

She turned to look at the Flower of Almhu who had remained subdued during the meal. 'Apart from two bandit raids, this settlement has successfully avoided conflict until your arrival, Muirne Muncháem. Both the Tainted One and the *fian* came seeking you and your child.'

There was a silence as all eyes turned to the young woman and her baby. Despite their inclusion to *Muinntir Bládhma* the other woman had remained silent until this point and it was Lí Bán who finally articulated what all of them were thinking. The big woman's face was strained with pain as she placed her bowl on the ground but she forced herself to sit up and hold the Flower of Almhu's eye. 'If you have knowledge of the forces who slaughtered our menfolk or the motivations behind them, you should speak now, Muirne Muncháem.'

Muirne turned her gaze down to her own bowl and scowled at the meaty broth. 'I know of no association with a Tainted One. Neither do I have familiarity with the tattooed men. All are strangers to me.'

Bodhmhall frowned. 'We cannot hope to survive if we remain in a state of such ignorance.'

Muirne reached down to take the baby into her arms and clutched him close. 'I am as oblivious to the motivations of these dire events as you. I do not know these aggressors. If you believe-' She paused suddenly and looked at the *bandraoi*, her eyes heavy with suspicion. 'I know you, Bodhmhall. If

271

you are revealing these thoughts so openly it is because you have already made a decision with regard to our fate.'

Bodhmhall shrugged. 'I do not deny it. It is clear Ráth Bládhma can no longer offer you sanctuary. Should you remain, those who seek you out will return and we can neither protect you nor survive another confrontation.'

'So you will cast me out? You would cast your own nephew out?'

'It is not my intent to cast you out. Neither is it my intent that you remain. I have given the matter consideration and there is but a single feasible route to our mutual security. You must leave Ráth Bládhma for a refuge where you are unknown, where you can live your life in safety.'

The Flower of Almhu looked at her coldly. 'And, no doubt, you have such a refuge in mind.'

The *bandraoi* confirmed the accusation with a sharp nod. 'There is a place. Far to the north-east. It is known as Fir Ros.'

'Fir Ros? That is a lifetime's march away.'

'And hence its attraction. You are well known in this region. No matter where you concealed yourself it would only be a matter of time before you and the babe were discovered.'

'And what do the forsaken lands of Fir Ros hold? There is no settlement there that I have ever heard of.'

'It is nomadic territory. Under the leadership of Gleor Red-Hand. He was once a friend and ally to my father before they had a falling out. Now he disassociates himself of any interaction with *Clann Baoiscne* but he and I remain on positive terms.' She pursed her lips in silent reflection. 'There is also a matter of a debt that is owed, one on which I must now call. When Ráth Bládhma returns to strength, I will accompany you there myself. I will solicit his assistance.'

From the hostility of her expression, it was clear that Muirne was unhappy with the proposed arrangement but she was not foolish enough to ignore the determined set to the faces surrounding her. There would be no alternative. She looked coldly at Bodhmhall. 'As a refugee,' she said, bitterness tainting her voice, 'I am dependent on your goodwill and have little say in the decision. Very well. We will travel with you to Fir Ros.'

Bodhmhall returned the Flower of Almhu's glare with a stony expression.

'You misunderstand, Muirne. You will be travelling to Fir Ros. The babe remains at Ráth Bládhma.'

Muirne Muncháem's eyes widened then flared in wrath. 'No! *An Cailleach Dubh*! Crone of treachery!'

The *bandraoi* displayed no emotion at the other woman's outburst. 'You must see reason, Muirne. Your enemy seeks a woman and a young babe living amongst strangers. Even far to the north-east they can locate you by that simple description and can then send their lackeys to confirm any suspicion. We will take you east towards Dún Baoiscne and you will carry a blanket formed to resemble the babe. When sufficient word had spread of your passage we will discard the blanket, amend your appearance and veer north. I have herbs that will change the colour of your hair.'

But Muirne was not listening. She had risen to her feet and stood to confront Bodhmhall with unconcealed fury. 'If my child does not accompany me then I do not travel to Fir Ros. If you withdraw your offer of sanctuary I will return to Dún Baoiscne.'

'That option no longer remains either, cousin. You are not of *Clann Baoiscne*. Tréanmór will give you and the babe to *Clann Morna* in an instant if he can make advantage of the matter. They will kill the babe. You know this. It is why you came to Ráth Bládhma in the first place.'

Muirne's hands formed fists of desperation and she trembled with rage but nothing could refute what Bodhmhall had told her.

'You intend to steal my child. You cannot have a brat of your own so you would steal the babe of a defenceless woman.'

'Come, Muirne. You sell yourself short. You are hardly defenceless woman. Consider the death that follows in whatever place you tread.'

With that, the *bandraoi* got to her feet. It was clear that for her at least the discussions were finished. She made to head for the roundhouse where Liath Luachra and the other wounded still awaited her but then paused to look back at the white-faced Flower of Almhu. 'Muirne Muncháem, I warned you once that there would be a price to pay for the survival of your child. At the time you indicated your willingness. Now we know with certainty the price that you must pay.'

***

The story will continue in Book Two: Traitor of Dún Baoiscne.

See Brian O'Sullivan's website irishimbasbooks.com for more information on Brian's other books, news on new releases and works in progress, and a Gaelic Pronunciation Guide.

The Irish Muse and Other Stories

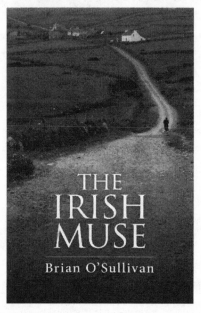

This intriguing collection of stories puts an original twist on foreign and familiar territory. Merging the passion and wit of Irish storytelling with the down-to-earth flavour of other international locations around the world, these stories include:

- a ringmaster's daughter who is too implausible to be true — despite all the evidence to the contrary

- an ageing nightclub gigolo in one last desperate bid to best a younger rival

- an Irish consultant whose uncomplicated affair with a public service colleague proves anything but

- an Irish career woman in London stalked by a mysterious figure from her past

- a sleep-deprived translator struggling to make sense of bizarre events in a French city

Beara: Dark Legends

Nobody knows much about reclusive historian Muiris (Mos) O'Súilleabháin except that he doesn't share his secrets freely.

Mos, however, has a *"sixth sense for history, a unique talent for finding lost things"*.

Reluctantly lured from his voluntary seclusion, Mos is hired to locate the final resting place of legendary Irish hero, Fionn mac Cumhal. Confronted by a thousand year old mystery, the distractions of a beguiling circus performer and a lethal competitor, Mos must draw on his unique background and knowledge of Gaelic lore to defy his enemies and survive his own family history.

Beara: Dark Legends is the first in a trilogy of unforgettable Irish thrillers. Propulsive, atmospheric and darkly humorous, *Beara: Dark Legends* introduces an Irish hero like you've never seen before. Nothing you thought you knew about Ireland will ever be the same again.

Made in the USA
San Bernardino, CA
23 February 2020